THE TIME BETWEEN US

J. RAE ROBERTS

For Scott
Who supports me in every way

CHAPTER 1

Sub-Level 3: Research Lab
Monday, 13/03/2175
2137 hours

FROM BEHIND A GLASS WINDOW, Dr. Sanda Luminita carefully tipped the test tube and poured the contents through a filter. This was the last batch for the night. If the results didn't show anything useful, she might as well turn in her resignation and get the hell off the planet. That is, if she survived the disease. So far, nothing was working, which meant more people would die.

This is not what she signed up for.

She pulled her hands out of the controller gloves and pressed her fists against her lower back in an arched stretch. It would take a couple of hours to get the results. She'd check the data from yesterday's trial to see if there was any progress, then go home and try to catch some REMs. She took a swig of jav from this morning's cup sitting on her desk and choked on the bitter sludge. Cold. Forgot to put the mug on auto-warm. How long had she been here?

She had come to Goliath well after the launchies had constructed the original, crude compound. In fact, she had been on the third wave of transports from Earth after the first medical doctor had done the hard part: setting up health and safety procedures, making sure quarantine protocol was followed, seeing to the physical, mental, and nutritional well-being of the first settlers.

All that was left was to maintain health regulations, patch up minor injuries not taken care of in the field, and to work uninterrupted on her passion: the study of chemical and organic compounds and their unique properties.

Now precious time and energy were focused on stopping the spread of this fatal disease.

"Research results, experiment Gene Standard, Sector 7-003," she said through an exhausted yawn.

"Retrieving," the room responded.

Wisps of a hologram materialized above her desk, showing rows of numbers, graphs, and chemical formulae.

Conclusion: no significant change.

Three workers from Sector VII died last week: Hamashi Benetti, male, four tours, Silver Class; Koringa Kolikulani, female, four tours, Silver Class; and Samulandon Dakota, three tours, Bronze Class. It was painful to see the tests fail again and again. Human physiology wasn't what interested Sanda, but now, it was all that mattered. She wasn't sure she could take much more of this, and neither could the colony. Humans were a limited commodity on Goliath.

Studying unique plant life, and testing different organic chemistries to see what could be used to generate alternate forms of energy gave Sanda the most satisfaction. Part of her job was to take care of the simple rejuvenations when workers came in from the outer limits. Seldom was she needed for more than that.

Eighty-four people lived on the planet, each had a vital job to do, and each had been specifically selected for their area of expertise. The loss of any one person was a hit to operations. The loss of three persons was devastating.

Koringa had been one of Sanda's favorites, always bringing her sprigs of colorful plants, or sticky thistles, and hanging around to see if Sanda needed any help, even after Koringa had spent a tough day in the mines. It didn't seem possible she was dead.

Now, a fourth worker from Sector VII had been brought in last night, having difficulty breathing, too weak to walk or even stand. Test after test came up empty. Sanda wasn't any closer to solving the problem than when she had started. Simple parenteral nutrition and pro-builders had no effect alleviating the symptoms. It didn't matter what pathogen was making them sick. What mattered was why the infected person's system wouldn't accept the modifications and produce the immunities needed to fight off the infection.

Sanda held her head in her hands, propped her elbows on the desk, and closed her eyes. What was she failing to see? The next set of recruits was over a year away. If she didn't figure it out soon, and the infection spread . . .

The room interrupted her thoughts, "Imitar Dubashi at the front entrance."

She met him at the clinic door. "What can I do for you, Imitar?" She did a quick visual assessment. He looked fine, thank the cosmos, except for the scraggly stuff on his chin. Was that hair? Maybe he was just here for a follicle-repressor.

"So, has CPO Schaefer called you?" Imitar asked.

"No. Why? Is something wrong? Is someone else sick?"

"Schaefer asked me to bring you this." Imitar pointed at the large oblong capsule floating behind him on a hover-pallet.

CHAPTER 2

SANDA GLANCED at the metal container.

"What is it?"

"That seems to be the question of the hour." Imitar shrugged. "CRYO34R is stamped on the top, but that's all the info we have. It came in on the oh-one-hundred shipment."

"I didn't order any medical supplies that would come in like that." Sanda frowned. A tight feeling pressed against her temples.

"That's what's weird. It wasn't on the shipping order. Zoleta and I double checked."

"And CPO Schaefer wants it brought here? To me? Is it clean? I can't afford to have any bugs. I already have a patient in quarantine."

"All checks came back clear," he said. "The cap was inside the sub-zero."

"This is just what I don't need. Well, we can't leave it out in the hallway. Help me haul it back to the last exam room. It must be some kind of viable tissue material supplies."

Sanda showed Imitar where to place the capsule against the wall under the IC monitors. "Leave it on the hover-pallet in case I need to move it again."

She took a hand-held scanner and ran it over the outside of the metal pod. "It's a human. No requisition order, you say?" She set the scanner down and crossed her arms.

"Is he alive?" Imitar's eyes grew wide. "We, Zoleta and I, thought it might be a new recruit, but he's not in a space-sleeper and this was a supplies-only delivery."

"The temp inside this capsule is minus 196 degrees C, well below the hypothermic state conducive to space travel. The question is what am I supposed to do with it?" She rubbed her temples. "Guess I might as well find out."

She called CPO Schaefer on the Zi-fi.

Ben Schaefer's profile came into focus on the screen. A series of holographic images he was working on could be seen in the background. His hands sliced through the air, whipping the pages around to line up in the order he seemed to want.

"Doctor Luminita," he said and glanced over his shoulder then back to his work. "What is it?"

"Perhaps you can tell me?" Sanda looked at Imitar, raised her empty hands, and waited for Ben's reply.

"I assume you are talking about the item from the cargo ship. Imitar tells me it sounds like a cryonics patient and I want you to take care of it." Ben stopped and turned to the screen, his gaze burning into hers. "Make it top priority. Re-animate it. It could be valuable to your research. Keep me informed. That will be all." He clicked off and the Zi-fi went dark.

Sanda stared at the blank screen. "Top priority? I don't have time for this. What is he thinking? There are workers dying that I can't bring back to life, and he wants me to take the time to defrost a human icicle?" She stormed around the room. Imitar jumped to get out of her way.

"Doc? If you need some help, I have the rest of the evening off. Just tell me what to do."

It took a moment before she said, "Thank you. Looks like it's going to be a long night. For starters, why don't you bring us something hot to drink?" She held her cup with cold dregs out to him. "I'll run the critical checks and see what we're dealing with. Not a deep-sleep space recruit? Re-animate? This guy is dead?" She sighed. "I'll have to search through some outdated material on this one."

* * *

Sanda watched the illuminated blueboard, as the procedure for re-animation of animal species scrolled down the page. The copy was grainy and blurred around the edges. She squinted and asked for a higher resolution. A message flashed across the screen: **extensive tissue regeneration may be necessary to restore healthy cell structure and chemistry before warming.**

Imitar breezed into the room and handed her the steaming java.

"Aren't you having any?" Luminita asked as she took the fresh cup.

"Nah, I'm going to be too wired to stay in orbit as it is. Already had my quota for the day. And tomorrow. So did you find anything on the IG-Net?"

"It better not be that complicated. I haven't ever done this, but it should be like warming a space traveler, only a little more intense. We didn't learn about cryonics in medical school. Rejuvenations and gene modifications had already eliminated any reason for freezing animal species to bring back to life at a later date."

"It won't hurt anything to open the capsule, will it? I mean, can we pull the face shield down and take a peek at him? I want to see if he looks like a Cro-Magnon, or should I say, Cryo-Magnon." He laughed.

Luminita gave him a weary smile and felt a tiny ember of interest start to burn its way into her curiosity. "Why not? Let's meet our new 'old' fellow."

They unclipped the fasteners on the sides of the capsule and pushed the shield back. The glass window underneath stopped just below the cryo's chest. They looked at the sleeping human.

The doctor raised her eyebrows. "This is interesting."

"For some reason, I just thought it would be a male. But it's definitely female," Imitar said with a smile.

They looked at each other, then down at the pale woman. Her hair fanned out in golden-red waves, like the setting sun melting over a calm sea.

A ten by fifteen-centimeter plastic card hung around her neck, resting across her breasts like a giant dog-tag. Sanda bent closer and read, "Rachel Elizabeth Allison McRae. Born: Feb. 27, 1960. De-animated: January 22, 1994."

"Wow, so she only lived thirty-four years? Do you think she was sick or had some kind of accident? Why would they freeze her instead of fixing her?" Imitar scowled.

"I don't know how or why she died. Remember, they didn't have rejuvenations back then. They didn't stick with cryonics for very long either, in the scientific scheme of things." Sanda took another sip of the strong jav. "1994, not very advanced medicine in those days. In fact, if I can remember some of what I learned in Ancient Medical History, they did some pretty crazy things, like using metal parts for hips and knees and such, sawing the chest open for heart surgeries, and using poisons in the bloodstream to fight cancers. All very barbaric."

"But she died and somebody had her frozen, right Doc? Why wasn't she reanimated back on earth a long time ago? Maybe she's lucky to be here with us. We can give her a longer life, can't we? Or a life, period. Don't you think?"

"Let's hope *she* thinks it's lucky." Sanda glanced toward the capsule. "I'm going to have to spend some time researching the reanimation procedure before I do anything that might jeopardize her prognosis. Feel free to head home, Imitar. I know it's late."

* * *

After Imitar left, Sanda conducted a full body scan then adjusted the pressure gauges and circulatory pump on Rachel's capsule. The scan showed glycerol as the main cryoprotectant used to keep ice from forming between cells while the woman was suspended in liquid nitrogen. Sanda knew she should start on the reanimation process: spraying the nanos through the med port and letting them begin to reconstruct Rachel's body and mind, cell by cell, neuron by neuron, but the doctor needed to proceed with caution. It was getting late. If she went too fast or skipped a vital step, Rachel could end up in an irretrievable state. The CPO would not be happy.

Giving a cursory glance over her shoulder, Sanda exhaled. "You aren't going to wake up for a few more days, so waiting a little longer isn't going to hurt."

Sanda started to pull off her lab coat, hesitated, then walked over to take a final look at the frozen woman left in her care.

Rachel's skin was almost translucent. "Well, what do you expect? All of those years you spent without any blood in your body, suspended in liquid nitrogen, plus eight more months on your ride out here. It's enough to make anyone look like an ice cube."

Bending closer, Sanda noticed a small brown spot on Rachel's left earlobe. A similar round bump snuggled on Rachel's neck above her clavicle. Sanda tried to remember what she knew about these blemishes. They were a normal feature of long-ago humans, nothing contagious or life threatening, but what were they called? "I'll search it on med-max tomorrow." She yawned and reached for her cup.

Empty.

Sanda ran through one last check of the data to make sure Rachel's values were in the normal range. She took a final peek at her unique patient. "You don't look like you'll be any trouble," she said to the sleeping form. "There isn't time for more trouble."

The doctor smiled a sad smile and rubbed the chill from her arms. *You've certainly missed a thing or two,* she thought. *You've been deanimated for a long time. This may take more work than I figured. It might be best to send you straight back to earth and let them deal with you. Darn you, Ben Schaefer.*

"Poor girl." Sanda patted the glass window above Rachel's cheek. "Good night, Rachel. We'll meet in a few days. Get your strength back—you're going to need it." Sanda pulled the metal shield on the capsule back up until she heard it click into place.

She started toward the door, turned and stabbed her finger in the air.

"Moles! That's it. They're moles!"

CHAPTER 3

Sub-Level 2—CPO Schaefer's private quarters
Tuesday, March 14
03:30 hours

BEN PACED BACK and forth across the four meters of his office. He'd worked nonstop since 06:00 Thursday morning. It was now Friday, 03:30. Sometimes, he wished he could go back to a simpler time. If only he could remember when such a time existed. He'd been doing too much wishing lately, and it wasn't getting him anywhere.

Damn it. He had a planet to run, people to direct, money to make.

That was the problem. He couldn't afford to lose any more miners. Two men and one woman had died and another was in isolation, not doing well. Dr. Luminita was working on it all hours of the day, an endless day, as the sun never set on Goliath. She didn't seem to be finding any answers, at least not fast enough to keep him from having to shut down Sector VII.

Ben needed to get a handle on the problem. No, he needed to solve the problem before the Intergalactic Council got involved. Life certainly wouldn't be simple then.

Arriving at his apartment too wound up to sleep, Ben pulled on a pair of gym shorts and a faded red T-shirt. The *n*, *f* and *o* were worn off the front of the shirt, making it read, "Sta_ _ _rd." He climbed onto the MFIT: part bike, part rowing machine.

"Play workout track. Sixty-five decibels."

The room's computer skimmed the audio library and locked on rock and roll music from over a century ago. The raw voice of The Boss boomed through the speakers. One evening Zoleta had stopped by, uninvited. He'd had the volume up full blast while he'd sweated away at his work-out. "What's that heinous noise?" she'd said. He'd turned it off. The next day he re-programmed his room to automatically switch to a popular galactic band if anyone came within range of his security sensors.

He pushed himself hard on the row-bike, the music hammering in his head, pounding the beat down into his legs as he attacked the pedals. Sweat poured from under his arms. More dripped down his forehead and stung his eyes. The pain kept him from thinking, or so he hoped. But it wasn't enough. The pull to see Rachel began to seep into his thoughts. He needed to fight harder.

Ben flipped the gear and changed over to rowing. The muscles in his arms and back strained as he worked the oars savagely. He rowed until he gasped for breath. If he could exhaust himself, he could go straight to bed and not care about anything. He could pretend she was still on earth, deep beneath the frigid waters of Lake Ontario. He'd dream about her though, which would be worse. Maybe if he laid eyes on her for a moment, only a moment, to know she was all right, he could sleep without Rachel consuming his every thought.

Ben slowed his pace until he began to relax and breathe normally. He coasted. The rowing reminded him of the days on the crew team at Stanford, gliding across the lagoon. He had been one with the boat, the team, the rhythm, and the water. He embraced it. It was his therapy. A great way to let off steam after grinding away all day at his studies in astrophysics. Much cheaper than booze therapy, although he did his fair share of partying on the weekends.

Five minutes later Ben slid off the MFIT and took several deep, cleansing breaths. He pulled his T-shirt off over his head and used it to wipe the sweat from his face, working his way down across his bare chest, tossed the shirt into the cleaning chute and pulled on a fresh one. Logical thoughts disintegrated, pushed to the back of his mind as his body took over control. He knew he couldn't trust himself, but he didn't have the strength to fight any longer. Nor did he really want to.

Avoiding the elevator tube and lighted hallways, he crept down the stairs to the third floor. The building was quiet. Outside the door to Medical, he glanced over his shoulder. No one. He tried to persuade his feet to turn around and leave, but the eye-scan acknowledged him and the door swooshed open before he could change his mind. He stepped inside and the door closed, leaving him where he knew he shouldn't be.

"Twenty percent lights," he whispered. The LEDs automatically dimmed and the soft glow illuminated the room enough to keep him from bumping into things. Although Ben had not been in Medical much over the years, he knew his way around. There were times when he needed to consult with Sanda on the status of the workers' health management. Every now and then a worker could not be effectively treated and had to be sent to specialists back on Earth. Lately it had been necessary to see the doctor more often, concerning the escalating crisis they were facing. Ben's job was to provide a safe environment for the inhabitants of the planet. And to make a profit. He was responsible for the lives of eighty-four people. Plus, one. And it was that "one" which tortured him.

Along the side wall, he passed the two outer examination

rooms and the pharmacy where rows of labeled spray-tubes had been placed meticulously on shelves. On the opposite wall of the pharmacy, an ID scanner stood guard over a large metal cabinet containing the narcotics, super stem-cell cultures and memory nanos – a locked area, accessible to only two people, the doctor and the CPO.

He approached the last room on the right, glad to see Sanda had locked it. He knew this was where she would be. To know she was here, on Goliath, was something he had thought about and wanted for a very long time. Coming to see her before she was re-animated was a mistake, but he couldn't make himself turn back. One more thing to add to his guilt-list.

Ben paused and blew out a slow breath. Finally, the opportunity to bring Rachel to Goliath, to have the excuse, the reason. It would take some time for her to adjust, but he knew it would become clear— *they* needed her. The problem was: how much time? *We need her now.* Or so he told himself.

"Open," he said and slid through the doorway into the dark room. A spit of anger flashed across his face. Why hadn't Sanda left the nightlight on? What if Rachel awoke and no one was there? She wouldn't know where she was. He relaxed his jaw, realizing his protective instinct was unfounded. Rachel would have to be reanimated and even then she might not know where she was, or who she was. It would take days, maybe a week before she would be conscious. There was no reason for Ben to be here now.

But, since he was already down here, he might as well make a quick check. He ran his hand down the side of the capsule, feeling the cool metal against his sweaty, hot palm. His blood coursed through his body and pounded hard across his forehead, his heartbeat speeding up with every millimeter closer to her. He touched the latch of the face shield and jerked his hand back as if he'd been scalded.

Calm down. This is all in the name of research. It's for the good of the colony. I have every right, in fact, it's my responsibility, to make sure the cryonic specimen is viable for experimentation.

"Lights steady up to eighty percent," he said. The lights came on gradually; the capsule emerged from the shadows like a mirage. He started to shake as he freed the lock and slowly pulled the face shield down.

"Rachel," he choked. "You're finally here. I need you, Rachel. I've needed you for so long."

CHAPTER 4

Sub-Level 3-Research lab
Tuesday, March 14
0635 hours

THREE HOURS later after Ben had left Medical that same morning, Sanda was just waking up.

"Jav-double caff," she grumbled and swung her legs over the side of the bunk. The brewing machine dropped a mug into place. A strong aroma filled the air as the brewer finished spitting out the liquid. "Add six mils soy." Pale fluid squirted into the cup and swirled on top of the dark beverage. She gulped down a few swallows and stepped into the blower tube.

"Wake-up-temp," she said and chilly bursts of disinfecting air prickled her naked body. The frigid blasts were invigorating though they made her shiver and suck in her breath. Some mornings she needed more of a jolt than she could get from strong java alone. It took less than eight seconds for her to spin around twice, the minimum number required for cleanliness, but she made herself stay for one more rotation. She hopped out of the blower and scrambled into her clothes. Ah, now she felt capable of beginning another day---even though it promised to be long.

Her apartment on Sub-Level 3, well below the unpredictable and sometimes destructive weather on the planet's surface, was at one end of the underground expanse, along with units for twelve other miners, mechanics and housekeeping personnel. One empty apartment was available, left vacant from the death of a miner from Sector VII. Medical, the Research Laboratory, and Sickbay comprised the other half of the floor. She was the only physician on Goliath, although everyone on the planet had first aid training, including emergency skin preservation and reconstruction. Accidents outside the belt could be fatal in a matter of minutes in such extreme temperatures.

She hugged her cup of jav to her, asked the room's computer to bring up the schematics on cryogenesis, downloaded the information onto a holo-stick, and trudged out the door to Medical. Normally, Sanda would have checked yesterday's lab results straight away, but now she had a new priority. It would have made better sense to leave Rachel on ice and attend to the more crucial matters. But Ben had fixed that, hadn't he? First, he had ordered her to find out what this mysterious disease was and how to combat it, then he had switched to having her concentrate on reanimating a dead woman. Why in the galaxy? Reanimating a person had never been done, even in the olden days, as far as she knew. At least, she had never learned about the process in all her years of schooling. They were wasting energy. Time was critical. Workers were dying.

The security scanner registered her ID and unlocked the door. Inside, she took another swig, set the cup down on the metal counter, grabbed a clean lab coat from the closet and started down the hall to check on her new patient. "Oops. Forgot my pep-punch." She turned back to pick up her mug of java and noticed the green flashing button on the switchboard

above the work table. "Room. Panel report please." Had she left
something on yesterday? She had been beyond tired by the
time she went home last night.

"03:30 South entrance. 03:47 South entrance. All clear," the
room responded.

That's odd. She cocked her head and frowned. *Looks like
the scanner was tripped at 03:30 this morning. Took it 17 minutes
to right itself? Probably just a shimmy in the bedrock screwing
with the timer. Seems okay now. If it happens again, I'll get
Lorensabio from repairs to look at it.* She shrugged, took another
sip of jav, and resumed her trek through Medical to Rachel's
room.

The locked door at the end of the hall opened for her.
Across the room the capsule floated, tubes holding it to the wall
like a lifepod moored to a space-shuttle. The capsule's shield
was down, revealing Rachel's motionless shape. "Didn't I close
that before I left last night?" She drained the last of her coffee.
Didn't matter. She looked at Rachel and saw that pink tinged
her cheeks and soft coral painted her lips. "Looking a little
more human today, are we? I see the blood synthesizers and
warmers were able to add some color. Let's see what else we can
improve." A smile started at the corner of Sanda's mouth. She
forced it down, back into a determined straight line, marched
over to her desk, and went to work.

"Locate procedure for reanimating humans."

Thirty seconds passed before the room's computer
responded. "No data in Goliath's files."

"Then search old IG files."

Rachel's temperature and hydration values lingered well
below normal. Not surprising. When new workers came to
Goliath, they hibernated on the eight-month space flight,
cooled to the point of slowing their vitals: heart rate, breathing,
and temperature. But they hadn't been vitrified as in Rachel's
case. Sanda wondered for a moment what story this young

woman had to tell. Why had she been frozen and why was she here, now?

"Why in the galaxy is it taking so long to retrieve the proper data!"

As if her annoyance sparked the air above her work station, waves of information began to materialize on the hologram. A waterfall of numbers, organic compounds and symbols cascaded down the wall. Luminita flicked her hand across the hologram, turning the pages. It was difficult to tell how long it would take for Rachel to regain consciousness. It could take up to two more days, depending on how well her body responded, and how well the perfusions had been done back in 1994 when she'd deanimated.

The bigger problem would be restoring her memory functions. Complete memory recovery is possible, depending on how much damage occurred from crystal formation deep within her brain, but it could be sketchy. If Rachel's long-term memory and personality were stored in durable cell structures and patterns within the brain, they wouldn't require continuous brain activity to survive. Once Rachel woke, assessment would be easier. Sanda glanced toward the capsule. "All we can do is rely on the nanos and hope for the best."

* * *

Friday, 17/03

Three days later, Rachel remained in an unconscious state. Her body responded to all the pokes and prods, by jerking and lashing out, but her mind remained adrift in some secret dimension.

"You should be coming out of this by now." Sanda crossed

her arms and frowned. Something was holding Rachel back; she didn't open her eyes. Obstinate maybe?

"The name, Rachel, must be an old biblical name. Certainly not a name used commonly in the 23rd century. Come to think of it, Ben's either. I wonder if Rachel means stubborn."

The doctor went over the procedure again to see if she had missed anything. She talked to the sleeping Rachel as she continued to fine tune the reanimation process: measuring, calculating and readjusting the diagnostic nanobots. Sanda added more cell and reconstruction bots as her patient showed gradual signs of improvement. The doctor explained what she was doing and why, hoping the sound of her voice or something she said might ignite interest somewhere in Rachel's mind, giving her a beacon to follow out of the darkness. The steady stream of conversation was not easy for Sanda, who worked a majority of her time alone in the lab doing research.

"I don't know what your name means but my middle name, Simone, means listening intently. But since I have to do all the talking, it doesn't quite fit, does it? And Sanda from my great, great grandmother means something about defending mankind. Doesn't seem too likely, either." She rotated her head back and forth and scrunched her shoulders up and down to relieve the tightness in her neck. "Or maybe Rachel means pain in the—."

Tiny bubbles rose to the top as Sanda shook the test tube filled with concentrated nanos and an atomizing agent. "This one goes straight up your nose. Hopefully it will work a little faster." She pulled a hover-stool over and sat next to Rachel.

"Might as well fill you in on a few things, in case you remember what I tell you. Where to start? For beginners, there are a lot of interesting people here. It takes a certain toughness to be a pioneer on a new planet. Well, the planet isn't new, but we're relatively new to the planet. Let's see. There's Imitar. Sometimes I wonder about him. He's slightly more than a century old, but sometimes he acts like a, what do you call them?" She looked up at the ceiling and bit the corner of her bottom lip. "A teenager—I think that's it." She shook her head. "One minute he's guiding space shuttles into the hanger or zipping across the hot-side to rescue a worker suffering from heat stroke. The next minute he's spinning out of orbit looking for that silly baseball cap of his. Or his latest, forgetting his hygiene. I wish he would get rid of that chin hair." She chuckled. "He's our best though. He can solve any programming problems, figure out codes using all those IG languages, and whatever else is needed. Imitar is always willing to help."

"Now Zoleta." Sanda wrinkled her forehead and started to speak, and stopped again. She patted the side of the capsule. "You know, I think I'll just let you make up your own mind on that one."

The doctor checked the monitors. No change in Rachel's state of consciousness. Sanda continued her monologue.

"The person in charge of this planet, the Chief Planetary Officer, is a highly intelligent man. He runs a tight compound and makes all of the final decisions, usually the right ones."

Sanda was beginning to feel like an archeologist trying to reconstruct the life of a primitive human, literally. Although she had to admit, it was more interesting than she thought it would be. Certainly less frustrating than watching failure after failure on her research into the deaths of the workers from Sector VII.

"That reminds me, I only have a couple more minutes. I had better check on my other patient and yesterday's results." She turned the temperature up two degrees and settled back on her stool.

"Where were we? Oh yes, the Commander. He works harder than anyone else on this planet and he's fair-minded, as long as it's logical to him. I think he has a primary life-mate, maybe a secondary and four or five offspring. More than one child was allowed back in his days, can you imagine? That makes me wonder if he might be close to your century. Anyway, he hasn't returned to Earth for years and it's a dangerous journey to Goliath. You probably won't see much of Benjamin Thomas Schaefer. He—"

A soft beep from the monitor drew Sanda's attention. Rachel's heart-rate jumped a notch.

CHAPTER 5

Sub-Level 3-Medical Ward
Saturday, March 18
1027 hours

RACHEL'S EYELIDS fluttered as she watched broken pieces of a dream scatter like leaves in a whirlwind. Her body twitched and cramped. She squeezed her hands into tight fists and pressed her legs downward in a spastic stretch, her left ankle rebelling against the command. Thoughts floated close to her consciousness, but the cold wind blew them away before she could remember. If she could just make her body move.

She forced her eyes open. They slammed back shut.

She blinked again, trying to clear grainy matter out of her eyes. It was like looking through a sandstorm. Her swollen tongue crept out and tried to wet her bottom lip. It was too much work and she gave up, letting herself be buried by the heavy sand.

There was the voice again, closer now. Rachel nudged her head toward it, or at least thought she had. A female voice, droning on and on, a hint of sadness softening the edges, taking away the crisp confidence, telling her things which didn't make sense or mean anything to her. Maybe the woman was speaking a different language. Or maybe she was cold and tired. Rachel certainly was. Her own chin must be chattering, she was so cold, and too tired to ask the woman for a blanket.

She had resigned herself to this chilly slumber when cruel fingers pulled her eyelids open, making the hot sandstorm scratch across her vision once more. Then something cool and soothing dropped into each eye. She wanted to keep her eyes shut, afraid the blinding pain would return, but her curiosity beckoned and she cautiously opened them again.

A woman with short hair, like a man's crew-cut, a pixy nose, and big, brown eyes, stood over her. Rachel studied her as the woman circled a light around Rachel's face, making her squint. She tried to turn her head but her neck muscles wouldn't cooperate and she only succeeded in sending shooting pains up into the back of her skull. She was sure she had screamed, but heard only a pathetic whimper.

"Someone is finally waking up. This should help," the woman said, and she sprayed something wet up Rachel's left nostril. She shivered and felt her muscles spasm in tiny jerks. The mini-convulsions stopped, leaving her tingly all over, like her body was one giant funny bone.

The woman was watching her closely. Rachel felt naked under her scrutiny. She wished she could lift her head to make sure she had clothes on. Was she in cement or something? She felt so heavy.

"Can you speak? Do you feel any pain? Are you cold?"

No duh, she would say if she could only move her lips and if her vocal cords weren't frozen.

"I'm Dr. Luminita and I'm in charge of your care."

"Ocker?"

The doctor grabbed a metal device, the size of a soda can, squeezed it in the middle and dragged it across Rachel's neck. "Try again. What did you say?"

Rachel cleared her throat, "Am. Am I in a hos. Hospital? What happened? What am I doing here?" She scanned the room with jumpy eyes and brought her focus back to the doctor.

"You're fine. You need to listen to me, and don't try to talk. I know you're confused and you probably have a lot of questions, but for now, try to relax. You're safe. I'll explain things after you've had more rest. You are in the final stages of reanimation and restructuring. It takes time."

The doctor waved her hand through the air as if she were brushing cobwebs from the ceiling. Strange symbols swarmed in the light above her and settled into columns. She used both hands to maneuver the array, switching one line of numbers with another, then spreading them out again.

Rachel squeezed her eyes shut, then peeked out, but the visions were still wafting in the air. "That?" she said and lifted a shaky finger to point at the hologram.

"This?" The doctor waved at the figures. "This is your chart."

"Ch. Chart? No. Ill. Usion?"

"No. It's an HC. A holographic chart. *Your* holographic chart. Your HC."

Rachel gave a slight shake of her head. No blinding pain this time.

Sanda continued, "The bots are taking readings and displaying the data on your chart. Is something hurting you?"

"The bots?" Rachel sucked ragged breaths into her tight lungs. Her eyes darted wildly around the room and beads of sweat broke out on her forehead.

"Where am? Not right. Home. I. Need to go—"

"Enough for today. Smell this."

"What. Is. It? So cold. I'm so. Cold."

"This will warm you up. Go ahead take a whiff. That's right."

Rachel hesitated then took a tiny sniff of the pink liquid in the vial held beneath her nose. "Smells good. Cherry . . . Cough syrup." Rachel's eyelids grew heavy. "Something. Bad. Must tell. You. Be. Fore . . ." She struggled, fighting the sinking feeling, like being pulled down into wet cement.

CHAPTER 6

Sub-Level 3-Dr. Luminita's office
Saturday
1247 hours

IT HAD ONLY BEEN two and a half hours since Rachel had gained consciousness, but it felt like days to Sanda. Rachel would sleep for the rest of the day and Sanda still had plenty of work to do and problems to solve. She opened the latest test results from Sector VII, hoping for a breakthrough, hoping today the data would give her the answer they needed. Skimming over the figures, she could see the experiment had failed. Sanda closed the hologram and hung her head. There was nothing to show how this disease started and why all her attempts to construct viable nanobots aimed at annihilating the invading organism had failed. No cure was within sight, no vaccination to support and enhance the patient's immune system had worked.

She had run out of ideas.

She plopped down at her desk, rested her chin in her hands and took a moment to think. What had Ben said about the cryo? About Rachel? Something about her being valuable to the research? Or did he mean in the Research Department? It didn't make any sense. Either way, it would be best for Sanda to get Rachel functioning and up to speed as fast as possible so she could be turned over to someone else and Sanda could continue with her life or death work.

The room chimed, interrupting her thoughts, "Thirteen hundred."

Right on cue, her stomach started to grumble. She didn't want to take the time to eat, but she wasn't getting much done at this rate. She pushed back from her desk and headed for the door.

Before she got there, it slid open and Ben walked in.

"CPO Schaefer. I didn't expect to see you."

Ben looked straight at her. "It's been five days since the shipment arrived."

"I was about to go to lunch. Would you like—"

"What is the estimated date when the patient will be ready for work?"

"What?"

"The patient. When will she be ready to contribute to your research?"

"Oh, you mean the cryo? I have her sedated now so her body can catch up and function properly. It'll take as long as it takes. Where did you get her? Is she a regular recruit? And what do you mean contribute to my research?"

Ben kept his gaze locked on Sanda's, making her feel a bit uncomfortable. "What has she told you so far?"

"She hasn't been awake long enough for me to find out anything about her. I've only been able to run preliminary med-bots to see what damage there might be to her system. She's been in a frozen, not a sleeper-state, for one-hundred-eighty years according to the tag around her neck. There wasn't a medical chart with her in the capsule or anywhere I could find. It could take several months to get her acclimated, let alone bring her up to speed, if ever, so she can help with data collection, evaluations, or whatever you seem to have in mind for her." Sanda crossed her arms and scowled at him. "I don't know how extensive her scientific background is. Either way, she's a century and a half behind. She'll most likely be quite lost. This will all be new. Why don't you just tell me what's going on?"

"Push the brain-function and reasoning-enhancers. We need to do all we can to keep more of our workers from dying. Maybe the cryo can help."

Sanda shook her head. "Believe me, I want nothing more than to have her up and out of Medical. But you must understand, I can't predict how she'll react to being thrown into a completely foreign environment without knowing where she is or what's she's doing here or recognizing a single soul. And the initial report shows some kind of congenital heart defect. It doesn't seem to be anything serious, but we don't see this type of thing anymore so I'm going to target a round of nano therapy. Normally it would only take a couple of weeks of cell turnover to fix the problem, but with her being frozen for such a long—"

"No. Do not do any gene manipulations on the cryo!"

Sanda gasped. "I'm not going to do gene therapy, it's a structural repair. One of her heart valves needs cell regeneration to help it close properly."

"Nothing is to be changed, re-arranged or modified on this patient's physiological makeup unless I give the order."

"This patient?" Sanda's nostrils flared. "Her NAME is Rachel. And she is MY patient."

"Dr. Luminita. Do not make the mistake of forcing me to use my authoritative power. As long as you are on this planet, you are under my orders."

Sanda couldn't let it go. She wouldn't let it go. Spending all this time on Rachel just to have her fall apart later? Ludicrous. Surely, he could see the waste in that.

She persisted. "What if a gene splice becomes necessary to

save Rachel's life? What if she can't fight off a disease that wouldn't affect her if she'd been previously altered like we've been?" She saw a slight shift in Ben's eyes, but the moment was gone and he stared hard at her.

"Is there a problem? I want you to hold off on doing anything other than what it takes to re-animate her."

"There's no problem. I just don't understand why we can't offer this young woman all the medical advances of our society." Sanda eyed the CPO. What was his stake in all this? And why does he care what happens to Rachel? Rachel certainly didn't look like someone who would work in the mines, which is what would matter most to Ben and his career.

"B-F-R-Es. That's it. I want a daily progress report. If anything else comes up concerning the patient, I want to know about it. Immediately." He strode toward the door. "And I want a TM embedded before she is cognizant of her surroundings."

Sanda's frown deepened. It hardly mattered what he wanted. This was her patient. "Is she supposed to live down here on Medical like some caged animal? Or will someone get her settled, if and when she becomes functional, and show her around? It's not going to be me. I can tell you that."

He turned to face her. "I'll have Imitar take charge of getting the woman used to her surroundings."

"But what about –"

"Not yet. Let's wait and see what we're dealing with before we change anything about her that's not vital to her recovery." He turned and strode out the door.

Sanda stood staring at the empty doorway, shaking her head.

What's he talking about? Why on Goliath wouldn't Ben want Rachel to have the same physiological strengths as they had? And a tracking marker on her? Rachel has nowhere to go. Sanda blew air out her cheeks. *I've never questioned Ben's authority before, but this just doesn't seem right. But why do I care? I have enough on my disc.*

There was something about the girl though, something innocent in Rachel's eyes that made Sanda want to care for her. Something that made Sanda remember why she had first studied medicine. A time before she had switched the emphasis to research. A time long ago.

CHAPTER 7

Sub-level 3, Medical Research Dept.
Tuesday, March 21
0800 hours

IMITAR SIGHED as he considered the order, disguised as a request, from CPO Schaefer to give Rachel a tour of the compound and get her settled in her quarters. Feelings of excitement and confusion battled in his mind. Number one, he was not female, not that that should make a difference. Maybe he wasn't as confused as he was nervous. But why wouldn't it be Dr. L's job, he wondered? Rachel was already under her care. Was Ben giving him an extra responsibility because he could be trusted to do a good job, or was he chosen because he wasn't as vital to operations as say, Zoleta? He had to admit it was Zoleta that was bothering him. He could never be sure how she saw things. Suspicion seemed to be her default. It was Zoleta who had encouraged him to breach protocol the day they had landed the unmanned cargo shuttle.

Imitar had pulled up the info and scanned down the report. "Looks okay, nothing different, same old—wait a second. This is interesting."

Zoleta had marched across the room and looked over his shoulder. He'd caught a whiff of freedenia, at least that's what he thought it was, as she pointed at the highlighted error.

"Looks like we received some extra supplies. Or supply, rather," she said.

"A large capsule, by the dimensions and weight. Doesn't say what it is."

"Let's check it out." She headed toward the doorway, stopped and turned to him. "Aren't you coming?"

"Shouldn't we call CPO Schaefer? Or security? What if it's dangerous? Or contaminated?" Imitar envisioned flesh-eating, bone-warping bugs crawling over his body. He picked at his chin whiskers.

"Don't be such a worry-worm."

"Here we go," he said under his breath.

He followed her down the ramp to the cargo area. She flashed her eyes at the retinal scan and stated her name and rank. He was impressed. She out-ranked him by several levels, but he didn't know she was able open the hatch before Schaefer had given the order.

The door to medical slid open bringing Imitar back to the present. "Morning, Doc. Anything new with— what's her name again?"

"You mean Rachel? Yes. She started to come out of it yesterday but I gave her a sedative. I want her to go a little slower on the re-entry. She should wake up more refreshed and coherent sometime this morning. Although how coherent can one be waking up one-hundred -eighty years later? It's going to take a lot for her to adjust to her new surroundings. I just hope the complete revival goes smoothly. I need to get back to my other obligations."

"Do you really think she's from 1994? I hope she has some good stories. I can remember begging my great-to-the-fourth grandfather to tell us tales from his time. The way life was before rejuvenations or deep space travel."

Visions of talking to a time-traveler tickled his brain. Maybe he could find out if some of the things his ancestors had alluded to were true or not. Did it really take humans that long to figure out the genome and to clone, what, a sheep? And maybe Rachel could tell him about the pioneers on the first space station, or the beginnings of the World Wide Web. *Craters. Maybe she can tell me about some of the ancient, what were they called, video games?*

"Will you sit with her, Imitar?" Sanda asked. "She should wake up soon and I need to check on another worker I just admitted to quarantine."

"Another worker? From Sector VII?"

Sanda nodded. "I'm afraid so."

"Holy craters! That's terrible news. We're going to be in trouble, as a team, as a mining operation, as a viable colony on this planet. What are we going to do?"

"I'm working as fast as I can on the problem."

"In that case, I'd be more than happy to stay awhile. Anyway, CPO Schaefer asked me to look out for the cryo. Show her around and get her settled after she's out of hibernation."

"That would be a big help, Imitar. I'll be in sick-bay if you need me."

*　＊　＊　＊*

Imitar sat on the hover-stool near the head of Rachel's gurney. He was glad Sanda had moved Rachel out of the space-pod and onto a regular bed. Maybe she would feel more comfortable when she came to.

Her pale skin glowed under the overhead lights and her chest expanded and deflated with steady breaths. Rachel's muscles twitched in random groups making Imitar wonder what she was dreaming, or if she was dreaming. Before he knew it, his mind had drifted off, wrapped around thoughts of Zoleta. He longed to watch Zoleta sleep. That was partially true; he longed for Zoleta, period. The few times she had brought him to her bed, he had stayed awake after they had melded. He wanted to memorize every line of her face. Sleep softened her features and smoothed her ambition. The only nights she had let him stay were the times when her father or brother had received another badge in his career, and she had felt left behind. Imitar had pulled her to him and let her cry softly in his arms, but no matter how much or how often he told her she was an amazing leader, she always needed to prove it. Zoleta was tough, but she could be compassionate and caring, especially if she didn't think anyone was watching.

Zoleta was never straight forward as far as Imitar was concerned. What was she thinking or plotting now? *If she'd let me in enough to tell me. Trust me. What am I saying? How could she trust me? If she ever found out I ran across her private files, even if it was by accident, she'd shoot me into the next galaxy.*

"God my head hurts."

Imitar jumped at the sound of Rachel's voice. "You're awake."

"What? Where?" Rachel turned her head back and forth, scanning the room. "Please. No. I don't want to be in this dream again." She rubbed her eyes hard and opened them. "I don't remember any of this. I don't know any of this. Oh God, make this stop."

"It's going to be okay. My name is Imitar. You aren't dreaming. This is the Medical area of the compound. You've been fro – asleep, off and on, for eight days. I'll get the doctor."

"You're a what? Did you say I've been here for over a week? What happened to me? Was I in a car accident? Have I been in a coma?" She jerked forward then fell back against the bed. "I'm so weak. My body feels trashed, like I've been out of it for a hundred years, not just three days."

"Would you like to sit up higher?"

"I don't think I can."

"It's okay, I'll help you. Raise head forty degrees," he said. The upper half of the bed slowly brought Rachel to a more upright position. She tried to bend forward and Imitar scrambled to the side, slipped his arm behind her shoulder, and held her so she didn't list to either side.

"Is that better? Are you dizzy?"

"A little, maybe. I think I'm just weak, like all my muscles have disintegrated."

"You should take it slow. You've been horizontal for quite a while and inverted for ages." He released his hold and stepped back.

"Yes. Eight days, you said." She opened her eyes wide, terror dilating her pupils. Then she snapped them shut and whispered, "This is the room that was in my crazy dream before. There was this woman and she conjured up images in midair. Then she made me smell something. That's the last thing I remember."

A loud, violent hiccup jarred Rachel's body and she pressed her fist to her sternum. "Ouch. That really hurts. I need to go home. Just help me get out of here will you –" Another hiccup forced her back against the bed.

"We don't have your quarters set up for you yet. They should be ready by tomorrow and I'll help you move in."

"My quarters? I don't know what you're talking about. I'm not staying here." She shook her head. "I have to go home. Please don't make me stay." She tried to get up but was too weak and fell back. Her chin trembled and she started to sob in-between hiccups which were coming faster and harder.

Unsure of what to do, Imitar tapped his ear bud. "Maybe I'd better call Doc."

"Oh my God," Rachel said between spasms. "I'm in a hospital's psych ward, aren't I? You aren't even using a phone. You're a patient too."

"You're in Medical, not a hospital. You're on Goliath, a planet in the Libra constellation. You arrived here eight days ago from Earth."

She clenched her fists and bit her bottom lip. The sobbing diminished into short bursts of sniffs but the hiccups continued unabated. "I suppose you are the head Martian?"

"We are not on Mars. Mars is a planet in the solar system you came from."

"I know where Mars is. So, you're telling me that you are an alien from another planet?"

"No. *We,* including you, are actually the aliens on this planet. But it's going to be fine. You'll like it here."

What am I telling her? Why did I say that? How do I know if she'll like it here? She doesn't know where here is.

Rachel sucked in a quick breath, held it, then let it out and sucked in another. She repeated the process four times and looked over at Imitar. "Okay, let's say we are on another planet, which is impossible of course. Why would *I* be here?"

Holding her breath seemed to have helped stop the chest spasms. Her tears were gone, but now Imitar was worried by the angry look she gave him. The CPO hadn't had time to tell Imitar much so he wasn't sure what he could or *should* tell her. If he was going to have to watch out for Rachel, Ben had better give him a little more information. Or Imitar might have to do some investigating on his own.

Rachel shifted her gaze past his shoulder. "It's you. You're that woman who was here before. Are you the Director of this warped experiment?"

Imitar turned to see Dr. Luminita coming toward the bed. "Glad to see you, Doc."

"Having trouble, are we?"

"She seems upset."

"Rachel. I'm Dr. Luminita and yes, I am the woman who was here yesterday when you woke. I'm going to tell you what we know. I'm afraid we have very little information about you. Are you ready to listen? I'm not here to hurt you or make things harder. Do you understand?" Sanda reached toward Rachel's shoulder but pulled her hand back without touching her.

Rachel closed her eyes and nodded.

"You arrived a week ago in a cargo shipment that left Earth eight months earlier. You were in a cryogenic state and I—how should I put this—revived you."

"Cryogenic state? Doesn't that mean frozen? You're saying I've been frozen for eight months? And I'm alive? That's not possible."

"You've been frozen for much longer than eight months."

Rachel hugged her body and rocked back and forth on the bed. "No. This isn't right. This isn't happening. It's not real. I'm dreaming. This is all a bad dream. Or, is it death? Am I dead?" She hugged her knees to her chest and mumbled to herself until Imitar couldn't stand it any longer.

"Do something, Doc."

"Would you like to try to stand and get some circulation going? You said your muscles feel weak. I can help support you if you want." Imitar looked over at Sanda.

Rachel kept rocking but moved her hands over her ears as if to block out Imitar and the doctor.

"Try to walk, Rachel," Imitar said. "It'll make you feel better if you get your body moving. Sanda, I mean Dr. Luminita, and I will both help you."

Rachel looked around the room then gave a small nod.

Imitar extended his hand for her to grasp as she raised herself
slowly off the edge of the bed and stood, swaying on wobbly
legs. When her stance finally stabilized, she glanced up at the
doctor and Imitar. "Oh God, I'm hallucinating again. Either you
two are the tallest people I've ever seen, or I'm shrinking."

"People born back in your century were much shorter
compared to the average height of most people today."

"In my century?"

"Yes. The name-tag you had on said—why don't you tell
her, Imitar?"

"Name-tag?" Rachel checked her wrists.

*Great, thanks a lot, Doc. I don't think this is going to be good
news for Rachel. I can see she's terrified.* He took a deep breath,
"Rachel, when I brought you down to Medical from Space
Control, you had a tag around your neck with your name on it.
It is Rachel, right? It had the date of your birth."

Her hand automatically went to her throat, feeling for the
identification. "February 27, 1960, was the day I was born. Why?
Is it my birthday today or something? If it is, it's the worst
birthday I can ever remember. I think."

"No, sorry, it's not. The tag also had the date you died –
January 22, 1994."

"What!? This is a weird joke." She looked at both of them.
"Died, what do you mean, died? I'm obviously not dead. Did I
fall into the river and my heart stopped? Is that what you
mean? So I was semi-frozen? How long was I out? Wait. What's
today?"

"Today is Tuesday, March 21st. But . . ." Imitar rubbed the
back of his neck and shuffled his feet.

"But what?"

He glanced at Sanda.

"Rachel. The year is 2175."

Imitar caught her as she fell. He held her tight to his chest and felt the anger in his jaw and the heat in his face. *How could CPO Schaefer do this to someone? Take a person from her home and bring her to a far-off planet. Rachel couldn't have planned to come here. Why would Ben bring her to Goliath and what was he trying to gain?*

CHAPTER 8

Compound
Wednesday, March 22
0930 hours

THE NEXT DAY, Rachel's head felt groggy and her mouth tasted like she had partied all night long. She was still in the room with no windows, lying in a bed that was not her own. The walls were white, devoid of pictures, and there was an odd smell that she couldn't quite place. That proved it. She was still on the hospital ward and it was time to get out of there.

Something blue at the end of the bed caught her eye. She reached down and pulled up a one-piece midnight-blue jumpsuit with silver stripes running down each leg. It looked like it was made for a ten-year-old. The silky material slipped through her fingers. Surely the guards or whoever they are didn't think this was going to fit her?

Sanda burst through the door, startling Rachel. "Better today? Go ahead and put on the uniform. Imitar will be here in a few minutes to show you the compound."

"Um. I'm quite a bit shorter than you people, but I'm not

this small." Rachel held up the outfit. "You must have given me your daughter's clothes."

The doctor's face paled. "I don't have a daughter. It will fit. Try it."

"There's no zipper."

"Step through the opening at the top."

"Right." She'd show this woman, this so-called doctor. The garment would never make it past her thighs. But when she pulled up one pant leg then the other, and put each arm through the sleeves, the uniform easily stretched and lengthened to fit her perfectly.

"Wow. What kind of material is this?"

"Excuse me. Am I interrupting?" A male voice called from the doorway.

"Imitar. Good morning. I was just about to show Rachel around the lab. Are you here to take her to her apartment?"

"If you give the go-ahead."

"Fine with me. Rachel?"

"This is the most exhausting dream I've ever had."

"Let me get her some footgear and you can take her." Sanda left and returned with a pair of tiny slippers.

"I've always wanted blue moccasins. Do you have anything bigger? Say in a size six and a half?" Sanda gave her a blank stare. "Okay. Whatever." Rachel shrugged, then tugged one shoe on, amazed at how it formed comfortably to her foot, and then followed with the other, pulling it farther up past her ankle. She evened out the pair by pulling them both up to below her knees. "Boots! Now this is a delusion of grandeur I can deal with."

"Ready to see your own place?"

Dream or no dream, the Imitar man/boy was slim, but very tall and could overpower Rachel if he took a notion. He didn't look scary though. He had a nice smile and seemed kind of sweet.

CHAPTER 9

Three weeks later
Sub-Level 3
Wednesday, April 12
2200 hours

IT HAD BEEN a full and challenging three weeks since Rachel woke not knowing who she was or where she was. She learned the layout of her living quarters, the lab, and the compound as if she was underwater, not engaged, just going through the motions because she didn't know what else to do. Every now and then she was amazed at the science and technology that existed on this planet but never enough to do anything more than learn the simple skills she was training to do. It all still seemed like a complicated nightmare. In the time that she had been 'the living dead', earth had had its own problems. Imitar had given her the history lesson: back in the twenty-first century, global warming melted the ice caps causing the oceans to rise. Across the globe, less land resulted in dwindling food supplies, resources, and living space. Millions of people starved to death and the rest fought to keep what they had to themselves.

Rachel dragged herself down the long hallway toward her one-room apartment, wanting to crawl into her bunk and sleep for a month. Had she eaten anything all day? She could check with Imitar. No, he was probably already up at the D.C. right now eating with the other giant, robotic people. Or maybe not. On Goliath, eating was only for refueling. No conversations, no socializing, just shove it in and move on. No one had yet to go out of their way to welcome Rachel when she sat down at a table with her meal. Face it. She had no contacts other than Dr. Luminita and Imitar. Sanda seemed patient enough, but Imitar was the one who seemed genuinely interested in her.

Does this corridor seem to slope uphill tonight? Has it always done that? The running lights along the floor aren't as bright as usual either, or maybe it's just me. She trudged on, squinting at the numbers above the portals. She rubbed her eyes to make the numbers above the door hold still long enough to see if it was the right room. *Yep, this is it. Home.*

She lifted her head for the recognition scan. God, her head was heavy. The door must have opened because she ended up inside the small room. How she made it over the threshold, she couldn't say. She stepped out of her boots, ignoring the pungent odor wafting up from her feet. She fumbled with the shoulder-clips on her tunic, fingers refusing to help. The shower tube beckoned, but she sighed and pulled herself up into her bunk, and burrowed into the side of the wall, like a hibernating animal.

Down, down, she sank into a deep sleep filled with heavy, exhausting dreams. She tried to move her arms, her legs, but the more she thrashed, the more trapped she became, shackled in viscous lead, trying to keep her head up to breath. Her heart pummeled against her chest. No. She didn't want to be here again. Stuck in a place without time. Without life.

Someone in her dream –a man – tried to pull her out of the cement setting up around her body, slowly hardening, solidifying. The man's muscular frame seemed familiar. His shirtless broad shoulders strained with a frantic effort to free her. Sweat poured down his neck and across his chest. His face was a blur. He screamed at her, "Rachel. Rachel!" as he wielded a sledge hammer, smashing at the cement. Pounding and pounding. Trying to break her free.

* * *

Saturday, April 13
0700

"Rachel!" Imitar hollered as he banged on her door. "Are you okay? You missed mess call. Rachel? Can you hear me? Open the door."

"What?" She sat up and whacked her head on the low ceiling of the berth. "Shit." She rubbed the knot emerging at her hairline. "Imitar. What? Oh, sorry. Open."

"Craters! You've been sleeping for over seven hours. Are you sick? Sanda sent me to check on you."

"What's the deal with you people and only four or five hours of sleep a night? Isn't eight the recommended number?" She crawled out of her bunk and sat on the edge, holding her head in her hands. Yuck, her mouth tasted nasty.

"No one sleeps seven hours unless they're ill or had too many Rang-O-Tangs. Six hours is sleeping in. And what is that awful smell?" He grabbed his nose, eyes watering.

She looked up at him and pointed a weary finger at her boots heaped in the middle of the room.

"Well. Uh, why don't you get in the blower, take those in with you, then come down to Medical when you're dressed?" Breathing through his mouth, he looked around the room and scratched his stubble. "I think Sanda wants you to go with her to meet Ben and go over the—"

"Ben? The CPO Ben? I'll be right there." She jumped out of bed and rifled through her clean clothes, chattering to herself as she threw various tunics over her shoulder. She picked out the jade green uniform and held it up against her. "This look okay?"

"It'll be great, as long as you take care of that . . . that aroma." He waved toward the boots and fanned his nose at the same time.

* * *

Twelve minutes later, Rachel, face flushed and out of breath, darted in to Medical, tripping through the doorway. She banged her arm on the counter as she caught herself.

"Rachel. Slow down, don't kill yourself," Sanda said in a scolding tone. She placed her hands on her hips, "You're starting to be helpful around here. I'd hate to lose you now." A smile crept across her lips. "Please be careful. Let me look at your arm."

"It's okay Dr. Luminita. I don't know why I'm so clumsy. But thanks." And she held her arm out to Sanda.

Sanda felt along the elbow and carefully rotated Rachel's wrist back and forth. She smiled, "Yes, I think you'll be fine." She lowered Rachel's arm and gave her a gentle pat. "You'll have a bit of a bruise. And please, call me Sanda. You've been working with me for how many weeks now? Speaking of which, we need to get busy. Lots to do."

Rachel took the lab coat Sanda held out to her. "Imitar said something about going to meet Mr. . . . Commander . . . General . . ." She shook her head, searching for the right title. "The CPO man. Person."

"He hasn't called for us yet. I've been keeping him up to date on the research and with your progress. He's occupied with bigger problems right now."

"He wants to know about my progress?" Rachel bit the side of her lip.

"He's concerned with every person on this planet. And whether or not they are working hard."

"Am I working hard enough? Do you think I should be doing more? I'm tired but I feel I could take on more responsibility with the research. If you think I'm ready."

"You're doing fine. I'm impressed with how far you've come these past few weeks. You seem to have a natural talent for analyzing data. Do you remember what you did . . . before?"

"Before?"

"What type of work you used to do?"

"Not really. Just bits and pieces. It all jumbles together most of the time. I've had glimpses of an older man and woman. I think they're my parents, but it makes me sad so I don't let myself focus on the memories for very long."

Rachel walked over to the lab window and stared at the robotic arms waiting to be programmed. She squeezed the flesh on her own arm. She didn't know how much to tell Sanda about her dreams. They haunted her more than they gave her a sense of who she was. It was hard to distinguish between what was a true memory or her imagination trying to fill in the blanks. If she could find out who she was, maybe she would know what she was supposed to do.

"It's all still right here, Rachel." Sanda tapped the side of her own head. "It'll just take the right stimulus, something to make it click. Could be someone's name, a picture, or maybe a smell, to unlock the pathway. It'll come. Don't try to force it or hold it back."

Easy for her to say.

Rachel looked at the test tubes as she placed them in the rack. Colors swirled inside each one like wisps of smoke. She thought about the Chief Planetary Officer again, curious to meet him. *Kind of.* From all she'd heard, she pictured him as huge, commanding, and cold. What did Imitar say the miners called him? Sub-Zero Sarge. That sure didn't make her feel competent. She tried to swallow around a non-existent chunk of cotton that seemed to be stuck in her throat. Why should she be nervous or scared to meet him? It wasn't her fault she was here. She didn't ask to be brought to Goliath. If anything, they should start answering her questions. No, she needed to meet him, the sooner the better.

"Rachel?" Sanda chuckled. "Are you going to take those samples over to chromatography, or analyze them yourself by staring at them?"

"Sorry." Rachel turned quickly. The rack of test tubes slipped from her sweaty hand and crashed to the floor. "Oh no." She bent to pick up the broken glass, cutting her pinky finger in the process. Tears rolled down her cheeks. She blinked hard, trying to hold them back, not let Sanda see.

"Did you cut yourself?"

Sanda's voice was soft, like a voice from somewhere in Rachel's past. Someone she wished would hold her, stroke her hair, and make all her problems disappear. Why did she always feel like such a little kid? Was she this inept in her other life? Rachel couldn't answer Sanda. It was only a tiny cut for God's sake. Nothing really. But it was everything. Everything and nothing. She kept her head bent, struggling for control.

Sobs escaped, despite her attempts to hold back the tears, and echoed off the barren white walls.

"Use the mini sanitizer, while I get you a stem-wrap," Sanda said.

Rachel nodded, dabbed at her tears, and wiped her nose with the back of the uninjured hand.

"In fact, use the sanitizer on that hand too." Sanda pointed as Rachel made another swipe.

Rachel rolled up her sleeve and placed her arm inside the sanitizer. The air felt cool and tingly on her skin, making her shiver. She pulled it out and stuck in the other arm while she stared at the cut finger. The bleeding had stopped, but the gap in the flesh looked jagged and angry. Sandra brought the bandage to her.

"I'm so sorry. All those samples . . . and time . . . and maybe lives."

"Hold out your finger." The doctor touched the white piece of plastic substance to Rachel's finger. It wrapped around her pinky and sealed itself together at the seam. Sanda placed a small cast over the bandage to protect it while it healed. "The repair stems infused in the bandage will mend the cut in four minutes, but you can leave the whole thing on longer. It will dissolve in a couple of hours, cast and all."

The bandaged finger looked like a marshmallow on a stick, ready for toasting over an open campfire. The image made something click in Rachel's mind, like a gear slipping into place. She used to do that, go camping with her family.

Excitement grew in the pit of her stomach, replacing some of the sick feeling from just moments before. "I think I remember my family. My mom and dad. And my older sister." She turned to see if Sanda had heard her.

But the doctor had left. Was she so upset with Rachel she couldn't stand to be in the same room? *Stop thinking like a two-year old. This isn't about me.* Rachel shook off her doubts, went to find Sanda and apologize again for her clumsiness and possibly jeopardizing the lives of Goliathians. She checked down the hall and found Sanda standing in her office with her back to the door. As Rachel raised a tentative hand to knock on the door frame, Sanda's raised voice stopped her mid tap.

"But it might help if we give her tonins—" Sanda was shaking her head, held prisoner by the person on the other end of the call. She threw her hands up to the ceiling in surrender. "Fine. I'll bring her up in twenty minutes."

Something about the tone in Sanda's voice made every

muscle in Rachel's body stiffen. All thoughts of telling Sanda about the small breakthrough in her memory vaporized. A throaty 'ahem' would have been proper at this point, but Rachel's vocal cords were constricted as well, leaving only her hearing.

Sanda tapped off her earbud without a goodbye and turned toward the door, her face red, lips tight. "Oh. Rachel. I didn't see you." Her features smoothed quickly, leaving only a pink flame visible on her cheeks.

"Were you just talking about me? What are tonins? Do you mean serotonin, mood enhancers? And help me what?"

"Rachel, I think you are exhibiting signs of depression. We have simple meds that might help. The CPO doesn't want you to take anything but he does want to meet you today, so I will talk to him about what would be best for you."

"Meet him? Right now?" Rachel managed to choke.

Sanda nodded. "I need to go back to my place to get something first. I'll only be ten minutes at most, and then we can head over to Command Center. Why don't you prep the next sample batch while I'm gone?"

Rachel gathered another set of test tubes from the 'clean' cupboard, her puffed-up finger not helping any with dexterity. She sighed. *I'm such an idiot.* Had she always been this uncoordinated or was this something new? Maybe space flight had messed her up. "I'll have to ask the Doc if other passengers—

A deafening siren slammed her body, knocking her back like the recoil from a rifle shot. She covered her ears with both hands, her bandaged pinky sticking out like a fat antenna.

No one had gone over any emergency procedures with her. She had no idea where to go and Dr. Luminita wasn't back yet. Rachel didn't smell any smoke.

Then the shock waves hit.

The lights went out.

She ran into the hallway.

Flashing lines of yellow, orange, and red lights ran along the floor in time with the blasts from the alarm. The combination was enough to make her feel like she was in the middle of an epileptic seizure. The lights seemed to illuminate a path toward the elevator tube. But that couldn't be right. Weren't you supposed to take the stairs in an emergency? She had yet to see any staircase and now was not the time to look for one. Where was everybody? Wasn't there some kind of back-up generator for lights and air circulation?

Air.

Suddenly, it seemed harder to breathe or maybe it was the panic that threatened to disable her. All this time not understanding where she was or who she was but finally feeling she might have a purpose, and now she was going to die from asphyxiation.

"Get ahold of yourself," she whispered, and willed her feet to move toward the elevator.

CHAPTER 10

Command Center—Ground Level
Saturday, April 13
0900 hours

"Ben, we need to boost the neutron diffraction with thermal processors," Zoleta said. "You know, if we use the standard matrix, it's not going to work. We need to use the MX-3."

He stood with his back to her, flipping through images of data on the H screen. He didn't want to listen to Zoleta right now. Letting his mind wander to Rachel and what she might be doing was how he wanted to spend his energy. Or better yet, to be with Rachel and have the chance to explain to her how he should be the one to take care of her. That it was him. The one who had taken care of her. Yes, life- times had come and gone but he loved her no matter if she wasn't able to love him back. Maybe—

"Here, let me show you." Zoleta walked toward him. He felt the purposeful brush of her shoulder against his.

"Zoleta, I'll take your suggestions into consideration when we get to that aspect of the problem. But right now we need to check the meteoric ground-water values. We can't just push blindly ahead. We have to determine what minerals are there and if we even want to waste our time mining if they don't possess the desired properties." He kept his gaze glued on the information in front of him.

As if I've been able to concentrate on much of anything since Rachel arrived. I had better focus or Zoleta will sense that something is going on and use it to her advantage. All I want to do is see Rachel, be with her, hold her in my arms . . .

"But this will save a lot of time and be more accurate."

Ben stepped away from the screen and turned to face her. Though she was thirteen centimeters taller, he held himself as a commander should with a presence which exuded authority. Most of the citizens of the colony were taller; having the benefit of prenatal genetic planning. It wasn't a problem. Usually. Only Zoleta seemed to confuse height with power. She was smart, he'd give her that. And she knew what she wanted. Unfortunately, so did he. There were times when Goliath was a very lonely planet.

"Get Imitar's correlations on the sector inputs and we'll run them. In fact, tell Imitar to bring them to me."

Zoleta snorted and turned on her heel.

The blast of the alarm hit before she could get out the door.

"Rachel," Ben whispered.

Zoleta turned back, "What did you say?"

"We only have two minutes before we find out if we're in the path of the asteroids. Shut down the programs and the analyzers. Back up the systems to the underground safe-blocks. I'll make sure the compound's shields are on full repel and run a tracker list. And silence that blaring."

"On it." Zoleta moved to the screens, syncing her earbud with the main feeds to enable verbal commands.

Ben's hands flew over the open holograms, saving and storing the information before it was lost. "As soon as we're set, take the emergency e-vac route and get below. I'll meet you there."

"Finished." She ran to help Ben with the last of the computers. "Now we can both go."

He nodded and glanced out the window, scanning for the asteroid shower that was on its way. Nothing within sight. Yet. Only the far-off explosions and shaking of the ground – like a giant stomping across the land – let them know this was not a drill.

They needed to get to the second level, to the reinforced safety bunker, to sit out the storm in the off chance that any of the rocks were large enough to penetrate the force-field. The auxiliary generators had kicked in, on low, allowing for the use of the elevator tubes but enabling the bulk of the power to re-route to the outside shield.

Zoleta and Ben squeezed into the elevator with several other workers and shot down a floor. The door opened at Level II and the passengers got off. All but Ben.

"Where are you going?" Zoleta called. "The bunker is this way." Zoleta stuck her nose in the air, a scowl seared across her face. She tried to push her way through the clump of people, back to the elevator. "Hold that door," she commanded.

The door closed.

"Medical," he said, and the tube descended. He ran his fingers anxiously through his hair and let his breath out just as the elevator touched down three floors below the surface.

* * *

The lights were dim on Sub-Level 3, but bright enough if you knew where you were going. Rachel would probably be in Research with Sanda, if they hadn't already left. He quickened his pace, racing through the empty corridor.

Ben turned the corner in a rush and smacked full-body into

a woman, slamming her backwards. He made a frantic grab, catching hold of one wrist before she hit the ground.

Rachel.

"Ouch. Damn, that hurt." She frowned at him.

He kept hold of her wrist as he scooped her around the waist with his other hand. "Sorry. I didn't mean to run over you." His eyes locked on hers.

"Will you please let go of my arm, or are you trying to dislocate my shoulder?" She rubbed her deltoid. "Never mind. I'm the one who's sorry. I tend to react first and think later when I've been hurt. Glad I didn't punch you. I heard the alarm. I'm sure they could hear it all the way to Earth. Those shockwaves. Are we having an earth-quake . . . or whatever you call it here?"

He let her voice melt over him. *Say something to her.* "The emergency shelter for this alarm is up a floor, but I need to check out the backups in MCC. You can follow evacuation procedures or, if you like, you can follow me."

"I don't know what the evacuation plan is. And what is MCC?"

"Main Control Center on Sub-Level 4, next to the library. Energy backup systems, all of our programs, communication satellite relays, etcetera, in the MCC." He snuck a glance at her. She was chewing on her bottom lip. God, she was beautiful. He released her arm. "We need to hussle."

Another shock wave hit, causing the two of them to fall sideways, bumping into the wall. Ben braced his arms around her to keep from crushing her with his weight. His heart ached when he saw the terror in her eyes. *Oh Rachel. I would never let anything happen to you. I have always watched over you and I always will. I wish you could know that.*

"Don't worry. This building is underground for a reason. The outer shield will deflect any debris and the tremors will probably be over soon. There. See, they're fading already." Still he made no move to drop his arms from around her, but instead looked deep into her eyes. "Think you'll be okay?" he said with a warm smile. For an instant, she seemed to recognize him, and for a moment he was both excited and afraid.

As much as he hated to, he finally stood back and freed Rachel from his protective embrace.

She blew out a deep breath, "I'm sorry. I don't mean to be a wimp but I'm new here and I'm not sure . . . I'm Rachel, by the way." She held out her hand with the bandaged pinky.

He clasped his hands behind his back and made no attempt to return the handshake, nor did he give his name. "I know who you are." The look of confusion on her face as she dropped her outstretched hand made his chest feel tight. He swallowed, and then turned to lead the way.

"Should I let my boss know where I am? Do you know Dr. Luminita? Oh, of course you do. Sorry, I'm not thinking. I'm a little shaken up. Where are we going?"

The elevator door opened and he stepped back to let her enter first. She was quiet on the ride down to Sub-Level 4. For one-hundred-eighty years he had thought of everything he wanted to say to her, still keeping the fantasy alive, though time had squeezed the memories down to a flicker, and now he couldn't think of anything to say. Where would he start? He looked at the top of her head, covered in golden-red hair. He ran his hand through his own hair.

They reached the bottom. "To the right. Follow me." Another shockwave rumbled from above. Ben glanced at the ceiling.

At the door marked MCC, Ben looked at the retinal scanner and stated the authorization code. "Ben Schaefer CPO 1221994 Code-All Entry Allow."

"Ben Schaefer?" Rachel gasped. "As in the main-man? I'm sorry, I mean, commander. Now I'm really glad I didn't punch you."

"Yes, well." He moved quickly to the circuit boards covering the back wall. The room was large but cramped with the machinery. The computers generated heat, making it warm and dry. Bundles of wires ran across the low-hung ceiling and snaked through openings in the corners. What the room lacked in sophistication, it made up for in solidity. It was a fortress, the heartbeat of the colony.

"Why does this equipment look so much older than everything else I've seen in the rest of the building? In the rest of the whole compound for that matter."

"It's what we started with when we first landed here on Goliath. Just the basics. More durable on the voyage." Ben flipped switches and studied the lone computer screen, checking for damage reports from the outlying sectors. "Looks clear in Region 2." He glanced over his shoulder at Rachel, who was only three steps into the room, biting on her thumbnail. "Can you give me a hand over here?"

She nodded and came closer. "What do you want me to do?"

"See that switch? The yellow one? Flip it up and tell me when you see the light next to it blink green." He continued to scan the data, looking for problems.

"It's on, but it's not blinking," she said.

"It'll start blinking when the drones have finished sending in the vids, Rache."

Did she catch the slip? He cleared his throat and wiped the beads of sweat from his forehead. "It'll be another minute. Just keep watching."

"There it goes. It's blinking."

"Good. The data is coming in." He turned toward her, "Why don't you come see? I'll explain what's happening."

She seemed to hesitate for a moment. "Okay."

"Here, stand in front of me. See that quadrant? In the upper-right corner where the lights are flashing green?" His hand brushed her shoulder as he tapped the spot on the computer screen. "That's our location. The area the compound is in, Region 2. No damage."

"So, this is us?"

"Yep, it's good news."

"Thank goodness." Rachel pressed her hand against her chest and breathed a sigh of relief. "So, what happened? Is it over? How long do we need to stay below, and is this where we're supposed to be, so we're safe?"

"It was a Level-three asteroid shower. We have them periodically, usually later in the year. This one came up suddenly and for some reason we didn't get the proper forecast. Don't worry, I'll be looking into the cast-prediction program and satellite feed."

"Mr. Schaefer. CPO Schaefer. This is probably not the best time to ask. But since you are in charge of this planet, perhaps you could find the time, not right now of course, but maybe sometime, soon, to help me understand how I came to be here. I mean. I. Well, no one seems to have any answers to my questions and I've been here long enough to—"

"What did you do to your finger, by the way?" He turned from the computer, took her hand in his, and scrutinized the bandage.

"Just a little accident. I seem to be a klutz."

"And we have you working in research?" He chuckled. He ran his thumb gently across the back of her hand, in no hurry to let go.

CHAPTER 11

Main Control Center, Sub Level 4
Saturday, April 13
0910 hours

"Well, isn't this the picture of teamwork. Do you two have the damage reports ready?" Zoleta leaned against the door-frame with her arms crossed.

Ben dropped Rachel's hand and stepped away from her. "They're just coming online now. How'd you get in here?"

"The door was wide open. Seems someone used the All-Entry-Allow code." She marched toward the screen, forcing Rachel to take a step back. "Looks like Region 2 and 4 are damage free. Good. What about the mine?"

"Flip toggle Blue, and we'll find out," Ben said, back to business.

Rachel moved closer to him, squared her shoulders and glared at Zoleta. "I'm Rachel, by the way."

"I know who you are," Zoleta said. "I just don't know why you're here."

"CPO Schaefer asked me to follow him."

"I didn't want her in the way."

Heat rose in Rachel's cheeks. Her shock morphed into embarrassment in two milliseconds. "Oh, sorry, I'll get out of your way," she said and slipped out of the room.

When she got to the elevator, she punched the door open instead of waiting for the eye scan and took the tube up to Medical. The closer she got to the lab, the more her injured pride was replaced by a slow simmering anger. Her jaw began to hurt from clenching her teeth. These people had the social graces of piranha. Yes, there was an emergency going on but really, did they have to act like such jerks? *Couldn't that woman, Zoleta, have been a little nicer? She made me feel like a waste of oxygen. And the CPO. He almost seemed, well, like he cared. Until he said he only brought me along because he didn't want me to get in the way. Useless. That's what I am. Useless and in the way. I'm done with these robotic imbeciles and this planet. The hell with it all. The hell with them.*

Rachel stomped back to Medical. The room was dim, the power not fully restored. The silence welcomed her. Sanda wasn't back from wherever she had gone during the evacuation. Rachel took a deep breath and let it out, her anger slowly dissipating. Her shoulders slumped.

"The problem is: Zoleta is right. That's the question. Why AM I here?"

Rachel cradled her head in her hands. The ache in her heart emptied her, making her chest collapse and her stomach hollow. Anger was better. It made sense. She could rip off a piece of it, chomp it up, spit it out. Anger gave her a focus, made her alive. But she couldn't keep up the steam. It took too much energy that she didn't have. Unless she could hang around Zoleta more, she might stay in a perpetual state of pissy-ness. Oh God no. She wasn't that desperate.

But Ben was another story. There was something familiar about him. Or maybe she just wanted there to be. It wasn't his smile. She wasn't sure he had one. He certainly didn't flash it around. Of course who would be smiling like a looney during a life and death emergency. No, it was more of a spark in his eyes when he looked at her. She envisioned his square jaw and strong shoulders and felt the brush of his arm and the stroke of his voice soft in her ear. A shiver ran up her spine and she hugged her body.

Well, at least she didn't have to worry any more about meeting The-Big-Chief-Planetary-Officer. Wouldn't Dr. Luminita be surprised to know that she had already run into him, literally. Sanda still might want to officially introduce her. The two of them would need to confer with Ben about their findings on the research and what direction he wanted them to take. It would probably be best if she could meet with him, maybe later in the evening sometime, and ask questions about the planet and life on Goliath, without all the interruptions of work.

Oh, who was she kidding. She wasn't all that important to warrant his time. Dr. Luminita could, and probably would, give him the reports on her own. Sanda didn't need her. A little know-nothing—what did Imitar call her— a nebula—tagging along.

A sharp whistle pierced her thoughts. Lights flashed on full, signaling what she hoped meant the danger from the storm had passed.

Rachel was sitting at the desk when Sanda swept into the room. "Rachel. What are you doing here? Have you been here the whole time?"

"Sort of. I didn't know the evacuation procedure so I just . . . yes, for the most part."

Sanda touched her fingers to her forehead, and then dropped her hand. "We've been so busy I never thought about going over emergency contingencies with you. We are some-what safe down here, three stories underground. A good place for research and sickbay."

"Sickbay? Do we have sick patients? Here?"

Sanda stuffed her hands into her lab-coat pockets. "Not usually. Most of our workers come in for quick rejuves, spinal spacers, tonins, and things like that. But . . . something is happening. Two men and one woman were brought in from Sector Seven with vague respiratory symptoms. I tried every combination of stem cell vaccines that I could think of and nothing works. Both patients died within a week. I admitted a third man late last night."

Something gripped Rachel by the throat and the guts at the same time, making her freeze as if taking one more breath would plunge her over a cliff. It wasn't a memory. It was more like an instinct. It felt purposeful. It felt right. It was connected to her somehow, this feeling, and she knew she had to follow it quickly or risk losing a glimpse of who she once must have been.

She jumped off the chair. "Where is he? The man in sickbay? I need to see him."

"What? Why? What good would that do?" Sanda frowned. "He's in quarantine. Watched twenty-four hours a day. All his vitals and medications are online and controlled by remote."

"Online? You mean checked and controlled by a damn robot? No—I need to see him. Now."

Rachel's breath came in rapid gulps. Her heartbeat raced at jackhammer speed. It took all her concentration to force herself to calm down.

She started over, looking directly into Sanda's eyes. "Please, Sanda."

"There's nothing you can do that's not –" The doctor stopped and met Rachel's pleading look. This was the first time Rachel had ever called the doctor by her first name. Sanda gave a slight nod. "All right. I'll take you to the infirmary."

* * *

Rachel peered through the viewing window at the form propped on a gurney. A pale man clothed in a sleeveless white smock, the same color as the walls, opened his mouth barely enough to dab his tongue across his bottom lip. He was the only living organism in the stark room and maybe not for much longer. It was impossible to tell his age. He had no gray hair, no hair at all that Rachel could see, and not a wrinkle on his smooth, anemic face.

The man opened his red, watery eyes and looked around the room. His vision wandered across the window and passed over Rachel, without a hint of finding anything to focus on.

"Can't he see us out here?" Rachel asked.

"No. This is only a viewing window."

"That poor man. He doesn't even have a blanket."

"The room is held at precisely the right temperature and humidity. He's being closely monitored. Any deviations are noted and taken care of in a safe and accurate manner. He has everything he needs."

Rachel pressed her palm against the cold glass. The man turned his head and seemed to stare passed the wall at her for several moments. Then he tipped his head back and closed his eyes.

"What's his name? What are his symptoms?"

"He's Alpha twelve dash seven."

"That's his name?"

"No. That means he is one of the original fourteen colonizers and he works in Sector Seven. Not a good sign." Sanda touched a panel below the window and the patient's holograph materialized in front of them. "His symptoms include: inflamed pharynx, rhinitis, repetitive forceful exhalations, convulsive expulsions of air through the oral and nasal orifices. Temp thirty-eight degrees C. His name is Georgesbernhardmoro de Fanspana."

"Are you kidding me? Why does he have such a long name?

Never mind. How do his lungs sound?" Rachel reached for the stethoscope draped around her neck. "Oh. I . . . I'm missing my stethoscope."

"Your what?" Sanda looked at her.

The base of Rachel's skull tingled and warmth melted through her body. This time, memories bubbled to the surface. She turned to Sanda, her mouth agape. "I'm a PA. Or was. A physician's assistant. I need to assess this patient." She stood back and looked for the eye-scanner. "Open," she said.

Nothing.

"Open," she said, louder this time. The door remained closed. "Please open this door for me, Doctor."

"No. I can't let you go in there. You would be exposed. I shouldn't have brought you here."

"Sanda, I don't know how to explain it, but I know I'll be fine. But the patient won't, if you don't let me go in there."

"This is not protocol." Sanda shook her head.

"Well, how do we change that? Who do you report to?" Rachel raised her chin. "Ah, straight to CPO Schaefer I'm sure. Call him." She crossed her arms in a defiant stance.

"Why are you so determined to do this?" Sanda's frown deepened.

"Because he needs help. He needs more than that chunk of metal in there can give him. I can't watch a man die without at least offering him comfort, and that includes human contact." She clenched her fists until her nails bit into her flesh. "– and a damn blanket."

* * *

Rachel paced in front of sickbay while Sanda put a call in to Ben. Rachel looked through the window again. The walls were bare. Not even a blinking light interrupted the nothingness. A sixty-centimeter-tall, white cylinder, the sensor-bot, floated in the corner of the room outside of the man's line of sight. From here she couldn't tell if the bot made any noise. Probably not. Maybe the only stimulation the patient had experienced since he'd been in quarantine was from the scream of the sirens and the jarring of the asteroids bombing the compound.

"Rachel is here with me at sickbay. She wants to see the patient. I told her she can't and she insisted that I call you." Sanda looked up at the ceiling. "No. Inside quarantine. She says she needs to help him." Sanda strode back and forth while the person, the CPO, on the other end continued the conversation for several long minutes. "No, I don't think it's wise. What –? Are you willing to risk it?" She blew out a breath, tapped her earbud off, and turned to Rachel.

"And—what did he say?"

"CPO Schaefer said to give you the entry code." Sanda's eyes were wide. She shook her head. "I think we should wait and ask him again tomorrow. He's distracted with the damage reports. This doesn't make sense."

"He's the boss." Rachel said, and then softened her voice, "I promise it'll be okay." She touched Sanda's arm.

"I still don't like it, but here's the plan. You have to decontaminate before I let you in there. And double purify when you leave. I'll give you eight minutes with him – then out."

"Of course. And, can I get that blanket?"

"I'll see what I can do." Sanda huffed off, mumbling to herself.

The sensor-bot whirred on and swerved toward the patient. It thrust out its robotic arm a few centimeters above the man and scanned him from head to toe and back, then disappeared again into the corner of the room.

Sanda returned with a small, white sheet. "Take this with you. When you go through the door, you will be in the shower. It's important to keep your eyes open and inhale slowly through your nose for as long as you can. Then take a second slow breath through your mouth. The inner door will open when you are decontaminated and coated."

Rachel draped the make-shift blanket over her arm and stepped into the separation room. The five second count-down made her skin prickle. A greenish mist suffused the room. It smelled like ammonia. She fought to keep her eyes open, take a steady breath, and not gag. Her skin felt like it had been completely singed off her body and then replaced with a slippery coating of potent smelling slime.

The door opened and she emerged, blinking hard and trying to clear her throat. She rubbed her tongue over the slickness in her mouth.

The man stared at her with tired eyes.

She started to say hello, but it sounded like she was trying to talk with a burning -hot marshmallow in her mouth. After several more swallows she was able to try again.

"Hi. I'm Rachel. I'm working with Dr. Luminita. How are you feeling today?"

His eyes roamed around the room while his head remained still. He whispered, "Am I dreaming?"

"Do you know where you are?"

"I thought. I thought I was in sickbay," he said barely above a whisper, "but I've never seen you in here before." He had to stop for air. "I've never seen anyone in here before. This has to be a dream." He closed his eyes again. "But it's a nice one, a lovely one at that." He chuckled. A brutal coughing spell seized his body, forcing him to double over in the bed.

Rachel hurried to his bedside and stood helpless while he struggled. His eyes clamped shut, knuckles white from clutching his fists to his chest like he was trying to keep from blowing apart.

The violent coughing finally abated, leaving him out of breath, with sweat beading over his bald head and running down his temples. He flopped back like he had just finished running a marathon.

She unfolded the blanket and gently draped it across his lower body. He looked up, thanking her with his eyes.

"You're welcome," she said. "May I call you George?"

A meager smile tugged at the corner of his parched lips.

"I'll take that as a yes." She checked for levers along the sides of the gurney. "We need to prop you up a little higher to make it easier to breathe. I don't see any control buttons." She walked around the bed.

The patient pulled his arms slowly away from his chest and unfurled a hand which held the tiny remote.

"Thanks George. That'll do it." She raised the head of the gurney and pulled the sheet up. "I can only stay a few minutes today. Would you mind if I checked your vitals?" She smiled.

His eyes moved upward, toward the vital-bot in the corner of the room, she guessed, since he didn't turn his head and couldn't see the machine behind him.

"I know," she said. "The robot scans your body, but it doesn't ask you how you feel. I'm going to do my own assessment. If that's okay?"

He managed a slight nod.

She took hold of his large, clammy hand and pinched several of his nail-beds, checking for the color return. She felt his wrist, carotid, and pedal pulses. She didn't think. She moved through her assessment automatically, explaining things as she went, asking him questions and watching his reactions, making sure she didn't tire him out.

"Just one more thing. I don't have a stethoscope so I'll need to listen to your lungs. Will that be okay with you?"

It felt strange to her, and yet it didn't. She wasn't sure how much she could hear without a stethoscope. "Can you sit up a little higher for me and lean slightly forward?"

He nodded and she helped him up in to a better sitting

position. Placing her ear as tight as she could against his upper back, she asked him to take a deep breath in through his nose, and then blow it out. She listened four more times on the left side, then moved to the right side of his back and repeated the process. "Hmm," she said.

"I'd like to listen to your heart next," she said, and looked at George with the question in her eyes.

He nodded again so Rachel moved around in front of him. "I'm going to place my ear against your chest and see how the 'ol ticker is tickin. So just think about something relaxing."

Rachel was listening intensely to George's heart sounds when she felt his hand gently caress her hair, soothing like a mother's touch, petting her with tender strokes.

She raised her head and smiled at him. "Do you like my hair?"

"Yesss," he croaked and a small spark ignited in his burnt-out eyes.

She stood and placed her hand on his bald head, wiping back sweaty hair that didn't exist. A whisper of content escaped in his quiet sigh.

"Ni . . . s. Ray-chel."

The voice in her earbud made her jump, and she snapped her hand off his clammy scalp. She paused for a moment, then slowly nodded her head at the air in front of her. "I have to go now George. But I'll be back tomorrow, okay?"

He raised his fingers in goodbye; a peaceful look floated across his face.

* * *

Rachel left George's room, passing through the cleansing port on the way out. It wasn't as bad as going in. It didn't taste as foul anyway, but it certainly wasn't a day at the spa. The sanitizing shower had been rough, blasting away at her hide, like being shot at close range with an air gun, but she didn't care. She had seen the patient, touched him, listened to his heart and lungs, and was going to check on him tomorrow. She couldn't wait.

"You look like you're on a planet with no gravitational pull," Sanda said as she welcomed her back in the lab. "How did it go?"

Rachel smiled, "It was great. I mean – he is definitely a sick man,

and that isn't a good thing. But I felt – I felt like I was doing something to truly help. Something real. You know, Sanda," she looked hard at her, "There's a lot to be said for human contact. Especially when you're sick."

A vision flickered in the blind spot in the back of her mind. The room and Sanda fuzzed around the edges, then dissolved altogether. Rachel squeezed her eyes shut and covered her ears as a waterfall crashed in her head.

The picture focused on a little girl lying in bed with the covers pulled up, her favorite doll tucked in the crook of her arm. The mother snuggled close beside her, finishing the story she had been reading. "Mommy, put your hand on my head again. It feels nice and cool."

Sanda's voice broke through her trance. "Rachel? What is it? You seem to be in another galaxy. Your face is flushed. Are you ill?"

Rachel stared at her hands as if they belonged to someone else. She cleared her head with a shudder. "Memories, I think. Just snippets. Stuff that doesn't make sense. It was such a sweet picture though." She touched her cheek, "I'm sure I do look flushed. Raw is more like it. That 'shower' felt like being scoured with forty-grit sandpaper."

She forced a laugh, looked up, her index finger pressed against her lips. "I'm not sure how I know about forty-grit sandpaper"

"I'm sure I don't," Sanda said and shrugged. "Do you think

you could run the labs before you drift completely out of Goliath's orbit?"

* * *

By the time Rachel finished her work, the high from taking care of George was waning, like a dying sparkler. Glad to be heading to her unit, she thought about another shower. Not that she wasn't clean. Oh no, she was beyond clean. Relaxed and soothed is what she longed for.

She made herself a quick protein shake and gulped it down. "A glass of wine and a nice warm bath would be so incredible." She looked at each corner of the ceiling, hands on her hips. "Do you hear me? You stupid room. How come you can turn on everything in here, but you can't figure out a simple bubble bath?"

She sighed and wiggled out of her garments. She pinched the clothes between her thumb and index finger, dropped them in a heap in the middle of the floor, and stepped into the blower.

"Soft. Warm temp. Lavender. And moisturizer," she said as the door closed around her.

The air enveloped her and she closed her eyes, imagining a real shower with warm, caressing water. She rubbed her palms together, pretending to lather up a bar of soap. "Ahh," she said and let the soft jets carry her away. She smoothed her hands over her face and slowly down her neck. She was gentle, almost timid, with her touching. A sharp intake of breath turned into a groan as she lingered over her breasts. She pushed her hands lower, across her abdomen and down the inside of her thighs.

Ben's face, with his powerful blue eyes and rugged square jaw, materialized in front of her. In her mind, he held her with one strong arm and stroked her hair with his other hand. Her heart was pounding and she began to tremble. He leaned in toward her.

She snapped her eyes open. *Did someone say something?*

The room repeated, "Ben Schaefer. Allow entry?"

"Holy shit."

CHAPTER 12

Saturday evening
Rachel's quarters

RACHEL SCRAMBLED, looking for something to throw on, and ran quick fingers through her hair. She grabbed her robe, pulled it tight around her, and scooped the pile of clothes off the floor and pitched them into the closest space, her bed-cubby.

"Come in. Um. Allow access."

The door opened and Ben stood at the threshold. His eyes traveled down her short frame and back to her face, a hint of a smile at the corner of his mouth.

She felt her cheeks burn as he inspected her. *I've been on Goliath for over a month and now he shows up on my doorstep?*

"Sorry. Come in."

His smile vanished, replaced with a commanding presence which unnerved her. Had she done something wrong? Was it because she had demanded to be let in to sick-bay and now she was in trouble? It wasn't looking like a social call. She gripped her thumbs inside her fists to keep them away from her nervous biting and shoved them deep into her pockets.

"Is there something I can do for you? Sir?" Better to stick to protocol till she knew what was happening.

"I heard you saw the patient in quarantine." His hands clasped behind his back made the muscles across his chest stand out.

She shifted her gaze upward to meet his. At least she didn't have to strain her neck like she sometimes did when she was talking to everybody and anybody else on the planet. No, Ben was just the right height. "Yes. Dr. Luminita said you gave permission for me to go in."

"That is correct." He took another step into the room. "May I?" He held his hand out past her.

"Oh. Yes. Sorry." She turned to lead the way and rolled her eyes while her back was toward him.

He reached the kitchen area in two strides and swung an athletic leg over the stool at the one-person counter. A whiff of his fresh after-shave scent made her feel a little swoony. She couldn't avert her nose so she averted her eyes to the dirty laundry oozing over the side of her bed. He looked good, smelled good, and if they accidentally brushed up against each other in this dinky room . . . *Oh for heaven sakes, what was I in my past life, a teenage hooker or something? Geez.*

Ben cleared his throat, "Rachel, I came to ask your permission for something."

Yes, I'll marry you—Oh, my God. Stop it. What is it about this guy? I don't even know him, why am I so attracted to him?

She blew out a breath, wiped her sweaty palms down her robe and tried to stay focused. "Oh?"

He stood and pushed the stool neatly under the counter and faced her, arms straight by his sides, stern look on his handsome face. "I – we, would like to have your permission to get samples for DNA and genetic testing."

"Samples? From me?"

"Yes. From you." He cleared his throat again. "Your genetic

code hasn't been tampered with and, therefore, may have certain properties that the average Goliathian's genetic make-up no longer contains. Factors that may, in fact, be beneficial to our ability to self-regulate."

She rubbed her hand over the soft inside of her opposite arm, pressing gently on the vein, and looked up into his eyes, the color of deep-blue glaciers. Could her knees actually melt and leave her in a puddle on the floor?

"Rachel?"

"Oh sorry. You asked me –? Self-regulate?" She bit her lip, trying to remember what he'd said. *Don't think about his eyes. Don't think about those muscular quads.* All moisture had left her mouth and somehow found its way under her arms. And else-where. *And for God's sake, don't think about everything in-between.*

He laughed. "You say sorry more than anyone I've ever met. In fact, you've said I'm sorry more often in the two times I've seen you than everyone else on this planet put together. And I've been here over thirty-four years."

She scowled at him and fisted her hands on her hips in a playful manner. "If you recall, you said sorry to me first."

His body recoiled as if she'd slapped him. He looked down at his hands and rubbed his thumb over the knuckle on his pinky finger. Was he searching for something to say? She seemed to have wounded him, or maybe he just wasn't used to having people call him on something he'd said. She was only teasing. He unclenched his hands and splayed his fingers out. The kink in his little finger remained.

"Remember? When you ran into me in the hall during the asteroid shower?" She felt her cheeks burn. If he couldn't remember something like that? Geez, that's all she could think about lately, replaying it over and over in her mind, wishing she could add a little touch here, a little rub there. *God Rachel you're pathetic.* "Never mind. So anyway. Yes. I'll let you take samples. I'm happy you actually asked me for permission and didn't just sneak in sometime in the middle of the night," she laughed.

Ben's body went ridged. What had she said? Now Ben was the one with the red face, looking like he was trying to swallow a stone. Or maybe he just realized that she was flirting and was embarrassed. Maybe he really did want to sneak into her room late some night. She could only hope.

"Very well. Dr. Luminita will set up the tests." He turned and walked out. The door swooshed shut behind him, leaving Rachel wondering what had just happened.

"Whoa. Good-bye to you too. Thanks for coming." She waved a hand at the closed door. "Guess he doesn't get my sense of humor. He's odd. Sexy-hot. But definitely odd."

She wondered what it would take to make him even.

* * *

Saturday
Medical/Sickbay

The day after the encounter with Ben and his request for DNA samples from her, Rachel woke early, the first time on her own, not forced by the scheduled daylight of the compound. Today she would get to spend more time with George's care. She hummed a tune and didn't try to figure out the lyrics or where she had learned it. She opened the door to her closet. Four clean uniforms hung at the back. She seemed to recall there used to be more to doing laundry than dumping it down a chute and having it pop up in your closet clean, pressed and ready to go.

She felt light this morning, like she had stomped two kilos of mud off each boot. Maybe they had turned up the anti-gravity frequency a notch.

She let herself in to Medical, put on her lab coat, and

hurried through her samples and calculations from the day before. It took forty-five minutes to get the next set of specimens placed in the analyzer and start the automatic titration system. She was bringing up the hologram when Sanda came through the door.

"Good morning Sanda. I was just transferring the results from yesterday's experiments to your hologram so you can look them over in your office. I also started the next round. They're in the analyzer now and then I'm going to clean up." She brushed her hands together. "I can run the stem-vaccs for you if you want, but you'll have to show me how first."

Sanda looked around the room, eyes wide. "Have you had a liter of double-jav this morning?" She raised her own mug and took a sip.

"Ha. No. I want to get my work finished so I can check on George."

Sanda squinted. "George?" She drank the last of her coffee and set the mug on the counter.

"George. In sickbay." Rachel pulled up the hologram from the sensor-bot showing the vitals on the patient. "Look at his chart. His temperature is down and his oxygenation level is up. He's doing better."

Sanda scanned the graph in front of her. "He does seem to be improving. I suppose it's fine. You say you've started the next round of samples?" She closed the chart and turned to go into her office.

"Yep, all set." Rachel paused a moment, then added, "I'd like to bring him a glass of water. How do I get it through decon?"

"First a blanket. Now a drink of water," Sanda muttered, but Rachel caught the half-smile. Sanda opened the small vault of the sanitizer, took a thermos from the chamber and filled it with water from the irradiated spigot. "You'll need to carry it through. Leave the spout open." She handed it to Rachel. "I'll be in my office if you need me."

"How long can I stay with him today?"

"Use your own judgment."

* * *

George was awake when Rachel entered the room. The sheet lay across him with his arms over the top. He raised one hand in hello.

"Hi George. You look better today. How are you feeling?" She gave his shoulder a gentle pat.

He tried to speak but only scratchy fragments came out. He shook his head and touched his throat.

"Too hard to talk? I brought you a drink of water. That should help." She smiled and held up the thermos.

"Wa. Ter?"

"Yes. Water. To drink. Moisten your mouth. Soothe your throat. Wet your whistle." She uncapped the straw from the lid and held it to his lips. "Start with just a sip."

George sucked the cool liquid into his mouth and swallowed. He downed two more swigs before Rachel eased the thermos away. "That's enough for now I think."

He tipped his head back, eyes half-closed.

"That seemed to do the trick." She smoothed the sheet over him and was checking his pulse when his eyes flew open.

"Whistle?"

"What?"

His voice was stronger, soft but clear. "You said water to wet your whistle."

"I did say that, didn't I? You don't know what that means?" He didn't reply. "Well, it comes from an old saying. At least I think it does." She cocked her head and tapped her lips with her finger. "Anyway. Whistle. You know." She took a deep breath, puckered her lips and began to whistle a tune. It was a spunky little ditty and she liked how the notes echoed around the room and came back to her. *What is this song? I know it from somewhere.* Three notes into the second stanza, she stopped whistling and squeezed her eyes shut. Something nagged at her mind and pressed upon her heart. "*Good Morning Merry Sunshine* is the name of the song." She softly began to sing the words: "*Good morning merry sunshine why did you wake so soon? You scared away the little stars and chased away the moo-oon.*" She suddenly stopped. Her throat constricted and her chest felt tight. "My mother used to sing it to me when . . . I was little."

"It's very pleasant. Keep going if it makes you feel better."

"I – I can't. There's something more to it. But I don't know what." She grabbed the side of the bed to steady herself. *I feel so strange. How can my head and heart feel so empty, yet so unbearably heavy at the same time?*

"I don't know who you are." George shook his head and chuckled. "But I'm glad they let you in here."

His comment snapped her out of it. "I'm sorry, George. I'm being a real idiot, aren't I? But I thank you for your kind words." She smoothed the sheet where her hand had crumpled it. "I used to work in the medical field back on Earth as a P.A. I'm having a little trouble remembering where I was employed or what my specialty was. Hope that doesn't scare you."

"Not at all. I'm sure you made an excellent P.A., whatever they do. And now? Do you enjoy –" His voice caught and he tried to clear his throat. He pointed at the container of water. She gave him another drink. He swallowed and began again. "This is a small colony, Rachel. Everybody knows everybody else. I don't recall seeing any notice of your arrival. When did you get here? We haven't had a shipment of recruits in two years." He scratched the side of his head. "And we aren't expecting one for another twelve months."

"Are you sure? I've only been here a month and a half."

"Positive. There haven't been any new workers. What's your ISO?"

"ISO?"

"Intergalactic Station Orders. Who sent for you?"

The automatic sensor-bot kicked on. Rachel moved away from the bed so it could run the scans, thankful for its timing. She subconsciously chomped down on her thumbnail while she mulled over what he said.

Did someone send for me? I don't know anyone here and I would never have voluntarily chosen to go to some planet in God knows where . . . would I? Maybe Imitar or Sanda knows something. Trying to figure this out makes my head feel like hairline fractures are splintered through my brain. She jerked her hand away from her mouth. *Stop it. Just focus on taking care of George.*

The bot finished its assessment. George was watching her.

"You ask a lot of questions, George. But enough about me. You're the patient. Tell me about yourself. What do you do when you're not lazing around in sickbay?"

"I'm not all that mysterious. I'm a miner. Was in the first class of recruits. Back in '41. Came here with CPO Schaefer, Doc, and fourteen other space-junkies. We're known as Launchers, a team sent to build and run the temporary compound, explore the resources of the planet, and in general, to get things going."

"Do you have a family here? Or back on Earth?"

George took a deep breath and let it out slowly. "Now who's asking lots of questions?"

"I'm sorry. If you don't want to talk about it, I understand."

"No. It's okay." He rubbed a hand over his hairless scalp. "I had a lifemate not too long ago. She meant the universe to me."

Rachel leaned in toward him. "Tell me about her, George. What was she like?"

"She was special. Always thought things through, weighed the pros and cons of every issue before making a decision." He glanced at Rachel, a hint of a smile at the corner of his mouth. "She knew me down to my bag of nucleotides. But she never tried to tweak me or get me to slip-splice out my – shall we say – enterprising, qualities. Told me she liked my spontaneity. Said I was adventurous. The complementing strand of her double helix."

Rachel touched his arm. "What happened?"

George grew quiet, took a careful breath and began. "I wanted to travel. You know, to check out other galaxies. When this venture came up, I applied and was chosen as a Launcher. Once the initial facility was operational and safe for habitation, I had the choice to stay on and work or go back to Earth – all expenses paid."

"Ah. So you obviously chose to stay. You liked the excitement of being a real pioneer? But what about the hard work? I can't imagine what it must take to get a compound like this off the ground. Or under the ground, as the case may be."

"It's extremely hard work, but you can see your efforts pay off. You're basically your own boss, except for reporting to CPO Schaefer, and free to solve problems as they come up. After things are on-line and running, you can go exploring. Be the first to see what's out there." Rachel caught the gleam in his eye before it disappeared. "But I wanted it all."

Her heart skipped a beat with the mention of Ben's name and she wanted to query George about him, but now wasn't the time. Instead she asked, "What was it you wanted, George?"

"I wanted the adventure. I wanted the hard work and the freedom. I wanted to stay here and make a life. But I wanted Shirleena with me."

Rachel gave him time to collect himself. "Would you like another sip of water?"

He brought a fist to his mouth as if to cover a cough. "No. I'm okay. She wanted me to come back home. To Earth. I wanted her to come here to Goliath."

"She chose to stay back on Earth?"

A heavy smile hung from the corners of his mouth and he

lowered his head. "The opposite. She was willing to give up everything for me. She made all the arrangements, sold all she owned – we owned – and borrowed as much as she could from my family and hers. She signed an agreement to send all wages earned back to B of U to pay off the loan she took out." He shook his head. "It's a very expensive trip for those of us who've been recruited. But for the average citizen from Earth, it's almost impossible to procure the funds."

"What happened?"

"She did it. Shirleena was able to get the money for the trip. She had her ticket for the next recruiter ship leaving Earth's orbit. She was on her way. You know it takes three years for a spaceship with humans aboard to reach here. Half that time if it's only a supply ship."

Rachel's mouth opened and then closed again quickly. She rubbed the tiny mole on her earlobe. Something didn't feel right. Things didn't add up. "Please go on."

"The ship was two days out," he said, his voice barely audible. He turned toward her. "Tail end of asteroid debris took out the entire ship. All fourteen recruits were lost in an instant . . . and my Shirleena." He turned away again.

Rachel used the cuff of her sleeve to wipe the tears from her eyes.

George reached for her hand. "I've upset you."

"No. It's okay. I seem to have leaky eyes these days." She smiled. She liked it that he still held her hand. It was the first time anyone on the planet had opened up to her and shared more than the day's data.

"You know, you remind me of her. Of Shirleena."

"I do?"

"You're a strong woman, like her. Determined."

"Me? How do you know I'm strong? I don't feel very tough."

"You were able to get someone to let you in here weren't

you? This is quarantine, a restricted area." He squeezed her hand tighter.

She laughed. "And I better get out of here and let you rest. I promise I'll come see you tomorrow." She stood, feeling a little sad when she pulled her hand away.

"And George – thank you."

CHAPTER 13

Command Center
Sunday, April 14
1700 hours

SANDA STORMED in to Command Center. Zoleta stood next to Ben, marking points on a holographic zoning map. Their backs were toward her. "I want to know why you ordered codes on Rachel. What were you thinking? It'll knock her out for days, maybe longer if it throws her into a memory sink."

Ben continued to work on the graph. Zoleta moved to the console. "We need to find out if she has any cells in her body that have been genetically altered," he said without turning around.

"And why do we need to torture her just to find that out?"

He faced her. "We can use her tissues to construct modified arrangements of DNA."

"What for?"

"Dr. Luminita, from the results of the mixes you've tried on your patients, nothing has worked to regenerate their immune responses. According to your data, I would say, their systems are shot. Like re-charging a battery only so many times, then it's just – dead. Maybe our cell rejuvenations have passed their expiration date and we don't have any clean DNA to use. We need a brand-new battery."

"You're going to use Rachel for this purpose? She's just some kind of new battery to you?"

A loud "Humph," came from Zoleta. "Ben, I think we should try moving the vector twenty degrees to the right." She pointed to the map.

"Try it. But be sure to align the other variables to account for the change."

"Am I missing something? Or is this some way of satisfying some morbid curiosity?" Sanda's teeth clenched, like she was trying to make dental impressions in wrought iron.

"Of course not. If Rachel holds the genetic key, she could help prolong or even save the lives of everyone on this planet."

Zoleta snorted. "We could call her 'The Goddess of Goliath'."

"Do you think this is a joke, Zoleta? Ben, this could really harm her. All her memories could return at once. She would be overwhelmed, too much loss to deal with, for anyone to deal with, let alone someone who doesn't have any family or friends near to support her. Splicing could cause a cognitive fracture."

"Then you wouldn't have to waste your time babysitting anymore, Doc."

"Zoleta!" Ben and Sanda snapped at the same time.

"That's enough, Zoleta. Let's finish up the mapping; I have other things I need to work on."

"I'll bet you do," Zoleta said.

Sanda continued with her plea, "The two men and . . . Koringa were from the same sector. They worked in the same mine and I believe their illness was caused from a bacteria or fungus they came into contact with."

"It doesn't matter," Ben said.

"What do you mean, it doesn't matter?"

"Sanda, have you been able to isolate a bacterium or fungus?"

"Well. No."

"Then how can we develop a vaccine or specific stem-cell enhancement?"

"From the immunity response of the patient –." Sanda stopped. Her shoulders sank. "I don't like this, Ben. How am I going to explain the risks to Rachel and get her permission?"

"You don't need to. I got her permission."

Zoleta's head jerked back and her eyes narrowed.

Sanda felt heat creep up her neck and singe her cheeks. "And when was it that you got her consent for this procedure?"

"The day after the asteroid wash."

Sanda hadn't expected Ben to answer her. He was the Commander and didn't have to answer to anyone, and he usually didn't. *What is going on with him? First, he puts me in charge of teaching and caring for Rachel and now he usurps my guardianship.*

"Did Rachel bonk her head during the e-vac," Zoleta said. "Or is she truly as dumb as a space-slug?"

Ben and Sanda ignored Zoleta's comment. Ben turned around and started on the maps again, leaving Sanda baffled and somewhat defeated. Her thoughts went back to Rachel and how much she was starting to accept the young woman's help and her fresh outlook on things. She was even starting to enjoy the enthusiasm Rachel brought to the lab every day, especially since taking over George's care. *She's got me calling him George now.* Sanda's stomach twisted with the thought of Rachel slipping into a depressed-catatonic state.

"When? When do I need to start the tests?"

"Zoleta, take this mem-chip to Imitar. I need it reprogramed to the proper boost capacity for the propellants."

Zoleta held out her hand for the chip. "Sure you do." She snatched it from him and walked out the door.

Ben turned to Sanda. "The sooner you initiate the procedure, the faster we'll get some answers. I'd appreciate it if you'd start this evening."

A flash of anger gripped her. "This evening? Ben, I need time to go over things, get her permission on my own, make sure she gives her informed consent, not just some smitten-yes because you're the CPO." Sanda's tone was ugly, but didn't he realize what he was asking of her?

"Of course, Doctor. Do what you need to do."

Ben hadn't said much, but something was different. Sanda sensed a slight change in his bearing, like a miniscule thawing around the edges of his rigid posture. His gaze floated beyond her as if he were searching for an answer on the other side of the wall.

She tried to get him to look at her. "Ben," she said and then a little louder, "Ben!" He let go of whatever had held him and focused on Sanda's eyes. She waited for a long, awkward moment for him to say something. *This is unlike him.*

"Please, Sanda, make it as painless as possible for her. For Rachel."

The soft tone of Ben's words made the last vestiges of her anger disintegrate. She felt numb except for a heavy sadness that settled deep in her chest. The weight of what lay ahead made her move slowly as she tried to tell herself that she had the strength to make things right. She didn't understand why Ben, who was always so in control, now seemed lost and anxious. Sanda was beginning to feel the same.

As she left Command Center to take the elevator tube, Zoleta was just getting off. They looked at each other, and for a moment, Sanda wondered why Zoleta seemed more antagonistic toward Rachel than her normal unfavorable disposition to all the other workers. Something about Rachel really split Zoleta's nucleus.

"Back so soon? Did you give the chip to Imitar?"

"That little quasar? He wasn't there. I don't know where else he'd be at this time of day, but he failed to check in with me. You wouldn't know where he went, would you? No matter. I have more important things to do than run silly errands and keep watch for Mr. Chin Scruff."

"Yes Zoleta, I'm sure you do."

CHAPTER 14

Sub-Level 3
Medical Research
Sunday evening

IT WAS quiet in the medical lab when Imitar entered. He had come to check on Rachel before she went under the nano-slicers. He shivered at the thought. Was it so far removed from the torture chambers of Medieval Times that he had been reading about? Snipping from the inside versus the outside. At least in this modern day of torment the subject would be anesthetized, sedated, and cared for afterwards. And kept alive. Hopefully.

Rachel is . . . Well, she's nice. I like her a lot. Course, not in the same way I like Zoleta. Now that woman throws me into orbit, makes me sweat and shake like I'm standing on The Hot Side of Goliath during a quake. But Rachel doesn't deserve to be experimented on like some space-bug. I know Ben brought her here. I just wish I wasn't the one he needed to cover for him.

He found Rachel sitting in front of the robotic testing window, humming as she worked. He took a deep breath and cleared his throat.

"Oh hey, Imitar. What brings you down to the dungeon?" She looked up at him with that warm smile and pulled her arms out of the simulator gloves.

His heart bunched into a knot. *She really doesn't know what she's in for or she wouldn't look so calm.*

"Came to see how my favorite girl is doing."

"Ha. You and I both know who your favorite girl really is, now don't we? And don't try to act like it's not true."

"I am quite fond of the Doc," he said, rubbing his chin whiskers.

"Since when do you call Zoleta, Doc?" Rachel gave him a friendly punch on the arm. "No, really. What can I do for you this evening?"

"I thought you might like to have a drink with me at The Bucket. I know you've been here for a few months, but you haven't had time to check it out, have you? We missed it when I gave you the compound tour and you haven't been up top since. It's the best place in the belt. *It's the only place in the belt.* Why don't you dump your smock and let's go? If we hurry, we can get a good niche."

"Sounds nice, but I'm not sure where Doctor Luminita went or when she'll be back. Maybe I should wait. Or we could go another time. I just need to finish this last assay."

He knew where Sanda was and he wondered what she was saying to Ben, not that it would make any difference in the outcome. There was a definite change in Sanda over the past few weeks. She seemed softer somehow, with a more relaxed demeanor, sharing more smiles, and laughter. Even under incredible stress trying to find a cure for this illusive disease, there was a definite lightness in Sanda's step, despite the gravity. It had to be due to Rachel. Admittedly, he found that Rachel brought out the best in him as well. And Sanda was becoming more protective of Rachel each day. No, the doctor would not be happy with what Ben was going to ask—order—her to do.

Imitar ran his fingers through the stubble on his chin. "I think I saw Doc taking the elevator tube up to Command Center," he said. "Probably going to see Ben for something." He forced a nonchalant look. "She might be a while. Let's go on up and have that drink."

"Sounds wonderful, but I'm just not sure. I have so much work to do and it is getting kind of late."

"Ah, come on, Rachel. The work can wait, I mean, I know it's important but so is your well-being, right? We'll only stay a little while. Please?"

"You really want me to see this place, don't you?"

He gave a single nod and bowed slightly with a flourish of his arm across his torso. "Yes, milady."

"Well, since you put it like that. How can I refuse, oh kind sir? Okay, what the heck, maybe I do need a little break." Rachel took off her lab coat and dropped it in the laundry chute.

As they rounded the corner, they met Sanda in the hallway.

"Hi Doctor L. Imitar and I were just leaving to go to The Bucket. That's where you said, right?" Rachel looked at him for confirmation.

"I thought Rachel might enjoy a little respite and a chance to see more than the walls of Medical before . . . well, before— um. She's only been topside once when I first showed her around the compound. She's got to try a Zang-O-Rang. Can't say you've been rejuvenated until you've had the Z-Mahn's Zang-O-Rang. Right, Doc?"

"What a great idea. Yes, she must try it and meet the Z-Mahn. Very unusual character. Interesting insights. Far from scientific, but knowledgeable in his own way," she said and gave Imitar a darting glance.

"Hey, why don't you come with us, Doc?"

"Oh. No. No thanks, Imitar. You and Rachel go ahead. Have a good time. You will bring her back tonight, won't you?"

"Do you need my help tonight, Doctor?" Rachel asked.

"Yes, but we can discuss it later. Enjoy yourself for now."

* * *

When the door opened topside, Rachel gasped. White, puffy clouds passed overhead outside the transparent bubble shield. The dwarf red star painted a muted sunshine across the sky and the air smelled fresh, though technically they were still inside.

"My goodness," Rachel said, and Imitar grabbed her elbow to steady her. "Thank you. I do feel a little disoriented out here."

"It's expansive. The dome covers half of a square kilometer. Behind that building across from us is the garden, remember? I think I pointed it out before – where all our food is grown and harvested and then it's taken below for enhancement. Speaking of food, maybe we can get something to eat at The Bucket, as long as we're there."

"You always have two things on your mind, don't you? Your stomach being one of them. And the other you have an appetite for as well." She winked at him.

"How do you do that? Squint one eye?"

"What, wink? You don't know how to wink?"

"No. Why? Does it mean something?"

"It can mean a lot of different things depending on how and when you do it and who you do it to. It's a form of expression . . . which there doesn't seem to be a lot of around here."

"What did it mean when you winked at me?"

"It meant, I knew that we both know what we're talking about even though we didn't spell it out."

"I don't understand."

"Tell you what, you practice and when you get it down, give Zoleta a nice slow wink when she's looking directly at you."

"Why?"

"Just try it. Trust me."

Imitar swallowed. "My throat's dry. We better get moving. We'll take the sky-bridge across to that granite hillside." He directed her vision to a long arching tube high above them and then to a rock outcropping barely visible in the distance. "The entrance is inside the dome but The Bucket is actually outside the protection of the shield. It's a natural cave where the Launchies first set up camp. They realized it was too dangerous out in the open when the first asteroids hit. It's somewhere else to go instead of to the DC for a bite to eat."

The sky-bridge, a moving walkway, spanned the dome from east to west, and a second bridge crossed from north to south. They climbed a spiral staircase fifteen meters upward to reach the onramp. "It's two hundred meters across. I'll explain some of the buildings as we go."

"I don't think I want to look over the edge."

"You don't have to. You can look down at your feet. See, the ramp is transparent."

"Oh lord."

"Don't you remember, I showed this all to you before when I gave you the quick tour?

"You pointed to things. We didn't actually walk everywhere, especially not on this. Besides, I was still in shock and didn't believe what you were showing me. Now I believe you, but I think I'm getting that shocky feeling again. Yikes, this is crazy high!"

"See, look how well you're doing now," Imitar continued, "And that's Command Center, the larger building coming up on the right. See, the double-bubble? Two reflector shields. CPO Schaefer's headquarters." His mind wandered.

I wonder if Zoleta is working right now. Probably. She always is. Maybe she'll ask me for help on the z-line codes. No, too stubborn,

*she'll try to do it herself even though we could get it done so much
faster if she'd let me frag it out.*

Rachel had stopped walking. Imitar turned around to see
what she was looking at.

"What's wrong?" he asked. The walkway shuttled them
along at a slower pace. They had moved directly across from
Headquarters.

"It doesn't seem like a very big building."

"It doesn't need to be. It holds the information relay center,
the main connector burst drives, some viewing screens. Stuff
like that. But it can all be disconnected and re-booted in a
matter of flashes. The backup systems are kept in a safer place
– Sub Level IV."

"Yes. I've been there."

He didn't know whether to believe her or not.

"Does he work in there? Alone?"

"Does who work where?"

"The CPO? I mean, is there room for other workers?
Assistants?"

"Of course. There's Ben's station, Zoleta's station, and I have
a tiny console in the corner."

He didn't know why he bothered with a desk. He could do
most of his work from anywhere on the compound and Zoleta
and Ben never seemed to notice if he was there or not.
Although he liked being at the office just because Zoleta was
there.

They were barely past the Command Center, both still
focused on the building, when a huge shadow swooped overhead. Rachel grabbed Imitar's arm.

"What is that?"

A large green and yellow bird flew across the dome. Rachel
staggered and he had to catch her. "Careful. You don't want to
dizzy-out and pull us both over the railing. We'd land on top of
the CPO and Zoleta." *I'd like to land on top of Zoleta but falling*

from this height is not what I have in mind. Course with my luck, this would be as close to an intimate meeting as I'd get.

"Rachel. If you are going to stare at all the scenery, we can stop and look around."

"No. I'm okay. I just haven't been outside in – well, since you brought me up here before, and I didn't want to believe that this place was real."

Her sad empty look made him uncomfortable. He scratched the toe of his boot along the edge of the walkway. It was suddenly hard to swallow. "Let's go get that drink and we can plan a real outing for you when you're better."

"When I'm better?"

Craters. I did it again. "I just mean when you've had a couple jaunts up to the surface to acclimate outside of the compound's dome." He pulled at his chin.

She squinted at him. "You know, you do that when you're nervous, or not telling the truth."

"Do what?"

"Pull at your whiskers."

He dropped his hand. "And how did you figure that out?"

"Not too tough. Every time Zoleta is near or you mention her, or someone else mentions her, you scratch, or rub your beard. And why are you trying to grow a beard anyway? You're the only one I've seen around here with any facial hair."

"I was hoping that doing a little something different might make me seem . . . I don't know, more interesting?" He hoped she was buying it.

"You are interesting. And I will like you even better when we get off this moving mountain goat trail-in-the-sky."

"We're getting close. The elevator, if you can call it that, is just up ahead." They continued down an incline and rounded the corner.

A steel cage surrounded a large, gaping hole in the ground. A cable looped over a metal girder and ran along an overhead track. When Imitar pushed a button, gears ground as the cable pulled up a huge rusted-out bucket, complete with teeth for digging into the hard surface of the planet. It was a recycled part of machinery left over from the original tractor used to excavate the first underground living station. He opened the cage door and climbed over the edge of the giant scoop.

"I'm supposed to get in that? It looks ancient compared to the rest of the structures on the compound. Is it safe?" Rachel had a worried look on her face.

"Sure it is. Adds to the ambiance." Ready?"

"I thought it's called 'The Bucket' because that's what we are going to drink out of. Not ride in."

He held a hand out to her which she grasped tightly. Shaking her head, she shimmied over the side to join him. Imitar slid the outside door shut and pushed another button. A bell rang and a moment later the oversized iron bucket lurched downward into the darkness.

"Don't hold on to the edge," he warned her. "This heavy thing might hit the side of the tunnel and crush your hand between it and the rock wall. Hold on to the cross-bar in the middle."

They descended at a bumpy pace, banging along the vertical tunnel in several spots, the light from above fading as they went. Imitar enjoyed the ride. "Having fun, Rachel?"

"Wonderful. Are we there yet?"

"Good. I like it too. We'll hit the bottom in a minute."

"Imitar, I'm being sarcastic. Can't you tell by the tone of my voice? I find this unnerving. I don't like dropping into an abyss where I can't see a thing. And what do you mean, we'll hit—"

The jolt sent Rachel to her knees.

"We're here," Imitar said.

"Obviously."

He reached out and slid the cage door open, then helped her climb over the side. Soft music and laughter floated from up ahead. They worked their way along the tunnel toward the din. Phosphorescent splashes crisscrossed the ceiling a few feet above their heads, and a greenish glow carpeted the floor. The lighting was barely sufficient to show the way, and definitely not enough to see the faces of the workers they passed.

The tunnel opened into a lounge area with a circular stone bar in the center and individual niches carved into the rocks along the walls. Faint running lights outlined the granite tables and benches, and circumscribed anything else jutting out where someone might hurt themselves. The bar featured the only area bright enough to see, which included the top of the counter and the lone bartender.

"Why is it so dark in here? Are you not supposed to know what you're really drinking?"

"When you live on a compound where everyone knows all about everyone else, it's nice to have a place to go to be by yourself, or with a few friends, without having to go clear out to The Dark Side." Imitar stepped up to the bar, pushing Rachel in front of him. It was difficult to tell, by the volume of the voices, how popular The Bucket was tonight. He couldn't tell how many workers might be enjoying a drink in the shadows.

The up-lights on the inside of the bar cast a shimmery light on a tall, dark-skinned man with knotted hair that hung to his waist. His white teeth glowed in a huge smile and he tipped his head back and let out a deep, rich laugh.

"Ah, Imitar. Bring you to me, eh? Click-click."

"Rachel, I'd like you to meet Zuluzimbabanganga. Just call him Z-Mahn."

"Ah. Lay-dee, not before come here." Zulu extended a long, skinny arm across the bar, placed his palm on the top of her head and held it there. "Different. Ah, click-click. Long ago. Many years." He brought his hand back and made a steeple with his index fingers and touched them to his forehead. "But you not know. Click-click. I close see? Yes?"

"It's very nice to meet you Mr. Zulu man. But I'm sorry I don't understand a thing you're saying."

Z-mahn stuck his arms out, palms facing downward with his elbows bent. "Do like this. Click-click," he instructed Rachel.

"Go ahead, Rachel. Z-mahn is a good guy. He helps everyone with their problems."

"I don't have any problems."

"Me neither. Go ahead and see what he has to say."

She held her arms out over the counter. Zulu placed his arms under hers, his palms upward, and suddenly grasped her by the elbows with his long skeletal fingers. "Ouch," she cried, "do you have to squeeze so hard?"

"To me. Hold now. Quick-quick."

She clasped Zulu's boney elbows. "That's better, thanks. Am I supposed to feel something? Are you going to hypnotize me or tell me my future?" She gave a quick snort.

"Breathe you now. Soft. Quiet." Zulu's eyes rolled upward. "Good. Slow." His face morphed through a series of expressions, like a sleeping newborn. Smiles, frowns, eyes squeezed tightly shut, and then opened wide, and finally a look of disbelief, crossed his gaunt features. He broke the bond and took a step back, leaving Rachel holding her arms awkwardly above the bar's surface.

The music twanged in the background. "What? What is it, Mr. Zulu?"

"Ah. Small, happy. Click-click. More little happy. Sad. Questions have you. Needs." He wiped invisible spills off the counter.

"Craters, Z-mahn. What in the galaxy are you talking about? Can you elaborate?"

"Ah. Don't know I. Very old is she. Very young is she. New. Old. Not from time this. Same. Same as CPO is she."

Rachel turned to Imitar and whispered, "Is this guy for real? He's not some kind of alien, is he?"

"He's just a very cosmic soul. Likes to think he can see in to the past and the future. Who knows, maybe it's true." This is interesting, Imitar thought. *Rachel and Ben? I'm going to run a check through the net-feeds to see if there's a connection and if I don't find anything I'll try the archives. If the Z-Mahn is right . . . I know Schaefer is from way back but I never really thought about it. I wonder . . .*

"Imitar? You're sure quiet all of a sudden. I think I'm ready for that drink now."

"Of course. Z-Mahn, do your thing."

"Yes, yes. Z-Mahn best give you." Zulu turned toward the bottles tucked into the rock shelves in the center of the bar and pulled out three. First, he poured a reddish, watery liquid and then a thick silvery one into two tall glasses. Finally, he squeezed a glob of dark brown sludge on top, watching it sink slowly to the bottom. "Ah Lay-dee. Imitar. Talk you good. Over there, follow blue."

"Very nice Z-Mahn. How much do I owe you?"

"Her for? Nothing. All save you she will. Clean. Last of clean. No owe." Zulu bowed to Rachel and held his hand out for hers. She slowly placed it in his. He turned it over, kissed her palm, and pressed it to his heart. "This time. Okay be you."

"Thanks, Z-Mahn. I think." Imitar picked up both drinks. "Let's sit over here in the corner. Grab the back of my suit and follow me."

They sat in a niche along the far wall on cool, smooth rocks with a granite shelf jutting out between them for a table.

"That was strange. Do you have any idea what he was talking about? And what did he mean I was like CPO Schaefer?"

"Did Zulu say that? I don't have a nano-clue of what he's talking about."

"Well, it's the first time anyone has seemed to know something about me, even if he is from the twilight zone. I have so many questions, Imitar, and nobody will answer them or they tell me they don't know. At first, I just thought my being here was all a bad dream. But someone put me, or my body, on a spaceship and sent me off to Never-Never-Land. Don't you think it's time I get some answers? I don't even know where to start. Maybe Doctor Luminita is right and the blank spots in my memory will fill in after the DNA procedure."

"Try your drink, Rachel. I think you'll like it. It should help you relax."

"Okay. That's twice you've circled around something but haven't told me. What's up?"

"What do you mean?" Imitar took a long drink, set his glass down and shuffled his feet under the table. He had no idea how they were going to ask Rachel to do the splicing, but he knew she'd do it no matter how much it cost her. He was her friend and he should probably tell her. He wanted to tell her, but it'd be like space-walking without a safety-line. And he'd be overstepping Ben's orders.

"Imitar, I can feel you jiggling your leg up and down under the table. I'll bet you're pulling at your whiskers right now, too."

He dropped his hand into his lap. "No, I was wiping the drips off my chin."

"Is something bad going to happen? Can't be that bad or Zoleta would be first in line to give me the news."

"Why do you say that? That's not really true, about Zoleta. She is incredibly intelligent. She's driven, yes, but she's always working hard, trying to do her best, be the best. She doesn't have the time to worry about people's feelings. There's a lot of pressure on her. Of course, not as much as she puts on herself."

"Is she ever nice? Other than to you? Although honestly, Imitar, I'm not sure I've ever seen her be nice to you, either. You're right, this drink is good."

"Depends on how you define nice. Her father is a top military commander in Federation Security. Tough guy. She has a brother who is very accomplished. Her parents don't really care about her. The brother is the star."

"She told you all this? That's amazing. She doesn't strike me as a woman who would ever let her guard down and let someone in. Unless it's someone . . . special. This drink is absolutely delicious, by the way."

"Well, she didn't exactly tell me everything." He could feel Rachel giving him that questioning look of hers. *If she could see my face right now, she would figure me out in an instant.* "To be honest, I am quite good, well, more than good, at breaking security codes – not that I would ever use information I . . . obtain. Unless it were absolutely necessary."

"So, you're telling me you broke into her personal files? Hmm, interesting but don't worry, Imitar, your secret is safe with me. I can see you trying to find the good in people. And any good you can find in Zoleta is probably worth the risk. Go on. Tell me."

He leaned forward with his elbows on the table. "Zoleta has always been in her brother's eclipse, striving to do better and pull in her father's attention. She's higher in rank than her brother now, but she can't seem to stop wanting more. She joined the Star Cadets when she was only ten years old."

Rachel hiccuped. "I don't know what the Star Cadets are but I'm sure it had to be a huge deal, especially for a ten- year old. What about a childhood? What about Zoleta's mother? What about another one of these zingers, or whatever you called it? It's super yummy."

"Zang-O-Rang. Hold on I'll get you another. Be right back."

As Imitar stepped up to the bar, Z-Mahn slid two drinks across the counter toward him "Ah, Zang-O-Rang another. For Rachel-One. And Slow-Clear for you."

"Okay." Imitar said. "I shouldn't be surprised, but how did you know what I wanted to order?"

"Many things the Z-Mahn knows. You are the same. Know to protect and trust Rachel-One. Even her decisions, crazy to you. She must be."

"Thanks, Z-Mahn. I think."

Imitar picked up the two drinks and headed back to the table. "You might want to slow down on this one. Where were we? Right . . . Zoleta. Her father had enough points for a Class I ovum and surrogate. He paid for a male child but there was a centrifuge malfunction, power glitch, or something."

"Obviously." Rachel slurped the rest of her drink, smacked her lips, and let out a loud burp. "Ex-squeeze me."

"I can tell you enjoyed your Zang-O-Rang."

"Yup. Gracious, I feel a tad bit tipsy. Okay, time to sh-pill the beans. Tell me why I feel like thish is my last meal, not that it's not delishish, I mean, it's tasty, but is there a fire-ing squad I should know about or sumpthin? In fact, can you tell me anything, like who, or is it whom . . . oh boy, I'm kinda toasted. Tell me what happened to me and why the hell I'm here? You said you're good at finding out information. Pleez Imitar, this has been a long ashed dream and I'm getting tired of it. It makes me sad."

Imitar didn't answer her. His thoughts jumped from Rachel to Ben to Sanda. *Someone must know something. How could a person in a cryogenic state end up on a cargo ship bound for Goliath without any records? It just doesn't happen. Either Rachel does know what's going on, but can't remember, or she's deceiving everyone for some reason and she's not really from the past. That's what Zoleta believes; that Rachel is here to take her job. Or, Rachel really is innocent, which is what the Z-Mahn seems to be saying. In which case Dr. L might know more than she's letting on. No, the Doc has no reason to be dishonest. She couldn't lie.*

That leaves Ben.

"Rachel. I'm sorry, it's got to be tough, but I really don't know what to tell you."

"I just wanna remember who I am. Did I have a fam? Is anybuddy looking for me? There musht be records somewhere. Is there a phone book or old newsh-papers I could check?"

"A what? We have the Intergalactic Library. You might be able to find something there. I think we better head back up top. Ready to get going?"

"Whoa. Yeah, I'm ready, just need to find my foots, I mean, feet. Are these my legs? Ha, these aren't my lips. Everything is kinda numbly. Hey I remember something . . . from before, or maybe it's the Zang-O-Rang talkin."

"What is it?"

"A really strong drink, silly"

"No, what is the memory?"

"Oh, well there were these women and we were drinking punch with funny little ice cubes, and we were laughing. I can't see their faces. There was a cake with something on top that was making us laugh even harder. Shure wish I could remember. It was more of a feeling I have, like it was a siggy-nificant, happy time. Like we were celebrating something sh-pecial that was going to happen."

"Take hold of my elbow, Rachel. Time to get back to the real world." He stood next to her and helped her up from the table.

"Wouldn't that be great."

CHAPTER 15

Sub-Level 2
Zoleta's private quarters
Late Sunday evening

ZOLETA SAT in front of the buzz-screen, searching the intergalactic web for information on cryonics. Just as she had suspected: the deep freezing of human bodies at the time of death for preservation and future revival was obsolete over a century ago, and anyone frozen before then hadn't survived the uprisings by religious factions. So, what was this Rachel woman trying to pull? *First, she shows up acting like she doesn't know who she is? And now Imitar is following her around like the tail of a comet, orbiting her like she's a queen bee. I'm not as dumb as he thinks. I can snake files too, I just can't find anything on her – yet. Poor Imitar. As if I would ever let him see anything in my files that I didn't **want** him to see. Maybe it's time to find out what all he knows.*

"Delete search files." She said to the room.

"Search deleted. Menu?"

"Off. No wait – bring up tracking on Imitar Dubashi G83187."

"Retrieving."

The green dot blinked along at a leisurely pace on the screen-map, moving first vertically outside the domed area of the compound and onto the overhead skywalk where it steadily pulsed toward the main buildings.

Zoleta folded her arms across her chest and scowled at the tracking display. "For bit sake, what is he doing? It looks like he's coming from The Bucket, but he never goes there unless I'm with him, and he thinks he's going to help me through some personal crisis."

She waited for a few more minutes to see where he would head next. "I think this might be a good time to bump in to the little worm-hole."

Her hair was in a tight knot on the top of her head, covered with a green plastic mesh. She released the cap and let her hair cascade over her shoulders in jet-black beauty. She lengthened her eyelashes, outlined her lips, and sprayed a touch of perfume at the base of her neck.

This bottle of scent Ben gave me years ago has certainly lasted longer than his interest in me. At least Imitar likes it.

One last glance at the screen showed Imitar still on route. She was about to tell the screen to shut off but then stopped. "Hmm. I wonder. Show tracking on Rachel."

"Insufficient information," the room responded.

"The new citizen, Rachel Allison McRae. Arrived eleven-four, twenty-one-seventy-five."

"Password?"

"Password? What do you mean password? I have clearance to track anyone and everyone on this base."

"Tracking not available on subject without password."

"Is there a tracker on the subject?"

"Yes."

"Who has the password?"

"Not authorized to release information on subject."

If Zoleta hurried she should be able to intercept Imitar as

he was coming off the sky-tram before he went home for the night, if that was where he was going. She wanted to know two things: where he had been tonight and with whom.

Above ground the dusky light took the edge off harsh buildings and equipment abandoned for the evening. Most of the workers had come in from outlying areas and were either enjoying the last meal of the day or already on their way to bed. Zoleta loved the subdued feel in The Belt with its constant twilight. Many citizens of Goliath needed to venture to the sun-drenched hot-side of the planet every now and then, or take tonins to keep from getting depressed.

Ah, there he is. And look what we have here—Rachel hanging on Imitar's arm. Besides interrogating him, I may be able to get some interesting info from the green-eyed, red dwarf as well.

"Out for a stroll, you two?"

"Zoleta. Hi. Um, Rachel and I went to The Bucket for a drink. We were just heading back to Medical." Imitar tugged at the collar of his tunic.

"Hey, Goleta. Sorry, that's not right. I mean, Zoleta. Yup. Imitar took me to have a Zang-O-Rang. Good stuff." A lopsided smile was plastered across Rachel's face. "That Z-guy was sooo weird. Kinda spooky. All that stuff he was saying about me being like the C—"

"Come on, Rachel. We need to get you back to the lab." Imitar pulled her by the arm toward the elevator tube.

"You're heading to Medical? At this hour? It's a little late to be running lab rats around don't you think?"

"Oh, Doctor El had sumpthin 'portant to talk to me 'bout tonight. Purdy shure she'll still be there. Hope she doesn't want me to operate any heavy machinery. I'm a little un-coordinated right now. Ha. Right now. Get it?"

Zoleta crossed her arms and watched Imitar grind his toe into the ground. *I wonder if this has anything to do with Sanda coming down on Ben yesterday?*

"I think she is capable of making her own way back to Medical. Run along now, Rachel. Imitar, I need you to help me with something. It won't take long. Or, it could take the rest of the night." Zoleta smiled at him and brushed her hair behind her ear.

"Sure. No problema. I'll be back," Rachel growled in a low voice and then giggled.

Zoleta raised her eyebrows. "What's wrong with her?"

"C 'mon." Rachel tried to blow a strand of hair out of her face. "Didn't you ever watch the Term-nator? Im-tar, you mushed have. You know, it's that shy-fi movie 'bout this bad guy who comes from the future to get rid of this kid who's ack-ack shooly going to save the human race, and then the other guy ish a robot, too, only he comes to protect the kid from the firsht robot or cyborg or whatever he was. Or was that Term-nator 2? I'm show tired. I think I'll go to bed."

"No, Rachel. You can't. Remember the Doc wants to talk to you tonight about . . ."

So Imitar does know something and Rachel has no idea of what's going on or is pretending not to. Well, I intend to find out.

Zoleta dismissed Rachel with a wave of her hand.

Rachel pushed past Zoleta then stopped and turned around. "Wait a second. What's that smell? It seems familiar. It smells cool . . . or like cool something. Wait a minute. Are you wearing perfume? Oh my God. Is it – oh no. Think I'm going to . . ."

Imitar caught her before she slid to the ground. "Rachel? You okay? Guess I better get her to Medical now for sure. Sorry, Zoleta. Another time, maybe."

Zoleta stared at their backs as they stumbled toward the elevator tube. *You think I believe your little act? You fool. Sanda must be in on it too. I can see how Rachel will need Imitar to help run the next planet with her. Is that why he's orbiting her like a moon? No way is she going to snake me out of what's rightfully mine. I deserve my own planet. I'm the best. I'm certainly more qualified than CPO Schaefer.*

CHAPTER 16

Medical
Sunday
2250 hours

RACHEL SNAPPED out of her fainting spell before they reached the elevator tube. She was groggy and her head throbbed. Imitar had his arm under her and carried her with little effort as if she were as light as a puppy.

"You can put me down now, Ben."

He set her gently on her feet. "So, what happened back there? Do you think you had a delayed allergic reaction to the Zang-O-Rang? And did you just call me Ben?"

"I . . . I don't know. I fainted I guess. Sorry. I must have been about to ask you a question concerning Ben, so that's probably why I called you Ben."

Thoughts careened through her mind as she tried to make sense of the memory but it was like looking at scraps of photographs on a moving 3-D collage of her life. Nothing held still long enough for her to focus on it. How could she tell Imitar there was something from her past, something about the smell of Zoleta's perfume, if she wasn't sure herself?

I'm sick of these chunks of debris flying through my brain, never giving me any clues as to who I am or what I'm doing here.

"Are you feeling better now?"

"I think my little episode has passed. In fact, I don't feel the least bit inebriated any more. How strange."

"Good. Sanda will check you over anyway before she starts the procedure."

"What procedure?"

"Craters. I didn't mean to say anything. I'll let Doc explain. I don't understand it all myself and I don't want to screw things up."

As they descended in the elevator tube down to Medical, Rachel watched Imitar closely. His hand started toward his chin but he brushed the side of his face like he had crumbs on his cheek and then clasped his hands behind his back. Something was definitely going on.

Do I have a medical condition that they know about and have been afraid to tell me? Or maybe I have some kind of contagious bacteria or virus that'll jeopardize the entire population of Goliath. No, I would have been in isolation like George. That reminds me, I should check on him tonight after this meeting, or whatever it is.

Sanda met them at the door. "How was The Bucket, Rachel? Did you enjoy yourself?"

For the second time since waking up in an unfamiliar place, the rooms in Medical felt a bit chilly to Rachel. Perhaps she had never noticed before but the whole unit seemed bleached out, antiseptic, devoid of color. Of course, this was a medical area, but still, it lacked the touch of human warmth.

"I appreciate your attempt at being sociable, Sanda, but why don't you just cut to the chase and tell me what this is about? What's going on and why all the mystery? Let me guess. You don't know what cut to the chase means? Well, it means tell me the facts, the truth. I'm not a child and I'm tired of being treated like one."

The doctor sighed and gave a slow nod. "Okay, Rachel. I'll explain what is happening and how we hope you will help." She looked toward Imitar. "Imitar, thank you. You're free to go now."

"No," Rachel said. "I want him to stay. Imitar, would you mind?"

"If I won't be in the way, I don't mind hanging around, but I can't stay too long. Zoleta's waiting for me."

"Very well. Let's go into my office and have a seat. Imitar, pull in a hover-stool from the lab."

Rachel had never been in Sanda's office, other than sticking her head in every now and then to give the doctor a message or update her on any results from the experiments they conducted. The room looked much like the rest of the medical and laboratory units, only smaller and without the sterile equipment. Sanda sat on a slim white chair behind her large, metal desk. Flow charts and pages of data that she had been reading on the e-desktop blinked off when she tapped the center.

That's what's missing. Pictures. Nothing on the desk or walls or anywhere of people or places or even pets. Nothing to show who Sanda is. And I thought I had problems. At least I have an excuse. I wonder if her private quarters are like this.

"Did I do something wrong?" Rachel asked. "Or is there something wrong with me? Other than the minor, obvious things like clumsiness and lack of long-term memory?"

"No Rachel. It's quite the opposite. You have the chance to do something very right, for not only you, but quite possibly for every citizen on this planet."

"Why do I feel like there's a big 'but' coming next?"

"Let me explain. You know all the research we've been working on and how we haven't been seeing the results I've been hoping for? I think we've been looking at the problem from the wrong angle."

"Doctor, even with all of your advanced medicine and treatments, three people have already died. What other way should we look at it? And what about George?" Heat rose in Rachel's cheeks.

"Yes, that's true but we were looking for a bacterium or other organism as the culprit. But what we didn't look at was the workers themselves and what they had in common with each other."

"But they all came from the xeno mines in Sector Seven. Right Doc?" Imitar said.

"They also received more rejuvenations than anyone else on the planet. More than twenty times what the rest of us have needed over the years. Being in the mines aged their cell functions at a much faster rate."

Sanda paused in her explanation, giving Rachel time to let the information sink in. Something was tapping at her brain, trying to connect with what she knew from somewhere in her past.

"What exactly did the workers die from? What was the official cause of death? Was it the same for all of them?" Rachel leaned forward on her stool, her palms flat on Sanda's desk.

"They all died from their lung tissue's inability to repair itself and expel fluid."

"Pneumonia! Originating from . . . the common cold? Oh my God. George!" Rachel jumped up from her stool, making it spin backward, away from her. Imitar snagged it before it hit the wall.

"Rachel, it'll be okay. Maybe the Doc has figured out how to stop, whatever you said, from happening to George."

"Let me finish." Sanda continued. "What it looks like is happening is the human body is reaching a point where it can no longer use the stem-cell rejuvenations to keep up its immunity function. I've checked all intergalactic news feeds and this hasn't occurred anywhere else or in any other populations so far. But if we are right, the simplest disease could result in the death of everyone on this planet, and possibly billions more on Earth. Everyone we know has had multiple genetic modifications in order to live longer lives. Except . . . you."

Imitar gave Rachel's arm a gentle squeeze. "You aren't going to do that falling-down thing again are you? Your face looks white and sweaty."

"I'm fine. Sanda, what do you mean 'if **we** are right'? I don't know any of this so you can't mean you and me."

"CPO Schaefer is involved in every aspect of this planet and is concerned for the lives of every citizen. He's kept abreast of the results of the research and is alarmed that we haven't come up with a single thing which works. As am I. He believes that there may be some merit in having you tested to see if your DNA is clean, meaning not tampered with in any way. Do you remember when the CPO asked for your permission?"

Oh, my God. Like I could forget. I was standing there with nothing on but my robe and I wanted to take that off too. What was he asking me to do? Self-regulate? Damn it. I was too flustered to ask intelligent questions or to concentrate on what he was saying.

"Rachel. Are you listening? I'm sure Schaefer neglected to explain the risks of this procedure. And there are life-threatening risks involved."

"No. We didn't get that far." She cleared her throat. "What exactly are you hoping to find and why me?"

"If you did indeed come from Earth, from a time before man was able to prolong his life indefinitely, then you might have DNA which has never been manipulated and can be used as a fresh base."

"So, you're saying I'm like a sourdough starter? Everyone else is dying out or will eventually die out because they've used up the life of their DNA so it's no longer active? Is that possible?"

Imitar looked from Rachel to the doctor. "Do you mean we need to re-boot ourselves?"

"Genetically speaking, yes."

"If I can help anyone, especially George, sign me up. Let's get started, so to speak. Do you need to do a blood draw or something?"

"I wish it were that easy. The risk involved can be substantial. I don't want you to say yes just because there may be a chance that this might work. You could be out for several days after the splicing. If the nanos can't re-establish your sequences and connect the neural pathways, you could be lost in a vegetative state for the rest of your life." Sanda rubbed her finger across her lower lip. "Although there is also the possibility that the nanos could give your memory a boost. It's hard to predict which way it will go."

"What do you mean, a 'boost'?"

"If the prep-nanos do their job, they should clear out any extraneous material, allowing you to recall memories that have been buried deep within your brain."

"I could remember . . ."

Imitar wiggled in his chair. "You could tell me all about your life back in the olden days.

"Let's not get ahead of ourselves, Imitar. There's a possibility. I didn't say it was a given." Sanda folded her hands on her desk and looked at Rachel. "There is another drawback that you should know about."

Rachel glanced at Imitar and he shrugged.

"The splicing itself will be painful but the realigning will be excruciating."

Imitar gulped. "Can't you give her pain meds or something?"

"Of course, I will. She will be as far under the anesthesia as we can safely keep her. But when the sampling is done and the nanos reconstruct the dismantled pain centers, the body will react even if the patient is unconscious."

Rachel stood and walked slowly around the room. Questions ping-ponged through her mind. *What are they asking me to do? Physical pain might be a welcome distraction from all this . . . this what? Mental anguish and frustration I feel. And what if it works and I remember? Do I want to know who I am? What if my past was more horrible than my present?*

Yes, I'd give anything to know.

CHAPTER 17

Medical-Surgical
Monday
1247 hours

"COULD I DIE? I mean, like not be patched up, re-frozen, re-built, whatever?"

"I'm sorry, Rachel, but yes, it's entirely possible that you might not survive the splicing," Sanda said.

"You know the worst part is if I died no one would know. Who would you tell? You couldn't tell my family because I don't know if I have a family, or where they are, or if they know that I'm alive. So, I guess you really aren't asking me to give up my life, because I don't have one." Rachel seemed to collapse into her chair and held her head in her hands. "Imitar. If you were me, would you go for it?"

"Craters, Rachel. I don't know if I'd be strong enough."

* * *

After Imitar left, Sanda had Rachel step through the sterilizer, settled her in the surgery room, and began the preparations for the gene splicing. She pulled out vials full of colored liquids from the cabinets, mini scanners, and an atomizer. She connected a remote alarm between the holographic chart and the vital-bot which stood at the ready in the corner of the room.

With the surgical equipment in place, Sanda closed her eyes and took a calming breath. When she opened them, Rachel was staring at her.

"Sanda? Are you okay?"

"I'm fine. Just making sure everything is set to go." Sanda smiled at Rachel and patted her arm. "I know what you need. I'll be right back."

She returned with a small bed sheet and draped it over Rachel. "There you are."

"Thank you, Sanda."

"Let's get started. Here's your first cocktail snort: a mix of muscle relaxants and sedatives."

"Up my nose with a rubber hose." Rachel took the atomizer from Sanda, placed it in her nostril and sniffed. "Oh, and what time will I be up and around tomorrow, do you think? I promised George I'd check in on him."

"We don't . . . use rubber hoses any longer. Not that we ever have." Sanda chuckled then turned away and pretended to look over her instruments. *Did I not talk about how long she might be out from all this? If I tell her it'll be a couple of days, at the least, she might refuse the testing, and not because of the pain. It's George she's worried about.*

"Remember Rachel, this procedure will, more than likely, have you down for a while."

"Oh, that's right. Will you please tell him for me?"

The door to main medical buzzed. It was probably Imitar back from giving Zoleta the rundown on what was happening.

"I'd better see who's here. You relax and think of more odd things to tell me."

* * *

"CPO Schaefer. Did you come by to check on yesterday's results?"

"No. I want to know if you've started the splicing."

"You told me to get it going as soon as possible, so yes, I have. Rachel is in the surgical room now and she's had the first sedation dose. You didn't give me enough time to run the allergy panel so I hope she isn't allergic to anything."

"She isn't."

How would he know? If Rachel has a reaction to any of the meds, it's going to be on his head.

"I mean, let's hope she isn't." Ben looked at the floor then asked, "May I see the patient, Doctor?"

"You want to see Rachel? She'll be getting groggy, so you won't have much time if you're hoping to thank her."

"Understood."

I'm beginning to wonder just how much he does understand.

Sanda entered the room first. The vital-bot had just finished its checks and was whirling back to its corner. Rachel's arms were sunk down by her sides like they weighed twenty kilos each. She turned her head slowly when Sanda came closer. The overhead light enhanced the gold streaks running through Rachel's hair as it fanned out across the pillow. The flush of her cheeks contrasted with the milky white of her complexion. Even her freckles seemed to have lost their color leaving only the tiny mole on her earlobe looking lost and alone.

"The CPO is here to see you. May he come in?"

A silly smile bloomed across Rachel's face. "Did he bring flowers? Or balloons? I always liked it when they brought balloons. Especially the ones in the shape of cute little animals. The helium ones. Those are the best. We can suck the air out of them and sound like chipmunks on crack. Gosh, I sound silly, even to myself. Can't seem to help it. Please ignore me."

"No, Rachel. Sorry. I didn't bring you any balloons. I'll try to remember next time." Ben walked over and stood by the bedside while Sanda busied herself checking the values from the vitals-bot. "Sanda, what's this sheet on her for?"

"Oh, just something she did for George in sickbay. It seemed to bring him comfort so I thought it was a nice thing to do for her."

"Hellooo people. I'm right here. Why, Mr. CPO? Would you like me to ditch the sheet? Should I stop there? Too bad. I can't seem to move my arms, anyway. Damn, there I go again, my fantasies over-runneth."

"I see the drugs are starting to work. How are you feeling so far?"

"I'm GREAT. But ya know what?" Rachel lifted her chin in Sanda's direction. "Pretty soon she's going to give me some little bugs that are going to cut me into teensy-weensy bits and then she'll give me all the king's horses and all the king's men to try to put me back together again."

"That will be good. Um, Rachel," Ben stuttered. "I wanted to thank you for what you are doing. I know it won't be pleasant and—"

"I know, but Sanda says there's a good chance that I might get my full memory back."

Sanda came around the bed on the opposite side from Ben. "Time for your second dose. It will shut your body down in less than three minutes." She held it under Rachel's nose. "We don't have to inject it. Just take a big whiff."

"Is it some of that cherry-thought-suppressant that you gave me that one time?"

"Yes, thought suppressant." Sanda smiled and went to make sure the nano-splicers were ready to go, leaving Ben the last few moments alone with the semi-conscious patient.

Rachel yawned as Ben stepped closer to the bed. "Rachel, can you hear me?"

Sanda moved the scanner to the corner of the room where she had a better view and could see, or hear, if Rachel needed anything before the sedatives took full effect.

Rachel's eyes fluttered open and closed. "I . . . can hear you. You sound so far off. Like from a dream. Ben . . . that's funny. I'm on the wrong side."

"The wrong side of what, Rachel?"

"The bed . . . you're the one that should be in the bed. Remember? I remember now. The first time I saw you." She licked her lips and tried to open her eyes. "Skeeting. No, that's not right. Can't think of the word. How is your . . . leg? Penicillin. That's right. No penicillin for you."

"What's she's talking about, Ben? Does she think you're someone she knows or used to know? Is there something wrong with your leg? I can take a look at it later if you want."

Ben glanced at Sanda. "The drugs must be making her confused. Will she be asleep soon?"

"I'm not . . . confused. I'm . . . remembering. I'm going to remember everything about you. And about you . . . and . . . me."

A sigh escaped from Rachel and then she lay still.

"That took longer than I thought it would. She's a stubborn little thing but she's completely under now. I'm going to inject the nano-splicers. You're welcome to stay if you like, but there's nothing to do but let the bots do their job and hope for the best. The auto-scan will alert me if anything goes wrong. You might as well go home and get some rest."

Ben reached out and gently smoothed Rachel's hair back from her forehead, letting his hand linger at her shoulder. "I want updated reports on her progress every hour. Is that clear? I'll be back to check on her in the morning."

"Certainly. Good night, CPO Schaefer."

"Good night, Sanda."

CHAPTER 18

Wednesday
0300 hours
CPO's private quarters

BEN WAS TORN between staying with Rachel during the splicing or going to his apartment and trying to get some sleep. The thought of Rachel in pain was bad enough but he knew he couldn't bear to see her in agony. If he was lucky enough to get a little shut eye maybe he would be able to function when he headed back to Command Center in a few hours. It was early morning and he was exhausted. He swigged down a quick glass of water and sat on the edge of his queen-sized bed in his spacious bedroom, a luxury as well as a symbol of his highest rank on the planet. He kicked off his boots and fell back on top of the comforter, his arm slung across his eyes.

Oh, Rachel. What have I done? Will you be able to forgive me for putting you through this? And if you get your memory back . . . will you be able to forgive me for so much more?

The room was chilly but Ben was too tired to request a warmer temp. His eyelids drooped and soon he fell into a restless sleep, haunted by an old familiar dream.

* * *

Snow coated the windshield as the wipers swished back and forth, leaving soft angel wings.

"Hold on girl. It's not much farther."

A sob caught in his throat and he tried to force it down by swallowing. He reached over to the passenger seat and gently scratched Molly Brown between her ears. The chocolate lab attempted to raise her head and lick his fingers, but the effort made her whimper in pain.

"Easy girl. Just take it easy. Everything will be okay."

Ben glanced at his best friend, his solace for the past four-teen years, the last connection to Rachel. "We've had a lot of good times, haven't we, old girl?" Molly Brown rolled her eyes up at him. They were red and glassy, like they wanted to close, too tired to ever open again. She rested on her side across his favorite Stanford sweatshirt. "Do you know how much I will miss you?"

He turned off the main road into the industrial park. The two-story buildings all looked the same with their white concrete and small square windows. There wasn't any land-scaping to speak of, just endless pavement. Few cars remained in the parking lot on the weekends and this dreary Saturday morning was no exception. He continued until he arrived at the last, and only, building at the end of Sorrentino Court.

The Erfurt Runkle Building, saddle-brown in color with brick trim across the front, showed off its small patch of snow-dusted lawn. Juniper bushes snuggled together under the large picture window. Ben whipped the pickup around and parked in front of the twelve-foot-high double garage door. He barely registered the temperature drop, or the frosty puffs he exhaled.

Molly Brown didn't move when he came around to the passenger side of the pickup and carefully lifted her, feeling the deadly lumps through the sweatshirt. Tears burned his eyes and trickled down through the two-day-old stubble on his cheeks.

The director of the Cryonics Institute met Ben and Molly Brown at the door and ushered them inside. Dr. Ettinger wore a white lab coat, two sizes too big. Three ballpoint pens and a pair of reading glasses fought for space in the breast pocket. A blue ink-spot smeared across the pocket's bottom corner. The wrinkled collar of his plaid flannel shirt peeked from the neck of his lab coat, the garment tag sticking up against the back of his neck. Frayed bottoms of blue jeans ringed the tops of his worn-out tennis shoes. His gray hair fluffed out in every direction as it fled from the bald spot in the center of his head. The AWOL strands landed above his eyes in the form of one fuzzy eyebrow.

"Ben Schaefer? And this must be Molly Brown." Dr. Ettinger's voice was kind and his eyes were warm but sad. "You can follow me to the prep room and we'll make her comfortable."

Unable to speak, Ben lowered his head in a single nod.

Noisy generators banged and pressure valves hummed, steam escaping every four minutes. Ten metal cylinders, over eleven feet tall, stood like giant thermos bottles. A smaller tank, the size of a horse trough, squatted in front. This is where Molly Brown would rest, suspended in a liquid nitrogen bath, until the day technology could bring her back to life.

Ben followed Dr. Ettinger as if he were walking underwater on the bottom of a frozen lake. They entered a well-lit area, separate from the cryostats and the other large machinery. A wide table with eight-inch-high sides, like an oversized surgical instruments tray, sat in the middle of the room.

Dr. Ettinger spoke softly, "Would you like a few minutes alone with Molly to say good-bye? I'll give her a sedative before placing her in the ice bath. The perfusions won't take long and she won't feel any pain."

"Yes. Thank you," Ben croaked.

He laid her gently on the exam table. A weak moan used up one of her few remaining breaths. Ben cradled Molly Brown's head in his hands and whispered, "You have been a true and loyal friend for all these years . . . I will never forget you. Rest now. I'll see you again someday, on the other side."

Ben stirred from his dream; his pillow damp beneath his cheek. He wanted to wake up, he tried to wake up, but he was too exhausted from the worry. The dream pulled him under again, like quicksand sucking him below the surface. Thrashing only made him sink farther.

This time he was pacing, his stomach in knots, as he waited for Dr. Ettinger to answer the phone. "There's no time. You must move her now! They'll bomb the facility within the next two days! The new location is ready. Follow the plan, and don't tell anyone."

Ben's heart raced and his breathing was rapid as he fought to exit the dream. "Only room for one. No choice–got to save her. Transport should be there soon. It's her only chance."

CHAPTER 19

Medical/Surgical Unit
Thursday
0400 hours

THE ALARM from the vital-bot went off, jarring Sanda from two short hours of restless sleep. She threw on her scrubs and raced down to surgery.

For three days, she had watched and worried over Rachel, like a mother with a sick infant. Rachel was coming out of recovery and she, Sanda, needed to be there. She flew through the door and ran to Rachel's bedside.

Sweat matted Rachel's hair to her forehead and the sides of her face. Spasms racked her body as she screamed, "I'm on fire! Put it out. It's killing me. You have to make it stop. Help me."

Sanda grabbed the naso-tube with the Schedule VII pain-killer in one hand and held Rachel's head firmly with the other while she forced the medication up Rachel's nose.

Rachel's body shuddered for a few seconds and then relaxed. She took a ragged breath and looked up at Sanda. "Please, just let me die. I . . . I don't want to do this anymore."

"No, Rachel, I can't do that. You're going to be okay. I know you're in pain. We'll stay on top of it until all your nerve endings have healed. You're through the worst of it now, I promise. Try to take some deep breaths. As soon as you're able, I need to know how your head feels."

Rachel took her time and several deep breaths before answering. She reached up and rubbed her sticky brow. "It feels different. It still hurts like someone took a sharp knife and scooped my brains out, stirred them, and then dumped them back in. But there's a tingly sensation . . . like my head feels full. Of memories, maybe. I think. I can't really tell yet."

"That sounds like a good sign."

As long as your memories don't come flooding back all at once and fracture your mind. Sanda patted Rachel's arm.

"If I can only figure out how to retrieve them. At least I know they're there now." She licked her dry lips. "Sanda, how long will this pain last? How long do I have to be in here?"

"Later today we'll see if you're strong enough for a short walk around the room."

"I'd like to try now. Please, just let me try."

The pleading look Rachel gave her was more than Sanda could stand. "Okay, but let's take it slow." She held Rachel's arm and gently pulled her to sitting. "Are you feeling dizzy, or nauseated?"

Rachel shook her head. Sanda helped her swing her legs over the side of the bed where she sat until Sanda finally allowed her to stand. They circled the bed at a snail-like pace, and then three more times as Rachel gained strength and her balance returned. On the fourth pass, Rachel bumped the corner of the gurney with her hip and cried out in pain.

"I'm so sorry, Rachel. Your entire body is going to be very sensitive for a few days. It's best you stay here where we can manage the pain."

"No! I want to go home. Ha, like I have a home. No, Sanda, I'll be fine. I'll get more rest in my apartment. You can send whatever meds you want with me. Besides, you have to find out if all this is going to work."

"I don't like this, Rachel. I don't advise you leaving this room, but you make the call. I'll give you two more naso-seds, one for tonight and one for tomorrow morning, but you need to check in with me as soon as you wake up tomorrow. I'll get the hover-chair when you're ready to go."

"I want to walk. Please no wheel-chair, I mean, hover-chair."

They took their time getting to Rachel's apartment down the hall from Medical on the same wing as Sanda's. The door swished open and Rachel stumbled in. Sanda followed her, ordering the room to turn on the lights and set the thermostat. After setting the meds on the dining shelf, Sanda helped Rachel into her sleep uniform.

"Are you hungry? I can have something sent up. It's best if you take in as many fluids as you can. I'll get you some water."

Sanda brought the thermos of water to Rachel who had already climbed into her bed-cubby. Rachel drank the entire container. "Thank you. That's much better."

A few crusty dishes were stacked on the kitchen counter. Sanda scooped them up and placed them into the autoclave. She stuffed a jumble of dirty clothes down the laundry chute and looked around the room.

"Now that's better too. Looks like we took you straight in to surgery before you had time to clean up your place."

Who am I fooling? We didn't give the poor girl a chance to do anything before she went under the nano-splicers.

"Sanda, have you gotten the results back? How did the tests turn out? Did you get the answers you were hoping for?"

Sanda smiled. "Your DNA is clean. We were able to use it for a whole new family of stem-vacs, beginning with T-cell rejuvenators. We've already started applications on those who are most at risk."

"And George? Is he going to be okay? Does he know yet? Have you told him? I'd like to go see him."

Rachel struggled into a sitting position; a pinched look on her face and inched slowly off her bed. She took an unsteady step in the direction of the closet. Sanda grasped her by the arm before she could fall and hurt herself. *How am I going to tell her? She'll be devastated. I don't know how fragile she is and what the news of his death might do to her.*

"Wait. You need to rest," Sanda said. "You don't have all of your strength back yet." Rachel weaved toward her.

"Okay. Maybe I could use a little help."

"No, Rachel. I'm sorry."

"You won't help me?"

"It's not that . . ." A lump felt dusty and dry in Sanda's throat as she tried to gather what she would say.

"What? What are you not telling me?"

Sanda took a deep breath. "George died last night. We sent him on his final orbit this morning." She placed a comforting hand on Rachel's shoulder. Rachel stepped back and grabbed the counter for support. "He left a coded hologram for you. If you'd like to read it, I can have Imitar set it up," Sanda continued, the sadness in her voice emanating from her heart.

Rachel sank to the floor, taking the place of the puddle of clothes Sanda had cleaned up moments earlier.

"You helped him, Rachel, and he was truly grateful for your part in his care-taking."

Rachel held up her hand as if to ward off demons. "Stop. You don't understand. How could you understand? George was all I had on this God-forsaken planet. All I had to care about and the only person who seemed to care about me and what I was going through. Oh, what does it matter? He's dead. I'm breathing, but I'm dead."

"Rachel, let me get you something."

"Sure. Bring me your special: scrambled grey matter with a

side of grief. I'd like to be alone, now." She curled into a fetal position in her bed-cubby and faced the wall.

Sanda was at a loss for what to say, and how to say it. She finally walked toward the entrance. "Rachel, please remember to take the medications I left on the counter." She stopped and turned back. "And I think you are forgetting that Imitar cares a lot about you. So does Ben. And I hope you know that I do too. Please call me if you need anything. I'll be close by."

"Please, just go away," Rachel whispered.

Sanda stood outside Rachel's door, not knowing whether she should try to talk to her again or leave her alone like she'd asked. Rachel needed rest and maybe tomorrow would be better. If Rachel would only draw on that inner strength that she didn't seem to know she had, but Sanda knew it was there. She had seen glimpses of it, especially in her interactions with George. She just hoped Rachel would keep fighting.

Ben Schaefer was lucky in his guess about Rachel's unadulterated genetics. Her stem cells will deliver us. But if she slips into a catatonic state, I'm not sure I want to stay here on Goliath. And what if— cosmos forbids— the vaccine is defective? I will have failed, when I'm the one who should have been strong.

Sanda wiped the tears from her eyes.

CHAPTER 20

Command Center
Friday
1100 hours

IMITAR ARRIVED at Command Center as Ben and Zoleta were looking over a topographical map marked with locations of possible mining sites. He sat down at his console and brought up the software systems that he had been working on. The other two didn't seem to notice he had finally made it in to work until Zoleta spoke up. "So, how did the gene-harvest go? And how's the star sample? Did she make it through with A + B still equaling C?"

Imitar took a deep breath and ignored Zoleta's question. He shot her a look and started the quality checks on the programs he had tweaked a few days ago, days before all this upheaval, days before Rachel had undergone the splicing. He was worried about her, about Rachel. She had yet to come out of her room, even with his coaxing or Sanda's, telling them to go away when they tried to get her to let them in. Dr. L told him she hoped Rachel had at least followed her orders and taken the medication for the pain. Now an uglier worry emerged,

Rachel sinking into a deep depression. "If she gets too far with-drawn, we may not be able to pull her back. She'll be lost, not only to us, but to herself," Sanda had told him.

Ben was focused on his hologram, tossing his question casually to Imitar. "Do you know how Ms. McRae is doing?" He stopped manipulating the data and turned to Imitiar. "I haven't heard anything from Dr. Luminita."

Imitar was going to have to tell them something, though he didn't want to. For the first time in his life, he felt like he meant something to someone. It was important to hold that person's confidence, to be loyal, to be a true friend to Rachel, not just an informant for the CPO, or a string wrapped around Zoleta's little finger.

"Rachel needs some time to heal," he said.

"Does she really have anything we need? Hard to believe." Zoleta snorted. "What does she want? What's it going to cost us?"

"Why do you ask, Zoleta? All I know is it cost Rachel more than you or I could ever give. She's the one who's sacrificed herself so the rest of us can continue living with fresh, healthy cells. Do you think your life is more important than hers? No – don't answer that. I don't want to hear it." Imitar's voice had increased in pitch and volume. He forced himself to unclench his teeth.

Zoleta came and stood next to him. He felt the sizzle of her proximity but was too angry and disgusted to enjoy the close-ness. "Maybe you could be first in line for the new heart-stems, Zoleta. As long as there's enough substrate and they can survive in the bitter temperatures."

"Oh, don't get your electrons all in a bunch, for bits sake. All I did was ask a question. What do we really know about her?"

Ben waved off the hologram. "Imitar, go ahead and run the z-rams on the topographical sets. I'll come back later this evening."

"Do you want me to finish the probs and stats for the next section?" Zoleta asked.

"I don't care what you do. I'm going home. Goodnight."

For once, Imitar didn't care that he was alone with Zoleta. *Why did I even bother coming in to work? I've got too much on my mind for her games.* He cleared his throat. *Maybe I should forget it for tonight and come back tomorrow.*

He was about to leave when Zoleta placed her hand on his shoulder. "I'm sorry, Imitar. I just don't trust something, or someone, I don't know anything about. You can understand that. And this Rachel, who is she? She shows up here, no PO, no info, just a cryo lost in space? Maybe she was sent by the Federation, to oversee this planet, or be the CPO of the next planet on the list for exploration of viable resources. How would we know?"

"It's nothing like that, Zoleta. It can't be. Rachel doesn't have a clue as to what's going on. And besides, she really doesn't want to be here. She has no family, no memories, and no friends. Why would she choose this?"

"Exactly."

Imitar closed his eyes. *Am I really hearing this?*

"Zoleta, believe it or not, not everyone has an ulterior motive. If you only knew how incredible you are. Your mind is light-years ahead of mine, and yet, you can't seem to grasp the simplest concept of what it means to connect with another human being. If you'll excuse me, I need to get some outside air."

CHAPTER 21

Sub-Level 3
Rachel's quarters
Monday
0700 hours

IT WAS TRUE, Rachel had not left her room in the three days since the procedure. Ben checked the updates hourly on the tracker he had had Sanda insert under the skin of Rachel's forearm. He longed to go straight to her bedside but protocol held him back. Instead he headed for Medical to speak with Sanda.

When he arrived, Sanda was pacing the floor in front of her desk, not a good sign. Ben swallowed the metallic taste of fear rising in his throat. The splicing was risky but they had to take the chance, or so he kept telling himself.

"Dr. Luminita. What is the status of the patient?"

Sanda stopped mid-pace and turned toward him with a deep crease between her brows. "CPO Schaefer, I didn't hear the room bell. I'm sorry, what did you ask me?"

"How is Rachel?"

"The experiment was quite successful. I've already been able to culture the samples and inoculate the at-risk workers.

Another citizen was brought in with low T-cell replication potential and after administering the purified stem cells from the donor, the worker is going to be okay." Sanda went back to her pacing.

"Stop." Ben reached out and grabbed Sanda's arm. "That's not what I asked you."

Sanda shook her head and looked down at the floor. "I don't know how to help her, Ben. Maybe we should give her tonins. Try to elevate her mood enough to get her past this."

"No, I'm the one she did this for. I'll see if I can talk to her, let her know how much she has helped. Give her a sense of purpose. If that doesn't work then yes, let's start a course of serotonins."

"She won't let you in. She wouldn't even let Imitar in the door."

"I've got to try, Sanda. That's all we can do."

* * *

Ben left Medical and continued down the hall to Rachel's apartment. He was sure the room had announced his arrival but the door didn't open and there was no acknowledgment from within. He rapped on the door with his knuckles in the ancient old-fashioned way, his deformed pinky-finger bent out of place. Still, no answer. He took a step back and raised his eyes to the scanner. "Ben Schaefer CPO 1221994. Allow access."

The door swooshed open and he entered, squinting to see through the dark.

"Lights up, three clicks."

Corners of furniture emerged from the darkness as the room took on a dusky glow. In the bed-cubby niche on the far wall, Rachel lay curled in the fetal position.

"Rachel?" Ben whispered from across the room. "It's CP—

it's me, Ben Schaefer. I'd like to talk to you if that would be all right."

He made his way to the bed-nook and sat down on the edge. A faint "no" came from the small lump against the wall. His hand shook as he reached in and touched her shoulder. He rubbed lightly along her upper arm.

"I . . . can't," she said, so softly he wasn't sure he had heard her.

"Please, Rachel. Look at me."

He pulled her toward him, scooping her into his arms. He held her with one arm under her bent knees, the other supporting her back, her head slumped against his chest. A soft groan escaped her lips as he rocked her gently. Her eyes were closed and he fought the urge to lightly brush a kiss against each eyelid, her forehead, and her soft, pale mouth. Her hair was matted to her brow and he wiped it away from her face, letting his fingers trail down her cheek and across her lips.

What have I done?

Rachel licked her lips and a dry, pathetic cough barked from her hoarse throat.

"I'll get you something to drink," Ben said as he laid her carefully back on her side, went to the kitchen and returned with a cup of water. He put his arm around her again, propping her as she took a sip.

Rachel's body stiffened and she pulled out of his grasp. At first, she seemed to gaze past his face, then finally locked in on his eyes, making his heart slam in his chest.

"I was dreaming. So many dreams," she croaked. "No sense, all scrambled. *You* were in some of them. How funny. God, I'm so tired. I just want to sleep and never wake up."

"I'm going to make you a cup of Jav and get you a nutrient pack." *Is she talking about dreams of me from here and now? Or from . . . before?*

Ben ordered the brewer to make a double shot cup of java,

chocolate flavored, and requested a complete protein-carb crunch bar, with lifters, to be sent up from the DC.

In less than three minutes the food arrived in the vac-tube. He handed her the bar along with the coffee.

"I'm not hungry."

"I'm not leaving until you eat at least half of that and finish off the mug."

She bit off a chunk of the biscuit and rolled it around in her mouth. She took a sip of the java and swallowed. "Tastes like chocolate. I haven't had chocolate in such a long time." She took another, bigger sip.

"I know you like choc—I thought you might like it. The brewer will make it at your request."

"Chocolate," she sighed. "What I might be persuaded to do for some Belgian chocolate. Too bad you've never had the pleasure. You're missing out. If I can't have any, I'd just as soon go back to sleep."

"Sure. As soon as you finish your dinner."

Ben paced around the small room, keeping watch on Rachel's progress with the protein bar. "Rachel, doctor Luminita and Imitar and I, well, we've been a little worried about you. I was thinking that once you are feeling better, I'd like to take a survey group to the edge of the belt to do a little exploring in a cave-pocket that looks promising. I'd like for you to come along. It would give you a chance to see a little more of the planet. You don't have to answer now. Think about it. I'll send Imitar to check with you in a day or two. In the meantime, I'm sure Dr. Luminita would be happy to have your help in Medical as soon as possible."

She held out the empty mug to him and the half-eaten dinner-bar. "Is that enough?"

He took the cup and smiled. "You need to eat one more bite."

She rolled her eyes. "What are you, my mother?" But she

took another bite. "If this was chocolate, I promise I would eat the entire thing."

"I want you to think about the field trip. I know you'd enjoy it. And as far as chocolate goes, I'll see what I can do."

As he turned to leave, Rachel lay back in her cubby but she was no longer in a tight ball. He told the room to set the temp and turn off the lights. In the darkness, he said, "I need you . . . I need you to get better, Rachel."

CHAPTER 22

The Belt
Thursday
0800 hours

RACHEL STOOD beside her bed and scanned the small apartment, trying to decide what and how much to pack. It had been three days since Ben visited and a week since the procedure. Ben had insisted she eat something and return to work as soon as possible. Since then that she hadn't stopped eating, like she was making up for lost time and calories.

Oh lord. That's right, he came to my room. The CPO. Gorgeous hunk. I wasn't dreaming. I must have looked like hell. Maybe Sanda has some kind of nano-memory-eraser bugs I can slip him somehow. Stop it, Rachel. Why am I doing this again? How can I be acting like a sex-crazed woman when I've just had the crap knocked, or rather spliced, out of me.

At least I was skinny . . .

Sanda had given her an ultra-light backpack, but no hint on what she should bring along on their expedition. Breathing fresh air above ground and going off the compound sounded wonderful. Rachel had never really been outside the protective bubble, except for the short time to The Bucket and back. Working below in the lab day after day could get mighty depressing.

"Yummy. Real sunshine." She closed her eyes, already feeling the glorious warmth.

You can't go wrong with a snack or two. Water? A must.

Which jacket, she wondered. They wouldn't be going outside the belt really – so much for that luscious sunshine – just up to the base of the northern mountains. "To look for crystals with special properties," Sanda had told her. "It'll be a nice break to get out and stretch your legs a bit. Besides, Rachel, you'll get a chance to talk to someone other than me."

"Who all is going?" Rachel had asked.

She shivered, remembering Zoleta would be part of the expedition. What was it about her? Only a few people on the planet seemed kind of nice and Zoleta wasn't one of them. *They're probably just focused on their work.* But Zoleta was another story. Rachel had the feeling that she was the focus, like some pesky bug pinned under Zoleta's dissecting scrutiny.

She shook off the chill, forced her thoughts back to her packing and held up two jackets, one in each hand. The blue zerotex was lined with a soft microfiber and would be warmer. Made sense to take it. She started to lay it on the bed and put the dark-jade lightweight away, and then stopped. She pulled the green jacket close to her body. Another tingle shimmied along her spine but this time it started at her lips and melted down into her breasts, her abdomen and between her legs. It felt like small embers igniting long dormant stirrings. "The green jacket. It'll show off the color of my eyes. Maybe he will notice . . . maybe he will—oh stop it," she reprimanded herself. Grabbing the pack, she rushed out the door and up the elevator tube.

Ben was on the tarmac, standing beside the open door of the ZX. He glanced at her as she approached. She shot him her best smile but he didn't return one of his own. Instead he turned back toward the car without saying hello.

This might not be so fun after all. She felt the spark of hope fading fast. Someone was bending over the driver's seat only showing her shapely backside in a skin-tight uniform.

Damn. Zoleta.

"What are you doing?" Ben barked at her as she approached the vehicle.

"I . . . uh . . .," Rachel stammered and tried to swallow the dry knot stuck in her throat. Now she wasn't sure she wanted to go on this trip at all. Zoleta's voice floated up from the floorboards of the vehicle like a syrupy mist. Rachel breathed a sigh of relief. Ben was talking to Zoleta, not to her.

"I'm prepping the ZX so I can fly us out to the site. I like to have my own equipment," Zoleta said. Without looking up, she pulled a controller out of her bag to connect it to the steering column and continued with her adjustments. "We can go over the layouts," she said to Ben, "and maybe over some of your ideas on the future direction of this colony, like who should manage special projects. Besides, I am the best driver here."

"You're welcome to fight Imitar for piloting the Hubba, but you're not driving the ZX." Rachel felt Ben's frigid reply, like a frozen breeze blowing off an ice cap. She didn't think Zoleta even noticed.

"I have to," Zoleta said, in her phony-sweet voice again. "The Hubba is packed with the equipment and there's only room for Sanda, Imitar, and Rachel. I'll drive the two of us. Hand me that wrench in my bag." She reached her right arm back behind her and waved her open hand.

Rachel looked hard at Ben, but she couldn't tell what he was thinking. His face was a blank mask. "No, Zoleta, *you'll* ride with Imitar and the doctor," Ben repeated.

"That won't work." Zoleta gave up waiting for the wrench and backed out from under the flight console. "It only holds three passengers." She straightened up to face Ben. Rachel's mouth went dry as she felt Zoleta's cold-blooded gaze land on her.

"That's right, doctor Luminita, colonel Dubasi, and you. Rachel rides with me."

Zoleta opened her mouth to protest, but Ben sliced her with a razor-sharp glare, daring her to object. She mashed her lips together in a tight line and stabbed him back with her own poisonous look.

"I see," Zoleta said, with enough acid to disintegrate the metal on a Star-cruiser.

Oh yes, this is going to be loads of fun. "I'm going to go to see if . . . well, check on . . . I'll just wait for the others while you two discuss this," Rachel said and made her way over to where the Hubba was parked.

Sanda arrived at the garage the same time as Imitar, knapsack over her shoulder, the legs of her green trousers tucked securely into her molded hiking boots. The light-weight all-terrain, bright yellow jacket made her look like a beacon for stray hornets. She placed her backpack next to the equipment behind the driver's seat in the Hubba.

They both acknowledged Rachel, then Imitar mouthed, "Where's Zoleta?"

Rachel pointed a thumb in the direction of the other vehicle. "She's getting her stuff out of the ZX and she's not too happy about it." She hoped her feeling of satisfaction didn't show in her face.

"Imitar. Did you pack the EC?" Sanda opened the back door of the Hubba.

"The EC?"

"The electron coder."

"Is it that big cone shaped thing with the spin chargers?"

"Here it is," she said as she pulled back the solar blanket

covering all the equipment. "Just checking. Is everybody ready for some fishing?"

"I'm driving," Zoleta said.

Rachel and Imitar exchanged glances. He shrugged and climbed into the co-pilot seat of the Hubba.

Thank God, I'm not in that vehicle, Rachel thought. Ben asked if she was ready to go. She nodded, climbed into the ZX, and fastened the harness. They cruised slowly out of the garage hanger, through the compound's gate, and took off at full speed in a northwesterly direction with Zoleta driving tight on their tail like a guided missile.

The other vehicle was so close behind them, Rachel pushed her side-viewer outward so she didn't have to look at Zoleta's scowl reflected in the mirror.

They took the main road past the compound, leaving the giant dome of the city behind. Bubbled roofs of titanahexium stuck up above the surface like giant mole-hills scattered across a prairie. "What are those?" Rachel asked, breaking the silence.

"Those are the tops of the underground storage sheds for the mining equipment, old containers, tools, etc. We never really discard anything. Recycle, re-use."

"I've never been good at purging, always saving every little memento. I think. Of course, I wouldn't know where to find any of those things I've squirreled away. Wouldn't know where to start. Well, anyway." *Why am I babbling? Oh my God, I'm such a loser.* She crunched back further in the seat.

They continued through the middle of the belt, flying past hundreds of different plant species, some with draping foliage and enormous flowers, others stunted, scrubby, and needled. It was a medley of hodge-podge greens, browns, and blues. Rachel caught glimpses of animals and birds she had never seen before, or at least didn't recognize at this speed. Or worse, she had seen them somewhere in her past but couldn't remember. No, they weren't familiar, but they were certainly interesting and she would have liked to look at them more closely. Typical male. CPO Schaefer seemed bent on getting to wherever they were going without stopping or even slowing down to take in the scenery.

"Will we be going to the hot or cold side of the planet?"

"Neither. The caves sit closer to The Hot Side, but we'll still be within the belt. And it'll be a cool but pleasant temp underground."

"You never told me what we're going to be looking for."

"Nothing really. Just exploring. But we're taking the equipment along in case we luck out and run into a pocket of something that looks promising."

"Like?"

"Xenostone. Most of the xenostone is found on the Hot Side of Goliath where the high temperatures combine with the increase in asteroids bombarding the soil to form unique materials not found on Earth."

"How wide is the belt anyway?"

"Roughly three-hundred twenty-two kilometers across."

Rachel thought about the distance. It didn't seem like all that much for a colony to have as their home base. Kind of like living on an island, she guessed.

As she watched out the window, the terrain began to grow rockier, dryer, plants became sparser, and the air hotter. The stark landscape looked beautiful to Rachel. A simple calmness melted over her senses. She opened the air-duct on her side and breathed in the strong aroma. A smile hovered at the corners of her mouth, but then vanished.

Why can't I just enjoy myself and relax? Why do I have to go and think? I get to ride with Ben. Why? Probably because, I'm the New Kid on the block and he doesn't want me screwing anything up. I mean, I want to ride with Ben. Who wouldn't want to ride with him? Zoleta would probably jump at the chance. I'd have more to talk about with Sanda, and even Imitar, but here I am. She sighed and chewed the cuticle on her thumb. *Well, things could be worse. I could be riding with Zoleta.*

She forced herself to concentrate on the surroundings. The ZX climbed higher and once again the landscape changed. The gray scrub gave way to greener bushes which gave way to small trees. The air smelled moist and the turquoise sky wrapped around the land. The small trees surrendered to larger conifers until forests of pine, fir, and cedar grew dense and impassable except to the creatures that make the woods their home. The road squeezed down between these giants and dwindled until it was no more than a trail.

Ben slowed to navigate a sharp turn to the right. Up ahead, a huge pine sprawled across the road, its massive trunk blocking the path. He braked hard and Zoleta missed slamming into him by a fraction of a centimeter.

"What have we here?" he said, glancing over at Rachel.

"Now what are we going to do?"

"Hang on, I'll check it out."

He climbed out of the craft and stood in front of the tree. It looked like a dead giant with broken arms and legs lying in an open coffin, ready for viewing. Even on its side, it was taller than Ben by several meters. He stepped up onto one of the branches with his right foot and grabbed another with his left hand, working his way up the side of the trunk. Rachel watched from inside the ZX, impressed at how easily he climbed to the top.

This would be as good a time as any to stretch her legs she figured and hopped out of the vehicle. Tilting her head back and shading her eyes from the sun, she looked up and watched Ben jog a few steps down the trunk, stop, and come back. "How does it look up there?" she called to him.

He gave a quick nod, jumped from the top of the trunk, and landed right beside her.

"Geez! Couldn't you have warned me?" She whacked him in

the stomach before she could catch herself. "Oops, sorry, I didn't mean to smack you. Did that hurt?"

Ben grabbed his stomach and doubled over.

She put her hand on his shoulder and leaned over to check on him, feeling both embarrassed and concerned at the same time. He stood up with a frown on his face, but the corners of his mouth soon gave way to a big grin. His eyes sparkled with mischief.

She slugged him again, this time in the arm.

"Ouch," he said and laughed, bringing out his dimples. "To get back to your question, the forest on either side of this little sapling," he jabbed his thumb toward the tree, "is too thick to drive through. And we can't go over it in the ZX. Let's get back in the car."

"Oh—kay." Rachel wondered if they were going to turn around and find another path.

Ben waved at Zoleta to back up, and then swung into the driver's seat. "I'll have to blast it."

"Blast it!? With what, may I ask?" Rachel glanced at him nervously.

Not bothering to explain, Ben looked over and gave a wink that made her melt, pulled the drive bar toward him, and threw the vehicle into reverse.

"Ready?" Rachel wasn't sure if he was talking to her or to the tree.

"Does it matter?" She looked over at his profile. A boy-man excited about blowing something up.

"No."

He flicked up the two covers in the ends of his control handles, revealing red buttons underneath. "Here we go," he said, and pressed the triggers simultaneously with his thumbs.

A flash of light erupted from the front of the craft. Two surges of power snapped out and intersected in the center of the tree trunk, like synchronized lightning strikes, blowing a gaping hole in a split millisecond.

They passed through the newly blasted tree-tunnel with room to spare. Smoke wafted up from the hole and a few hot embers still danced around the edges. The bigger vehicle had less space to maneuver but didn't seem to pose any problem for Zoleta.

The road wound around two more curves then ended abruptly in front of a huge granite slab, four stories tall. Rachel gasped.

"We'll park here. It's a short hike to the other side of this outcropping," Ben said and climbed out of the ZX. Rachel followed and they both turned as Zoleta and crew pulled up behind them.

The same mean, nasty look was still plastered across Zoleta's face when she stepped out of the Hubba. Imitar and Sanda slid out and started unpacking the equipment from the back. "Throw me my bag," Zoleta barked and Imitar chucked the silver pack toward her. She caught it in mid-flight, hefted it over her shoulder and stomped off in the direction of the cave.

"Just a mili-sec, Zoleta," Ben called. "We need to group up for safety and figure out who's going where."

"Now what?" Zoleta turned back toward the group. "Let me guess. Me, Imitar and The Doc—one way. You and her," Zoleta jabbed a finger toward Rachel, "in the opposite direction. I say, quit wasting time and get going."

"Stay in communication range. That's an order. The connection might go in and out depending on the crystal depth —" Zoleta took off before Ben could finish his sentence. Rachel bit her lip to keep a smile from sneaking across her face.

"I'll go first—or next, rather," Ben said. "Imitar, hand me the crystal-analyzer when I get around to the entrance. Rachel, I want you to follow Imitar. Sanda, bring up the rear. Once we get into the cave proper, we can set up the equipment and go off exploring."

Ben turned sideways to squeeze his broad shoulders between the granite walls. When he was past the opening, he reached back for the coder. The machine, a meter long and forty-five centimeters in diameter, weighed forty kilograms. Imitar carried it and his pack and hadn't broken a sweat. *Impressive. He's really strong for such a tall, skinny fellow. No bulging muscles. Maybe some bionic parts? Definitely some mods.*

The team turned on their helmet lights, casting shadows on the walls and ceiling of the cavern. As they entered the largest open area of the cave, Rachel noticed instruments and other supplies left from previous expeditions sitting in the middle of the room, like the left-over dregs of an old party, cold and alone. The farther she tried to see, the more blurred the cavern boundaries became. Something about this place felt familiar to her. Then she realized – the scene was like her – like her memories, too far away to see clearly through the shadows. A shiver ran down her spine. Like the old equipment, she was cold and alone.

"This is the main chamber," Ben said. "Not much to look at but wait until we get to a few of the outer rooms. Some are impressive with incredible formations and colors I can't quite describe."

"And beautiful. Like the diamond tailings of a comet hitting the frozen air of the Dark Side and shimmering across the sky," Imitar added in a soft voice.

"Hmph," came from Zoleta in the far corner of the room, shaking Rachel from the vision back to the present. Zoleta's headlamp swung from side to side in a disgusted shake. "Is anybody going to throw out a light-bot? Or are we just going to stand around in the dark?"

"Got it," Imitar said and reached into his pack. He brought out a round metal object, the size of a walnut, pulled a clip out of the top, and set it on the ground. A tiny spark flickered. The ball grew brighter until a burst of light fractured the darkness, blinding them momentarily. The huge room lit up like a star had exploded.

"Couldn't you have put that behind a rock or something?" Zoleta screeched, throwing her hand up across her face, shielding her eyes.

"Sorry."

When her eyes adjusted to the brightness, Rachel scanned the large cavern. Ben was right, there wasn't much to see. The ceiling of the cave rose to the height of a five-story building, then curved across to a sharp flat edge down the eastern wall. Boulders, stacked like giant marbles, lined the other sides.

No sign of water. That's probably why there aren't any interesting formations. No sign of creatures either. Creepy-crawlies are one thing, but creepy-crawlies in the dark are another.

"I have the portable analyzer. Let's set it next to the sorter and purifier and bring the coder with us to the pond." Sanda broke through Rachel's worries.

Imitar carried the heavy instrument across the dirt floor and placed it on a flat spot near the old equipment. One of the tripod legs stuck and he fiddled with it, trying to get it to release. Zoleta gave another disgusted grunt, picked up a rock, and hit the end of the latch. The tripod sprung open, surprising Imitar, who stumbled backward, falling over the machine.

"Uh thanks, Zo."

"Hmph."

Sanda and Imitar set up the coder and began the calibrations while Zoleta pulled out her Galactic Positioning System to see if it worked inside the cave. Ben checked the tracking and communication devices. He tapped his earbud.

"Testing check."

"On clear," Imitar replied.

"Clear," Sanda followed.

"Yes, I hear you," Rachel said.

Zoleta looked up from her GPS and yawned.

"Good. We're all set." Ben picked up his pack.

"What should I be doing? Can I help with the equipment or something?" Rachel ran her hand along the metal edge of the analyzer.

"You're fine. When we get the samples, I want you to help with the data entry and note any deviations. Don't worry. I need – we need your help here." He held Rachel with his gaze until Imitar broke the connection.

"This cave has levels with various passageways joining different sections. It's like a giant three-story maze with lots of dead-ends. We're in the middle layer where we've explored only about a quarter of this eighteen-kilometer wonderland." Imitar spread his arms out wide to encompass as far as the light allowed.

"Can't you just throw out a probe-bot or something to find whatever it is you're looking for?" Rachel said.

"No. The readings aren't consistent and we get a lot of false positives. So, it ends up taking more time following erroneous data than looking for the mineral traces on our own." Ben flashed Rachel a grin. "Besides, what fun would that be when we can go exploring in the dark instead?"

Did Ben just smile at me? A warm tingly feeling fluttered in Rachel's chest. Her armpits felt suddenly damp even in the cool temperature of the cave.

The team headed toward the back of the cavern, walked up a short incline, wound around a large boulder, and finally came to the entrance of a long passageway. The path was wide enough for two people to walk comfortably alongside each other. Zoleta made her move and slipped ahead of Rachel to be in the lead with Ben. Rachel followed beside Imitar. They seemed to have lost Sanda around the last bend.

Rachel half listened as Imitar droned on about the types

and formation of caves, physical patterns, and geological distri-
bution. "And there's a mammoth cave on the Dark Side that
only Ben has seen. It must be incredible because he goes out
there all the time by himself."

*Hope Imitar doesn't notice I haven't been listening. Damn.
What I wouldn't give to hear what those two are talking about up
ahead.*

The tunnel arched high enough so the group didn't have to
stoop over, but every now and then a sharp slab jutted out
above eye level. Rachel would have scraped her head more
than once if it weren't for her helmet.

Rachel rounded the corner in time to hear Ben laugh and
see Zoleta rub her hand down his arm. Rachel gritted her teeth
and picked up her pace.

"Hey, slow down Rachel," Imitar said. "It's not safe to go too
fast. You could hit a—."

Rachel glanced behind her while she stomped forward and
slammed her head hard against a low-hanging chunk of
granite.

"Shit," she said and staggered back a few steps.

"—nasty piece of rock," he finished. "That must hurt."

"Well, it sure didn't feel good."

"That's why I said it must have hurt."

"Imitar, I'm being sarcastic. It hurts like hell."

Ben came around the corner. "What's going on?"

"Nothing." Rachel felt the top of her helmet, amazed there
wasn't a crater-sized dent.

"A rock clobbered Rachel in the head when she wasn't
looking."

Ben dropped his pack and stepped in front of Rachel. "Let
me take a look. Imitar, you and Zoleta go on ahead. We'll catch
up and meet you at the pond."

The thought of being alone with Ben would have made
Rachel smile if only the pain didn't radiate clear to her jaw. Her

teeth must have chomped together hard when she struck the rock.

A loud harrumph came from Zoleta. "I'm sure Rachel will be fine waiting here alone a few minutes for Sanda, and you can come with us, Ben."

"You know how doctor El is," Imitar chimed in. "She can get distracted by any little thing she finds that she hasn't seen before. Who knows how long it might take her to catch up."

Zoleta turned and glared at Rachel, then stomped ahead of Imitar into the darkness.

CHAPTER 23

North of the compound
Monday
1100 hours

THE TWO HEADLAMPS of Imitar and Zoleta faded off in the distance, leaving Rachel and Ben alone in the solitude of the cave. He gently slipped off her pack and unfastened her helmet.

"Let me see your pupils," he said, as he brushed her hair away from her forehead.

Rachel looked up and felt herself melt under the scrutiny of his deep-blue eyes. His warm breath whispered across her cheek.

"Are you feeling dizzy or nauseated?"

"A little dizzy." But she wasn't sure if it was more from his touch than from the conk on her head.

"Sanda should be here in a few minutes and we'll have her check you over. You need to rest." He guided her to a flat rock and helped her sit. He knelt and held a small water vial to her lips. "How's that?"

"Much better. Thank you. I'm sorry to cause so much trouble."

"You have no idea," he whispered. He took off his helmet and sat next to her.

"What's that supposed to mean?" A flash of anger erupted before she could stop it from spilling out in her tone.

He shook his head, stood, and started to pace. He rubbed his crooked finger and looked like he was trying to decide what to say. A feeling of dread replaced Rachel's quick anger. Maybe he wanted her off the planet.

"It isn't anything bad. I'm concerned about you. More than you realize." He massaged his forehead as if he had a headache coming on. "It's complicated."

Ben turned and looked at her. She exhaled slowly, waiting for an explanation, wondering if she would be devastated, scared, or ecstatic. And wondering if the explanation would be the truth. Either way, she knew she would most likely still be confused.

"I'm obligated," he continued, "to see you're taken care of. That you have everything you need. But . . ."

Uh oh, here it comes . . . the BUT.

"I also need to tell you something. I want you to know I—." Ben's eyes suddenly focused past her. "Where have you been?"

"I didn't realize I'd fallen behind. I couldn't help taking a reading on that huge rock in the alcove back there. Did you see it? The one with the greenish rings circling the top and bottom? I hoped it was a giant geo with a fossil of some pre-historic, Goliath-like beast hibernating inside. But nothing. Just an interesting shaped boulder." Sanda looked from Ben to Rachel. "What's wrong? Has something happened?"

"Oh, you know, klutzy me," Rachel said. "I wasn't watching where I was going. I had a little fight with a chunk of the cave. It won."

"Well, let's do a quick neuro-check, shall we?"

Sanda pulled out the portable diagnostic bot, PDB for short, from her satchel, unclipped the cover, and fastened it like a suction cup onto Rachel's forehead. The device emitted a soft whirring noise. All Rachel could think about was how ridiculous she must look with this contraption stuck between her eyes. And Ben right there watching.

The PDB beeped off, signaling the evaluation was complete. Sanda released the neuro-scanner and read the results. "Your neuros are sound, Rachel. How do you feel?"

She wanted to say she felt like an idiot and hoped she didn't have a hickey on her forehead. "I'm fine. Just a little shaky."

"Where are the others?" Sanda asked.

"I sent them on. They should be at the pond by now," Ben said. He turned to Rachel. "You. Sit. I don't want to have to carry you out of here."

In those muscular arms? I'd definitely be okay with that. I wonder how much I weigh? Oh God, Rachel, don't even go there.

"Go on ahead, Ben. I'll stay with her until she feels ready," Sanda offered.

"No. She's my responsibility. I told Zoleta and Imitar we would catch up and meet them at the pond. I want you to collect any samples they've found and run them through the analyzer. Rachel will stay with me."

"But I'm the planet's physician," Sanda countered.

"Hello people. I'm right here," Rachel raised her voice to be heard above their arguing.

Ben and Sanda looked at her with blank faces. Sanda nodded at Ben, patted Rachel on the shoulder, picked up her pack, and headed down the passageway.

A few minutes passed before Rachel said, "I'm fine. Really. Maybe we should get going." She started to get up but Ben's tone stopped her.

"Rachel. I'm sorry. I'm sorry I haven't taken more time with you. To see that you feel comfortable and a part of this team. We're all so busy we forget this can be a lonely place for newcomers. I hope you'll let me make it up to you. Maybe we can meet two nights a week to go over any questions or concerns you might have. I can show you more of the planet. How about it?"

She took a deep breath, pushed her shoulders back, and tipped her chin toward him. "Will you help me find out about my past?"

Ben touched his ear-bud. Rachel's chest sank. *Now he gets a call? Of all the timing.*

"Of course," he said. "We'll be right there."

* * *

They wound through the passageway for several more kilometers, then the ceiling sloped sharply and the path grew tight. Rachel followed directly behind Ben's crouched figure. He hadn't answered her question. Instead he'd answered a phone call.

Probably from Zoleta.

They reached a place where the cave finally expanded upward and outward again. Ben stood and stretched his back, then turned and smiled at her.

"How's the head now?"

"It's okay. You'd think hitting it that hard would've jarred some memories loose." Her attempt to bring the conversation back to where they'd left off failed. She leaned her hand against the wall and adjusted her boot, waiting for his reply, not wanting to appear anxious. Cold water seeped through her glove. "Hey, the wall is wet here," she said.

"We're getting close to the pond, an underground lake really. The water trickles in and drips off the xenostone, creating formations similar to stalactites and stalagmites, like you see in limestone caverns on earth. Only more unusual."

"Why aren't there any formations in this part?"

"Because there isn't any xenostone here. It's all granite," he said. "The water just runs off the rock. But up ahead, you'll see."

They went through a low archway and came out into the center of a massive cavern. The moist air smelled sweet and Rachel started to stick out her tongue to taste it but stopped. "Is the air poisonous or anything?"

"We haven't found any traces of toxic substances in the areas we've explored."

She tilted her head back and opened her mouth wide, feeling like a child trying to catch falling snowflakes.

"What are you doing?" Ben said, with a chuckle.

She quickly pulled her tongue back in. "Nothing."

"We're at the tip of the pond. From here to the farthest edge, it measures one-hundred thirty-seven point seven by ninety-seven point eight meters. It's deceivingly deep. Temp. thirty-eight degrees. Warm from a geothermic fissure in the bottom."

Rachel rolled her eyes. *He can be so technical. Do romantic thoughts ever cross his mind?*

"The lake is shaped like a teardrop. We have to be careful on this narrow part of the path. Give me your hand." He reached back. "Stay against the wall. It's only a short way, then we can relax with more room."

This is more like it, she thought. An electric buzz hummed through her body from the contact.

He was right. It was only a short way before he let go of her hand. Much too early as far as she was concerned.

They came around the bend to an open area that looked like a huge indoor parking lot. Rachel squinted at the smooth, dark surface. "This is it. The Pond," Ben said.

It didn't appear deep. It looked like wet pavement: a thin film you could hydroplane on and lose control if you took it too fast.

"So, where's the pretty stuff?" she asked.

"Hang on." Ben reached into his pack and pulled out a

round object. "Watch this." He tossed a glow-bot out into the center of the lake.

The bot sank into the depths, illuminating jagged rocks and pinnacles: a maze of pink, green, blue and purple formations like a city of underwater castles. Yellow fish with red fins swam through the castle windows and doors and under the drawbridge.

"Oh my God," Rachel said, as the magnificent colors overwhelmed her. "It's indescribable. I've never seen anything so beautiful."

Before she could stop herself, she blurted out, "Wanna go skinny-dipping?"

CHAPTER 24

Cave B-1
Monday
1300 hours

BEN ARCHED AN EYEBROW. A smile hid at the corner of his mouth. "I do know what skinny-dipping is," he said. "You first."

Ooh, there might be hope for him yet. Maybe he's just shy. I can fix that.

"If you insist." Rachel started to pull off her pack when Imitar interrupted.

"Over here," he called.

Ben shrugged. "Guess we'd better see what they've found." His smile disappeared. The tiny hole in his all-business-like armor seemed to weld itself shut. He turned and headed for the far side of the lake where Imitar and Sanda waited for them.

"I wish they'd find another cave. Or better yet—another planet," Rachel grumbled under her breath. She plodded along behind Ben, in no hurry to meet up with the others.

"Took you two long enough," Imitar said. "Did you find anything?"

"No. We were taking it slow," Ben replied and glanced back at Rachel.

"Are you okay?" Imitar asked with a concerned look at Rachel. "Let me take your pack. Do you need to sit?" He leaned the xenometer against the wall and started toward her.

"Thanks, I'm—"

"She's fine," Ben stepped in Imitar's path. "Where's Zoleta? I specifically said for ALL of us to meet here. She had better be in communication range."

"She had a high reading on her meter and went to check it out. We're setting up the coder, in case she brings back a sample." Sanda said. "She'll let us know as soon as she has something."

Ben tapped his earbud, "Zoleta! Where the hell are you?" He waited for her reply, and then nodded. His voice changed from pissed to pleasant. "Great. Sounds good." He grinned.

Rachel's jaw tightened. *A real smile? For Zoleta? Just because SHE might have found what he's searching for, and I don't even know what to look for in the first place.* Rachel took a cleansing breath and willed her teeth to unclench.

A low, far off rumble made the smile on Ben's face drain away, like water through a crack in the earth.

Rachel's eyes darted around the cavern, then back to Ben. "What is it? What's wrong?"

"Quiet." He held up a hand and squeezed his eyes shut. "Probably nothing. Imitar, check the seismograph. What's the level of activity for the next thirty minutes?"

Rachel had always been able to read people: their body language, their subtle change in stance or facial expression. Ben said it was probably nothing, but she knew. Something bothered him. At least he's been here before. Maybe it isn't anything to worry about. She didn't much like the thought of being trapped underground, even if it was with Ben.

Imitar looked down at his hand-held meter. "Seismograph shows trembling north of here. Can't tell if it's from Goliath's core or outside conditions. Hold on. Let me change the mode." He pushed buttons on the gadget. "The signal isn't strong enough to tell for sure, but it looks like there's asteroid tail eighty kilometers to the north. Atmospheric currents are moving east to west. No, south to . . . I can't tell. I've lost the signal."

Sanda stood next to Rachel. "Will we have time to evaluate what Zoleta has found? We should at least mark the location so we can come back later if we need to."

Ben tapped his ear-bud. "Zoleta? We need to pick up the pace. There's been some activity outside. Don't know if it will affect us, but—" He was cut off while Zoleta replied. Then he continued, "Okay. Follow it as far as you can. Rachel and I will come help you." He chuckled and glanced at Rachel. "No. We're both coming. And I'm sure all of her body parts will fit through the key-hole."

God, and Ben, only know what that woman is saying. But if it concerns me, it isn't flattering. Rachel's face felt on fire.

Ben checked the tracking device to get Zoleta's locale. "She's over to the left. And up." Rachel followed the direction of his pointed finger. "She's found a promising vein but it doesn't sound easy to get to. She's close to being out of com-range." He twisted his watch band back and forth and looked at Rachel. "Ready?"

He hefted his pack over his shoulder and headed out. Rachel scrambled to catch up with him.

This time she kept her concentration on following Ben's footsteps and not letting her mind wander like a silly teenager with blazing hormones, although she would like to have stayed at the pond longer. She'd be darned if she was going to let Ben out of her sight with Zoleta lurking around the next corner.

Focus, Rachel. Focus.

Imitar and Sanda stayed behind to wait for the samples and to relay any new information on what was happening outside the cave, while Ben and Rachel wound their way through a small side tunnel. They hiked for fifteen minutes until the roof sloped and Ben had to crouch to continue forward. Rachel was still able to walk upright. Short is beautiful, she thought. And more comfortable.

Ben spoke over his shoulder, "Time to activate our knee pads."

Her smugness was short-lived; the ceiling dropped drastically, now they had to crawl. Broken chunks of rock tried to bite and bruise, but the caving-uniform did a good job of protecting her elbows and shins. The slow going on hands and knees was starting to wear on her. She had a moment of admiration for Zoleta—the woman was a lot tougher than Rachel thought.

The air was heavy in the confined space. Rachel tasted the dryness and had to swallow several times to clear her throat. She started to cough. *If only there was a little more room. If only I could see more than just Ben in front of me. These walls are close. Really close.* Her heart jack-hammered against the inside of her chest and her breathing tried to keep up with the wild pace. *I've got to get out of here!*

Without warning, Ben stopped, and Rachel smacked into his back-side. "Rachel," he said, "Take some deep breaths. Just follow me. Don't think about anything. Only about following me."

"K-kay," she said, trying to calm her ragged breathing and will her heart-rate to slow down.

It took five minutes, but it felt like an hour before they came to what looked like the end of the tunnel. Ben stood, but she could only see his bottom half; his head and shoulders had disappeared through the narrow hole above. He pulled himself through and reached down to help her.

"You doing okay?"

"Better. Thanks. Felt a little tight in there," she said.

He stared at her like he was about to say something but bit the corner of his lower lip instead. "I need a drink," he said, in a slow, quiet voice.

That did sound good. She envisioned a margarita, blended, no salt, with a slice of lime. Sipping it in the shade on a tropical beach, enjoying the refreshing breeze coming off the ocean . . .

"Ahem," Ben cleared his throat. "You look like you were off somewhere else. Here, have some water." He handed the bottle to her.

She thanked him and took a swig. All traces of her tropical paradise vanished, leaving only the salty taste of the electrolyte water. *Salt? Didn't she say, "No salt" on her margarita?*

"It's not much farther," Ben said. "Then we have to go up. Don't know if it'll be a gradual slope or if we'll have to do some climbing. Are you up for it?"

"Has Zoleta found what we're looking for?" Rachel fisted her hands on her hips. "Maybe she just says she has, so you'll follow her."

"Why would she do that?" He frowned. "No, she's discovered a good-sized vein and needs to trace it back to the source," he said.

"Well, no problem. I'm up for it." She brushed the dirt off the front of her pant legs and looked over at him while she brushed off her bottom. He twisted his watchband back and forth on his wrist. He jerked his gaze away. Too late, she'd caught him staring.

"I think we better go," he said.

After twenty minutes the tunnel emptied out into a chamber, the size of a small pagoda. They checked along the perimeter for any off-shoots, but their helmet lights weren't strong enough to illuminate any hidden passageways.

"Zoleta must have climbed up somewhere in here," Ben

said. "But I don't see any openings. I'm going to set a glo-bot so we can get a better picture."

He set the light and Rachel covered her eyes with her hands, then slowly removed them to let in the brightness in incremental doses. They craned their necks and looked upward, following the walls of a smooth, vertical shaft rising over nine meters in height.

Ben continued to inspect the alcove, searching for any possibilities until, finally, he pointed toward the entrance they had come through. "Ah, there it is. See that slab? It jets out from the wall above us, about three meters up? It's casting a shadow. My bet is there's an opening behind it."

"But how could Zoleta get up there?" Rachel followed Ben and stood below the outcropping, staring at the smooth rock. "Don't tell me we're going to climb up this?"

Rachel's heart seemed to jump-start again, not that she was afraid of heights, the opening wasn't that high up. It was more of the not-knowing-what's-up-there that bothered her. Or, worse yet, how confined it would be once she got there.

"I'll give you a boost until you can reach the bottom of the ledge. There's a notch for your foot about two meters up. Can you see it? Try to find the hand and footholds as you go."

"I have to go first?" Rachel gulped.

"I can catch you. Not the other way around. I'll hand your pack up, then mine when you give the okay."

"Wonderful."

"Come here," he said.

She came closer. He reached for her and slowly released the shoulder straps on her backpack. His touch sent a shiver down her spine and she was suddenly back on the tropical beach, letting him pull the straps down on her bathing suit top.

He put his hands on her waist, turned her to face the wall, and lifted her easily.

She found a small crevice and worked her fingers inside.

Searching with her toes for the indentation they had spotted from the ground, she pulled and struggled, not gaining much ground. Ben moved his hands under her rump and continued to push her higher.

One more foothold and she pushed away from him as she gripped the solid ledge of the opening and pulled her body into the tunnel.

"How's it look?" Ben called up to her.

She took a moment to catch her breath. "The hole's a little tight, but it opens up inside. You should fit."

"You're killing me."

"What? What is it?"

"You. Never mind. Reach out and grab the pack when I lift it up."

She lay flat on her stomach in the entrance, arms and head dangling over the edge, reaching down as far as she could. She smiled at him. "By the way, thanks for the boost."

"My pleasure," he said and melted her with a magnificent grin.

He snatched her backpack off the ground and pushed it against the face of the rock toward her outstretched hands. The pack was half-way up the wall when Ben stopped, lowered it to his chest, and looked behind him.

A deafening boom split the air, like a lightning bolt destroyed by Thor's mighty hammer. A small crack opened in the chamber floor and Ben scrambled to stay on his feet as half of the ground shifted forward and dropped.

"BEN!" Rachel screamed.

The ceiling rained rocks and dust down on him. The shelf above the opening where Rachel lay paralyzed began to break loose.

"Rachel! Get back inside the tunnel. TURN AROUND. NOW!"

The urgency in his voice broke through her shock and she

jerked herself back from the edge. She crawled as fast as she could. The shaking and rocking grew stronger.

She took one last glance over her shoulder.

CHAPTER 25

Celtic Cavern
Monday
1320 hours

SOMEONE GROANED.

Rachel lay prone in the dirt. Lifting her head carefully to see where the sound had come from, she spat and struggled to blink the grit from her eyes. She groaned again.

Her headlamp cast a fuzzy beam through the thick dust as it settled over the rubble of fallen rock. For a moment, she couldn't remember where she was or how she got there. She swung her head to look behind her and wished she hadn't. An avalanche of granite was all that remained.

Gone.

The opening had been sealed off.

As she tried to pull herself to her hands and knees, pain zinged from her ankle up her leg like an electric current. She screamed and grabbed for her ankle, ramming her fingers against the rocks that buried her foot.

It took several deep breaths until the pain subsided enough

for her to inch her hand slowly down again and try to pick and brush away the debris that covered her injury.

Two heavy stones lay across the top of her foot, smashing her ankle trapped beneath. She pulled on one of the rocks. It shifted, but the pressure increased on the injured joint, making her bite down on the inside of her cheek. She stopped and studied the angles. If she loosened the wrong side first, the other side would slip and crush her ankle.

Her head-lamp flickered.

She would have to work quickly.

To see what to do next, she pushed herself up onto her elbow and cleared the smaller chunks of granite and rock from around her ankle. From this awkward position, it would take a great deal of strength to hold up one of the heavier rocks and pull her leg out at the same time. She took a deep breath and reached again toward the stones.

The head-lamp flickered for a second time, and then went out.

"Oh, please, no," she prayed. She waited for a glimmer, a faded ray, anything. She tapped the helmet and wiggled the light.

Nothing. Nothing but blackness.

She lay still, trying to clear her mind, trying to control the rising panic. *I've got to do this now while I remember how it looked in the light.*

She twisted her body around as far as she could and stretched both arms down her leg until her fingers touched the jagged edges of rock. She felt with her hands, trying to picture the way the heavy stones were aligned. She vacillated between which rock to pull out, deciding first one, then the other, and finally back to her first choice, hoping she'd picked the one that would cause less damage when she pulled . . .

Her scream shattered the darkness.

She collapsed on her side, breathing hard, choking on sobs.

A wave of nausea swept over her and she bit down on her lower lip. Tears streamed down her face, mixing with snot. She tried to wipe them away, smearing dust and mucus into a dirty streak across her cheek.

Her foot was free.

After several minutes and between ragged gulps of air, she drew her leg toward her chest and gently probed the area below and to the side of her calf. Where there used to be bone, she now felt a spongy indentation. Her fingers gently probed a four-inch long gash separating the flesh above her ankle, coating her fingers with a sticky wetness. Blood.

Without moving her legs, Rachel searched for something, anything, she could tie around the cut and hold her flesh and bone together, and for anything she could use as a splint. Panic rose in her chest as her hands grasped nothing but dirt, rock, and more rock. She slugged the ground with her fist in desperation.

"Nooo," she wailed. "My pack."

She had no delusions that the loss of her backpack was crucial to her survival. There was nothing to do but marshal her energy and focus on the path ahead. *Must keep moving forward.* She took a deep breath and began to crawl, feeling her way slowly over the rubble, dragging her useless foot. The pain from her ankle thudded through her body. Her helmet scraped the ceiling several times letting her know she was still in a low-hanging part of the shaft.

She had no idea how much time had passed, or how far she needed to go. She only knew she couldn't go back. The tunnel opening no longer existed. She inched along.

She didn't have her pack.

She didn't have any water.

Thoughts of dying began to push up through her control and twist into knots in her brain. Slower and slower she crawled, struggling along, fighting the pain, fighting the thirst, fighting her mind. Over and over she placed each hand in front of the other, making little headway except to sink further down into despair. Time became a vague, evil presence, torturing her for fun. Had she been dragging her body through the tunnel for minutes, or hours?

"Must think of something. Anything to keep going," she said to the constricting walls.

Ben.

Yes, think about Ben. She conjured his face in the darkness: handsome, but stern, military-like, always in command, intimidating, almost cold. Except when he smiled. Then the harshness melted away and the dimples came out. His teeth, straight and white. His lips, full and inviting . . .

But then she remembered. Ben was below the cave-in. He could be hurt. He could be dead!

She was hurt, but she wasn't dead. "I will make it through this," she ordered the darkness. She began a mantra with every movement. Left arm forward fifteen centimeters— "I am strong," right arm forward ten— "I can do this," pull body along floor of cave pushing with good leg, dragging injured leg, "I will not give up."

Her eyes burned trying to gather any speck of light they could find. Reaching out in the dark, she felt along the rough walls of the tunnel, her progress, achingly slow.

The sides of the tunnel began to feel smoother and fewer chunks of rock ground into her hands and knees. She reached above her and couldn't touch the roof of the tunnel. *It's widening out and up.* She took a break and leaned her back against the cool wall, pulling her legs in toward her, being careful not to bump her damaged ankle. She took off her helmet, let her head fall back, and closed her eyes.

A trickle of spit leaked from the side of her mouth and she jerked awake. *How long have I been out? Can't stay here. Got to keep going.*

Forgetting about her ankle, she moved too quickly, pain stabbing a sharp reminder, making her head swim with tiny bursts of light. That's all she needed was to faint. She put her head down on the cool, rough floor, and breathed deeply for several minutes. After the danger passed, she clipped her helmet back on and returned to her brutal trek.

Did the cave look lighter up ahead?

Light. Am I dead? Is this heaven? Do I crawl toward the light? Everything hurts. I'm so tired.

She continued to drag herself through the cave, feeling woozier with each passing minute, weak from the loss of blood and lack of water. The light grew stronger. She could see the roof of the cave now, it was higher, and there was a bend in the path up ahead.

As she inched around a huge granite outcrop, the last of her remaining strength faded and she collapsed onto her belly. This was it, she knew, the end of her journey.

The muffled sound of drums, from somewhere far below the water's surface, interrupted her ascent in to heaven. When she lifted her head, trying to make sense of it all, a brilliance, like she had never seen before, blinded her. *This is the light the dying speak of . . . I must be in the presence of God!*

"Well. If it isn't Little Miss Rachel." Zoleta boomed. "Where's Ben?"

CHAPTER 26

Celtic Cavern
Monday
1320 hours

BEN JUMPED BACKWARD, away from the collapsing ceiling. The ledge, where Rachel had smiled down at him only moments ago, gave way, raining huge rocks in front of him. The crashing and grating of stone on stone bombarded his ears. The cave-in lasted less than twenty seconds but dust continued to billow out in thick clouds. The major impact was over.

He slapped at his earbud, "Rachel? Can you hear me? Rachel! Come in. Please!" Tiny avalanches skittered randomly down the sides of the walls, adding their rubble to the chaos.

He tore at the rocks like a drowning man. With each stone he moved, three more shifted to take its place. He was breathing hard now, too crazed to think straight; sweat poured into his eyes, mixing with the dust. Still, he attacked the fallen rock with all he had. Blood gushed from somewhere above his elbow. It was impossible to see. Impossible to move the granite. Impossible to get to her.

He wasn't a praying man, but he offered up a quick request;

that Rachel had made it clear of the cave-in and was safe until he could find a way to rescue her.

He tried his earbud again, "Rachel?"

Burst of static scratched along the line, morphing in to chunks of unrecognizable syllables. He held his breath and concentrated on making out the words.

Please, by the stars, let it be Rachel.

"Ben, are you okay?" Imitar's voice came through. "What happened? Sanda and I heard an explosion. The seismograph jumped off the charts."

Ben deflated as if a stalactite had punctured his heart. He spoke in a slow monotone. "The ceiling collapsed. In the cave. Rachel's trapped. I can't get to her. We need the excavation equipment—the big stuff. Call the base. Have the drillers get them ready."

"We can't reach the compound from here. We're out of range," Imitar said.

Ben forced himself to think. There'd been emergencies in the past, snap decisions had to be made, people's lives had depended upon him. And he had made those decisions, rationally and logically, and they had been the right ones for the most part. But this was different. This was Rachel's life.

He couldn't lose her. Again.

"Go back to the Hubba and call on the satellite phone. Have them on stand-by."

"All the way back through the cave? It'll take a while. Have you heard from Zoleta? I—we can't reach her either," Imitar said.

"Go. Now."

"I'm on my way."

Sanda came on the line, "What's going on Ben? Imitar just took off like a comet."

"There's been a cave-in. Rachel and I were separated and I

can't reach her. I sent Imitar to call from the Hubba. I'm on my way toward you. Stay put if you're in a safe spot. Out."

Ben raced back the way he and Rachel had come, scrambling around piles of fallen rock. He slowed at the key-hole, dropping through the tight opening and army crawled as fast as he could through the rest of the narrow tunnel. Luckily it hadn't collapsed in the quake.

His legs and chest burned as he rounded the last corner and stumbled toward the pond. Sanda motioned for him to sit, but he shook his head as he stood, bent-over, with his hands on his thighs and gasped for breath. She offered her thermos of water and when he had recovered enough to take a drink, he raised it to his lips. Blood ran from his elbow. "Ben, you're bleeding. Let me take a look at your arm."

"What? No time. Is Imitar on his way to make the call?"

"I guess so. He said something about Zoleta and flew out of here." She tried to lift Ben's arm but he jerked it away.

"It's nothing. Leave it. I've got to get back to the base." He tossed the thermos back to her and headed for the side tunnel.

She grabbed his shoulder. "You might be losing a lot of blood. I can put –"

"You don't understand. I've got to get to her. I've got to dig Rachel out."

"Don't you mean you need to dig *them* out?"

"I want you to stay here and try to make contact."

* * *

He left Sanda standing by the pond, yelling at him to come back and let her take care of his wound. He pressed on as quickly as possible, despite his waning energy. And worse, he couldn't afford to let thoughts of Rachel dying claim his mind.

At the entrance to the cave, Ben slowed to squeeze through

the jagged rock slabs, and out in to the open sky. The Hubba was parked casually next to the ZX, as if there was nothing to worry about on such a glorious day. Imitar sat ridged in the driver's seat, a set of headphones covering his shoulder-length hair, rapidly mouthing directions into the speaker. Ben yanked the door open.

"Did you get hold of base?"

"Yes. They are on the line now. I told them what we need and they say they can't change the location of the digger without proper authorization."

"Give me the phone." Imitar took off the headset and handed it over. "This is CPO Schaefer. I want Big D prepped, re-fueled, and ready to go in twenty-four hours. I'm sending the coordinates. I need a five-man team to accompany."

"But sir. Big D is working on the xenoline in the far sector, top priority. We can't just pull it from the site. Besides, it will take at least three days to re-boot."

"God damn it! Do it. That's an order. I'll be back on base in minus four hours. Out."

Ben yanked the headset off and threw it against the dash-board. He clenched his fists, wanting to hit something.

"Sir? Do you want me to go back to the compound with you, or stay here and relay any info from Zoleta or Rachel?"

Ben shut his eyes, trying to gain control, but the image of Rachel, lying broken beneath slabs of granite, made him feel like every muscle in his body had been incinerated, leaving nothing but a useless pile of ash. He forced his eyes open and willed strength into his every cell.

"Go back to the pond and wait with Sanda. I'll bring Big D and move heaven and earth."

Imitar climbed out of the vehicle and turned to head back through the passageway when Ben reached into the rear seat and pulled out a bag. "Wait. Take this extra supply kit." He gave Imitar a steady look, "Rachel doesn't have her pack."

Imitar stared down at the pack in his hands. "Yes sir."

"I'll be back as fast as I can. Just stay with Sanda and wait for my call unless the ground becomes unstable then get the hell out of there. And Imitar, Rachel is going to make it. Zoleta will too."

If only he could make himself believe it.

* * *

Ben jammed the thrusters into reverse and spun the ZX around. It screamed out of the opening, past boulders and trees, and down the mountainside.

His mind flipped through different scenarios of how he could get Big D, the excavator, inside the tunnel without causing more damage. He would have to widen the entrance first. It would take time and he wasn't sure how much he had. Or Rachel had.

He pushed the ZX beyond its limits, racing against time, racing against loss.

Ben reached the underground hangar, stumbled out of the vehicle, and struggled to the elevator tube. Blue smoke boiled from beneath the craft's belly. A safety droid sped from the far corner of the garage toward the ZX and sprayed a quick coat of white foam to the undercarriage. Ben ignored it and continued to the elevator. The head of Maintenance stepped out of the tube just as Ben was getting on. She held the door open for him.

"CPO Schaefer, is everything okay? What happened?"

"Run diagnostics on the ZX and do whatever needs to be done to have it ready for me as soon as possible."

"Yes, sir. And, excuse me, I think you're bleeding."

Thorian, the head mechanic, met Ben in Command Center. Thorian's massive frame filled the doorway. A knot of shoulder-length blond hair fell across his brow and he brushed it back with a quick swipe. He rubbed the side of his nose, leaving a skid mark of axle grease. At the end of his burly forearms hung his huge hands and, not knowing what to do with them, he clasped them behind his back.

"Sir, you wanted to see me?" His voice was deep and rumbly like the machines he worked on.

"Big D. The excavator. I need it and the trailer in Section B-North, grid 23. Immediately."

"Sir. The equipment is beyond the belt, in the perma-frost. It's clear out in Section BBPF-7. It'll take two days to extract it and haul it back here. Then, depending on what shape it's in and if it needs any retrofits, it could take another day or two at best."

"Not good enough!" Ben slammed his fist on the desk.

"Sir?" Thorian pointed at Ben's arm. "You're bleeding."

Ben had forgotten about the cut on his arm. He must have sliced it on the edge of a rock when he was trying to get to Rachel. Fresh blood oozed from the gash. He stared at the red splotch smeared across the top of the desk like he was trying to interpret a Rorschach Inkblot test. He looked around for something to wipe it with.

Thorian reached behind to his back pocket for his grease rag and handed it to Ben.

Ben ran it absently across his elbow and passed it back. "Where's the other excavator? Big D-Two?"

"Junked. Smashed beyond repair from the Category Four shower last month." Thorian said as he jammed the greasy, blood-soaked rag back into his pocket. "It was all in the damage report."

Ben flipped on the hologram, drew a circle around the cave, and spread his fingers apart to enlarge the picture. He studied the map for a moment and turned toward Thorian.

"Get Big-D One. Here. In two days." He stabbed at the spot on the hologram. "Dismissed."

"Shit." Thorian muttered under his breath as he headed out the door.

* * *

Back in his apartment, Ben rubbed his fingers across his forehead. There was nothing more to do but wait. He hadn't had anything to eat since morning, not that he was hungry. He needed rest. If he could only turn off his thoughts . . . The buzz from his phone made him jump.

"Ben. Can you hear me? We're at the transport. The aftershocks are getting stronger. We need to get out of here. I repeat. We are leaving the area."

Ben stumbled through the short hallway to his office. An ancient teakwood desk stood proud and reserved in the corner. He picked up the lone picture from the desktop and stared at the image of a young man holding a chocolate lab puppy, a smile slathered across his face as the puppy licked his chin. Replacing the photo, he brushed his hand across the top of his old leather chair, circa 21st century. When he wasn't officially at work, he spent most of his time in this room, working. Would there ever be a time when he would take it easy and enjoy life's simple pleasures?

He staggered over to the sink, wet a cloth and wiped his face and the crusty blood from his arm. He ran his fingers through his hair and looked up at the ceiling.

"What in the hell am I going to do now?"

"Unclear directions. Please repeat," the room responded.

"Unclear for you and me both." He shook his head and sighed, "Quinceberry ale. Make it a double."

Back in the kitchen, the quencher hummed and a yellowish-green liquid poured down the side of a frosted glass. He took the mug to his office, sat back in his chair and took a long drink.

"Music," he said.

"Specific request or Galactic Station?"

"Regular station. No. Wait. Play something from Favorites, circa nineteen-ninety-four."

"Searching archives."

A sweet melody floated around the room, the words of the song gathering Ben's memories like cirrus clouds, sending them to rain into his heart.

CHAPTER 27

Celtic Cavern
Monday
1510 hrs

RACHEL PULLED herself up into a sitting position against the cavern wall, biting down hard on her lip to keep from screaming as her ankle rubbed along the rough ground. The beam from Zoleta's headlamp drilled through her tightly shut eyes straight into her brain. She raised a hand as cover.

"Where's Ben?" Zoleta demanded for the second time.

"Water?" Rachel licked her cracked lips.

"What did you do now? And where are the others?"

Rachel let her head slump back. "Do you have any water?"

"I have water. Where's your water? Where's your pack?" Zoleta rummaged through her backpack, pulled out her hydration bottle, and held it out to Rachel. "Oh, for bit sakes. Here." She grabbed Rachel's hand and slapped the bottle into it. "Drink."

Rachel brought the water to her lips with shaking hands. She took a long swallow and slowly opened her eyes. "Thanks."

The light from Zoleta's headlamp traveled down Rachel,

scrutinizing every millimeter, then paused over her mangled ankle.

"What'd you do to your ankle? It looks like it was caught in a ventilation shaft with the fan still running. Why didn't you use the quick-staunch spray on it? Oh wait, let me guess. You don't have any meds because . . . you don't have your pack? Where is the rest of the group? Why are you here and they're not?"

"God, Zoleta. Believe me, I wish they were here and not me. I don't know what's happened to them. Didn't you feel the quake or whatever it was? The cave collapsed right after B— CPO Schaefer boosted me up onto the ledge. We were following your route. He could be . . ." Rachel turned away and covered her face with her hands.

Zoleta took the water bottle from Rachel and gathered up equipment, stuffing items into her pack. "We better get going."

"What are you doing?"

"What does it look like I'm doing? Why don't you turn on your light and you can see what I'm doing."

Rachel pulled off her helmet. "Dead."

"Who's dead? They're dead or your flashlight? I'm going back to the pond. You coming, or staying here in the dark?" Zoleta hefted her pack over her shoulder and headed toward the tunnel Rachel had just crawled through.

"There is no back. The shaft is blocked with a few tons of rock."

Flecks of silver sparkled in the xenostone as Rachel followed the beam from Zoleta's headlamp across the wall. Then it swung around directing the light at Rachel's face. "Oh great galaxies, let me guess—I have to share all my supplies with you for the next, who knows how long?"

"You don't have to do anything, Zoleta. I'll be fine."

"Humph. I can see that."

The words hung thick and heavy in the air like the darkness

that surrounded them. Zoleta paced back and forth, dropped her pack on the ground next to Rachel, and crouched beside her. She opened the flap and pulled out a small square kit with vials of liquids, mending tape, a hand-held scanner, and an atomizer. She plucked out one of the vials, inverted it several times and snapped it into the atomizer.

"Straighten your leg."

"What for? I know my ankle is smashed. I just need to splint it. After a little rest."

"I'm going to take a look." There was a slight change in Zoleta's tone, like going from standing in burning sunlight to standing in the shade of a high floating cloud. Not quite so scathing.

Rachel extended her leg, sucking in a sharp breath as she set her heel on the ground in front of her.

"I'm going to get this boot off and see what's left of your ankle." Zoleta set the vial down, grabbed Rachel's foot in one hand, released the fasteners in quick succession, and yanked the boot free.

Rachel's scream exploded off the walls of the cave.

With the snips from the med-kit, Zoleta cut away the pant leg. The scanner emitted a quiet buzz as she ran it over Rachel's open wound.

"I'll do what I can but this calls for more than a field-fix. Probably needs reconstruction—if we ever get out of here."

Rachel rolled to her side and retched. "The pain," she gagged between dry heaves.

"Oh no you don't. You are not going to get sick on me." Zoleta grabbed another vial from her pack, pushed the hair away from Rachel's neck, and slapped the atomizer against her exposed carotid.

The cold sting of the injection instantly made Rachel's pain seep into the shadows. She carefully pushed herself back to sitting and wiped a hand across her crusty forehead.

"What did you give me?

Zoleta unscrewed the empty vial and tossed it back into the first aid kit along with the atomizer. "Class-III pain blocker. It should last eight to twelve hours. Then we might have to try something else to keep the screaming down so I can think." She took off her helmet, turned the light to low power, and set it on the ground in a clear spot between them.

The muted glow stretched their shadows up the walls of the cavern like vines searching for a hidden sun.

"I can't feel my ankle. And my lips and tongue feel fuzzy, like the dentist gave me too much Novocain. Better than Novocain. That's some good stuff. Am I talking funny? Everything is numbly."

"Good. The hexathal is working. We can have a nice chat before bedtime."

"I thought you said you gave me a pain blocker. What else does it block?" Rachel squinted through the dim light catching the half-smile on Zoleta's face. "You are the last person I would want to have a chat with and unless you have some kind of mood enhancer in your bag of tricks, any conversation we have will be a far cry from nice."

"Being honest, are we? How does it feel to say what you think? Quite liberating for you I'm sure."

Rachel could have slapped herself if only her hand didn't seem to be attached to someone else's arm. She fought against being sucked into the black hole of Zoleta's snare, but whatever drug Zoleta had given her was too strong. Whatever thought crossed Rachel's mind fell directly out her mouth without passing through any filters.

"I don't like you."

Zoleta chuckled. "We don't have to talk about me. We can talk about someone you *do* like. How about Ben?"

"CPO Schaefer?" Rachel bit down hard on her lip. No help.

"I think he's hot. For an older man that is. I don't really know him—but I'd like to. Damn it."

"Is there something causing CPO Schaefer to have an elevated body temperature? Is he working on the Hot Side of the planet on some secret project?" Zoleta leaned in closer to Rachel.

"What? No. I mean, you know. He's hot. As in tall, dark, and handsome." She raised her eyebrows a couple of times for effect, or at least she thought she did. Images of Ben raced through her mind: sitting next to him in the ZX, Ben climbing up on the tree trunk looking like a Greek god, Ben helping her in the cave when she banged her head—all wrapped in an electrified tingle which shot straight to her center. She gasped.

Then the image suddenly changed. A feeling of terror gripped her as tires slid across an icy road and tumbled over the embankment.

"Tall?" Zoleta's voice broke through Rachel's flashback.

Rachel was breathing hard, her pulse racing as she tried to focus on something Zoleta was saying. "What?" Rachel was finally able to croak.

"You were definitely somewhere else. You said, tall, dark, and handsome. What do you mean by tall?"

Rachel tried to shake off the helpless feeling. They had been talking about Ben. "Oh. Right. Maybe not tall to you, Zoleta, Amazon woman. There's just something about him." Rachel shivered. "Like I've known him, or someone like him, before. But that's not possible. Is it?"

Zoleta turned to her pack and brought out a small pouch which she squeezed in the middle letting the ends fall loose. She shook the thermal blanket, draped it across Rachel's shoulders, and offered her another sip of water.

"Tell me more."

Rachel took a drink and handed the container back. She

pulled the wrap tight around herself. "I don't know what there is to tell. I had hoped the splicing would trigger more of my memories. I do have this weird feeling that I took care of Ben, CPO Schaefer, that he had hurt himself and was in the hospital."

"Did Dr. Luminita bring you to Goliath?"

"I don't know. Why don't you ask her?"

"Did Ben bring you to Goliath? Did he plan your arrival to coincide with his re-up?"

"I told you I don't know. Why would Ben, I mean CPO Schaefer, bring me here? And what's a re-up?"

"All personnel, including CPO Schaefer, have to go back to Earth for a six-year leave before they can re-up. Re-enlist. Are you here to direct planetary operations while he's gone?"

"Ben's leaving?" Rachel's head slumped back against the rock and she closed her eyes. "Apparently, I'm just here because of my genes."

A warning beep came from some device in Zoleta's pack as the cave ceiling showered dirt and small rocks down on the two women. Rachel cowered beneath the thermal blanket as the rumbling grew stronger.

"Are you trained in Galactic Admin.? Do you work for the Federation or some other corporate enterprise?"

"What? Do you ever give up, Zoleta? For Christ's sake, we're probably going to die and you keep asking me stupid questions. I have no idea what you're talking about. You're giving me a headache. I'm so tired. I just want all of this to be over."

"Over? We are just beginning, so get used to it. If you aren't going to cooperate, let's just call it a night. I'll spray a steri-coat on your ankle to help protect it and numb it up. Maybe I should spray some on your lips as well."

"Aren't you funny. Do whatever you want."

Zoleta sprayed the soothing barrier on the wound, tucked the bottle away, and pulled out another square packet. A few drops of water from her canteen morphed the packet into a spongy pillow which she tossed to Rachel.

"You brought a pillow?"

"I'm turning off the light. Need to save power. Get some rest, Rachel. We have some long days ahead of us."

"But I have the blanket and pillow. What will you use?"

"Humph. Go to sleep."

Rachel pulled the pillow under her head and felt the fuzzy corners of her thoughts diffuse throughout her mind.

Maybe this time I'll fall asleep and never wake up.

CHAPTER 28

Goliath Compound
Monday
23:50 hours

SANDA AND IMITAR scrambled to break down the equipment and throw what they could into their packs. Sanda had wanted to leave hours earlier but was unable to persuade Imitar to give up trying to reach Zoleta and Rachel until strong tremors made the decision for them. They had better clear out of the cave while they still had the chance.

"We can leave the analyzer. It's too heavy for just the two of us to carry and too tough to wiggle through the narrow passage at the entrance." Sanda tried to keep up a steady dialogue so Imitar wouldn't worry.

Imitar stopped abruptly on the path in front of her. Sanda missed slamming into him by a nanometer.

"Did we set the locator? Will we be able to receive the pings from base?" He faced Sanda, his eyes wild.

"Yes. You set the beacon. The best thing for us to do is to get to the compound and help with rescue plans. If we leave now we can make it back by 0500." She gave him a nudge, half pat, half push.

They reached the vehicle and quickly loaded the gear. "I'll drive," he said and hopped into the driver's side of the Hubba.

"I'll call Ben and tell him we're on our way." Sanda tapped her earbud and waited for Ben to connect. Nothing. She tried two more times and still no answer.

"Something wrong?"

"Ben's not answering. I'm sure he's busy setting up the rescue team and going over procedure."

Why in the galaxy doesn't he pick up? She hoped he was working furiously on saving the two women. She would track him down as soon as she and Imitar arrived back at the compound.

Sanda knew Imitar would be too worried to set the auto-pilot and get some sleep on the way home. She drifted off for only a moment and the next thing she knew they were pulling beside the ZX in the parking bay.

Ben's vehicle sat unattended at an odd angle outside of the running light-strips used to mark his official parking space. The driver's door hung open. Imitar slammed it shut as he strode by.

"Imitar, why don't you go get a few hours' rest? We can unload later. I'll find Ben."

"I'm going with you."

The determined look in Imitar's eyes silenced her. "Then after you." She held out her hand for him to go ahead.

Command Center

As Imitar and Sanda entered, Ben stood in front of the Z-screen talking to Goliath's head mechanic. A four-and-a-half-meter tall studded tire rolled past Thorian in the background.

"Big D transporter is heading out now, Sir," Thorian said on the vid.

"Bring all tools you need so repairs can be made on location. We don't have time to bring anything back here to fix. I want Big D en route as quickly as possible. Out."

Imitar slapped his hand against the wall. "How are we going to use Big D to dig them out? We don't know how much of the tunnel collapsed. There isn't enough room for the digger to make it to the pond, let alone to the place where we lost contact with Zoleta." Imitar shook his head. "Wait. You're not planning to—you can't. It's too dangerous!"

"What are you thinking, Ben?" Sanda held her palm up toward Imitar cautioning him to keep quiet. It didn't work.

Imitar answered, his voice rising. "He can't have Big D chomp its way to the cave-in and then start digging. It would take too long. You're going to blast. Right? Sir? But that could kill them!"

CHAPTER 29

Celtic Cavern
Tuesday
0600 hours

RACHEL WOKE to the sound of someone, or something shuffling near her head. Maybe she was dreaming because she thought she had opened her eyes but only blackness existed. It was like being at the bottom of a deep well. A well with rats scurrying around. Hungry rats. Rats that were coming closer.

She jerked herself up to sitting and cried out in pain as she grabbed for her ankle.

"Well. Look who's awake," Zoleta said as she clicked on her helmet lamp. "Day two. As fascinating as it has been spending time with you, I've got lots of work to do back at base, so let's get moving."

The horrors of the day before pounded their way back into Rachel's brain making her head throb. Her body felt bruised and the nasty metallic taste in her mouth made her want to spit.

"The tunnel collapsed."

"You said that yesterday. Here. Have some breakfast." Zoleta tossed half a dried fruit wafer at her. "You can have a sip of water when you finish."

"If I had the sip of water first, I might actually be able to eat this."

"Humph."

Rachel chewed slowly willing her mouth to produce enough saliva to swallow. She reached for the water bottle, took two long swigs and handed it back. "But shouldn't we stay here and wait for B—for a rescue party?"

"You're welcome to stay here and wait, but I'm going to find a way out."

Or die trying, Rachel thought. *But, if I stay here alone in the dark without food or water I'll be dead anyway.*

"I'm not sure I can walk."

"Well I'm sure I'm not going to carry you. I'll give you another dose of analgesic."

Zoleta coated Rachel's ankle with a fine spray from the vial she'd used yesterday, tossed the empty into her pack and brushed off her hands as if she was done with an odious chore.

What did Rachel expect? A little sympathy? A smidge of compassion and human understanding? From Zoleta? They were likely to die as soon as the water ran out, which was in half the time with the two of them. What was to keep Zoleta from leaving her behind? Perhaps, Rachel thought, Zoleta will leave me and I'll die quickly by falling off into a black chasm. Or, another tremble of the cavern walls might put an end to them both. Either way, maybe this time she'd wake up in the right place, in the right world, in the right century. Or better yet, be dead for good.

Zoleta is helping me. Why?

Rachel pushed against the wall and stood balanced on her good leg. She sucked in a deep breath and blew it out as she shifted her weight to the injured ankle, took a step, and gritted her teeth against the pain.

Zoleta nodded, turned, and headed down the tunnel. Every few feet she stopped and shined the light for Rachel.

The women inched along moving in the opposite direction from the pond, following the vein of xenostone. An hour had passed, Rachel leaned against a boulder jutting out from the wall, and gasped, "Please stop, Zoleta. I need a minute."

"Now what?" Zoleta swung her headlamp and looked Rachel up and down. "Fine. One minute."

"Never mind. Let's go." Stepping beside Zoleta, Rachel stood as straight as possible, trying not to let the pain show in her face, as Zoleta brandished the light on her.

"Well, since we've already stopped . . ." Zoleta took a noisy swig from her water bottle, making Rachel lick her own dry lips, aching to quench her thirst, but refusing to ask for a drink. "Here," Zoleta said, finally holding out the precious liquid.

As Rachel reached for the water, she knocked Zoleta's hand, launching the bottle to the ground. Both women froze as the sound of the container clattered swiftly downhill then faded into silence. "Oh God, Zoleta, I'm sorry. We'll find it. Shine the light over here."

They looked along the sides of the tunnel, slowly sweeping back and forth with their steps and the lamp, going farther and farther downhill until Zoleta suddenly stopped. She threw her arm behind her to halt Rachel and pointed at a murky shadow on the ground. At first it looked like a small crack in the floor and surely if the water bottle had fallen into the fissure they could reach down and retrieve it. The crevasse was only twenty-five centimeters wide.

But the bottom was nowhere in sight.

There would be no more water for either of them.

* * *

God, will Zoleta ever stop and take a break? Rachel clamped down on her lower lip; she'd be damned if she'd ask for another rest, no matter how much it killed her ankle to keep walking. She had a rhythm going: breathe in, step with her left foot, exhale as she put weight on the right. Repeat. Focus on breathing, not on the pain. Breathe. Step. Breathe. Don't stop. Don't ever stop.

Zoleta came to a halt and panned her light across the ceiling of the tunnel.

"What? What is it?" Rachel strained to hear above the hammering of her heart.

"Shush. I need to think."

"Think away," Rachel said, thankful for the chance to rest. She lowered herself against the wall and watched Zoleta pace back and forth swinging her head lamp up one side of the tunnel wall and down the other.

"Hmm. Yes. Possible."

"Is there anything you'd like to share, Zoleta?"

Zoleta repeated her movements. "Hmmph. The xeno-layer may be running out."

"Is that a good thing or a bad thing?"

"If Ben survives he'll come back for you. If Imitar makes it, he'll come back for me. Let's hope Imitar is alive."

"My how your compassion knows no bounds. But what does that have to do with xeno—whatever?" A flicker of hope caught in Rachel's breast. Would Ben come back for her if he could? Would it be because he felt something for her, or only because he wanted her DNA?

The headlamp followed the path of Zoleta's finger along the wall, pausing at each sediment layer. "If this vein gets any thinner we might be able to patch-pulse through. If Imitar thinks to link the sat-sone coordinates . . ."

"The what?"

"The satellite-sonar. They should be able to get a reading on our location without interference. We might be able to re-establish communication."

Establish communication? Get out of this dungeon? And then what? Back to all my unanswered questions? Back to my unanswered life?

Rachel swallowed the dry lump in her throat. "Onward and upward as they say." She pushed herself off the rock and hobbled past Zoleta.

CHAPTER 30

Celtic Cavern
Wednesday
0430 hours

THE TOPS of the palm trees waved from the oasis far in the distance where he would be waiting for her. He would brush her hair back from her forehead and tell her how much he loved her and wanted her in his life. He would hand her a cool drink . . .

But with each step the sand shifted beneath Rachel's feet, dragging her farther away from the haven. If only she didn't have to walk. If only the plane—or was it a helicopter—she could hear in the background—would pick her up and take her to meet him. The whir of the blades increased in volume until she was forced to plug her ears.

The buzz of Rachel's earphone jarred her awake. She sat up and tried to blink away the darkness. Then the sound stopped and she heard only the soft breathing of Zoleta asleep on the other side of the tunnel floor. Rachel fumbled for the helmet, managed to find the lantern switch, and flicked it on. The light threw itself up the walls then seemed to settle down as Rachel's eyes adjusted to the brightness.

A low hum returned in her earbud, followed by a crackle of static.

"Zoleta. Wake up," Rachel croaked. "I think someone is trying to get through on my earphone."

"Father? Can't you see?" Zoleta whimpered.

"Zoleta." Rachel reached over and prodded Zoleta's shoulder. "I hear something. From my phone."

Zoleta jerked fully awake. "What is it? What's happening?"

"It might be a call. Listen."

Zoleta pushed on her earbud, stated her name and ID number. "Can you read? Imitar, are you on line? Do you catch? Is anyone out there?" She tried again, waited for a reply, and finally shook her head.

The two women, not a drop of water between them, their throats dry and scratchy, took turns desperately trying to make contact. Over and over they called. There was no more buzz. No more static. No one. Nothing.

"Need to. Keep moving. Clean re. Ception," Zoleta managed to squeak. She struggled to her feet, reached for the helmet, and held on to the wall. "R. Hold on. To me. I'll ssport you."

If there was ever a time in her life when Rachel was too exhausted to keep going, it was now. And she would have given up, let death fall as it may, except for a tiny seed that began to burrow its way in to her bones. It wasn't only about her survival anymore. Someone needed her, even if that someone was Zoleta. It was not going to end here, not if Rachel had an ounce of strength left in her tattered body. And someone out there was trying to help them. How would she feel if a person she was trying to help gave up? With trembling legs, she raised herself up to standing and let Zoleta put her arm around her waist. She leaned heavily on Zoleta and together they took a step.

Their progress was excruciatingly slow, but they kept a steady pace and every five minutes one or the other sent out the distress call. The tunnel continued the downhill grade following the dwindling vein of xeno-ore.

They concentrated on each step, wasting as little energy as possible, until there was no more energy to be had. They had nothing left and sank to the cave floor.

"Ray. Chel," Zoleta croaked. "I never meant for you to—"

"Shh. It's okay, Zo. Wait. Call. Coming."

"From?"

Rachel held up her hand to silence Zoleta. A smiled formed across her cracked lips. "Yes." She cleared her throat as best she could. "I'm here. Yes. Zoleta. Too. No. Not going. Anywhere."

The call was like a small shot of pure, clean, revitalizing water and energy bar all in one.

Zoleta tapped frantically at her earbud, "Come in. Control Center, do you catch? Senior Commander, Zoleta Murjanah." She stopped to swallow. "Calling Control Center. Come in."

Rachel shook her head at Zoleta. "He said he'd call again in three hours. To give them time. To re-align the something-or-other and ping, the vector thingy." A dry, rasping cough made Rachel grab her throat.

"It's Imitar. He's figuring out the extraction route."

"You got all that from my vague relay of information? And what were you going to say before when you said, I never meant for you to . . . to what?"

"Hmph. Can't recall. Guess we wait now."

"Guess so."

"Ankle? How is it?"

"It's there."

"You rest. I'll stand by and wake you if I hear something." Zoleta tossed the space blanket to Rachel.

"Zoleta. What are our chances of getting out of here?"

"If the xenostone isn't too thick and they can determine our location within a fifteen-meter radius, including depth, and if there is enough integrity left and they can drill down above us, or if they dig from below us and we fall to our deaths—"

"Zoleta!"

"We have about a twenty percent chance of surviving."

CHAPTER 31

Celtic Cave
Wednesday
0500 hours

Sorry, Red Dwarf, but I'm the one with the twenty percent chance of getting out of here. Yours's is more like five percent. Maybe they had even less; no water and now it was getting harder to take a deep breath even though they were still going downhill.

Zoleta flicked on her headlamp for a quick check of the air content on her hand-held meter. As she suspected, the oxygen level was falling rapidly. If they could make it a little farther through the cave they would be more likely to be out from under the impenetrable xenostone. Unfortunately, they would probably be out of breathable air as well. Dragging Rachel along was a strain on both of them and maybe pointless. She may have to leave her behind. But first, it was time to see what Imitar was capable of. Either he could figure out where they were, or he couldn't. Zoleta was sure not going to sit around waiting for him. She didn't wait around for anyone, unless it served her well.

"Hope he turns on the jets."

"You hope who does what?" Rachel sucked in a breath, "and why did you turn the light on?"

"Imitar. Hope he figures out something. Soon. Oxygen depletion." Zoleta held the meter up to Rachel.

"My chest. So tight. Thought I was panting because I'm struggling and the pain is making me—"

"Best thing to do," Zoleta broke in, "Is quit talking. Think you can do that?" *Then I can think without you jabbering at me.* "I want you to listen for any contact. I'll see what I can do to help us get out of here."

Zoleta shimmied off her pack, pulled everything out and spread the items along the ground. Sitting back on her haunches, she studied the array. After a few minutes, she picked up the tripod. *If I can just find a thin spot in the stone.* She ran the head-beam slowly across the ceiling, stopping on a slight indentation in the roof a few feet away. *Might work. Have to try.*

The ground was uneven beneath the crevice so Zoleta pushed small rocks and dirt into a pile with her feet and set the tripod in the center. Next, she clamped a metal cone shaped device to the top of the tripod and flicked on the pulse-laser.

"Is that some kind of radar?" Rachel asked.

"We've been lucky this tunnel hasn't been so low that we've had to crawl our way through." Zoleta paused to take a breath. "This is a pulsar, a type of signal. I need to get closer to that crevice above us and drill a notch." The light from her headlamp swung across the floor and landed on a sixty by sixty-centimeter chunk of granite. "See that rock? We need to put it here." She pointed down between her feet. "Give me the blanket."

Rachel removed it from around her shoulders and handed it to Zoleta who rolled it up and placed it in front of the rock. "I'm going to push it up on end. You unroll the blanket under as far as you can."

They repeated the process until the rock was completely on top of the space blanket. "Bed-making 101. With one heavy patient."

"Yes. Well, now for the hard part."

The women worked together; Rachel seated on the ground pushing with her one good leg; Zoleta pulling with all her strength, until the stone rested in the level spot.

"How does this help us get out of here?"

Zoleta ignored the question, stepped up on the rock, and felt above her head for the deepest part of the crack. Satisfied, she stepped off and picked up the wedge and hammer from the tools still spread out on the floor. The smack of the hammer rang out in a steady rhythm for the first twelve hits, then five slow, sporadic strikes, until the only sound remaining was Zoleta gasping for air.

"You don't want me to talk? Looks like you're going to use up every last liter of O-2 with your hammering away at the roof."

In response, Zoleta went at the ceiling again more ferociously. She let the memory of her father and brother flying off to the prestigious galactic flight school fill her with boiling anger. It wasn't that she hated her brother, or even her father for that matter. It wasn't her brother's fault that he was their father's favorite. But she had worked so hard and placed first in her class for seven years in a row, earning 'Exceptional Cadet' honors. Her brother had only received 'outstanding' in those same classes. Maybe she did hate him . . . She had raced out to the launch pad on that day so many years before, waving her arms wildly and yelling for them to stop. "Go back to the terminal, Zoleta." Her father had barked over her earphone. "But I'm ready for GFS! My Seventh Level Master handed me my diploma. I get my pick of flight schools." She was confused— she was the one who was supposed to be on the shuttle. "I overruled his orders," her father had said. "You are to stay here and run international flights only."

It was obvious what her father had done. She had let the anger burn into her every cell.

She would show them. She was the best and some day she would be in command and her father would be the one who had to follow her orders.

"Zoleta. Stop. You're going to pass out at this rate."

The flashback vanished. Zoleta dropped the hammer and wiped the sweat from her face. "Good as I can get it. Have to do."

The hollowed-out area was only slightly bigger than the size of a light-globe like the one Imitar had thrown how many days ago? Zoleta settled the tripod in the center of the rock, secured the pulsar to the top, and aimed the beam up into the drilled hole.

The likelihood of the pulsar penetrating through the roof and sending out a signal was slim. It all depended upon how thick the layers were above them and what the sediment consisted of. The two women had been descending gradually through the tunnel as they followed the vein of xenostone. They could be meters below the surface. There was no way of knowing.

CHAPTER 32

Control Center
Wednesday
0500 hours

THREE DAYS HAD PASSED since the women had been trapped in the cave. Imitar tried to stay optimistic, but things were not looking good. He plied Ben for as much information as he could get on which way the women had been heading when the collapse took place. The search perimeter was still too large, no matter how Imitar calculated and recalculated. Time was running out. They had to move on rescuing Zoleta and Rachel. Now.

With a little luck, Imitar might be able to get a track on a reading once he got out to the site, if and only if Zoleta was lucky enough to set up the pulsar.

Thank the cosmos Zoleta never relies on luck. What she can't make happen she ignores, and that's not often. If there's a way, she'll do it. If there's a nano of a chance, she'll take it.

As Imitar entered Control Center, Ben sat at the console with his head in his hands.

"Sir. Here is my best estimate of where we should start digging. I propose we dig a shaft as close as possible to their last known position."

"What are we looking at with the layers? What kind of rock do we have to bust?" Ben ran his hand through his uncombed hair and looked up at Imitar through blood-shot eyes. Imitar hadn't stepped into a blower in three days and knew that he looked just as bad.

"We don't know, sir. But we have to start digging. We can make adjustments after we see what we're up against."

"Big D will be here in zero-minus-four hours. Thorian will run the digger. You direct. Take doctor Luminita and whomever else you need with you."

"Aren't you coming?"

"No."

"But—"

"Dismissed."

Imitar hesitated for a nanosecond, wanting to call out the CPO, but instead turned and stomped out of Control Center.

* * *

Ten minutes later Imitar arrived at the garage in time to help Sanda load her medical bag and diagnostic equipment.

"Is that everything?" he asked, trying to keep the anger out of his voice.

"I think so, but where's Ben?"

"He's not coming." Imitar slammed the vehicle's back door shut with his fist.

The two climbed into the Hubba and Imitar set the Galactic Positioning System for the upper end of the belt. Neither spoke for some time until Sanda broke the silence. "Imitar, I hope Zoleta is okay. I hope they are both okay."

"Me too. Thanks, Doc."

* * *

They reached the cave orifice in warp time considering they had driven the slow but reliable Hubba. It would be hours until the digger arrived, but they worked to ready what they could. Before Imitar set up the radar, he made his way as far into the cave as possible until he came to an impassable pile of rock where the collapse had occurred. He yelled several times for Zoleta and Rachel, but his voice died against the wall of stone. Silence was the only answer on his earphone as well.

Back outside at the Hubba, Imitar glanced at Sanda and then hoisted his pack, which contained the hand-held positioning calculator, communication booster, and portable radar scan, over his shoulder.

"Any sign of either of the women?" Sanda asked. "I've been trying my earphone. Nothing."

He shook his head. "Nothing here, either."

The load was heavy but Imitar ignored the weight and hiked around the outside of the cave and up over the hill. Sanda followed close behind with her pack containing extra food, water, and her medical kit. The brush was thick, and they had to backtrack several times until he found a path well-traveled by some Goliathian beasts, which to his relief were nowhere to be seen.

The trail meandered for another three kilometers until it opened out in a grassy meadow. A rocky outcropping stood alone on the far edge of the field. At its base, Imitar marked the spot with a red flag for Thorian to start digging. He hoped it would work; it was the closest he could get with his calculations. *What was that funny superstitious thing Rachel was always saying? Cross something? That's it—cross your fingers. How ridiculous.* But he did it anyway.

After he set up the marker, he trudged back through the

grass to the center of the meadow, where he had left Sanda and his pack.

"I assume you are going to set up some kind of locator around here?" she asked.

"Pulsar."

The shiny metal cone, the pulsar, served two purposes: the narrow end sent out a signal, the open end picked up transmissions. He hooked the cone to the rotating tripod. It was possible Zoleta might be able to send out a radar location, but between the amount of earth and rock, the signal would have to travel through, and the shape Zoleta might be in . . . he didn't want to let morbid thoughts enter his head. The chance of detecting any sign was slim.

Imitar achingly watched the machine rotate 360 degrees every five minutes in its search for any possible blips across the terrain, while Sanda busied herself organizing her instruments. After nine complete rotations, there was no change, not even an aberration to raise his hopes. He had been three days without sleep. As his gaze continued to follow the circular motion of the pulsar, they began to close. He lay down in the soft grass with his arms behind his head and thought about the past seven years he had spent on Goliath and all the things he wished he'd said to Zoleta. Now, he may never get the chance. Feelings weren't something people shared much these days; there was too much work to be done, money to make, staying one step ahead of the hundreds of thousands of others waiting in line for your job. But he had always been the one, to the horror of his parentals, who showed concern for the people around him.

There was more to Imitar's attraction to Zoleta than just the initial physical admiration but putting his reasons in to words was beyond him. Deep down he knew she cared, but she would never allow herself to look weak in front of others. If he only had a little more time. Wasn't it ironic? People now lived many more decades than in the olden days, and yet failed to tell those they loved how they felt.

Maybe if Zoleta knew how he felt she would be more . . . what? If she would just let him be a part of her life, more than the bungling teenager she seemed to think he was. Zoleta was driven and that was okay with him. Would she ever be as confident on the inside as she portrayed herself on the outside? She was really the child. The one who needed someone to hold her and tell her she was a brilliant, capable, woman worthy of respect and dare he say it—love. *If I get the chance to be that person . . .*

Imitar drifted off to sleep.

* * *

He woke with a start and scrambled to check the equipment. Sanda was asleep on her back with her arm flung across her eyes and her mouth agape. The pulsar had been rotating for over three hours while the two of them slept, but hadn't detected a thing, not even a trace of a blip. Still, Imitar refused to believe Rachel and Zoleta were, more than likely, dead. Try something else, he told himself, and started to scrape a small hole to set the tripod lower, enabling it to pick up weaker signals closer to the ground.

"What's going on?" Sanda asked as she sat up and squinted at him.

"I'm—" Imitar had barely turned the pulsar back on when its alarm-beep sounded.

"I hear a beep. Is that the signal?" Sanda moved next to him.

"I can't believe it." His heart jumped, and then quickly sank as he realized the radar had picked up Big D. "No. It's not from Zo."

The huge dozer rumbled across the meadow, dropping chunks of sod from its tracks as it went. It stopped several hundred meters from Imitar and Sanda's campsite. Thorian turned off the engine and hopped down from the cab. Imitar ran toward him, waving frantically.

"I'm here." The deep baritone of Thorian's voice boomed. "Took a while to get around that last bend and up that bank. Been serviced back at the compound. Ready to drill." Thorian patted the side of the huge machine. "CPO said to give you the reins. Where do you want me?"

"See the marker over by that rock pile?" Imitar stopped to suck in a breath. "I need you to start immediately. Did you bring different drill bits? I'm not sure what soil types we'll be dealing with."

"No worries, little boss. That's my department. Let's get this toplander going."

* * *

Imitar directed Thorian to the site, then went back to digging his own spot for the radar equipment. By the time Imitar had scraped a ninety-centimeter circle by sixty centimeters deep, sweat ran down the back of his neck and his arms ached. Zoleta probably wouldn't believe he could work this hard. He wasn't much of a physical labor kind of guy. His favorite games didn't call for much athleticism, either. The only exertion while gaming involved manipulating controllers and shouting quick-voice commands.

Thank the galaxy; they were finally doing something constructive to rescue the women. That was more than he could say for the CPO. Better not go there. Being mad wouldn't help anyone.

The sound of the auger pounding away in the background gave Imitar something else to focus on besides staring at the pulsar as it spun slowly in the dugout, throwing its red needle-light across the grassland like a high-powered infrared surveillance system. "Come on Zoleta. Just give me something. One little ping."

Before he could finish his wish, the digger screeched to a halt.

CHAPTER 33

Wednesday
Control Center
1600 hours

BEN WENT OVER and over the last few days in his mind as he sat at his console with his head in his hands. What had he been thinking, taking the group out to Celtic Cavern? He should have been paying more attention. He should have checked the astro reports before they left the compound. He wasn't thinking about anything except spending time with Rachel. And now look what had happened. For the second . . . no, third time he was the one to create havoc in her life.

The com buzzed, making him suck in a sharp breath. A millisecond of hope mixed with fear scorched him like a fuel-pack. He quickly wrangled his emotions. "CPO Schaefer. Go ahead."

"Sir. This is Four-Four-Nine-Seven. I'm bringing in two sick workers, Two-Seven-Seven, and One-Eight-Seven. I called Medical but no one answered, so I thought I'd better call you."

Schaefer swore.

"Sir, they need the vaccine."

"Goddammit. They're Firstwave miners. They've already had the shot."

"Excuse me sir?"

"Just get them to Medical. I'll have someone there to place them in quarantine. Out."

Maybe the two sick men had different symptoms. Maybe this wasn't related to the disease that had already claimed three lives. A feeling of dread tightened in his stomach. Two-Seven-Seven is the twenty-seventh mine recruit and One-Eight-Seven is the eighteenth recruit. Both from Sector VII. Both original miners. They would have had multiple rejuvenations to keep in top physical condition.

Both had already been vaccinated with Rachel's immunity stems.

This can't be happening.

"Communications. This is CPO Schaefer. Patch me through to Dr. Luminita." Ben paced the room. "I don't need excuses. Just do it. Now."

CHAPTER 34

Somewhere above Celtic Cavern
Wednesday
2210 hours

BOTH SANDA and Imitar ran toward the drilling site as soon as they heard the screech of the digger followed by silence as it jammed solid. Thorian jumped down from Big D's cab and was surveying the hole when Imitar yelled, "What happened? Why'd you stop?"

Thorian shrugged. "It's okay, Boss. Just hit some bedrock. Broke a bit. I'll change it out to diamond-frac."

"Do whatever you need to do. Just keep digging. We've got to find the women." Imitar paced around the opening.

"Any contact yet with either of them? How long they been down there?" Thorian asked as he flung open his huge tool box.

Sanda answered. "No contact. But we'll keep trying." She shot Thorian a look.

"Well, it's going to take a little time, but we'll get there." He squinted at Sanda. She hoped he got the message to be careful with his wording. "Hard-ass rock we're trying to drill through.

Can be done, though. Done it plenty a-times before. If you haven't heard from the two, it's probably 'cause they're down under a-ways. You can give me a hand switching out the blade, Boss. Then we can get this big-boy back to bustin' balls."

Good, Sanda thought. Thorian understood and was putting Imitar to work to keep him focused. It could take hours to break through the layer of rock, so Sanda went back to the small campsite where they had set up the pulsar. She occupied herself by sending out a call to the women every four to five minutes, hoping for some sign, any sign, of life. Imitar finished helping set the bit and was now trampling a permanent path around the hilltop, staying out of the way of Thorian and Big D, but, Sanda was sure, close enough to know if there was any news.

Of all the time Sanda had spent studying and conducting research on this far-off planet, never had she anticipated that part of the job description would include caring. Sure, she had the medical background to treat those needing rejuvenations or quick repairs to their systems, but to deal with the emotional requirements of the citizens of Goliath was not what she had signed up for. Wasn't that some illogical notion left to those on over-populated Earth? It was all Rachel's fault. Sanda could see that now. The way Rachel dealt with patients was very different from the way Sanda did. Was it better? And now here she was, a research scientist caring about Rachel, about Imitar, even about Zoleta. As she watched Imitar pace, a strange feeling in her stomach made her push her clenched fists into her belly. If she could just give him a tonin, or at least ease his worry with a dose of Lift.

If they lost these women . . .

Sanda glanced at the pulsar. It continued to circle without any interruption. "Poor Imitar," she sighed.

A call on her earbud startled her out of her thoughts.

"Imitar!" Sanda shouted and waved to him before she realized the call was not from the women, but from base. Imitar called out questions as he sprinted to her. "Is it Zoleta? Are you talking to the girls? Are they okay? Do they know their location?" He was out of breath by the time he reached her.

Sanda held up a hand to silence him. "That can't be," she said. "No. Not good. Yes sir. Right now?" There was a pause. "I understand. Out." And she clicked off.

When she looked up, Imitar stood in front of her. His face drained of color. "What is it Doc? What's happened?"

"That was CPO Schaefer. He needs me back at base. Immediately."

"What? Why? What'd he do—stub his toe?" Color returned to Imitar's cheeks. Now they were brushed with a red tinge. "Get a sliver in his ass?"

"Imitar. I have to go back to the compound and see what I can do to save the lives of two more workers brought in from Sector Seven."

"But what about Zoleta's life? And Rachel's?"

"It's been over three days and we haven't heard a word from the women. We don't know if they're alive. You and Thorian are doing everything you can. I'm more valuable back at base. I'm sorry Imitar. I'll leave my field bag with you and I'm sure Thorian has an emergency first aid kit as well."

* * *

Sanda took the Hubba, leaving Imitar to ride back with Thorian when they either found the women, or gave up the search. The look on Imitar's face haunted her and the same odd pressure as before, traveled from her stomach to her chest and tightened around her heart.

On the trip home, Sanda went over all the possible scenarios in her head. How could two workers be sick? The vaccine using Rachel's DNA immune base should have allowed the men to develop their own antibodies. It had seemed to work. Even the men who had shown signs of illness seemed to recover after being given the vaccine. Maybe this was a different disease they were dealing with. But it shouldn't matter. Their immune systems should have responded and protected the host from any and all types of foreign microorganisms.

Sanda squeezed her temples. Her head throbbed and her stomach felt clumpy, like when she ate the entire plate of neuvo-figs. Never had she felt so spent. She reached a hand up to feel her throat. "Am I getting sick? No. I can't be. I don't have a cough. My throat isn't sore. Is it?"

In the distance, she could see dusky light reflected off the protective bubble which covered the compound. The closer Sanda got, the more exhausted she became.

* * *

As soon as Sanda stepped through the door of Command Center, CPO Schaefer handed her the stick-files on the two men from Sector VII.

"I had Tiernan clean and ready your lab and put Josepheno and Romeran in quarantine. The autoscans are running the vitals so preliminary information should be available as soon as you get down to Medical. Is there anything else you need, Sanda?"

"I could really use some sleep, but I'll get right to work. Would you please have a liter or two of strong jav sent down? That should help." She looked Ben over quickly and was dismayed by the dark circles hanging under his eyes and the pallor of his face. "Ben? Can I do something for you before I head down? What do you need?"

Ben rubbed the knuckle of his pinky finger and spoke so softly Sanda had to lean toward him to hear. "News? Is there any news on Zoleta? And . . . Rachel?"

"We hadn't heard from them before I left, but Imitar has the pulsar going and is watching for a signal. Thorian is drilling as fast as possible." She paused. "I'm sure we'll get some good news soon."

Now why did she say that? Giving false hope was not something she pandered to. It was so unrealistic and unlikely. She was sure Ben knew it and wouldn't fall for it. Still, he seemed to need something to hold on to.

Ben gave Sanda a weak smile. "Thank you, Sanda."

* * *

Sanda had forgotten how rough the scrub down was in de-con but she did her best to breathe slowly and keep her eyes wide open. Normally, she relied on the sensor-bot for assessing the patient and running the info through the med computer for her diagnosis and treatment. Workers ending up in quarantine? This was not what she had expected. The vaccine had worked, hadn't it?

She brought a thermos full of water and a blanket for each patient.

* * *

The two patients were in serious but stable condition for the time being. They presented with the same initial symptoms that eventually led to George's demise, only these men had been given the vaccine using Rachel's immunity stems. Sanda ran blood, urine, skin, and bone tests on samples from Josepheno and Romeran.

The need for sleep pulled at Sanda's mind and body but she continued to belt down cup after cup of jav and pore over data for the next six hours. Her head had barely touched the desktop when she snapped alert.

She knew what was missing from the vaccine.

She grabbed an empty holo-stick, loaded the vital data, and went to see Ben.

* * *

"Come in." Ben's voice was rough around the edges.

"I brought the results of Josepheno's and Romero's immunoassays." She waved the stick. "I thought the vaccine would work. Well, it did work but it didn't last because—here let me put it up on the screen and you can take a look."

There were dark circles under Ben's bloodshot eyes. He rubbed the back of his neck. "Just give me the report. Verbally."

"Of course. The vaccine works initially but after a certain amount of time the patient's body stops replicating the gene and the system shuts down. The immunity function is lost and the body becomes susceptible to infection once again. Which is ironic because the workers are building immunity against Rachel's stems and rejecting her DNA."

"And you can give the men some type of agent to stop the rejection? Right? You do have a solution to this problem, do you not?"

"All we can do right now is to give the patients rejuves to buy us some time."

"Time?"

"I need to configure a new batch of vaccine with a splice added to the strand so the receiving host cells won't recognize it as a foreign invader and attack."

"How long will the converted vaccine take before it'll be ready?"

Sanda studied the floor. "That depends."

"You can do that with the remaining samples of DNA?" The intensity of Ben's gaze and tone made her feel like she was plummeting through Earth's atmosphere at too sharp of an angle.

"It's imperative that we have a viable batch of fresh samples."

The muscles in Ben's jaw tightened. "You mean, we need Rachel."

CHAPTER 35

Somewhere above Celtic Cavern
Thursday
0230 hours

THORIAN REPLACED yet another drill bit, restarted Big D, and hammered into the hard ground. Imitar pulled at the scraggly hair on his chin and tried to reach Zoleta on his earphone for the umpteenth time.

Nothing. No reply from the trapped women.

For once, he wouldn't mind Zoleta telling him what to do and how to do it, and that he was such a nebula. But if things didn't work out . . . and no matter the outcome of this rescue mission, it was time for him to make a change; time he focused on himself and his career. Leaving Goliath would be the first step. He would ask for a transfer.

A buzz from his earphone made him jump, step backward, and knock over the tripod. He scrambled to his feet. "Yes? This is Major Imitar Dubasi."

"Have you found the women?" Ben demanded.

"No. We're still digging." Imitar righted the tripod and

pulsar, and picked up his thermos, wishing it contained a double jav instead of water.

"Any radio contact with them?"

Imitar's nostrils flared. "Not yet. Sir. We believe we are getting close but they may be deeper underground than we anticipated. They must have descended several kilometers from where you said the tunnel started."

"Do whatever you need to do but get them out of there. Bring Rachel . . . or, her body to the compound as soon as possible."

"What do you think we are trying to—?

Schaefer clicked off.

Imitar threw his thermos as hard as he could against the rock outcropping. Shards of tetraplastone sparkled down its face like twinkle-lights over a waterfall.

And then he heard it, or thought he heard it, and prayed to the universe he had heard it.

PING.

Imitar held his breath.

Yes. He had heard it. The pulsar had been activated. It was reading a signal. A signal from somewhere underground. He dropped to his knees and watched the radar complete two more full circles. The ping was faint but steady. His heart raced as he took note of the co-ordinates, then ran to the digger and motioned frantically for Thorian to stop.

Thorian shut down the engines and hopped from the cab, wiping his sweat with a dirty red kerchief. "What's-up, Boss? First you want me to keep on digging no matter what. Now you want me to pull the scoop?"

"Yeah, I know, Thorian, but there's new info. We need to change the site. We need to drill fifteen meters south-southeast from your current position."

"But that will take too—. Whatever you say, Boss."

Imitar measured off the meters and directed Thorian to the

new spot. "And we need to double-time the drilling. CPO's orders."

"Speeding up could destabilize the sed. Make the whole works come crashing down on those girls."

"Then we'll have to be as careful as we can, but don't stop until we find them."

*   *   *

The grinding chug of the digger signaled it had started up again. Imitar gritted his teeth as he stood over the hole and stared at the cold, steel pipe pounding into the ground, willing it to get to the women in time.

Bucket loads of rock piled up alongside Big D as it spit out the tailings. Bucket. The Bucket. Imitar wished he had a Zang-O-Rang about now. In fact, he wished he was at The Bucket and none of this cave catastrophe had ever happened.

What was it the Z-Mahn had said about Rachel the day Imitar took her to The Bucket, before the splicing? The Z-Mahn seemed to have a strong feeling when he had clasped Rachel's arms. *What did he mean Ben and Rachel are the same? They are nothing alike. Maybe it has something to do with—*

A scratchy sound in Imitar's earbud broke through his thoughts. He waited, not sure of what he had heard. The voice repeated: "An oo ear me? Ver."

"Yes! Yes. I hear you."

"Tar. Get . . . out . . . here."

"Zoleta! Is Rachel there with you? Are you okay?"

"Weak. Need . . . air."

"Hang on. We're coming. Tunneling toward you. We'll have you out soon. I promise. Keep in contact."

"Hur . . . ee."

CHAPTER 36

Celtic Cavern
Thursday
04:30 hours

DARKNESS ENVELOPED Rachel's body and mind, shutting down her senses, leaving her with nothing. Her soul seemed to float lazily upward, as weightless as a single atom. It felt good to be done, to let go and no longer be a part of life.

Catching a small draft of air, she drifted higher. It was like flying a kite, only she *was* the kite. It was easier to breathe up here. There was more air.

More air.

A far-off sound made her curious, drawing her back toward her broken body. Her mind fought against it, not wanting to leave the sacred refuge it had found. But the sound grew louder and morphed into words that she recognized.

"Rach L. Found us. Rachel. Wake up."

Someone pinched her shoulder hard.

Rachel sucked in a breath and croaked, "Ouch. Not morning. Let me sleep." She tried to grasp her dream and let it take her away again but the nasty person shook her and told her to move to the other side of the rock. What was the problem? Rachel was fine where she was.

"They're tunneling in from below us at an angle. We need to move back."

"What?"

Rachel sat up and tried to make sense of where she was and who was hollering at her. At least it felt like the person was yelling at her. She felt dizzy and her head throbbed.

"Can't you hear? It's Big D."

Zoleta. That's who was yelling at her. It all came flooding back: the cave, the collapse, her life, or lack thereof, on some God-forsaken planet, Ben...

The pounding in Rachel's head matched the rhythmic chomping of the drill as it bit chunks of rock and dirt out of its way to get to the women. The noise grew louder.

Rachel yelled over the machine, "What's that? Zoleta, I see something on the ground beside you. It's blinking." She pointed to a fist sized lump of metal.

"Molebot," Zoleta shouted back. "That's why we have air. They sent the drillbot to tunnel an airhole."

"I like air."

"That may be all you have underneath you if you don't move—"

The ground beneath Rachel began to open; dirt and rock fell inward toward the center, and slid down through a funnel, like sand through an hourglass.

Rachel was sliding with it. She leaned backward and pushed with her legs, trying to keep from slipping over the edge of the widening hole, but her left foot and ankle were useless. Her arms couldn't hold her much longer.

It'll be over soon. Why can't I at least have my life flash before my eyes so I will, once and for all, know if I've had a life?

"Oh-no-you-don't! I didn't let you drink up all my water for nothing." Strong hands grabbed Rachel under the arms and yanked. Zoleta fell backwards, dragging Rachel with her.

Dust billowed out from the hole, covering both women. They were centimeters away from the edge—not that they would have fallen very far. The huge metal blades of the auger would have stopped their fall if only to kill them instantly by pureeing them into a bloody gruel.

"Well. They've certainly broken through. Couldn't get any closer," Zoleta panted.

Rachel rolled off Zoleta and wiped the grit from her eyes. Her mouth was full of dirt. "Zoleta, shine your light down there," she sputtered.

The women watched as the drill-bit retracted downward, like a giant metal snake, and lost sight of it as it reversed its path through the tunnel it had been digging for the last three hours.

"I never thought—. What do we do now? Should we climb down the hole?" Going any deeper underground was not what Rachel wanted to do. But if they had to first go down in order to get to the surface, she would find the strength. The thought of a gentle breeze across her face, of being able to see the stars at night, of seeing Ben . . .

"No. We do the same thing we've been doing. We wait."

CHAPTER 37

Celtic Cavern
Thursday
08:30 hours

ZOLETA AND RACHEL listened closely for Imitar's call. The wait
grew painful. How deep had the rescue team had to dig? And
how long was the shaft connecting to where the women were
trapped? Had something else gone wrong?

Rachel looked at Zoleta but in the dim light her muted
features revealed nothing. "Zoleta? Why aren't we hearing
anything?"

"Hmph. Taking time to pull out the snake."

"The what?"

"The digger pounds or drills vertically through the earth.
The Snake can cut in sideways. It's more flexible. Take a rest,
Rachel. Make the time pass faster." Zoleta shook her head. "I
can't believe he did it. He found us. Impressive."

"Like, take a nap? There's no way I can relax until we're out
of here. Why don't you tell me about your childhood, since we
have air now and you think I talk too much. Get our minds off .
. . You did have one, right? A childhood, I mean? Tell me about

your family, your friends, the silliest thing you ever did when you were little."

"I don't think so."

"Come on. What's your happiest memory?"

"I'm about to make my happiest memory by throwing you head first—"

"Hush," Rachel ordered. "Listen."

A scratching sound followed by gravel skittering down a steep bank came from the hole. Soft light filtered its way up through the tunnel. The women looked at each other. Rachel tried to swallow the lump in her throat. Her nose burned as if she were going to cry but dehydration kept any tears from forming. They might just make it out of this god-forsaken cave.

Heavy panting grew closer until finally a set of gloved hands reached up, searched for a hold, and pulled a long body onto the cavern floor.

"Blind us with that headlamp, why don't you?"

"Zoleta. You. You're okay?"

"Took you, what? A hundred light years? I'm okay. Could be better." Zoleta's voice dragged.

"And Rachel?"

"Over here, Imitar. Can't you even give him a hug, Zoleta? I would, if I could stand."

"Oh craters. Are you hurt? What do you need?" Imitar scurried over to where Rachel was propped up against a rock.

"A little water, food, medicine, new ankle. She's pretty needy if you ask me," Zoleta answered for her.

"Thanks, Zoleta. As if you didn't need all the above yourself, except for the ankle part."

"I brought water and a kcal bar each. And a local numbing med. No room in the tunnel for much of a pack. Let's use the goop on your ankle and then what do you say we get you ladies out of this hole?"

The ground pitched beneath them.

"Is that the digger starting up again?" Rachel felt her heart jump and stay at a fast beat.

"I think it's time to get moving. Rachel, I'll take you first."

"No, Imitar. I'll slow you down. Zoleta should go first. She's more valuable."

"See what I have to put up with? Please. Take her. I could use some quiet time. Ben is probably burning power cells waiting for her."

"Zo. I'll come back—"

"Don't take too long. I've got lots of work to catch up on back at base."

* * *

Imitar climbed over the edge, dropped three meters, and reached up for Rachel. It was a long way straight-down. "I can't climb. My ankle is broken."

"Lower yourself over the side and I'll catch you. It's not far," Imitar said.

"Easy for you to say. You're what, seven feet tall?"

"I am two point two meters tall."

"How are we going to fit? The hole doesn't look very wide."

"We have to go one at a time."

"Would you two quit with the chatter? Grab my hands, Rachel. I'll lower you closer to Imitar."

Rachel hobbled to the edge, lay on her belly, and swung her legs over the opening. She knew Zoleta had to be as exhausted as she was, but the two women clasped arms. Before Rachel descended into the hole she looked at Zoleta and whispered, "Thank you."

"Hmph."

Rachel's legs hung in mid-air. "She's all yours," Zoleta called from above and released her hold. Rachel squeezed her eyes shut but Imitar's long arms quickly grabbed her before any free-fall was involved.

There was more room at the bottom. They could stand together, but not turn around. "Now comes the tricky part. There's only space for one body at a time, so I'll go feet first and pull. You get to travel head first. That way you can't get stuck. Push as much as you can with your good leg. Once we get to the main shaft, it'll be a fun ride to the top."

Imitar tipped his headlamp upward so Rachel wasn't blinded as they began their descent through the narrow tunnel. He felt his way along with the tips of his boots. Rachel was thankful he only glanced in the direction they were crawling a few times. Instead, he kept his gaze locked on her.

The two continued, slowly inching their way along. "How far does this go?" Rachel was breathing hard.

"We're getting close. Do you want to stop? We need to keep going if you can."

"No. I'm okay." A rock poked her in the ribcage, making her push harder to get past it. "Imitar, why you? Why did you come down here to rescue us? Are you under orders or was it your choice?"

"I was here when the cave collapsed for one thing. Two—my shoulder width is right for the job, and three . . . I care about you and Zoleta. Yes, I have orders from the CPO to get you out as fast as possible, but I would have come regardless."

"I'm glad, Imitar. So many times I just wanted to give up. But then I realized I felt less alone trapped underground with only one other person, Zoleta no less, than I've felt in the months I've been on Goliath. I guess I just need to accept who I am now and who I want to become instead of worrying about who I was. I may never remember—

A muffled explosion shook dirt from the sides of the tunnel. Imitar stopped and listened. Rachel stared at him. "Was that the digger?"

"No." He tightened his grip on Rachel's arms and quickened their pace. Rachel pushed harder with her good leg and they wiggled through the narrow tunnel as fast as they could.

"Ah, we're at the vertical shaft. It's wider here. There'll be a safety vest on the floor. You need to put it on and I'll lift you up to the cable. You'll have to hook yourself in."

Imitar dropped over an edge, pulled Rachel through after him, and set her gently on the ground.

"Wait a minute. What do I have to do? Is this it?" She picked up a pile of tangled straps. "Can it hold both of us? You're coming up too, right?" Rachel looked far up the shaft. It was like looking from the bottom of a deep well. Only a smidgen of light filtered from the opening at the top.

A meteorite hit somewhere on the surface, closer this time, causing dirt and rock to rain down on them. Imitar covered Rachel with his upper body, shielding her as best he could. She coughed and tried to rub the grit from her eyes. They waited for a few minutes until the rumble passed.

Imitar grabbed the harness and held it out for Rachel to put her arms through. He pulled hard on the straps to tighten it. "We can't bend down in here at the same time, so you'll have to step through the other two loops. Put your bad leg through first then I'll hold you up while you get your other leg in."

Rachel gritted her teeth. "Okay. I'm set."

"There's a rope with a carabiner on the end dropping down from the cable spool on the digger. See this hook here?" He waggled the metal loop attached to the center strap of the vest in front of her sternum. "Pinch the carabiner open and hook this part in. You'll have to reach up and feel for the rope."

"Can't they lower the cable? It'd make it a lot easier. And how are you going to reach it?"

"I'm tall, remember? And I have long legs so I can straddle-walk up the sides of this shaft without difficulty."

Imitar's strong fingers dug into her waist as he lifted her

above his head and held her steady. She reached a hand upward and waved it around until it connected with the dangling cable. "I've got the end of the rope but I don't feel the hook thingy."

"Keep trying. It'll be there and then I can support you under your back-side while you hook in."

"Good thing you're strong."

"True. I wonder why you are so heavy for such a short person."

"Thanks. I love you too." Rachel used as much strength as she could muster to climb the rope. "Gaud. This reminds me of gym class. I think. Ah, here's the little devil." She pulled up on the fastener attached to her vest with one hand and down on the carabiner with her other. With a final squeeze the clasp snapped into place just as the ground lurched. Imitar pitched sideways, catching himself on the wall but letting Rachel fall in the process.

"You okay?" Imitar recovered quickly and reached for Rachel's dangling legs, slowing her from spinning and bumping on the sides of the shaft.

"A little whiplash is the least of my worries."

Imitar tapped his earbud. "Rachel is on. Prepare for retrieval. Going back for Zoleta." He crawled through the side tunnel before Rachel could tell him good luck.

The cable drew taut and Rachel felt herself being reeled through the dark, rocky hole. The assault on the surface continued, the blasts shaking the stability of the tunnel. Rachel willed the spool to wind faster and prayed for Imitar to get to Zoleta before the entire shaft collapsed.

CHAPTER 38

DiggerCeltic Cavern
Thursday
10:30 hours

THE GLOW from Imitar's headlamp faded into the darkness as Rachel ascended the shaft. Up above, more explosions pounded the planet. The air was full of dust, and fragments of rock bombarded Rachel as the winch bore her, turn by turn, toward the surface. She tried to take a quick glimpse at the bleak light coming from the opening, but without eye protection the falling debris made it impossible to see anything.

Suspended from the harness, her eyes shut tight, Rachel thought about inner strength. Didn't she know someone in her past that she admired, a person who always made the best of adversity, learned from it, and went on with life? Who was it? It wasn't her, she felt, but maybe it could be. Did she have enough strength to care? Her ankle was killing her from all the blood pooling in her legs, making her injury throb with pain. The one thing she was certain of; she was, indeed, alive.

At least she didn't have to put any weight on her ankle. Hooray for small victories.

Yes, she was alive and she was going to live. What did that mean to her now with all she had been through? And since she was going to be around awhile, maybe it was time to find out about her past, and to decide what she wanted her future to be.

But what she really wanted was a long, hot shower.

The closer to the opening Rachel got, the more she noticed how cold she was. She had spent three, or was it four, days in the cool, dark cave. Had her teeth been chattering the whole time, or did they just start now because she was almost free of this disaster and that much closer to salvation, to seeing . . . Ben?

Ben is alive. He gave Imitar orders to get me out of here as fast as possible.

Her heart rate sped up a notch with each centimeter she rose. Would Ben be waiting at the top for her? She knew he would be. He just had to be, and that would mean . . .?

The cable suddenly jerked to a halt with Rachel dangling less than a meter from the opening, like a fish caught on a line. Before her eyes could adjust to the light, muscular arms reached down, lifted her out of the hole, and set her carefully on the ground.

A hulk of a man wrapped a thermal shawl around her shoulders. Rachel looked up into the handsome face. "Thank you."

"Here's water and some food. Your ankle bad? I'll get a stabilizer. Be right back." Another boom hit somewhere off to the north before he could take two steps. "On second thought, I'll carry you to Big D—might be safer under its roof. Let's get this contraption off you." The man helped her out of the harness, hooked the vest back on the rope and pushed the button to lower the cable into the gaping hole. Then he scooped her up like a load of delicate laundry, placed her on the seat in the cab, and climbed in beside her. "I'm Thorian," he said in the deepest baritone she had ever remembered hearing. "I might as well wait in here with you until I get the signal from the boss. I know you've had quite the ordeal, but you're going to be fine." He pointed to her ankle. "Let's get that injury wrapped. You shouldn't have to put any weight on it, but just in case, this will help." Thorian took a small package from the first aid box on the floor of the digger, removed the outer plastic, and squeezed the item in the middle. "Put your leg up here and I'll get this set."

Rachel nodded as she sipped the water and glanced up at Thorian. His eyes were light blue, and he had long, golden lashes that matched his shoulder-length blond hair. The man was huge and incredibly handsome.

But he wasn't Ben.

Ben isn't here.

She turned her head away from him and slumped lower in the seat. "I'm Rachel. Thanks. Thanks for pulling me out."

"Not a worry. How is Colonel Z? Is she hurt?"

"Zoleta? I don't think she's hurt."

"Let's hope not. We don't need injury added to inconvenience. That's not a good combo for her. She can be quite the supernova, exploding over the least little thing, taking out everyone in her path." Big D suddenly dipped abruptly, throwing Thorian across the seat into Rachel. "Well, shit," he yelled over the deafening noise. "They better hustle it up and get out of there, or we're going to have to start shoveling again. Or clear out of here without them."

The massive machine rocked back and forth with the shaking surface. Even with the auto-stabilizers doing the best they could to maintain the digger upright, Rachel had to grab on to the door handle to keep from being tossed around. So much for being cold. Sweat ran between her shoulder blades. A thick slurry of vomit rose in her mouth and she swallowed it back down. The ache in her hands, from the death grip on the door, burned the length of her arms, and into her neck. "We can't leave them!" she shouted over the cacophony.

* * *

The bucking slowed and Thorian pushed himself back to the driver's side of the cab. "Are you okay?" The blood felt like it had drained from her face and pooled in her bad ankle. She looked up at Thorian and gave a weak nod. Thank God, the roof of the digger was directly over her head and only sky above that; no chance of being buried alive, unless the trembling ground split open and she and the digger tumbled in. But what about Imitar and Zoleta?

"We won't leave them. I promise." Thorian opened the door. "I'll check the shaft. You stay inside."

"Don't worry, there's absolutely zero chance I'm going out there."

Rachel watched as Thorian bent over the opening she had emerged through only thirteen minutes earlier. He straightened, pulled a red cloth from his back pocket, and wiped his forehead. When he turned toward her, his furrowed brow and tight jaw made her stomach tilt. He marched to the rear of Big D and dug in an oversized tool box.

"Are Zoleta and Imitar on their way out? What's wrong? What's happened?"

"When we tipped, the winch got bent. I need to hammer it back in place." He swung the huge sledge and pounded on the reel until Rachel felt her head would explode. Then he tried the crank. The winch screeched and wound the rope around twice before stopping; making the motor rev. No use. Thorian slammed it into the off position. Smoke drifted toward the digger. A whiff of scorched metal stung Rachel's nose.

"Will it work? Did you fix it?"

"The winch is okay, which is more than I can say for the

shaft. The line is caught on something. Most likely pinned beneath fallen rock at the T."

"But the rope was able to wind a few turns."

"That was the slack. The vertical tunnel is blocked."

"But how do you know that? Can you see all the way to the bottom? I don't understand. They can get out, can't they? They can clear out whatever is clogging the tunnel, right? Use some kind of digging-robot thingy, or something?"

Rachel sprang from the cab and limped quickly toward the site. Thorian took three long strides and reached out a muscled arm, pulling her away from the edge. "Hold on there. I thought you said you would stay in Big D."

"I need to see for myself."

"Okay, but do me a favor and hang on to me while I shine the light."

Rachel gripped his arm and leaned out over the opening. The tunnel was deeper than she realized. No wonder the trip up in the harness had taken so long. A jumble of large rocks lay at the bottom, or what she thought was the bottom. "Oh, my God. It did. It collapsed." She pulled back from the gaping mouth, still holding tight to Thorian. "Phone. What about calling them? Have you tried to reach them? Have they been trying to call us?"

"Haven't been able to pick up a signal. You try. I'm going to see what we have to work with."

Rachel let go of his arm and sank to the ground. A lump stuck in her throat again, hard and thick and putrid tasting. Thorian went back to the digger and continued to rummage through various tools, stopping to rub a hand across his square jaw. She watched his broad back as she kept repeating her call, first to Imitar, and then to Zoleta.

After ten minutes, Thorian returned with an oblong, metal container and placed it on the ground beside Rachel. His face was red and sweat dripped from his brow. Heavy straps of iron secured the lid of the case. Thorian pulled bolt cutters from his tool chest and grunted hard on the handles, snapping the straps to unlock the lid. Rachel clicked off her earbud and looked inside. "Is that some kind of missile?"

"Digger-bomb."

"Bomb! You plan to blow something up? What is it with you men and blasting things?"

"It's all we've got. There wasn't time to equip Big D properly after the damage from the Sector Seven asteroid shower. I was lucky to get the repairs done and refueled before CPO Schaefer called with the order to get my butt out here. We're going to have to give it a try."

"Looks like this would be a good time for me to get back in the truck."

Thorian shook his head. "I need you to do something. My shoulders are too broad to fit down that shaft."

"Don't say it. Don't even say it."

CHAPTER 39

Somewhere Above Celtic Cavern
Thursday
10:50 hours

Once again bile threatened to erupt from Rachel's throat. She couldn't hide the tremor in her hands as she reached for the loop of rope Thorian held out to her. She didn't know if she could do this –go back down into that hell-hole, without a harness, and with only one good leg.

And plant an explosive.

"There's a small pack we can put the device in and strap it to you. The bomb will be heavy but all you need to do is hold on to the rope and I'll lower you down as smoothly as I can."

"I don't think I can do this."

"This loop is for your foot. There will be a lot of pressure on your good leg but there shouldn't be much swing in the rope."

"I think I might be sick."

"When you get to the bottom, take the digger-bomb and place it with the propeller end down. Nose up. You'll have to dig a small hole or clear a spot in the rubble. Just make sure it's standing vertical on its own. We don't want it tipping over on its side."

"No, we wouldn't want that," Rachel mumbled.

"See this small latch here by the nose cone? Unhook it and open the top. You'll see a toggle switch. Flip it, close the cone, give two tugs on the rope and I'll pull you back up. Simple."

"Can't we call the compound and have them . . ."

Thorian smiled at her. "Time to go." He settled the explosive into the pack. "More protection if it rides in front."

"More protection?"

Rachel took a deep breath and willed herself to lift her arms so Thorian could strap the bomb to her chest. She stared at the metal cone, directly in line with her chin, as Thorian gently let the full weight bear down on her shoulders. He took the other end of the rope and tied it around his waist.

"We'll be able to communicate, but if anything happens, just remember; two tugs and up you come."

"Are you sure this rope is long enough? I don't want to have to drop while cradling a bomb to my chest."

"I replaced the light in your headlamp. I'm turning it on now. Ready?"

Before she had a chance to make him see how this was not a good idea, he scooped her off the edge, straddled the opening, and began to lower her down.

She wanted to scream, "No! I'm not ready. I will NEVER be ready," instead she froze. The only thing moving was her heart, which hammered against her sternum and the bomb, like a pile-driver. Any logical thoughts she tried to focus on seeped into the dirt walls.

Thorian was right, she thought. At least she wasn't swinging; there wasn't enough room to swing. She closed her eyes, not wanting to see a rerun of the nightmare she had already survived. The sides of the tunnel were a mere exhale away, threatening to squeeze the life out of her. She struggled to keep her thoughts from slamming her into an all-out panic attack by concentrating on slowing her breathing, and unclenching the muscles in her jaw, as the bomb continued to drag them both deeper into the abyss.

A strange sensation drifted through her. Did it have something to do with this weight against her chest? There was something familiar about the heaviness, like she needed and wanted to protect it. She carefully let go of the rope with one hand and rubbed the back of the bomb, giving it a little pat. "Now, I know I've lost my marbles."

"You dropped what? What did you lose?" Thorian's voice shot through her earbud.

"Sorry. No, I'm okay. Still have this little baby tight against me. Maybe you should keep talking so I stay alert."

"Hard to do while I'm lowering you down. You aren't as light as you look."

"As if I haven't heard that before. Maybe you're not as strong as you look." But she could hear him huff and grunt over her earbud as she descended a meter at a time. It was getting harder on her as well. She pulled up on the rope with both hands to ease some of the pressure on the foot wedged in the sling. It didn't take long before her arms began to shake and she had to sink back down with all the weight on her one good leg.

How much longer is this going to take? Wait a minute—is there a count-down on the bomb? Won't the explosion kill me on my way back up the shaft?

She was about to ask Thorian how much time she had for him to get her out of the tunnel, when the earth shuddered violently.

The rope went slack in her hands. She was in free fall.

She threw her arms out to the sides, raking them along the sharp walls, trying to slow herself down. A scream tore from her throat as her injured ankle banged hard against rock. It took every millimeter of Rachel's strength to wedge her body with her two hands and one good leg to keep from plummeting to the bottom. She pushed hard with her leg, enabling her to use her shoulders to bear the weight and come to a stop.

The light in the shaft began to dim, becoming fuzzy around the center. Tiny bursts of green wobbled in a halo design.

She should just let go. This would all be over with. It would be so easy.

She exhaled a ragged breath and forced her weakening limbs to hold on.

"Thorian? Are you there? Can you hear me?" she croaked.

Think Rachel. Think. I could inch my way down to the bottom. It might not be that much farther. If I set the bomb and it explodes, I'll be killed, but the tunnel might open and Imitar and Zoleta could make their way out over my dead body. Ha ha. Over my dead body. And I thought that was just an expression. My mind is babbling. I need to—

"Sorry, Rachel," came Thorian's husky voice. "The blast knocked me flat. I hope you didn't let go of the rope. I don't feel your weight."

She looked around in search until the knotted piece of hemp rubbed against the back of her head. "I got it right here." How did she manage to get the rope behind her?

"Good. I'll start lowering you."

"Give me a second to get re-adjusted."

Pushing hard against the walls, she reached for the rope and pulled it around in front of her. Damn. The loop for her foot dangled somewhere below. She would have to rely on her arm strength alone. It was difficult to tell how far to the bottom with all the dust particles reflecting off her headlamp. Besides, she didn't really want to look down. Pulling the rope up until the loop was in reach might be the better option. But then how would she hook her foot in and keep it in?

Nope, it was all up to her to hold on.

Rachel clenched the rope in both hands and slowly pulled

her shoulders away from the tunnel wall and eased her leg below her. "Okay. I'm ready now."

Thorian quickly lowered her, hand over hand; the safety of his strength getting farther from her sight with every meter she dropped.

"You must be getting close. The line seems to be twisting. Push harder with your foot that's resting in the loop, so you don't start spinning."

Great idea. Maybe next time.

She dangled on the end like a plumb bob. No, like the planchette on that mystic board game she and her sister used to play; staying up late, asking all kinds of questions like what was the name of a boy who had a crush on one or the other, and what was the number of times they would kiss when the mystery man came forward . . . Ouija board, that was it.

Why could she remember immature stuff like a stupid game, when she couldn't remember more grown-up things, like romance, love, lust, and who in the hell she is?

She needed to concentrate on something other than her arms being pulled out of their sockets. God, they ached. As she sucked another breath through her teeth, her toe touched solid surface.

"I made it," she called to Thorian. "I'm at the bottom."

The pile of dirt, rock, and not so solid surface, shifted under her as she jockeyed for footing. It was like standing on the edge of an avalanche.

At least now I can get this hunk of dynamite, or whatever it is, off me.

She unhooked the straps from her chest and carefully set the bomb on the ground. Her body had that floating-away feeling, like the lighter-than-air sensation after piggybacking her older, heavier sister around the room. As much as she wanted to hold on to that sweet memory, she allowed it to slip away. It was time to get down to business.

There was no sign of the side tunnel where she had come through with Imitar. How far below the rubble was it? Was it still open? Were Zoleta and Imitar buried alive? Rachel swallowed hard and forced herself to focus on setting the bomb.

With little room to work, in a bent over position, and with one leg all but useless, Rachel did her best to smooth a spot in the rubble. It took three tries to get the bomb to stand straight with the nose -cone pointing upward. The hairs on the back of her neck prickled with the realization of what she was about to do.

What was it she was supposed to do?

Open the nose and flip some switch. Then get the hell out of here.

Only when she tried the latch, it didn't budge.

Her fingers cramped as she pulled and wiggled and growled at the clasp. She had come too far; giving up now . . . well, she just wouldn't. Maybe she could hammer it off with a rock. As she looked for a hand-sized stone to use, the metal buckle on her pack clanked against the missile.

It took some maneuvering to get the sweaty pack shrugged from her arms and chest, and to use the buckle to pry open the lock on the bomb. A ball of tangled wires was jammed inside. Where was the toggle switch? She carefully pulled the wires aside and looked underneath.

Her head pounded. She licked at her dry lips. Her hand seemed to have an acute onset of Parkinson's disease. Wait a minute; before she flipped the switch and detonated the bomb, she had better be ready to be pulled out. The rope hung loose at the wall, with the loop for her foot in a pile on the floor.

"I found the switch," she relayed to Thorian. "I'm turning it on."

Her lungs felt as if they had collapsed. She struggled to suck in a breath then blow it out slowly as she forced her fingers to pull the trigger.

A high-pitched screech echoed off the walls, making her

clasp her hands over her ears before her eardrums exploded. A strong smell of sulfur permeated the air.

A small rock hit her in the thigh, followed by another which smacked her arm. The spew of debris came faster and faster as the bomb dug its way into the dirt.

Time to get out. She grabbed the rope and yanked hard.

"Come on Thorian!"

The rope pulled taut; her body jerked upward, but her foot remained in the loop.

The rumbling grew louder all around her. She couldn't tell if it came from below. The bomb digging through the rubble, clearing the escape route for Imitar and Zoleta, or from above; more meteorites hitting the surface near Big D.

"Get me out of here!" she screamed.

* * *

Not until Thorian wrapped his arm around Rachel's waist and dragged her from the shaft did she open her eyes.

"Did you get the digger-bomb placed vertically?"

It took a moment to swallow the dry clump in her throat and answer. "I don't know if it stayed straight. I didn't want to hang around to see."

"We'll find out in the next twenty seconds." He picked her up and ran behind Big D just as the earth blasted loose, spewing dirt, rock, and smoke from the shaft.

Chunks of granite pinged off the metal sides and roof of Big D, like grapefruit-sized hail off an aluminum shed. Rachel stayed hunkered down out of firing range, tucked safely in Thorian's broad embrace.

After the last cloud of debris belched from the opening, Thorian took a deep breath and started to move his limbs. Rachel felt his arms uncoil from around her shoulders.

"No. Don't go. Please don't leave me," she pleaded.

"Rachel, I've got to get the rope ready for Imitar and Zoleta in case there's any chance..."

His unfinished sentence was like throwing ice water in her face. This wasn't about her. Why was she falling apart now? Why did she always seem to be swinging from capable, to a useless basket-case from one moment to the next?

"You're right, I'm sorry. How can I help?"

"Keep trying to contact Zoleta or Imitar on your earphone. Get the first aid kit from Big D and have it ready. We'll have to work fast."

Rachel pulled herself up off the ground and hopped, on one foot, around to the front of the cab. As if her legs weren't shaky enough, not having the complete use of her ankle threw her off-balance and slowed her down as well. It seemed to take forever to go five meters and left her winded from the effort.

A corner of the first aid pack peeked out from under the seat of the cab. When she tugged on the pack, it came out easily, along with a wooden-handled shovel caught on the strap. The shovel's handle was tall for her, but it would do for a crutch. She hefted the pack over her shoulder, grabbed the shovel, and hobbled to the shaft.

She stood by Thorian, next to the gaping hole. "Anything? Can you tell if the bomb blew the side tunnel open?" she asked.

"Nothing yet. How about you? Any contact?" He pointed at her makeshift crutch. "Good idea."

"I'll try right now." She tapped her earbud, "Zoleta? Imitar?" Can you hear me? Please answer me. Are you okay?"

Time slogged by. The dryness in her mouth and throat constricted her vocal cords until the repeated call was barely a whisper. She strained to hear over the throbbing in her head. Sinking to the ground, she watched Thorian as he paced back and forth beside the shaft. With each pass of the opening, Thorian pulled on the rope, which dangled into the bottomless pit, then dropped it back down, as if he were trying to entice a fish onto the line.

And finally, there it was. The line drew taut in Thorian's hands. "Something is either caught on the rope, or they're yanking on it. Anyone talking to you, Rachel? I'm going to start hauling on the cable. Let's hope we have a couple of keepers hanging on the end."

Thorian gripped the rope, straddled the opening and pulled hand over hand; his muscular arms and back rippled with effort. The coils of rope slowly mounded in a pile beside him. How did he have such strength? Probably another 'enhancement' somewhere in his genetic make-up, Rachel thought. She doubled her efforts to make contact, but the phone seemed to be dead. It was all she could do to keep trying to reach them on her earbud, and, at the same time, pray that Imitar and Zoleta were safe.

"I see a helmet! Rachel, get the first-aid kit over here." Thorian hollered.

Rachel stood beside him as he dragged Zoleta's body from the hole. The rope was cinched tight across her chest and looped under her arms. He laid her limp body next to Rachel, who did a rapid check of her vitals.

"She's unconscious, but breathing, and her heart rate is stable. She'll be okay. What about Imitar? Send the rope back down. NOW!" Thorian had already tossed the cable into the hole. "He'll be okay. I just know it. He's got to be." Rachel felt something move, like the universe had shifted beneath her. She looked around, but there were no asteroids hitting the ground causing the unbalanced sensation she felt.

Zoleta groaned, "What are you doing? Why do you keep shaking me?"

"Shh. Zoleta. It's me, Rachel. You're going to be fine. Just try to relax. We're going to take care of you. Everything's going to be okay."

"Wasting time. Get Imitar out. Pushed me first. Needs help," she said and passed out again. Rachel moved her from the opening as best she could, removed her helmet, and wiped Zoleta's face with a cool, wet cloth.

"Thorian, she says Imitar needs help. I can go back down. I can reach him. Maybe—"

"Wait. I think I've got him," Thorian's voice boomed.

For the third time in a row, Thorian's back and arm muscles bunched as he pulled hard on the rope.

"Imitar, can you hear me? We've got you. Hang on." Rachel threw Thorian a desperate glance. "He doesn't answer. Keep pulling."

Just as Zoleta stirred and pushed herself to sitting, a voice drifted up from deep in the shaft. The words were unrecognizable but the wonderful sound of Imitar's voice made a sob catch in Rachel's throat. He was alive.

By the time Imitar was free of the hole, the left side of his body, from his shoulder to his thigh, was drenched in blood. The white, pasty color of his face was the same life-less shade as the walls in the research lab. His gasps of breath were coming faster and faster.

"Lie back, Imitar. You're going to be fine. Let me take a look at what's happening here." Rachel grabbed the first-aid scissors and cut away his tunic. The damage made her gag, but she refused to slow down as she fought against time to staunch the bleeding and save his life.

"What are you doing to him? He needs a stay-pack," Zoleta said. "My bag. Bring it to me. I'll show you what to use."

Despite Rachel's efforts, Imitar continued to hemorrhage. His arm was all but shorn from his body and several chunks of rib bone jutted out from bloody punctures in his skin. "I've got to get this bleeding stopped or he's going to go into shock."

"Bring my pack," Zoleta said with more force.

"I'll get it," Thorian said.

He brought the pack to Zoleta and set it beside her. "Empty it. Dump it out," she commanded. Before Thorian could get the top unhooked and opened, Zoleta growled, "Hurry it up. We don't have all month." Thorian turned the pack upside-down and let the items clatter to the ground beside her. "Easy with that. Don't break everything." She scowled at him then started sifting through the items, finally pulling out a yellow-capped glass cylinder the size of her thumb. She twisted off the cap. "Inject this up his nose."

Thorian handed the tube to Rachel who turned it over in her palm and scrutinized it. A purplish colored vapor with flecks of gold swirled inside. "What is this?"

"Do you want a chemistry lesson, or do you want to help? Give it to him."

Before Zoleta had finished her sentence, Imitar's body went slack in Rachel's arms. His eyes seemed to focus on something behind her head and his mouth opened wide as if to take a breath.

"Oh, my God. I'm losing him."

Rachel lifted Imitar's head, held the tube against his nostril and pushed on the plunger at the bottom of the cylinder. "Nothing's happening. The plunger's not moving." She tried again, twisting and turning and pushing on the tube. "It's stuck. I can't make it work!"

"The cap is the lock. Puncture the bottom with it and then try," Zoleta calmly advised.

"There isn't a cap. I don't see a cap?" Rachel scanned the ground around and beside her. Panic began to rise and she fought to keep it from rendering herself useless to help Imitar.

"What? Are you saying you can't save him? *You* can't save everyone? Tsk, tsk."

Something in Zoleta's tone made Rachel stop cold and look at her.

Zoleta slowly uncurled her fingers from around the yellow

cap clasped in her hand. "I have it." With a smug look on her face, she held it out for Rachel to see, as if it were the final missing piece needed to complete a puzzle.

Rachel's panic dissipated quickly, replaced, not with relief, but by a different feeling. A cool breeze brushed the back of her neck, sending a chill through her body. She chose her words carefully, "May I please have the cap, Zoleta?"

"Of course. We all work together. Everyone has a job to do. Even you. And Imitar plays a vital part in keeping our systems running smoothly. I wouldn't want to see anything happen to him. Here, come and get the cap."

"I'll give it to her," Thorian offered and moved toward Zoleta.

"No. Rachel is, apparently, the medical expert. She needs to come get it."

If there was ever a time Rachel felt like killing someone, this was it. It took all the strength she could muster to keep from screaming and attacking this woman. Imitar's life was in her hands, no matter how much Zoleta wanted the power to be hers.

Rachel gently raised Imitar's head from her lap and unpeeled her legs from underneath him. Thorian grabbed the shovel to hand it to her as attempted to stand, but she shook her head and stared straight at Zoleta. A whimper escaped as Rachel pulled herself to standing. With most of her weight on her good leg, she limped the few feet to where Zoleta sat propped against Big D.

"Please, Zoleta. I know you don't want him to die."

"No, I don't. But I do want you to understand how things work on this planet."

Without taking her eyes from Zoleta's, Rachel took the cap from Zoleta's proffered hand. "Oh, I understand." She scrambled back to Imitar as quickly as possible and injected the tube of coagu-bots into his nostril.

The effect was immediate; blood coagulated around the injury, pulse slowed, breathing slowed and deepened, color returned to his face. He opened his eyes wide and coughed.

"Zoleta? Is she okay? Craters, my arm hurts," he said and tried to sit up. "Whoa, moons are spinning around my cortex."

"Glad you could join us. I was a little worried about you there for a few minutes. Just lie still, I'll get you something for the pain."

"I'm fine. I could use a drink of water though. Then we have to get back to the compound as soon as possible." This time he pushed to sitting and gulped the water, letting crusty rivulets run through his chin whiskers and drip on to his shirt in brown splotches.

"I think we should wait before trying to move you. The storm has quieted, so we should be okay for a while. Right, Thorian?"

"No. Imitar's right," Zoleta said, as she rose on wobbly legs and brushed off her pants in a show of authority. "I've got lots of work to do back at base."

"Sorry, Rachel. But I agree with the two of them," Thorian added. "The sooner we get out of here, the better. Besides, it's going to be a slow, cramped ride with the four of us in Big D."

"What? Why? Where's the ZX? Or at least the Hubba?" Dust filled the air as Zoleta stomped around looking behind the digger for another mode of transportation. "We could walk faster than riding in this ancient piece of scrap metal."

Caked-on dirt covered Imitar's entire body, sweat matted his hair to his head, and whiskers sprang out in patchy outcroppings over his face. The flesh under his eyes hung in dark, droopy half-circles. He stood on weak legs, his arm dangling lifeless at his side. "Thorian, thank you. For all you've done."

"No problem, Boss. I'll gather our packs and we'll see what Big D can do in high gear."

"Hmph." Zoleta sighed.

CHAPTER 40

Above Celtic Cavern
Friday
0200 hours

RACHEL CLIMBED INTO THE CAB, followed by Zoleta, and Imitar beside her, swinging the door shut with his good arm. The two women were squished between the two men but too exhausted to care. Thorian started the engine and the four set out on the long, slow journey back to base.

High off the ground, safe in the cab, they rocked gently over the terrain, skirting around the larger pockmarks left behind in the asteroid's wake. Rachel's ankle throbbed, but the ride was so mesmerizing that her thoughts drifted beyond the pain. Images lined themselves up in her mind along a timeline of when things had happened. It had been almost a week since Ben had left her in the cave. Had she dreamed all the insinuations and innuendoes they parleyed back and forth, teasing each other, flirting with each other? No matter how much she wanted to believe that he cared for her, the fact was Ben had not bothered to come out on the rescue, even though he was alive and well and nothing was stopping him. Maybe it just wasn't meant to be and she should let it go.

She had just drifted off when the digger jerked to a stop, throwing her forward into the muscled arm of Thorian who caught her before her head connected with the windshield.

"Why are we stopping?" It was more of a command than a question. As exhausted as Zoleta had to be, she was still in charge.

Thorian pointed through the window at the ZX blocking their path.

"Good. It's about time. I'll see you three back at base. Imitar, open the door so I can get out."

From tired, gritty eyes, Rachel stared at the man who emerged from the vehicle and strode toward them. Her quick intake of breath made Zoleta murmur a quiet, "This could be interesting."

"Thorian," Ben yelled, "I'll transport your passenger back to base."

"Passenger?" Thorian shut down the engines and the digger grumbled to a stop. "Why didn't he bring the Hubba? You could all get home a lot faster." He rolled down the window to hear what Ben was saying.

"Rachel is needed back at the compound. I'll take her with me."

"Rachel?" Zoleta snorted. "CPO Schaefer, I am second in command, and I have critical work that requires my immediate attention."

Ben stared at her through the windshield; his jaw twitched slightly, and his lips drew a rigid line across his face.

"Yes, sir." Thorian slid out of the cab and turned to Rachel. "Looks like your ride's here, Ma'am. It's been a pleasure. Allow me." He scooped her out of the cab, opened the passenger door of the ZX, and placed her gently on the seat.

"I've got it," Ben said as he looked at Rachel and closed her door.

Rachel gazed out the window at Imitar and Zoleta sitting in the cab of Big D. With an exhausted look of relief Imitar waved goodbye to her. Zoleta stared with a look Rachel couldn't quite define. A look that, once again, made her feel as if long, icy fingers reached out and encircled her throat.

As Ben spun the vehicle around, Rachel took one last look at the three stunned faces in her side mirror and sunk lower in the seat.

They drove for several kilometers before Ben finally said, "How bad is your leg?"

Rachel paused, ready for him to add something more, but that was all he said. He didn't even look at her. "My ankle? You mean—how bad is my ankle? I've been trapped for who-knows-how-long and that's what you want to know? It's nothing. I'm fine. I'm alive. Thank you for asking." She bit her bottom lip to keep from saying anything more. She couldn't believe she had just jumped all over him. What had she expected him to say? She clasped her hands in her lap and stared out the window, seeing only the scenarios she had concocted in her head, little fantasies and mini-dramas born of wanting. What happened to his playfulness, his protective flirtatiousness? Had she dreamed it all up? That's right, she had told herself to let it go, and now she was getting sucked back in. What was wrong with her?

She ventured a glance out of the corner of her eye. Ben's attention seemed to be focused on the road ahead, though the side of his jaw did that twitching thing again, and his fist clenched and unclenched on the controller.

"No, Rachel. That's not all I want to know. That's not all I want to say. I'm not sure exactly what I want to say."

"You're a big CPO. Try using your words. If I've learned one thing from dallying with death, it's: say it, or do it. It might be your last chance. That's my new motto."

Ben remained silent.

She had done it again, cut him off before he had a chance. Well, she was sick of giving chances. Time to move on and focus on other things, like work, or finding out what the hell she was doing in this nightmare.

They breezed smoothly over and through the landscape. Rachel tried to fight the gentle, mesmerizing rhythm, the feeling of being sucked down into a place without light, without sound. A place she desperately did not want to go. A place she had already been too many times.

Rain turned to sleet against the windshield. She increased the wipers a notch to keep up with the deluge as she drove toward the turnpike. Between the flurries and her tears, the road ahead was a watery blur. How could she have been so stupid? He was so vulnerable, so alone. Every time she entered his room and he looked up at her with that smile and his blue eyes, her heart slammed against her ribs. And his deep voice . . . she tried to keep from falling under its spell. Or did she? She had a job to do. She was a professional. It wouldn't be a problem. But did she try as hard as she should have?

Time, and circumstances, and caring too much. It was all too distorted, like looking at a Picasso painting. He had been discharged with a clean bill of health. He could return to his life and get on with it. But now he wanted her to be a part of it and she couldn't stop herself. The first time they kissed sent fire blazing through her body. And every thought of him, though she tried not to think of him, fanned the flames of her desire.

The affair was wrong. Not for him, for her, and she had remembered her loyalties and promises and put an end to it, before it was too late.

The wipers were useless against the frozen angel-wings of ice on the windshield. A sharp curve in the road appeared out of nowhere. . . No time to react. Brakes. Skidding. . . Oh my God! One last look in the rearview mirror. The car-seat . . .

CHAPTER 41

Compound
Friday
0540 hours

RACHEL WOKE from her nightmare trembling and gasping as Ben settled the ZX into its parking space inside the compound. She couldn't shake the Deja vu feeling as she stared at the profile of the man beside her and tried to make sense of where she was. How long had she slept? Had he asked her any questions? She smoothed her hair back from her forehead and wiped the dampness from under her eyes with her fingertips.

"Rachel. I—"

"Yes?"

"I'm glad you're back. I'm glad you're safe."

"Thanks. I'm glad you're okay too."

Sanda was waiting for them, a hover-chair floating at the ready for Rachel so she didn't have to put weight on her injured ankle. "I'll lift you out," Ben said as he hustled to the passenger side.

"I can walk. I'm sure you have more important things to do than waste your time babying me."

Before she could say anything more, Ben slid his arm underneath her legs, "Put your arms around my neck. I wouldn't want to drop you."

If I smell as bad as I know I look, he's probably doing all he can to keep from gagging. Oh well, he asked for it.

"Heavens. You look like you've been dragged through a black hole and back," Sanda said.

Rachel nodded. "Several."

"Dr. Luminita, please take care of Rachel's medical needs then take her to her room and help her get settled."

"But you wanted her to go directly—"

Ben cut her off. "I want her to go directly to her room and get a good two or three day's rest. Is that understood?"

"Of course."

"If I wasn't so exhausted, I'd be pissed. It's my ankle that's shot, not my hearing. Again, you people are talking like I'm three years old. I'm right here."

Ben and Sanda glanced at each other. It seemed as if some kind of signal had passed between them. Sanda shrugged. "Are you ready to go, Rachel? Let's get that ankle mended and get you up to your room."

The hover-chair reclined slightly and the foot stool swung up underneath Rachel's legs, elevating her injury. Rachel sighed and closed her eyes as Sanda turned the chair toward the doorway.

"Wait." Ben held up a hand, stopping Sanda. "Before you leave, I'd like to talk to Rachel for a second. In fact, wait at the elevator tube. I'll bring her over and meet you there."

"I'll give you five minutes, then come back for you, Rachel." Sanda stepped in to the elevator.

A wave of confusion washed over Rachel, like a rip-tide had pulled her under and she couldn't breathe. What on earth did Ben, CPO Schaefer want to talk to her about? What happened to all the time he had for conversation on the drive back to the compound?

The chair floated toward the doorway; Ben walked beside it. She glanced up at him. "You said you wanted to talk to me, but you haven't said a word." Back off, Rachel told herself. Give him time. Communication is obviously not a high-level skill in his repertoire.

"Rachel, I'm sorry."

"You're sorry? For what? For the cave-in? It's not your fault. I was having a nice . . . weren't you having a good time? It's okay. I'm okay. We all made it out of there. Alive. It wasn't your fault."

"No, Rachel. You don't understand. I'm sorry for . . . a lot of things."

"You're right, I don't understand. Please explain things to me. I'm listening."

"Let me float you to the corner where we can have a little privacy, then I'll start at the beginning."

What does he mean by 'the beginning'?

Ben knelt beside the hover-chair, eye level with her. "Rachel, I've known since you arrived here that—

"There you are sir. I've been looking for you. You're needed on the bridge. Immediately."

CHAPTER 42

Compound
Friday
0600 hours

RACHEL LOOKED up from where she sat in the hover-chair, still confused about what Ben said and curious about all he didn't get to say. Sanda marched over from the elevator tube, a worried look on her face.

"That was fast. How did your conversation go with Ben?"

"As usual, we didn't have one. He was called to duty before he could tell me anything."

"I'm sorry, Rachel. I guess we might as well get you down to your apartment and get you into bed. But first I want to look at that ankle, so we'll stop in Medical on the way."

Sanda maneuvered the hover-chair into the elevator and took Rachel to Medical. "It looks like Thorian did a pretty good job with what he had, but let's give you the good stuff now. I'm going to inject RNA-specific bone nanos to knit the bone fragments together in your splintered ankle. Then I'll wrap it and we can get you to your quarters."

"Thank you, Sanda."

"Rachel, you've been through a very traumatic event. Do you want to talk about it?"

Rachel sighed. "Sanda, ever since I arrived here it's been nothing but traumatic. The cave-in was just the event that made me *feel* the most."

"I'm not sure I understand."

"It was the closest I've come to feeling alive since I've been here. Since I could have died, being trapped gave me time to think about what really matters. Or, if anything really matters. I realized that deep down inside I don't belong here on Goliath, but this is where I am now and will likely be for a very long time. I have so many questions, but I'm not so sure I even care about getting the answers anymore. Does that make sense?"

"You're tired. You need rest."

"It's more than that. I need a reason."

The look in Sanda's eyes was a mix of confusion with a sprinkle of sympathy, like she was afraid of what Rachel would say next. "A reason?"

"A reason to keep from marching as far as I can into the blazing heat on the hot side of the planet until I turn into a briquette. Or maybe to the dark side until my lungs freeze. No, wait; I've apparently already been there, done that. Guess I'll go for the deep-fried version of 'non-existence' this time."

"Are you lonely, Rachel?"

"Is it always dusk in the belt?"

"Yes. The sun remains at the same angle every day of the year. Why do you ask?"

"Never mind. It wasn't really a question. But to answer yours; yes, I'm lonely and alone."

"Okay, we're all set here. Let's get you home."

Sanda hovered Rachel down the hall to her room, helped her into a sleep tunic, and ordered some concoction from the brewer. "Drink this, then I'll help you get into bed. And Rachel, I do understand more than you realize."

The warm, chunky liquid tasted bitter on Rachel's tongue. "Do you? You understand what, exactly? Are you talking about loneliness? How could you ever be lonely? You work eighteen hours a day with specific goals in mind and follow a pre-determined job description. You know who you are and what you're supposed to be doing. You don't have time to be lonely."

"Sometimes the busiest people are, in fact, quite lonely."

The drink was too strong for Rachel and she set the rest on the nightstand. Maybe she was too tired and cranky to look beyond herself and her own problems. A touch of pain in Sanda's voice and a far-off look in her eyes made Rachel feel ashamed. She took a deep breath and blew it out slowly.

"What are you saying? Are you talking about yourself? Are you lonely?"

"I . . . It's like you said. I'm too busy to be lonely, but sometimes I wonder what life would be like if I had made different choices."

Rachel was about to press Sanda on what she meant by choices, when the room chimed, "Delivery for Rachel McRae."

"Stay in bed. I'll see what it is." Sanda crossed the room in ten paces and opened the mail chute. She returned with a small paper box the size of a java mug and handed it to Rachel.

"What's this?"

"Looks like a hologram. Go ahead, open it."

The box was seamless: nothing written on it, nothing taped or tied to it. Rachel examined the package closely, turning it over several times in her hand. "How?"

"Probably activated by voice recognition. Just say, open."

"I wonder who it's from."

"At this rate, we may never know."

"Sorry. Open."

The box unfolded in her hand. Sparkles of colored light, like tiny fire flies, glittered from the center outward, revealing a holographic glass vase filled with a bouquet of yellow centered, pink edged roses. A strong, spicy-sweet fragrance filled the air. "Oh, it's beautiful! Where'd this come from? Is there a note or something, somewhere?"

"If I may?" Sanda took the hologram and placed it on Rachel's nightstand. "I don't see who it's from, but it is lovely. It will last longer if you close it. I'll turn down your lights if you like and you can get some sleep. I'll see you tomorrow."

"Tomorrow. Yes. Thank you for everything, Sanda. Goodnight."

As soon as the door closed behind Sanda, Rachel curled into a ball in her bed-cubby and turned to face the night table. "Open," she whispered. Once again, the sparkles of light swirled and then coalesced until they formed the fragrant bouquet. The scent reminded her of something. Something from long ago. She stayed focused on the roses, trying to piece together bits of memory, knowing its message was tucked away, like a secret, sailing from cloud to cloud, just out of her reach. As she stared at the holo-card, her eyelids grew heavy until they refused to stay open any longer. Sleep snatched at her thoughts, pulling her mind deeper into the darkness.

* * *

Thirty-three hours passed before Rachel stirred. She rolled her tongue around her mouth, testing for any moisture. Dry, crusty particles stuck in the inner corners of her eyes and in her nose, like barnacles on a pier. She dug the chunks out with the tips of her fingers and tried to focus. The room was dark except for one tiny spot; something glowed faintly from the table next to her bed. For one moment, she wondered if she could remain in this state: dreamless and inert. Forever. Where was she? Was this the same room she had lived in for the past eight months, the room in a foreign place on a foreign planet, in a time she didn't belong?

Rachel pushed herself to sitting, her head protesting the change in elevation. The last few days had seemed to last years. Maybe she'd caught up to these people in age while she slept. It felt like she was a hundred and fifty.

"Soft lighting," she croaked, and filtered light immediately suffused the room. Yep, she was still in her tiny room, on a compound, on planet Goliath. Pain from her ankle shocked her completely awake when she attempted to stand and threw her off balance. She grabbed for the corner of the night-table to steady herself, knocking it over in the process. The beautiful holo-card sitting on top fell to the floor. The roses glittered in one last gasp, and then sputtered out petal by petal.

"No. Oh, please, no." Rachel tried to scoop up the box and close it in time to save some of the magic, but she was too late. She slumped back on the bed cradling the empty container between her palms with tears in her eyes. A sob tore from her throat at the same time the door chimed announcing the arrival of CPO Schaefer.

"Allow entrance?"

What? Who? What is he doing here? She ran quick fingers through her hair, smoothed her rumpled tunic, and wiped her eyes.

"Yes. Come in. Oh, sorry. Allow entrance."

The door opened, and Rachel caught a glimpse of Ben squeezing the bridge of his nose between his thumb and fore finger as if he had a headache or was trying to keep from getting one.

"I hope you don't mind me stopping by unannounced. How are you feeling?" Ben clasped his hands behind his back. "How is the ankle? Healing well, I hope."

Rachel looked down at her injured leg and back up at him, meeting his gaze. "Was this from—did you send me this?" She held the remnants of the holo-card out to him.

Ben crossed the room in three steps, and gently took the

broken card from her. "Yes, Rachel. I wanted to tell you how sorry I am that I put you in harm's way. And to tell you ... well, to tell you how relieved I am that you're safe and back here where I can keep a better eye on you. If you'll let me, that is."

His touch sent hot shivers up her spine, erasing the soul-tired exhaustion she had felt only a moment before. A quick gasp escaped her as all the oxygen seemed to be sucked out of the room, and out of her lungs. Her hands were clammy in his and she pulled them away quickly, wiped them on her thighs, and clenched them together in her lap. Ben flinched. His eyes widened as he looked at her. "I can tell you are still upset with me. I better go."

Rachel released her breath. "I'm not upset with you. I'm upset that I look like hell right now. I do love, or did, the card, and you have nothing to be sorry for."

Ben turned back toward her. "I'm glad you liked it. I want you to know that I wanted—I should— have been there for you, with Imitar and Thorian. Let me make it up to you. If you feel well enough, I'd like to invite you to dinner. Will you join me at my apartment?"

"You don't have to do this—"

"It's not an order. I want to cook for you. I promise it will be good. Please say you'll come."

Rachel bit at the nail bed on her thumb. "I don't know . . ."

Thoughts bounced back and forth through Rachel's mind, like ping-pong balls. Should she go? What was the point? He did send her the holo-card, surely that meant something. He probably only felt sorry for her. *But those eyes. And what does he mean he'll cook for me? Don't you just push a button and food appears?*

"Are you worried about my culinary skills?"

"I'm sure they're better than mine."

"Good. I'll see you then, at nineteen-hundred tomorrow evening." He flashed a smile, making both dimples stand out.

CHAPTER 43

Compound
Saturday, 1900 hours
Zoleta's quarters

IMITAR PACED outside Zoleta's apartment. So many questions had weighed on his mind before the cave-in ever occurred. He had feelings for Zoleta, but those feelings were starting to change. Or maybe he was just getting tired of guessing how she felt about him. When she and Rachel were trapped in the cave, nothing mattered but saving their lives. They were safe, but where did he stand now?

What am I doing here? What does she want from me?

"Enter, Imitar Dubashi," the room announced. Zoleta stood with her arms crossed. "We've been back from that cosmos-forsaken cave for over a day and you haven't come in to work or over to see me. I heard you did check in on Rachel though."

"Is that why you ordered me over here, so you could ask me about Rachel? I've been resting, Zoleta. I'm exhausted, and you are too, but you just won't admit it."

"Hmph. First, I didn't order you to come here. And second,

yes, I'm tired. We spent twelve hours chugging along in that heap-of-rust with Thorian, the Barbarian."

"That barbarian saved your ass and you never even thanked him, so if you don't need anything else, I'll see you at work tomorrow."

"No, wait." She grabbed his arm. "I wanted to see you. I know it was you who figured out how to get to us, to me and Rachel. You are very good at what you do—"

"I need to go."

"I'd like to talk."

"Talk?"

"I'm sorry, Imitar. Please, come in and sit for a while. I could use the company."

"Use?"

"Okay. I need company. I need you. I spent days trapped—how many meters below ground? With only the 'Red Dwarf' from the Outer Limits to talk to. Rachel is not my idea of a stimulating conversationalist, nor did she contribute to figuring out a way to survive."

"I'm sure she's aware that she's alive, thanks to you. I'm tired. It's been a long—however many days. It's better if I just go."

"I think it's better if you stay. Ten minutes, that's all. I'll jump in the blower. You can fix us a frutini."

It didn't seem to be a request. Zoleta hustled off to the bathroom before he had a chance to reply. *I'll wait, but I'm not fixing any drinks.* He tipped back in the anti-gravity chair just to let his head quit throbbing . . .

In his dream, the planet was shaking violently, and tree branches were slapping against his arm. He woke to Zoleta calling his name and shaking his shoulder.

"Hmm? What?" She stood in front of him wearing a wispy, see-through sleeping tunic, her hands fisted on her hips.

"Imitar? Hello. Goliath to Imitar."

"Okay. I'm awake. Can I go now?"

"Do you know if Rachel and Ben knew each other back on earth? Do you know if he somehow managed to bring her here?"

Imitar rubbed his eyes and yawned. "How would I know? Craters, Zo, why aren't you in bed? Shut that genius brain of yours off for once and get some rest. I'm going home."

"But she, Rachel, knew things. She told me things. You were right though, she doesn't have any plans to take over Goliath. There's something else going on. Don't you think it's strange that she just happens to show up here when we find out some of us might die without her ever-so-vital genetic code?"

"What are you talking about? Rachel hasn't been able to remember anything. What happened in the cave? Did something trigger her memory?" Imitar paused; a scowl crept across his brow. "What did you do to her? What did you give her, Zoleta?"

"I did what anyone would have done. Her ankle was smashed. She was in a lot of pain."

"And you just happened to have some vycotlin in your bag, didn't you?"

"It's an analgesic."

"Come on Zo. It's a lot more than that."

"I had to give her something. She was ready to give up. Wanted me to let her die. And then where would all of us be?"

"And she told you things that you believe now?"

"She couldn't fabricate under the influence of the drug—medicine. Too bad I only had a little bit with me. Rachel said she took care of Ben, like he had some terrible injury, but she couldn't remember what it was exactly. She was a physician of some sort."

"And why does any of this matter?"

"I'm not sure yet."

Imitar pulled himself up out of the chair and gave Zoleta a sad look. "You didn't even notice."

Zoleta scanned him quickly from head to toe. "Notice what?"

"Never mind. Good night, Zoleta." He walked out the door.

* * *

Zoleta was right, he thought, there was something between the CPO and Rachel, if not from a long time ago, certainly a connection existed now. Even Z-mahn had sensed it. Ben seemed to care about her and yet he made such poor choices. But then again, Imitar wasn't exactly the brightest star in the universe when it came to showing he cared about Zoleta. Why had he felt it so important that she notice he had shaved off his whiskers? Maybe because he always noticed every little thing she changed and how she changed it.

CHAPTER 44

CPO Schaefer's apartment
Saturday
1900 hours

IT WAS SATURDAY NIGHT, not that it made any difference from any other night of the week on Goliath. Everyone worked continually and took their respite whenever they got the chance. The higher up in seniority, the less free time was available. Ben had already taken a so-called vacation, venturing out to the caves in the upper northeast quadrant, which turned out to be a disaster. Tonight would be different. It was important that everything was just right.

He hadn't slept more than a few hours a night since the cave-in. Now that Rachel was back and under his protection he should have been able to relax. But he needed her once again. Goliath needed her, maybe even mankind; all needed her unadulterated DNA. It was up to him to ask her to endure the torture and possibly sacrifice her life, one more time. How could he do this? He wasn't sure he had the strength.

A heavy lump in his stomach pressed itself clear up into his throat. Tonight he would see her and that's all he wanted to think about.

He prepared the salad, using the freshest greens he could get from the garden staff and made up his own dressing from mashed ginger root soaked in dilvinegar. The potato-yams were baking in the hot box while the steaks soaked in marinade in a pan on the counter. It had been a long time since Ben had had real beef. He hoped he could still cook it to perfection. It had cost a fortune to have the meat sent from earth and he didn't want to ruin it. Over the years he had also commissioned the Z-Mahn to experiment making different wines for his personal cellar. A year before Rachel's arrival he explained to Z-mahn what he wanted, and the Z-mahn bottled a red as close to Ben's specifications as possible. The label: a yellow rose with pinkish-tinged petals.

The dining room table in Ben's apartment was big enough for four people, although he never had time for guest and usually ate standing at the counter. Tonight, he would sit next to Rachel. The overhead lights were dimmed as he lit three tapered candles in the center of the table. The small flames cast a comfortable glow over the room.

"This is a safety precaution. Detection of possible fire hazard. Extinguish flames advised. Repeat; fire hazard detected. Extinguish flames."

"Damn. Room—override precaution. Safety is maintained. Return to 'run program' at twenty-three hundred hours."

"Order received. Program override. Delayed until twenty-three hundred hours. Current time: nineteen-eleven hours. Arrival: Rachel Allison McRae. Allow entrance?"

She's here. Ben glanced around the room. Everything was in place. The room, lit with soft candlelight and background music, was warm and inviting. "Affirmative."

The door opened and Rachel stood before him, her thick, red hair cascading over her shoulders. Her pale complexion accentuated the soft-pink of her full lips. Cold fingers wrapped around his heart when he saw the dark circles that hung below her beautiful green eyes.

"Please come in," Ben said as he stepped to the side and watched her enter the room, keeping his hands clasped firmly behind his back.

"I hope I'm not late. You'd think I could find my way—wow, your place is really nice. It's so big." Rachel's eyes darted around the room, then widened as they settled on the dining table set with real china, silverware, and candles as the centerpiece. Soft music suffused the room as she ran her finger over the amber-colored linen napkin. "This is amazing, and it smells wonderful in here. Is this how you always have your meals? I never see you at the DC. I can see why."

"May I pour you a glass of wine?"

"Sorry, am I babbling? Wine? Really? You know, I don't think so."

Ben raised his eyebrows, "No?"

She motioned toward the table and the rest of the room. "Something tells me I'd better not."

"Rachel, I want everything to be special for you tonight. To make up for your terrible ordeal."

Perhaps he shouldn't have mentioned it. A shadow crossed her features, making the edges of his heart tighten.

"I have had quite the experiences, haven't I? I have to admit . . . there've been times when I was ready to give up, but, you know, I'm a lot stronger than I thought." Ben held the chair out for her. "I'm sorry. I don't mean to be so serious. Everything is lovely. I think I would like that glass of wine, if the offer still stands."

It had been a long time since he had opened a bottle of wine, but the cork came out easily. He filled the long-stemmed crystal glasses. Rachel took a tentative sip and closed her eyes.

"Well?"

"Incredible. I already feel warm and tingly all over."

"Then by all means, drink up. Wait a sec. Maybe we should have a toast? To you, Rachel. For your courage to live for today, to keep an open mind, and to always know that . . . people care about you."

"Well, I'm not sure about all of that, but I am sure, this is delicious. And thank you." She laughed and took another sip. "It tastes—wait a minute—you poured this from a bottle? It didn't come out of the beverage unit? Is there a vineyard hidden somewhere on Goliath?"

"Unfortunately, no, but the Z-Mahn enjoys a challenge." Ben took a sip and let the flavor remind him of a time long ago. "And I must say, this is exactly what I ordered."

"What a beautiful label." Rachel turned the front of the bottle toward her. "The Z-Mahn is quite an artist too," she said. She gave Ben a coy smile, "The rose looks just like the hologram card you gave me. Hmm, the bottle is dated 1994—ancient. How did it not go bad? Ha ha."

"That tiny print on the label actually says, "in memory of the year 1994". But you're right, now that it's opened it will go bad, so it's better if we drink it all tonight."

He topped off her glass, placed a salad in front of her and one at his chair. The smell of warm, fresh bread wafted from the basket in the middle of the table between them.

"May I?"

"By all means, enjoy it while it's warm."

Rachel reached beneath the cloth covering the bread basket and pulled out a thick slice. She held it to her nose and breathed in. "This is absolute heaven."

They finished their salads, the bread, and their wine. "I'll start the meat." As he turned to retrieve the steaks marinating on the counter, he stopped and turned back toward her. After all the time between them, Rachel was finally here. How long had he dreamed of this? Of being with her? Of taking care of her. There had been a time when she had taken care of him, when he had no one. Now the roles were reversed, but he wanted it to be more. He wanted all of her. He wanted her to love him like he had loved her, for so long, for so many years.

"You're staring at me."

Ben swallowed the lump in his throat. "It's because you're so damn beautiful."

Rachel smiled. Her cheeks were a rosy pink and she reached a hand up to touch one as if her skin had raised a couple of degrees in temperature. "This is either very strong wine, or you had a cocktail before I got here."

He grinned and put the meat on the cook-range.

* * *

"Ready for your steak?"

The meal took him back to another place and time when he had cooked for her in his apartment back in Michigan. Would the flavors or delicious smells jar any of Rachel's memories? She finished off her yamato with another glob of butter, and then closed her eyes as she put the last morsel of succulent beef in her mouth.

"I can't eat another bite. Everything was so good, I could cry."

He'd always liked that about her; no prissy piece of cucumber and glass of water for her. She could eat and enjoyed eating. "We can wait awhile before dessert. Chocolate mousse."

"Oh, my God. You're killing me. Everyone keeps telling me how heavy I am. How will I ever keep my girlish figure at this rate?"

"Your figure—I better get these dishes in the autoclean." Rachel stood to help, but Ben waved her to stay put. "No, you sit. Enjoy the rest of your wine."

"But you did all the cooking. The least I can do is help clear the table." He reached for the bread basket at the same time she did, brushing his hand over the top of hers. They both stopped and slowly turned toward each other as he brought her hand toward his lips and kissed it gently along the ridge of her knuckles. "You know," Rachel stammered, "I don't think I'll be much of a help after all. My legs feel like they're made of goosh all of a sudden."

"Goosh?"

"Um. Yes. It's a technical, no, a medical term."

"Whatever it is, it sounds like I'd better hold on to you, so you don't fall and hurt yourself."

Ben took Rachel's arms and placed them up around his neck, then put his arms around her waist. She looked at him and smiled.

"Better?" he asked.

"Yes, but now I seem to be having trouble breathing."

"I can fix that too."

He brushed his lips across hers and felt her body shudder. He held her from him, questioning. She pulled him back for more, her need adding to his desire. Years of longing for her ached from his very core.

Rachel made a soft sound, like a purr, in her throat. "Now who's shaking all over?"

They wrapped their arms around each other. Each kiss grew harder and longer, the hunger rising with every breath, promising more. So much more.

"God, Rachel. I think my lips are melting."

"Yes. Well, Mr. CPO, you've certainly melted more than my lips. I think I need to take a cold shower."

"Then come with me."

"Hmm, this sounds ominous?"

Ben took her by the hand and led her down the hallway. On the right, an open door revealed a small room with an ancient teakwood desk and large leather chair. Light glinted off the frame of a lone picture on top of the desk.

"Wow. Look at this room. Is this your office?" Rachel stepped inside. "What's the picture of? Oh, sorry. Never mind. It's really none of my business."

Part of Ben wanted her to remember, but if she did, what else would be unveiled? He cleared his throat, "You are more than welcome to go ahead and take a look."

Rachel crossed the room and picked up the picture. "Is this you with a cute little puppy? A chocolate lab, right? I wonder if I had a puppy like this once. She looks familiar. Maybe not. And you, Ben, so young and handsome. What are you here, late twenties, early thirties maybe? But why do you look kind of heart-broken with such an adorable little pup sitting in your lap? What's her name? I'm assuming it's a she for some reason."

Ben gently took the photo from her hand and placed it back on the desk. "I bought her for a good friend, but the friend wasn't able to keep her. She was a good dog. She died many years ago." He guided Rachel out the door, past his workout room, and entered his bedroom.

Rachel gasped. A reddish-gold bedspread covered the queen-sized bed in the middle of the room. Its cherry-wood headboard matched the cabinets that ran from floor to ceiling against one wall.

"This room is gorgeous," she sighed. "Your whole place is amazing, so different from the other apartments. Very homey. Or is it just your bachelor pad for enticing women?"

Ben pulled her into his arms. "Does it work? Are you enticed?" Instead of waiting for an answer he tipped her chin up to him and kissed her long and hard. He fought with himself to slow down and give her time, when all he wanted was to make her his in every way. He cleared his throat, "Oh, that's right, I'm supposed to be giving you the tour. The bathroom. The bathroom is over here."

"What's the matter, Ben? You seem a little out of breath. Oh, my gosh, what's this? Why do you have two blower-tubes?"

"One's a shower."

"What do you mean a shower? Like with real water?" Rachel's eyes grew wide.

"Yes. With good, old-fashioned water."

"You have no idea how much I'd give—never mind." Color rose in her cheeks.

"It's quite all right. I want you to partake. My shower is your shower."

Rachel looked from Ben to the shower and back again. He loved the sexy smile forming at the corners of her mouth. Those lips he so wanted to kiss again.

"But I didn't bring a clean change of clothes."

"You can get a new outfit . . . in the morning."

"Oh, really?"

"Go ahead. Hop in. Would you like me to set the temperature for you?"

She shook her head, turned the knob on the left, and let the warm water run through her outstretched fingers. "You don't mind?"

Before he could answer, she had pulled her tunic over her head, shimmied out of her undergarments, and stepped in.

A huge smile plastered itself across Ben's face as he leaned casually against the wall and drank in her body. "As long as you don't mind me standing here admiring the view."

She laughed and let the water soak her face, run through her hair and over her breasts. "This is heaven. I feel like . . . like humanity does exist. Like I exist." After a few more turns under the faucet, she looked out at him. "Your mouth is still hanging open, you know."

"Hmm."

"I'm sorry. I'm not thinking. I'm using up all your water

supply. Shouldn't we be careful about conserving? Maybe we should share. You could join me."

"I doubt if you have the water cold enough to keep me thinking straight. Believe me, there's nothing I would love more than to hop in there with you, but I can't. Well, I can, but I shouldn't." He pulled away from the wall and looked up at the ceiling. "Rachel, I need to tell you something, before we go too far. There's something you need to know."

"You mean you need to tell me that you're married? Or have a life-mate, or whatever you call it? I already know."

Ben shook his head. "There's—"

"I don't care about that. All I need right now is for you to hold me. Please, Ben. I want you to hold me."

She didn't have to ask twice. He stripped down, closed the shower door behind him and stood facing her, all rational thoughts gone. Rachel stepped toward him and he took her in his arms as the water sprayed over them, washing away the rest of the world, leaving only the two of them and their need for each other.

Her head nestled against his chest, the weight of it feeling like a missing part of him was finally back where it belonged. He pushed her wet hair back from her forehead and tipped her mouth up to meet his kiss. The soft feel of her wet skin was almost more than he could stand. He ran his hands over her entire body, groaning as if in pain. He felt her shiver in the warm water, and then push her body tighter into his.

CHAPTER 45

CPO Schaefer's bedroom
Sunday
Early morning

RACHEL REACHED over her head in a deep stretch and untangled her bare legs from the silky sheets. The red-gold bedspread lay in a crumpled heap on the floor. Ben's breathing was soft against her cheek; his head resting partially on her pillow, a peaceful look on his sleeping face. It was hard to resist the temptation to smooth the hair from his forehead and kiss him gently. She moved so as not to wake him and tiptoed to the bathroom to splash water on her face. Her tunic from the night before hung on a peg by the door and she slipped it on, all the time wishing she could climb back in the shower and have that luscious water run over her body again. One last peek at Ben and she made her way down the hall.

As she passed by Ben's office door, the picture on his desk caught her eye. She entered the room, picked it up and examined it. There was something so familiar about the lab puppy. She started to set the photo down when a name popped into her head. "Molly Brown, "she said. "You're Little Molly Brown."

A clicking noise startled her and she turned to see a drawer slide open from the cabinet behind the desk. It wasn't like that when she came in, she was sure, so she made her way around the desk and bent to push it closed. Something pink lay inside.

She hadn't meant to snoop, but for one silly moment anger flushed through her body when she scrutinized the neatly folded pink sweatshirt. Why would Ben have this? And who did it belong to? A small, blue-velvet box peeked out from beside the sweatshirt; just the right size and shape for a piece of jewelry. Like, a ring? She glanced around the room. She was alone; Ben was still sleeping. The box felt light in her palm. It was none of her business what mementos Ben might save from his conquests, but who was to know if she peeked? No, it wouldn't be right, she told herself, but when it came down to it, she couldn't seem to help herself and tugged the lid open. Inside, a breathtaking heart-shaped silver pendant nestled in the velvet lining. It was beautiful and delicate. Rachel felt like a criminal just looking at it. In the center of the heart, tiny diamonds glittered in the pattern of a capital 'R'. She closed her eyes and clutched the necklace to her breast.

The room tilted beneath her feet. Her head swam with bits of memories spinning toward a center like a whirlpool sucking everything downward. Coldness seeped through her bones. She was being pulled under, and there was nothing she could do but try to swim at an angle and hope to surface with some fragment of her past.

And then, there she was, a hundred years in the past, tears streaming down her face as she held the locket out to him through the car window. He refused to accept it, to take it back and shook his head, pleading with her to reconsider. She tried again, but he wouldn't take it, and the necklace fell from her outstretched hand into the snow at his feet. She put the car in drive and glanced in the rearview mirror, pain and loss shredding her broken heart. He stood, frozen, as still as an ice sculpture, disbelief etched in his grief-stricken eyes as she sped away into the storm.

Ben groaned from the bedroom, snapping Rachel back to the present. She dropped the necklace into the box and placed it beside the sweatshirt, the way she had found it. The drawer clicked shut as she hurried out of CPO Schaefer's apartment.

Rachel made her way back to her dwelling and checked the time: zero-four-thirty. The compound would be rousing soon; the bubble shades would lock in DR, dawn-replication, within the next hour.

The night with Ben had been incredible, but now what? Things were likely to be awkward in the morning. Where would she go if things didn't work out? It wasn't like she could move out of town. Maybe it was all a bad mistake. But it had seemed so right at the time. She had felt so normal in his arms, so at home. And then there was the necklace.

A tiny green light blinked above her counter. "Now what the heck does that mean? I haven't seen that before."

"Not enough input. Unable to process. Please repeat question."

Talk about feeling like you couldn't say anything out loud without being accosted. This would teach her not to talk to herself. Some robotic room, elevator, or vehicle always replied. Maybe she could find out if there was a way to turn it off, or at least tweak the program to only answer direct questions. Imitar would know.

"Room? What does the green blinking light over the counter mean?"

"Mail has been delivered to your inbox. Do you accept?"

"My inbox?" Rachel looked around the room, wondering what and where. Then she remembered Sanda had gotten her last piece of mail for her—the rose from Ben. "What is it?"

"Info-strand. Do you accept?"

"I guess so." Rachel waited. Nothing happened. "Yes, I accept."

A small glass tube the size of her little finger appeared in the four by four-centimeter window below the blinking light. The window slid open revealing a compartment she had never noticed before. As soon as she picked up the tube, the window slid shut, and the green light turned off.

Rachel held the empty-looking tube up to the light. Thin, hair-like strands of something like shiny metal wound themselves through the center of the tiny container.

"Room," she asked, "What is this mail and how do I read it?"

A soft whirring sound skittered around the room as if it were thinking, and then responded, "From archives. Suggest library. ROM. Code, Archives 22.01.94NPMIOBit. Fourth level, basement. Access encrypted within mail."

"Great. That helps a whole lot. Room, who sent this?"

"Undisclosed sender."

CHAPTER 46

Command Center
Sunday
0730 hours

FOURTH LEVEL, basement, that's what the room had told her. She would have asked Sanda, or Imitar, how to "read" her mail, but they were probably busy at work, so she made her way down the hall. As she passed by the doors to medical on her way to the elevator, Sanda stepped out of the tube, holding a rack of blood samples.

"There you are, Rachel. Are you all right? Do you have any questions or need more time to think it over before you give us your answer?"

Rachel's forehead scrunched into a frown as she tried to recall schedules, projects, or work she might have overlooked, but nothing that Sanda just said made any sense. "I'm sorry. My answer? I don't think I've heard the question. I have no idea what you're talking about. Is there something I'm forgetting to do? I didn't realize I was missing anything. Unless it's on this info-mail thingy that I just got. I haven't had the chance to read it yet."

The doctor's shoulders slumped; she exhaled with a pained expression. "Didn't Ben, CPO Schaefer go over things with you last night?"

Rachel's face felt hot with the memory of making love with Ben. A warm smile crept from the back of her mind and threatened to seep across her lips. "We didn't really do all that much talking."

Sanda frowned and rubbed her forehead as if she could make whatever was bothering her disappear. "He didn't tell you?"

"Tell me what?"

"We need to go see the CPO. In his office. Now."

"But I was just on my way downstairs to—"

"Rachel, this is critical, and it concerns you."

Now what? Things always seemed to be at Defcon 2 at the compound. What was the problem this time? Rachel certainly didn't want to see Ben right this minute. It would be better to go at a slower pace, kind of feel her way around how he'd react to seeing her after such an intimate night. Would he act as if nothing happened, all business, or did he really care about her? And what about her discovery? The tone of Sanda's voice finally punctured through Rachel's romantic dilemma.

"You're serious? We have to go now?"

"Don't move. I'll put these blood samples away. Back in two nano-seconds."

For the first time, Rachel noticed Sanda had on her lab coat and held a twelve by twelve rack of test tubes. What time did she get to work this morning? And what was so important it brought her in so early? A tightness in Rachel's chest seemed to spread to every muscle in her body. What was critical, and what did it have to do with her? She tried to tell herself that maybe Sanda was over-tired. One thing for sure, Rachel would find out soon enough.

The two women entered the Command Center and found

Zoleta working on vids. The screen blinked off as Zoleta turned to them, "If you're looking for CPO Schaefer, he hasn't come in yet this morning."

"Where is he? Did he take the land-glider somewhere?" Sanda asked.

"How should I know? I wasn't with him last night." Zoleta stared at Rachel. "Maybe he's exhausted for some reason and still asleep."

"That's ridiculous. In all the years I've worked with Ben, he's never slept more than four hours a night."

Rachel dug the toe of her boot into the floor and bit back a smile that threatened to give her away. Part of her said to go ahead and flaunt it in Zoleta's face, but that wasn't really Rachel's style. Besides, she wasn't sure what Zoleta might be thinking. Better to act like no-big-deal.

The awkward moment vanished as Ben swept through the doorway. He looked around the room, his eyes lingering on Rachel. "Good morning," he said, followed by a slight pause, "Everyone."

"CPO Schaefer, did you, or did you not, bring Rachel up to date on the failure of the vaccine?"

Failure? The floor dropped out from beneath Rachel's feet. She grabbed the corner of the desk for support. Ben's glare flew from Rachel's face to Sanda's, turning from romantic to murderous in a flash.

A chill fell across the room.

"What do you mean?" Rachel asked in a whisper. "I thought everything was fine. Everyone was responding. Immune function was restored." She grabbed Sanda by the arm. "What's happened? Tell me."

"Do you want to tell her, or shall I?" Sanda spat the words at Ben, who stood rigid, nostrils flared, jaw tightly locked.

Rachel looked at Ben for an explanation. A minute slump in his posture made her uneasy. A bead of sweat trickled down his temple but he made no move to wipe it. The lingering gaze from when he first entered the room, that sent warm shivers up her spine, disappeared and now he avoided eye contact with her altogether. She scanned the room; Zoleta wasn't having any trouble looking at her. Zoleta's eyebrows rose in a 'this should be interesting' expression. Rachel turned back to Sanda, whose face was a volatile mix of anger with a touch of sympathy around the edges.

"Rachel," Sanda said. "Two new patients were admitted to Medical since you've been gone. Both exhibit the same respiratory symptoms, probably from the same virus that infected the others, and these workers have had the vaccine. Their bodies are rejecting the transplanted DNA. They're failing to replicate and produce functioning T cells."

A tremor ran through Rachel's body. "No." She closed her eyes, trying to wish away what she had just heard. "There must be something we can do. Stop the rejection somehow? This is supposed to be an advanced society; surely you have a way to fix this. You can't give up, Sanda." A horrible thought slithered its way from the outer edges to the forefront of her brain. She turned to Ben, "Did you know about this? Last night? Of course you did. Why didn't you tell me?"

A snort came from the back of the room. Zoleta cleared her throat and turned back to her work.

Ben took a deep breath. "Rachel, you'd been through a lot and I wanted you to have a special evening without anything to worry or be upset about."

Tears formed in the corners of her eyes, and her chin trembled. "Well I am upset. All we went through and people are still going to die. That's what you're saying, isn't it? And who are you to decide for me whether I should be upset or worried. You might be the CPO or whatever you're called, but you don't own me. You don't have the authority to make decisions for me on how I should or shouldn't feel."

"There might still be a way to make the vaccine work," Sanda broke through. "I would like to try and recombine the genes before delivery with an added enzyme to stop the formation of antibodies. The host should then be able to cycle through and form its own immunities."

"Then why are we standing here talking about this? I need to get out of here. Sanda, I can go to the lab and work on the remaining vaccine right now."

No one moved. Rachel looked from Ben, to Sanda, and to Zoleta who shrugged and said, "Don't look at me, I was with you in the cave, remember?"

A tight feeling clenched in Rachel's stomach and moved up into her chest. "There isn't any more vaccine is there?"

Sanda shook her head. "Not enough to work with."

"Are you asking me to go through the splicing again?" Rachel's mind whirled, then ignited into a ball of fury. She turned to Ben. "And you—you were supposed to ask me last night, weren't you? Get me all loosened up. Wine and dine me. Putty in your hands. You used me, Ben. What happened? Did you get so carried away with the acting job, you happened to forget to mention there was another opportunity for me to die?

"No, Rachel. I—"

"I'm not going through that again until I get some of my questions answered about who I am and where I came from. And if you won't help me, I'll do it on my own." She flashed the info tube she still held at him. "I'll be in the library. But then I don't really need to tell you that, do I? You seem to know where I am at all times."

Ben stepped in front of Rachel, blocking her exit. "Where did you get that? Who gave it to you?" As he reached toward her, she swiveled away from him, the information capsule tight in her grip. "Don't touch me. *You* don't know where this came from?" She said with a sneer. "What? The almighty CPO is clueless? How does that feel? Not much fun? Welcome to my life."

She stomped past him and out the door, wishing it was solid so she could give it a good, hard slam. Tears streamed down her face as she entered the elevator tube. Twice the elevator asked which floor before she could respond. A hiccup caught in her throat. How could these tiny strands tell her anything?

"Library floor."

CHAPTER 47

Command Center
Sunday
0800 hours

THINGS WERE CERTAINLY GETTING INTERESTING, Zoleta thought, as she watched Rachel storm out of Command Center. What was on those strands, and how was the Red Dwarf going to access the information? She didn't seem to be all that bright. Unless someone—

Before Zoleta finished her thought, Ben slammed his fist on the console. She flinched but kept herself from jumping. Instead she took a relaxed breath, "You seem a nano-bit angry, CPO Schaefer. Is there a problem?"

Ben turned to her, his eyes deadly. She had never seen him this crazed, like a trapped animal, furious there was no escape, prepared to fight to the death.

"Zoleta," he said, ice hanging off each syllable, "What have you done? I would have told her. I was the one who needed to tell her."

The crazed look was gone, replaced by a more terrifying determination locked on his face.

Zoleta snorted, "What makes you think—"

"Silence!"

She stopped. A small pebble of disbelief wrapped in anger began to grow in her mind. Memories of her past failures, dismissal by her brother and father, added to the layer, compacting it, making it harder to break apart. She struggled to keep from screaming the truth at Ben—she, she was the one who should be in command of this planet. She was the one most capable of ruling. How dare he silence her?

He looked at her with hatred in his eyes, but she held her controlled posture, standing at full height, looking down at him, her arms crossed.

"Lieutenant General, you are dismissed from duty. From this compound. Effective immediately. You are to be on the next spaceship back to Earth. That gives you slightly less than five months to prepare. You are to finish up all reports. I expect your resignation by the end of today. Is that clear?"

"I don't think it's quite clear to you. We'll just see who remains here, in command, Ben Schaefer."

"That is insubordination, Lieutenant. Don't push me, or you will never find another post."

Zoleta pressed her lips together. How could she have ever thought this man capable of running a planet? He was only in charge because of seniority. She had as many degrees as he did. In only two areas of study did he surpass her and hold a Level XII degree. But that was only because he had been around so much longer. He was old. Ancient. From the beginning of the Rejuvenation Period. Too old to command.

Dismissed? He thinks he can get rid of me? I won't be the one returning to Earth—ever. There must be some black-hole-shattering information on that info-tube. Big mistake, CPO Schaefer. You have no idea.

CHAPTER 48

Sub-Level IV
Sunday
0815 hours

FOUR LEVELS BELOW COMMAND CENTER, Rachel exited the elevator tube and turned down the same hallway where Ben had her follow him during the asteroid shower. It seemed forever ago.

Lights blinked on in front of her, illuminating her passageway until she came to the door marked IG-LIB. What if she couldn't figure out how this info-tube worked? What if she didn't even get the chance? Maybe Ben had already locked her out of the library. But why would he do that? What was it that had made him so furious? She raised her eyes to the scanner and the door opened.

Vague bits of memory from childhood darted through her mind. She expected a musty smell, or at least hoped for a comforting odor of leather-bound books. Instead, the same recycled air of the underground compound permeated her nostrils, and a metal taste coated her tongue. This room couldn't look anything like the libraries of her past.

The room was smaller than her living quarters, barely the size of the decontamination port in sickbay. Rows of glass drawers lined three of the four walls from floor to ceiling. A small padded stool was tucked under a round table which took up the center of the room.

There weren't any knobs that she could see, but as she reached for a drawer it opened automatically and closed as she pulled her hand away. The light reflected off the glass, twinkling like the solar panels surrounding the compound's garden.

"Where are the books?" she muttered as she passed her hand over a few drawers again, watching the effect. She paused in mid wave. A fragment of a memory skipped across her brain like a stone across a lake. Before she could grasp it, it plunked below the surface of her mind, piling up with other unreachable memories in a murky darkness.

What was it she wanted to remember but couldn't? Rachel shook off the uneasy feeling and pushed the hair from her clammy forehead. A green button blinked from the front of a toaster-size metal box in the center of the table. She pushed it.

"Welcome to Planet Goliath's Library Archives." Rachel jumped. The elderly female voice continued, "You may access inter-universal information from this location. Simply voice your request and the server will display the appropriate section. Select the reference stick and place it in the holo-reader. You may sort by planet, event, date, or subject matter."

She should be used to rooms talking by now, but still she hesitated. "Um. Room? I already have this reference stick. I think." At least it looked about the same size and shape as the other tubes she could see in the glass drawers.

"Be seated. Place the reference stick in the holo-reader. The information will display automatically."

She pulled the stool from beneath the table and sat. There wasn't any place to put the glass tube that she could see. She checked the sides of the box and felt along the top. Her fingers passed across a small indentation, releasing a beam of light from the center of the box. Two thin metal posts with clamps on the ends rose from the sides of the box, over the slit of light. She clutched the info-tube in her hand, wondering how this was going to work.

"Room? Are there any more directions on how to use the holo-reader? Can you show me an example?"

A drawer to the right of Rachel slid open. A tube in the front stuck out slightly above the others making it the obvious choice. "Take the holo-stick and place it between the holders."

The glass tube was delicate in her fingers. She held it up to the light, amazed by the twisted hair strands like the ones in her container. The tapered ends of the tube fit perfectly into the eyelets of the posts. As soon as she let go, the tube began to spin in the holder. The beam of light emanated from the box up through the filaments, forming a ghost-like hologram in front of her. The image sharpened. An article titled: Safety Precautions Using the Exothermic Template dated 14.12.2118, displayed in front of her.

"Got it," Rachel exclaimed and gently pulled the sample out of the reader and placed it back in its spot in the open drawer.

She took a big breath and blew it out slowly. After wiping her sweaty hands off on her tunic, she reached for her info-tube, sitting in front of the holo-reader where she had laid it. Her heart slammed against her chest so hard she was afraid the tube would be knocked from her shaking hand and shatter on the floor before she had the chance to find out what it contained.

CHAPTER 49

Imitar's quarters
Sunday
0820 hours

DID HIS DOOR BUZZ? No reason for Imitar to be surprised. He hadn't necessarily been expecting her, but he knew she'd figure it out. He just hoped it wouldn't be this soon.

Stepping out of the blower with only a towel wrapped around his slim waist, he stood back as Zoleta marched into his living quarters. "Do come on in, Zoleta. Something you need?"

"You know damn well why I'm here."

"No. Actually, I don't. Why don't you tell me?"

"As your superior officer, I have some questions requiring your full disclosure."

"Oh, come on, Zoleta, cut the crap. You're in my personal chambers. I have complete authority, unless it's a planetary issue and you know that. Why don't you have a seat and ask me what it is you want—excuse me—have to know."

"Humph. Zoleta stood her ground. "I want to know—"

"Just a sec. I think I'll put on some clothes before your little inquisition. Fix a drink if you like. The bev dispenser is set on low, but you can turn it up. In fact, I think I'm going to need something strong. Turn it on high."

It probably still worked, but he wasn't sure. He hardly ever drank alcohol and certainly not this early in the morning.

"I don't need a drink. I need you to tell me what was on the info strands you sent to Rachel."

"And what makes you think I know what you're talking about?"

"Now who should cut the crap, as you say? I can search through the access records and find out for myself, which I'm sure will prove it was you, or you can just tell me and save us both a lot of time. I'm sure you *scanned* the material you gave her. Your love of historical tidbits and all."

"Zoleta. I'm tired."

He yanked the towel from around his naked body and pitched it down the laundry chute. His glare stayed locked on her as he stepped into his lounging pants while she stared. She stood motionless, a show of her complete control, except for the faint jerk of her leg muscle, causing her to bump the Z-screen out of sleep mode.

"What's this? What were you working on?" she asked, pointing at the screen. "It looks like a resume—or a transfer request. Is it for you?"

Now he did want that drink and ordered the bev to make him a double. Bubbles rose to the top of the tall glass as he took a long, slow swallow. Thankfully the alcohol would hit his system quickly on an empty stomach.

"I'm putting in for a transfer."

"What an idiotic idea. Why would you want to transfer?"

"What does it matter to you?"

"You're not being logical. You're good at what you do, the best programmer on this planet, anyway. Your skills are needed here and you're on an advancing career path. You're not likely to get the same pay anywhere else, and obviously, you would lose your level of seniority."

"It's not all about money, Zoleta."

"No? Enlighten me, then."

Imitar took another long draught from his glass.

"I need—I'm ready—to get away from Goliath. Take the next step." Zoleta scowled at him. He knew she wasn't going to let it rest so he continued. "I need a break from never knowing where I stand with you. I don't want to care anymore. I've spent too much time caring. It's time for me to move on. You have your goals and ambitions, and that's fine. So, I'm leaving the first chance I get."

Zoleta paced around his small apartment, stopped and crossed her arms. A funny look washed over her face that Imitar couldn't quite interpret.

"You're saying that I'm the reason you want to leave?"

"Yep. That's about it." He downed the last of his cocktail, enjoying the soft burn in his throat and the warmth in his belly.

"Well, I have good news for you. Don't' bother. You can stay put. I'll be the one leaving on the next ship off this planet."

He started to laugh. What in craters was she trying to pull now? But the look in her eyes brought him up short. "What are you talking about?"

She ran her hand across the counter and shrugged.

"My turn to ask, why would you do that? You're second in command. You have everything you—"

"Schaefer fired me. I've been ordered to leave Goliath at the first available opportunity." Zoleta observed her feet for a moment, but when she looked back up, hurt had been replaced with a steely determination which made Imitar swallow hard.

Different scenarios vied for dominance in Imitar's brain as he tried to make sense of what he had just heard. In his heart, he wanted to take Zoleta in his arms and tell her everything would be okay. But time for that had long passed. Instead, he ordered the bev machine to mix another double and gestured toward the door. "I'm sure you'll be able to work your way around any obstacles or people unlucky enough to be in your path. No doubt you'll end up on top."

"I don't appreciate your tone. And, you haven't answered my question about the vial you gave Rachel."

Imitar led her to the doorway. "Good-bye, Zoleta. I suggest you start packing."

She took a step backward over the threshold, a combination of shock mixed with anger on her face. "Be careful, Imitar. You're right about one thing; I will get what I want, one way or another." She turned and the door closed behind her.

Should he have told her? He might have if she had acted like she cared. Who was he kidding; Zoleta didn't even know how to pretend to be nice. Anyway, there wasn't anything on the vids that would be beneficial to her. As far as he could see, the story of Rachel's life was tragic and sad, and why anyone would want to exploit it was beyond him. In fact, she had probably finished watching it by now and might need a friend to talk to. Maybe the holo would help trigger her memory and she could fill in the blanks of her past. But what if knowing her past made life more miserable for her? Would it be enough for her to know what happened? If he didn't know his full history, family, life, how would he feel? Would a simple piece of the picture be enough to satisfy him? He had thought he was helping Rachel. Now he wasn't so sure.

CHAPTER 50

Sub-Level IV, Library
Sunday
0900 hours

IN THE LIBRARY, Rachel placed the info tube into the clasps on the sides of the holo-reader. The tube began to spin as the light passed through the tangle of strands inside. A wavy image, like looking at a picture through a wet windshield, formed in the air in front of her, morphing into a jumble of words and then into paragraphs. She squinted up at the article. It was from the *New York Times* dated Saturday, August 31st, 2019 World News:

Coordinated dual bombings in Germany and Russia took place yesterday as protests against institutions storing frozen human beings escalated to violent levels. The so-called religious right, under the faction, the Army of God, claimed responsibility for the simultaneous destruction of the facilities. Although buildings were completely destroyed, no one was technically injured in the blasts, meaning; no living persons. However, all the liquid nitrogen tanks storing cryostatic patients, and even those containing beloved pets, were lost, leading to the question: were the persons contained in the liquid nitrogen chambers murdered since they are already considered dead in many peoples' opinion, including those of the alleged perpetrators?

Donald Rushman, the head spokesman for the Army of God, has been held for questioning in connection with the bombings. In an exclusive interview Rushman states: "Life and death is solely in the hands of the lord Jesus Christ, our one true savior. Man has no right to extend his life in abhorrent ways lest he thinks he himself to be the Almighty God. Woe unto him and all the corruption he spews with this act of abomination unto the one true God. We will take up our shields and march onward in the name of the Lord."

The holographic image faded and another newspaper clipping materialized. Rachel didn't like the feel of this. What exactly did it have to do with her? The article was dated two weeks later:

New York Times, Tuesday, September 17, 2019

Another double bombing of two cryonic facilities took place in the early morning hours on Tuesday. A homemade pipe bomb exploded at the Alcor Life Extension Foundation in Scottsdale, Arizona. No persons were injured but all suspended patients were lost as fire broke out in the storage buildings resulting in the shutdown of the container support systems. Three hours later a massive explosion at the Cryonics Institute in Clinton Townsend, Michigan, killed four employees whose names are being withheld until family is notified. The team of workers was in the act of perfusing a twelve-year-old girl, whose name is also being withheld, who died from a rare form of leukemia. Perfusion is the process by which the body's blood components are removed and replaced with amended fluids to ready the body for suspension in liquid nitrogen at minus three-hundred-thirty degrees Fahrenheit. A ten-foot wooden cross is all that remains of the site.

"Clinton Townsend? Michigan?" Rachel rolled the name across her tongue and through her brain. "Oh, my God. Was that where I was? Where I was frozen? But then how—I couldn't have survived. My body would have been destroyed like all the other patients. I don't understand."

The room interrupted the hologram, the last line of text still visible. "Please clarify request. Do you wish to replay hologram, or continue?"

Not again. Will I ever learn to keep my thoughts from spilling out my mouth? She needed to think. Whoever sent these articles was adding to her confusion. Was this information supposed to jog her memory? Her head felt like molten steel, sloshing back and forth, catching fire as memories tried to surface. Sour lumps tumbled inside her guts.

She swallowed the knot in her throat and requested the holo-reader to continue.

The rest of the articles were more accounts of the bombings, further interviews with the man behind the attacks, and responses from citizens living near the devastated areas. Rachel read for several more minutes until she could no longer ignore the name running through her mind.

"Room, did Clinton Townsend have a newspaper in the 1990's?"

The hologram paused as the room replied, "Conducting search. One moment please."

Rachel picked at the cuticle on her thumb.

"The Township Tattler, established in nineteen-fifty-seven. Last issue dated June 2007."

Beads of sweat gathered on Rachel's upper lip. She wiped them away with a trembling hand. A line of small green dots ran along the bottom of the hologram. She watched it trail from the left side of the page to the right and repeat in a kind of holding pattern. The room was waiting for further instructions. Rachel blew out the breath she was holding. "Please show me the newspaper articles from the January twenty-second, nineteen-ninety-four issue," she said in a whisper.

A picture of a large section of roadway buckling in an upscale neighborhood materialized on the front page of the Tattler along with the header: **Earthquake Hits Southern California.** There had been a major earthquake in San Leandro, California. Damage was estimated to be in the billions of dollars. It sounded devastating, but it didn't concern her right now. Another sideline on the front page talked about the new small animal rescue facility being built, time of completion near the end of March. There was nothing worth noting here either.

But at the bottom of the page in the lower right-hand corner, a small headline read:

Area pummeled by snowstorm. A six-car pileup on the turnpike occurred in the early morning commute but no injuries were reported. Everyone is advised to stay home unless travel is absolutely necessary or until further notice. One woman, however, was caught during the peak of the blizzard with zero visibility and skidded over an embankment. Her car flipped over several times before coming to rest headfirst in a huge oak tree. The woman was taken by ambulance to Henry Ford Macomb where she remains in critical condition.

A tingling sensation breezed across the back of Rachel's neck, making the hairs stand up, like someone was watching her.

"Room; please run the obituary column from the same date and from the following edition."

"Abort," CPO Schaefer commanded as he stepped in to the cramped space.

"High-level authority override. Information relay terminated," the room responded.

The light from the holo-reader blinked off and the hologram disappeared. Rachel jumped from the stool, her hands clenched at her sides. "What are you doing? Why did you do that?"

"Rachel, I'm sorry. You have every right to be angry with me. I should have told you about the vaccine not working. I should have asked if you—but I want you to know that last night was not a game. I've dreamed about being with you for a very long time."

"Well, now we can add this to the list of your fuckups." She flicked her hand at the non-existent hologram. "How long?"

"What?" A deep line creased the center between his brows.

"What do you mean—for so long? Are you talking about the months since I've been here on Goliath? Or something else?"

Ben rubbed his crooked finger, looked up at the ceiling, and then back down at her. The pain in his eyes, like the picture of him with Molly Brown, stabbed at her heart. "Over a century," he said.

Rachel staggered backwards but there was nowhere to go in the tiny library. He caught her as she bumped the table hard with her hip, jarring the holo-reader, and sending the tube of info-strands crashing to the floor.

"No!" she cried and dropped to her knees, sweeping the floor with her bare hands, trying desperately to salvage the pieces of her life. The hair-like strands disintegrated in her fingers. Shards of the glass vial and a few drops of fluid were all that remained. A guttural wail came from the depths of her soul as she rocked back, and forth hugging her knees tight to her chest. "It's gone. It's all I had. How will I know?"

Ben knelt in front of her and took her hands in his. "Rachel, look at me. It'll be okay. "

"It is not okay. I don't know what else was on it and now I've ruined any chance of ever finding out." She jerked her hands from his and stared at the drop of blood pooling in the middle of her palm.

"You've cut yourself. Let me take a look."

"No. Don't touch me."

The room grew dim; the walls of the library squeezed inward, the floor pulling her downward as her lungs fought for air. Hopeless. It was all so hopeless.

"I'll tell you what was on the info-strands. But not here. Will you go with me? Will you trust me?"

She sucked in a huge breath as if she had just broken through the surface of a bottomless lake. "I know what was on them. Well, one of them anyway. I read the article." She wiped the blood on her pant leg and tried to stand. Ben stood and grabbed her around the waist to steady her.

"Let go of me."

He released her and took a step back. "What do you know?"

"I know that the facility where I was, supposedly, frozen was destroyed. Clinton Township, Michigan. I lived near there, I'm sure of it. I don't understand how come I'm here. How I survived. Was I taken somewhere else before the bombing? Or was I ever really frozen back in time? How do you know what was on the strands? Were you the one who sent them?"

"Rachel. I need to tell you so many things. Please, just think of the other night. That was real. It was in the here and now and that's what matters."

His words calmed her trembling heart. She wanted to believe them enough to let herself give in just a little. The other night, yes, she could remember and believe, if nothing else, in his desire for her. But Ben wasn't the only one who wasn't being completely honest. He should have told her about the failure of the vaccine instead of her having to hear it from Sanda. But how honest was she?

"I need to tell you something. About last night—I"

"I'm sorry if I went too fast. I didn't mean to scare you."

Why did he have to seem like the vulnerable one and keep breaking down her defenses? She enjoyed the night just as much as he did. "I think I was the one doing the attacking, if I recall, but it's not what you think. I'm not upset about making love to you. That's not what I'm trying to say. When I was leaving your apartment, I was looking at the picture on your desk and I remembered." She searched his eyes. "I gave you Molly Brown, didn't I?"

"Oh God, Rachel."

"CPO Schaefer. Report to Command Center immediately," blasted throughout the compound. "CPO Schaefer report to Command Center."

"Rachel, I have—"

"Go. Just go."

"Please, just give me the chance to tell you everything. Will you meet me at the Dark Side in eight hours? Take the cruiser in C-3. It'll be pre-programmed to the exact location. Wear a thermal suit. I . . . I'll answer all your questions."

"Please," he mouthed and stepped through the doorway.

Rachel watched him go, then knelt to the floor and picked up the broken info-vial. It felt dead-cold in her hand.

CHAPTER 51

Imitar's quarters
Sunday
1200 hours

IT WAS ALMOST noon when Imitar awoke in his vid-recliner after having downed the cocktails three hours earlier. He tried to stand but his legs felt heavy and his eyes couldn't seem to focus when he turned his head. It had not been a good idea to drink but he didn't know how else to dull the pain from dealing with Zoleta. He slumped back into his chair and turned on an old-time show, hoping to take his foggy mind off the run-in he had just had with her. It didn't work.

Then he thought about Rachel. How things had changed since that day when he had brought the cryo to Sanda. Over the months, Rachel had shown everyone she met how to care for others above themselves. And what was he doing now? Putting himself first. He hung his head.

"This self-pity stupor certainly isn't helping anyone. Ha. Not even myself."

"Unable to process request," the room's soft, female voice responded. Imitar pushed himself out of the chair and weaved toward the kitchen. "Vid off," he said, thankful he didn't have to turn his head. The room would end the vid and he could keep the kitchen dispenser in his inebriated sight.

"Hyper-electrolyte detox," he slurred to the beverage dispenser.

The liquid looked nasty and tasted even worse.

* * *

Twenty minutes later, Imitar stood in front of Rachel's apartment door. Before he could announce himself, the door opened and Rachel stepped out.

"Oh, Imitar. Are you looking for me? I was just leaving. Can I call you later?"

A sincere, yet sad, smile crossed her face, making Imitar feel like a black hole. He might deserve whatever he got, but she certainly didn't deserve to be hurt over and over again. "I am looking for you. Wondering if you're okay. If you needed anything? Any help with . . . anyone to talk to?"

"Anyone to talk to? Is something wrong?"

"No. I just came by to ask you the same question."

"Are you ill, Imitar? Do you need to go to sick-bay? You look like you've been sucker-punched."

"I don't know what that means but it doesn't sound good." He ran his hand over his stomach. "Are you on your way to the lab? You said you were going somewhere?"

"I'm on my way to meet—"

A buzz sounded from behind Rachel. She jumped and turned to locate the source. "What the heck was that?"

"Sounds like you received a mailogram." Imitar stepped around Rachel to open the mail slot recessed in the kitchen wall but stopped midway and picked up the piece of broken vial from the counter top. "What's this?"

"My life." Rachel sighed. "In its usual broken state. It was a vial with info-strands. I don't know what to do. I was reading about a terrible time in history, in my history, I think. Back in 2019 all the storage centers containing . . . holding frozen patients, were destroyed. Every one of them, including the place where I was, if I was. I felt like I was finally getting somewhere. I asked the library to show me the obituaries from any newspapers when I might have been brought to a facility." Her shoulders slumped. "But Ben walked in and aborted the hologram. He says he will fill me in on everything. Imitar, I'm terrified, but I want to know so badly, to see if things will make sense. If I was frozen, and all the facilities were destroyed, where was I, or my de-animated self?" She looked up at him. "Say something, Imitar. What are you thinking? What should I do?"

He wanted to tell her that he could get a back-up of the strands but instead he said, "Be sure Ben tells you everything you want to know." Maybe it would be better if he gave Schaefer the chance to tell her the truth . . . if he would. Imitar changed the subject. "Did you want to take a look at your mail? It looks like a scriber. You don't see these anymore. Done in the ancient form—by hand. Look, there's some kind of characters. Can you read this?"

He handed her the paper.

"Of course, it's a note written in cursive. Sort of." She turned it sideways and back again.

She squinted at the piece of paper and read:

Lovely Rachel One,

You are yet to be.

Careful. Have not your heart chilled from anger. There is much to seek. Stars call to you and you must answer with the truth.

Z

"Imitar, is this the number two, or a letter?" She held the paper out to him.

"I don't know, but it sounds like it's from the Z-mahn."

"You're right. Has to be, but what the heck does it mean?"

"It's definitely from the Z-mahn."

"I'm not sure if he's talking about my being angry with Ben keeping me from finding out about my life. Or if it has to do with going through a second round of splicing."

"Your guess is better than mine, Rachel. But as your friend, I hope only the best for you in whatever you choose. Are you on your way to meet Ben now?"

"Thank you, Imitar. I appreciate your kindness. Yes, I'm going to meet Ben, but I want to talk to Sanda first. Maybe she'll have some input on what I should do."

This isn't right, Imitar thought. Either way someone's going to lose.

CHAPTER 52

Medical Lab
Sunday
1300 hours

"I'm sorry I stormed out of Command Center earlier this morning. I wasn't angry at you." Rachel went on, "Sanda, I just feel so frustrated, and useless. All this time we've, you've, worked so hard, and the vaccine worked, and now it's all for what? Worse, the people we thought we were saving are dying anyway. And no one is asking what I think. What I want."

"I'm afraid we asked you to go through something very painful, all so that we might gain a longer life expectancy. And my oversight cost us. I failed to project the outcome, both good and bad. I was taken by the initial results of the vaccine, so when it began to lose effectiveness over time . . ." Sanda sagged on the lab stool. "You have nothing to be sorry for, Rachel. I know it's too much to ask, so I'm not. It's up to CPO Schaefer to help you decide. But remember the pain you went through for others without any gain for yourself. You don't owe me, the citizens of Goliath, or Ben, anything. You certainly don't owe us your life. I'm afraid for you, Rachel. A second splice is far too dangerous. Your system has already been compromised. Don't do it."

"Sanda, it means a lot to me that you're concerned. I don't know what I'll decide, but I don't really have anything to lose."

"Yes, you do—your life, Rachel. You've tried so hard to access your memories while some of us have tried so hard to forget ours. I wonder if our life-span was shorter, would we put more effort into making our relationships work? Would we put more attention on caring about those around us?"

The tone of Sanda's voice made Rachel lay a hand gently on Sanda's arm. "Are you happy here on Goliath? You've never told me when you came here, or why."

"Research. I'm able to conduct studies unhampered by the various governmental agencies."

"I don't believe that."

"It's true, they have very little jurisdiction on this planet. I can—"

"Stop. That's not what I'm asking you and you know it. I can see it in your body language – there's something you're not telling me. You have that far-off look in your eyes that I've seen several times when you didn't think I was watching. Maybe I can help, if you want to talk about it."

"I am concerned about you, Rachel. If you undergo the splicing again so soon after last time, you might be so severely compromised that I can't—" Sanda clasped her shaking hands. "I can't. I couldn't. Save her," she whispered. Sanda's eyes seemed to drift toward something Rachel couldn't see. "I mean to say, I might not be able to save you."

Rachel knelt in front of her and gently peeled her gripped hands apart. "Who? Who was it you couldn't save?"

Rachel waited for her reply, but Sanda remained silent. "I want to thank you. For caring about me."

"No. Don't thank me, Rachel. If I had been strong and put your welfare first and been the kind of doctor I started out to be

—I would never have let you sacrifice so much. And I can't let you do it again."

Since awakening on this planet with few memories to call upon, the only things which seemed real were feelings, Rachel's and the feelings of those around her. How did they do it? How did everyone here always seem so stable, so flat? Was Rachel the only one who suffered from mood swings? One minute her heart nearly burst with love and caring, and the next minute it shrank into a withered leaf, brittle and ready to blow away with the slightest wisp of air. She was as hot and cold as the two halves of Goliath. Maybe the lack of memories drew her into a type of manic-depressive state, or was there something in her past that was trying to break through? Something too painful for her to bear?

"Sanda, if there's one thing I know, it's that I feel most alive when I'm helping care for others physically and emotionally. I think, maybe, you are finding the same holds true for you too. If I can't have my old life back, whatever it was, all I want to do is to be of use."

The stunned look on Sanda's face confused Rachel. "There it is again. A veil shadowed your eyes. Did I say something to upset you?"

It took a moment for Sanda to reply. "I'm just thinking."

"Are you going to be okay? I'm sorry, but I need to get going. Maybe I can come back after I meet with Ben, and we can talk."

"I'm fine. Really. I thought you were mad at Ben? But the blush of your cheeks suggests otherwise."

Rachel smiled. "There it is. You are an observant doctor. He came to my room and asked me to meet him so he could explain things. I remembered part of my past from a picture I had seen on his desk the night before."

"I wasn't aware there were any pictures on his console."

"Not in Command Center. On his desk in his office. In his apartment."

"I see. Go meet him, Rachel, and listen to what he has to say, but be careful." Rachel rose from the floor and turned to leave, catching Sanda's last words, "and as chief physician on this planet, and your friend, I strongly advise against undergoing the splicing."

CHAPTER 53

Command Center
Sunday
1430 hours

THE MINING CREW stationed on Grit Rim in the outer region of Sector III hit a sulfuric acid pocket four hours earlier, causing the collection tubing to melt and poisonous gas to escape. Back at Command Center, Ben was on the vid to the foreman. Emergency procedures to shut down and contain the area had already been initiated. One woman and two men were in critical condition, and another woman was dead. Things did not look good.

Ben squeezed the bridge of his nose with his thumb and forefinger. This was the hard part of his job, the part he didn't like, the part he wondered how much longer he could stand. Yes, he was paid well, but the responsibility of running an entire planet was starting to take its toll. He had made the journey from earth with only a year's supply of food, clothing, tools, and communication capabilities for himself and a small group of hardy men and women. He had come for the adventure and to test himself against unknown elements where resourcefulness translated into survival. And maybe, the chance to dream was a part of what enticed him. The huge corporation, Elements Unlimited paid his travel and a percentage of any usable discoveries that could be converted into profits back on earth. Ben was smart and lucky. Xenostone, found only on Goliath, was a new material capable of conducting electrical current at fourteen times the speed of substrates used on earth and required a fraction of the power. Ben didn't want for anything on Goliath, so his paychecks were sent home to his families. All except a chunk he secretly placed into account to take care of Rachel.

But how much money was worth losing good men and women? To be done with it all ran through his mind more and more often. He should take his pension and settle down on a quiet planet, far away from the ugliness of competition and demands. A place where he could enjoy simple things like riding off and exploring interesting landscapes, watching the beauty of stars and planets in their dance of life, or gazing at the sunrise or sunset smear vibrant colors across the sky.

How many times had his last life-partner, Regineela, begged him to leave the job and the stress and come home, until she, like the others before her, gave up and resumed her own life with someone else? He hadn't been fair to her, or to the others. Who was he kidding? He had kept working, always taking the next promotion; more and more difficult and demanding positions, knowing he would never return to his wives and families. There was only one thing, one woman, he ever wanted.

Ben had told Rachel to take the cruiser in spot C-3 and meet him on the dark side of Goliath. The vehicle was preprogrammed and ready to bring her directly to the rim of Ice Crystal Valley. Now he wondered if he would be able to meet her. Not until he received the 'all-clear' signal from the foreman at the site. Or until he could temporarily pass command authority on to someone else.

* * *

1530 hours

"Major Dubasi. I need to see you in Command Center immediately. Out."

Six minutes later, Imitar stormed through the door. "Why in a black hole did you fire Zoleta?"

"I will be out of communication range for the next four hours. Watch and wait for information from Sector III. There's been a breech. I have emergency personnel standing by in sickbay to manage the victims."

"Victims? Where are you going? Shouldn't you be here to take care of it? What could possibly be more important than the safety of those men and women out there? And what if I need to get hold of you? You can't go off-grid during a time of crisis."

"You'll be fine."

"No, I—"

"You're in charge while I'm gone."

"I'm not worried about being fine. I'm worried about what's right."

"Sector III. Four hours."

* * *

If Ben hustled, he would have a little time to organize his thoughts before he met up with Rachel. If he drove her, there would be no time to plan the best way to tell her everything. If that's what he was going to do.

The elevator tube seemed to creep down the two levels at

evolutionary speed. As soon as the door opened, he sprinted through the hallway, catching stares from several workers heading to the D.C.

Not much longer and he would be with Rachel. What was he going to tell her? How much was he going to tell her? What if she decided not to meet him? No, she'd be there, he was sure of it.

Thoughts flew around in his head, never settling on anything he could grasp. How many times over the decades had he envisioned things turning out differently? In his mind he had run through that last, horrible day over and over and what he should have said . . . and what he would say, if he ever got the chance.

He slammed his fist against his front door before he calmed down enough to look at the identification scanner.

"Molly Brown," he said as he entered his home office. The latch clicked and the drawer slid open. He reached in and grabbed the small velvet box in the corner. Strange . . . hadn't he left it toward the back of the drawer? "Close," he whispered. The case was soft in his hand like Rachel's skin against his fingers. The memory of sparks from her lips across his bare chest made the back of his neck tingle. He blew out a breath. What he would give to have that again, to always have it. What would he give? Rachel had given her whole being, and then some. She had trusted him and how had he repaid her?

He turned back to the drawer, opened it again, and pulled out a framed newspaper clipping from underneath the pink sweatshirt.

The elevator tube would be too slow, so he took the stairs and sprinted to the garage locker-room. His thermal suit hung on a peg at the back of his private locker; the helmet sat above on the top shelf. The face shield reflected Ben's worried face, like one giant, non-committal eye. He tucked the helmet and suit under his arm.

Good—the land cruiser for Rachel was still in its parking spot.

He climbed into the ZX and sped out of the compound.

* * *

Ben flew beyond the belt, greenery blurring by. Forty minutes later, he neared the glacial landscape. No one lived out here. Even the indigenous animals kept to themselves. But he liked the dark quiet and the way life and time stood still. Settling the vehicle on a level chunk of ice, he turned on his helmet light and crunched over the frozen tundra.

He brushed the snow from the side of a rock outcropping and leaned against the solid mass, taking in the cold whiteness all around him. Without the thermal suit and shield, the air would freeze his lungs in the fraction of a single breath. And yet it seemed his heart had been frozen for over a century while he waited.

The Dark Side was where his dreams felt real. And where he longed for absolution.

How many times in the last thirty-some years had he come here to think about her and sift through his mistakes? Over a century ago he had found the woman he wanted more than life itself. But she wasn't his to have. She was the one who had paid with her life on that treacherous day. Now the question was here, before him. Would she remember what had happened? Would she remember she loved him as much as he loved her?

The soft ring of his earbud alarm warned him he only had ten minutes left to get to Ice Crystal Valley in time to meet Rachel. He would have to race.

Face shields wouldn't be necessary on Crystal Rim, just warmer clothing, like one would wear on a chilly winter evening in Michigan. Evenings in Michigan with her . . . He scrambled back in the ZX and set the Galactic Positioning System for Ice Crystal Valley.

How could such a tiny woman hold so much power over him? He needed her. What was he going to do if she refused to go through the splicing again? Or worse, what if she did say yes? Would she remember her past? Would Rachel survive the procedure a second time? Oh God, how could he even ask it of her? In ten minutes, he would have his answers.

He made it to the rim before she arrived. He took off the thermal suit, walked to the other side of the vehicle, and checked his strobes and flare gun. The kaleidoscope effect of the light reflecting off the ice would be incredible, as romantic as a candlelight dinner—or so he hoped. Everything was set. He tucked the velvet box into the breast-pocket of his therma-lene jacket.

The framed newspaper article stared up at him from the passenger seat, its cold metal border ready to bite his fingers if he touched it. Across the page, the words found him guilty. He turned the frame over, face-down, and closed the door.

Half an hour passed. Where was she? Sending out a call would jeopardize their location, or worse, their privacy.

Time ticked on. Rachel was now over an hour late. A sense of Deja-vu made his insides tighten. Something must have happened. He would have to make the call.

He reached into the ZX for the relay booster, just as the land cruiser pulled up and Rachel climbed out. His heart flipped inside his ribcage.

CHAPTER 54

Crystal Rim
Sunday
1810 hours

A HUGE PART of Rachel wanted to meet Ben at Crystal Rim, but another part of her wasn't so sure. If she looked in those blue eyes of his, her resolve might vaporize and she would forget why she came. Maybe it was a good thing the only light to see by was from the ZX head-beams parked in the snow. She climbed out of the cruiser as Ben came around the side of the vehicle.

"Is everything okay? It was getting late. I was starting to worry," Ben said, as he came around to her door. "Wait a minute, what's wrong?"

Did her face show the turmoil she was feeling in her guts? "I'm fine. It's just been a long, complicated day. Or year. Or whatever. I was, am, worried about Sanda, but it'll wait. I'll talk to her when I get back."

"Then maybe this is just what you need—a chance to see the quiet beauty of Goliath. There's so much I want to show you, Rachel. So much I want to share with you." He held out his hand to help her out of the cruiser.

Warmth crept into her cheeks. They had already shared quite a lot the night before. She smiled with the memory. Ben stepped closer, then took a round object from his pocket and turned it on. A soft glow illuminated his features. "I think you'll like this."

"Please, Ben. We need to talk."

He bent his head toward her, "And I promise you we will. Take my hand. We need to get closer to the rim."

Their frosty breath mingled in the air between them. There was enough light to see the want in his eyes. He held out his hand to her. She hesitated and then twined her fingers with his. It felt so comfortable, so right. They crunched across the snow until Ben came to a stop.

"Where are we?"

"This is the rim of Crystal Canyon, in Ice Crystal Valley, one of my favorite places on the planet."

"It looks like black nothingness. I think we're close enough." She gripped his hand tighter.

"Just wait." He let go of her hand and showed the underside of the glowing ball. "I pull this pin and toss it over the edge. It'll light up the whole canyon."

"Like the glow-bots in the cave?"

"Better. It's more of a strobe with inner short-range propulsion capabilities. Kind of a cross between a grenade and a disco ball." He detonated the strobe and threw it outward and upward.

"Ben, I—I really want to know everything you can tell me. We need to—"

Beams of light exploded from the ball as it hovered over the canyon. The reflection off the ice made Rachel catch her breath. Light cascaded in every color from the sky, sparkling like a crystal chandelier. She had never seen anything more beautiful.

They watched until the strobe ran out. Only then did Rachel realize that Ben had put his arm around her shoulder. A hard edge pressed against the side of her ribs.

"I have something for you," he said.

She tried to answer him, but only nodded. It was suddenly difficult to swallow. Now would he tell her what was contained on the info-strands? Would it be good news that would help make sense of the missing pieces of her life? Or would the truth be unbearable?

The tip of her gloved thumb tasted dry in her mouth. She looked into Ben's eyes, searching for a clue. When he smiled back at her, she let out the breath she was holding, sensing that everything would be okay.

"Thank you for this, Ben," she waved out toward the canyon. "It's so incredibly beautiful."

"You're so incredibly beautiful." In his hand he held a small blue box. "I want to give you this."

"Oh no."

Ben's eyes narrowed. "You haven't even opened it yet. It's part of what I need to tell you. Please open it and I'll explain."

And how was she going to explain that she already knew what it was and that it had sparked a memory from her past? Her fingers shook as she slowly opened the lid. Tears welled up in her eyes as she took the locket from the box and held it in the palm of her hand.

"Ben, I—"

"The necklace is yours Rachel. It belongs to you. It always belonged to you."

"I know."

"You remember?"

"I remember . . . cold, so cold." Her body gave an involuntary shiver. "It was snowing outside; the car windows were fogged up. You, it was you. You were standing in the street. I—I tried to give the necklace back, but you refused to take it. You were upset. I was crying. Why was I giving the necklace back?"

"I loved you, Rachel. You loved me too. Do you remember when we met? You took care of me at the hospital after I suffered a spinal injury in a skiing accident. I was in rehab for almost a year. You checked on me every day. We fell in love. That's what's important. We can have that again. I know you still have feelings for me."

A prickly sensation crept between Rachel's shoulder blades up to the base of her neck. Everything Ben said was true, but still, something felt off. If they were so much in love, why had she hurt him? Why didn't she want to take the necklace? Why didn't she want to be with him?

"When I look at you, I can't help but know that deep down inside I loved you. But something is missing. I want nothing more than to love you again with all my heart, but I—I can't and I don't think I ever will be able to give you my complete love until I understand why part of me is hesitating. Do you understand what I'm saying?"

Ben closed his eyes, the tension along his jawline visible. "Please, Rachel. This is a new life. For you, for me, for us together."

"I'm sorry."

"I don't know what else to do. How can I make you see?"

The locket bit into her hand. She slowly uncurled her fingers. "By telling me the truth."

He hesitated; puffs of breath exploded in front of her as he paced back and forth. The pain on his face made Rachel want to tell him never mind, and instead, take him in her arms and comfort him. But before she could reach for him, he stopped, turned toward her and pulled an old-fashioned picture frame from inside his jacket.

"Here, take it before I change my mind."

"What is this? A photograph? It's too dark. I can't see." Cold from the metal frame seeped through her glove.

Ben reached over and pulled a cord on the side of Rachel's suit. She wanted so much for him to touch her, to hold her, but she wanted information more. Nothing, and no one, not even a man she felt so drawn to and knew she loved, would stand in her way. The cord was attached to a small flashlight which illuminated everything within five meters in front of her. She smiled at Ben, but he was staring at the ground.

It wasn't a photograph. What did she think it would be? An old prom picture of the two of them? As her eyes adjusted to the light, her breath caught in her throat. The typed words of her own obituary trembled in her hands.

> Rachel Allison McRae, 34, of Michigan, died Tuesday, January 22, 1994 after suffering severe trauma when her car crashed two days ago on icy roads during the most horrific storm this year. She was the daughter of John and Kathleen Allison of Auburn, Washington; sister of Tracey Allison Williams, and sister-in-law of Charles Williams, and aunt to their two boys, Scott and Ryan.
>
> Rachel leaves behind her loving husband, James Thomas McRae of 14 years and her most treasured gifts: beloved son, Thomas Kent, age four, and Emily Jo, age two.

Rachel's hot, rapid breath fogged the glass as she held the frame in a crushing grip. She peeled her fingers from one edge and wiped it with her shaking hand, afraid to read any further, and afraid not to. Children? The terrible ache in her abdomen; the emptiness in her heart. A little boy and baby girl. It was true, she knew it was. She could feel it now in every cell of her body. A fire ignited deep within her soul. To keep the inferno contained, she forced herself to read on, but the words swam in her vision, like air wavering off sweltering pavement. She swallowed down the dizziness.

. . . A celebration of life will be held at one o'clock, on Friday, February 27th at Macomb park.

And at the very bottom of the page, in tiny lettering:

Cremation services provided by Modetz Funeral Home.

The frame slid from her grasp and shattered on the ice.

"Ben." She spoke in a controlled whisper. "Look at me. It was you that I loved all those years ago, wasn't it? And the necklace. I was giving it back to you, because I couldn't live with the guilt. I had to go back to James; to my husband, even if we had been growing apart over the years. I needed to try one final time to make our marriage work. And now after hundreds of years, I end up here with you? This is all a lie! You've lied to me."

"No, Rachel, it isn't a lie. I sacrificed so much—I"

"You? You sacrificed? How dare you? I remember now, and here's a news flash; it's not all about you!"

"If you remember, then you know I have always loved you. And I still do."

"Did you? Do you? Or did you just want me? There's a difference. And I wasn't free to be with you. I was—am, married and I have a son and a daughter! Oh, my God! What right did you have to take that from me?"

"I didn't take anything from you. You left me, remember? I was just there to pick up the pieces and make it possible for you to live—someday, if the future ever came. And it did, Rachel. It's right here, right now."

"But why? For you? What gave you the right to save me? To throw me in a freezer. The obit says I was cremated. How did you pull that off because, obviously, I'm here. And you just what—defrosted me when it was convenient for you? My God. I may still have a family out there somewhere. Do I, Ben? Is my husband still alive? My . . . son? If you ever hope for me to love you enough to be with you, you need to tell me the truth and let me decide. It's my choice now."

Ben stepped closer and tried to put his arms around her. Rachel held up a hand and shook her head. "The truth."

He paced in front of her, then stopped and stared until she felt the pleading in his eyes. She fought the temptation to go to him.

"We had plans to be together. You were going to tell James in the morning that you were leaving him. You were going to bring Thomas and Emily with us. But something must have happened because I waited for you at the parking lot and you were over an hour late. The storm front had moved in and the temperature had dropped. Still I waited. Rachel, I did love you. You are the only woman I have ever loved."

Rachel put a fisted hand to her mouth. She wanted to stay strong, but sobs racked her body. "What happened?" she asked through strangled breaths.

Ben's voice was soft as he spoke, "You finally showed up. I could see you had been crying. Emily was in her car seat in the back, Thomas buckled in beside her. You said you couldn't do it. You couldn't be with me. I begged you. Rachel, I'm begging you now. I know you love me. Please don't throw it all away again."

"I don't understand. First, I'm frozen, something that's already beyond my comprehension, and then I seem to somehow survive an attack on the facility where I'm supposedly 'stored'. And cremation services? So, I was cremated? Well, I beg to differ. How did this happen? Were you behind this entire horror story, Ben? Does my husband know anything about me being alive? Is he alive? God, I don't know what to think."

"Rachel, let me explain—"

"So, I had made a decision, hadn't I? I remember, you were leaning in through the car window and I had told you I was staying with my husband, who is a good man and where I belonged. I started the car and threw it in reverse." She tried to keep up with the memories which overwhelmed her brain like a flash flood. "You tried to stop me. You opened the door and I slammed it shut. Your hand was caught. Your finger. That's why you never had it fixed when it was a simple thing to do."

"Yes, Rachel. It's all true. But I—"

"I should have died. It wasn't your decision to make. How dare you scoop me up and tuck me away somewhere. Now here I am on this God Forsaken planet, with a man that I don't know whether to love or hate. With a family out there, that thinks I'm long dead. Are they alive, Ben? My son? My daughter? You son-of-a-bitch!"

Anger filled her from the soles of her feet until it erupted through battering fists. She screamed at him as she slugged his chest with all her strength. Instinctively, he held up his arms to block the blows and stepped backward, away from her frenzied punches.

The edge slipped from beneath Ben's feet before either he or Rachel had time to understand what was happening. He threw his arms forward as his legs slid down the ice. He caught a few fingers on the rim with one hand but found no purchase. All thoughts left Rachel's mind as she dropped to her stomach and tried to hold on to Ben's fragile grip. "Don't let go," she yelled.

"I'll drag you with me—I can't. I'm sorry."

Their eyes met in a terrified goodbye; his hand slipped from hers, and he was gone.

A scream formed in Rachel's throat and shattered her lungs

as it burst from her soul and echoed down the precipice. She drew her trembling hands from the ledge and curled into a ball, hugging herself while she sobbed. "I'm sorry. I'm so sorry."

The cold, hard ground sent tendrils of frosty mist to embrace the fetal woman. The blankness beckoned to Rachel's mind and body. "Let go," it whispered, "come back into the ice where nothing matters. You'll be safe here. You were safe here once before. Yes, that's right. Let go, I will hold you and you won't be troubled by anything. No one will hurt or confuse you. You can stay with me for all of time. Rest now."

It felt like the answer she'd been looking for . . .

CHAPTER 55

Command Center
Sunday
1830 hours

THE CALL CAME in on the Z-feed, causing Imitar's heart to skip a beat. "Please don't let there be a problem. Or whatever it is, please let me be qualified to handle it," he said under his breath. Where in the heck was Zoleta right now? And why couldn't she give him a hand, since Ben was off somewhere not to be disturbed. It wasn't like Zoleta had been kicked off the planet. Yet.

Imitar took a deep breath, "Here goes nothing," and flipped the receiver to the on position. A far-off sound of someone screaming and sobbing made him lean closer to the vid as if that would make for better clarity. The picture wasn't any better; it blurred across the screen with the resolution of a tornado.

"Rachel? Is that you? Slow down. I can't understand you. What's happened? Where are you? Are you hurt?"

"Nooo. Yes. Can't breathe. Fell. It was an accident."

The crying grew distant again, muffled across the vid. He

was losing her. Imitar's fingers flew across the console, trying to boost the signal, trying to hold on to the fine line of communication long enough to start a tracer. Bits and pieces of words came through from somewhere far off. The voice changed. A slightly deeper voice. A voice without the desperate tone, almost as if another person were talking in the background.

"This is Imitar Debasi in Command Center," he yelled into the receiver, "Please tell me where you are. I repeat— this is Lieutenant Debasi in Command Center. Let me help you. What's going—?"

He was cut off and the vid went dead. He lost the signal. Or . . . someone had hung up.

It had to be Rachel who was screaming, but where was she and why did she cut the connection? One thing he was sure of —it wasn't a call from Sector III. This came from somewhere in the outer region.

Where was it Ben had said he was going when he so inconveniently stuck Imitar with minding the entire planetary operations? That's right. Ben hadn't said. All Imitar knew was Ben would be off the grid for several hours. Over three and a half hours was up. And what had Rachel told him? She was going to stop and see Sanda before she met . . .

Ben.

Imitar called the lab. "Sanda. This is Imitar. Did Rachel come and talk to you? Do you know where she is?"

"She left here a while ago. Said she was going to meet Ben but she didn't tell me where. Why? You sound upset. Is anything wrong?"

"Just checking. I'll touch back with you soon. Out."

Ever since Imitar had been unable to pinpoint the location of Zoleta and Rachel in the cave, he had promised himself he would create a new program, a code breaker, to enable him to boost the signal by relay. The program would blow through any firewalls and up the power push simultaneously. It wasn't a hack job. He had worked diligently on it every spare minute. Now would be the true test. Ben would be difficult to locate since he had never had a tracker placed, but Imitar knew that Ben had Sanda fit Rachel with a tracker right from the beginning. Outer limits or not, Imitar could, and would, locate her. His fingers flew across the console pad; bytes of data streaming downward until they sifted and finally locked into place.

Crystal Rim.

"Why in the galaxy is Rachel out there? And is Ben with her?"

The one thing he was sure of, was that Rachel had taken the cruiser. She had used the z-phone from the vehicle, not her earbud which wouldn't have a strong enough signal to clear the distance. He had that much to go on. It was a fluke that she had gotten through to Command Center at all, even from the cruiser, so why did she hang up?

A disturbing thought crossed his mind; if Rachel was with Ben and she was in trouble, why in the cosmos would she hang up? Was someone else with Rachel? Someone other than Ben?

It took a few more minutes to plug the data into the hand-held device, and then Imitar made a fast dash for the garage. For one quick moment, he thought about calling Sanda to go with him. Her skills might be needed, but there wasn't time.

"Wait a second. I can't leave my post." Imitar's heart continued to race even as his chest deflated. "I have to send someone else out there."

By the time he got back to Command Center, he decided he would call the next person in the chain of command and pass the reins. Or he could try Zoleta again. After all, she had seniority over him, and he just happened to be holding an advanced locator.

He plugged in her tracker information and waited for the display.

"She couldn't be." He shook his head in disbelief. Time to

try the booster relay and see if he could contact her. He'd have to call from the z-feed, not from his earbud.

Before he could get through to Zoleta, the radar on Rachel's tracker blinked. She was moving—in a diagonal direction away from Crystal Rim—toward the compound at a rapid pace. Was she headed back home in the land cruiser? Maybe she was okay. But what was Zoleta doing out there? He quickly switched to her tracked location. Zoleta remained in the same area. The tracker showed minimal movement. Nothing was making sense.

Imitar brought up the garage vid to see what vehicles were missing and cross-checked the facility use orders. Six parking spaces were empty; three were signed out and three were unaccounted for; the XZ, the land cruiser, and the Hubba.

Ben, Rachel, and Zoleta.

Imitar tried calling on each of the vehicle phones.

No one answered.

CHAPTER 56

Crystal Rim
Sunday
1712 hours

WITH NOTHING BETTER TO DO, Zoleta had set off after Rachel in the only vehicle left in the garage: the slow, plodding Hubba. At the time she thought that following Rachel might turn out to be interesting . . . but more than likely, not. Zoleta drove behind at a safe distance in stealth mode, letting the auto-pilot maneuver the vehicle over the terrain without turning on the headlights. The Galactic Positioning System showed she was approaching Crystal Rim in the Ice Crystal Valley. Rachel pulled over and parked next to another vehicle that had its headlights on bright. Zoleta stopped on a slight rise eight-hundred meters away.

Well, well. The ZX. A meeting with Ben.

"I'm not going to be able to see or hear those two—unless I can find something useful in this old jalopy. She used the minbeam she had grabbed on her way out of the garage to rummage through the vehicle. The light wasn't strong enough to be seen from anywhere but inside the Hubba. She pointed the ray at the compartment in the side door, reached in and pulled out a few kcal bars. Ugh—as if she could stand to ever eat another one as long as she lived. Next, she retrieved a pack of water clarifying tabs, some kind of a metal scraper, and a heat-shield hood. Again, nothing to spin out of orbit about.

She opened the compartment between the front seats and shined the minbeam. "Aha, now we have lift-off." A set of thick, silver-edged goggles were inside a small case. They could be worn in the daylight, in the night, in sub-zero temps, in the blazing sun, for near vision, or far vision.

She donned the eyewear, made a few adjustments, and gazed out toward the couple standing disgustingly close to one another.

Zoleta watched as Ben took Rachel by the hand and pulled her toward the edge of the rim. Suddenly, a burst of light from a strobe flashed strong enough for Zoleta to have to whip off the glasses and watch with the naked eye. It took a minute for her to acclimate to the brightness. She relaxed back in her seat and enjoyed the show from her vantage point.

"Nice touch, Ben. You never brought me out here."

The light show lasted a little over ten minutes. Zoleta put the goggles back on in time to see Ben drop his arm from around Rachel and face her, giving Zoleta a view of their profiles—much better than the view from their back-sides. It looked like Ben pulled something from his pocket and handed it to Rachel. Zoleta tried to focus the glasses, but it was too far to see what the item was. Now Ben was pacing like an animal that either didn't know what to do or couldn't get his point across. He was good with a lot of things, but words were not one of them. Zoleta chuckled.

A few minutes passed, and this time Ben reached into his jacket. "What? Another present? This is getting a little outside the galaxy."

From what Zoleta could see, Ben had pulled out something

flat and rectangular. Rachel took it and tried to what? Read it maybe? "Yoo-hoo, it's too dark. Try turning on your reading light. Bet she can't even figure out how to turn on her own suit light. Ben will have to do it for her. Yes, there it goes."

"Red Dwarf."

This was beginning to look like a big waste of time. Nothing much was happening and Zoleta had no desire to see where this was going. So many gifts. For what? Favors, perhaps? She had better things to do with her time, like start getting packed to get off this planet. She took one more glance toward the two standing on the edge of Crystal Rim and was about to take off the vision amplifier when something changed. Something in both Ben and Rachel's body language, or at least in Rachel's. "Hmm, maybe a few more minutes . . . just to see . . . "

So much for the romantic feel. At least this might be worth watching.

Wait. Was Rachel *hitting* Ben? Did he just step backwards? She's pounding on him, all right. "He'd better be careful; he's too close to the—"

Zoleta shook her head as if something was amiss with the glasses. Maybe the view finder had accidently slipped into another mode. She looked again, but it was the same scene.

Rachel had dropped to the ground and Ben was—gone.

CHAPTER 57

Compound
Sunday
2010 hours

BACK AT THE COMPOUND, Sanda was doing her best to follow what Imitar was saying over her earbud. "Please calm down. I can't understand what you're saying. Has Rachel been hurt, or Zoleta? Who's being sent back to base?"

The first thought that crossed Sanda's mind was what had Ben done? Had he coerced Rachel into undergoing the splicing again? Rachel was much too fragile and may never recover mentally, if she even survives. Is that all Ben ever thinks about; lining his bank with more money, no matter who gets hurt in the process? Where's his sense of compassion?

Compassion. She knew the word. She herself had pushed it down so far in her soul, shoved it back so far in her mind, and researched it right out of existence. She had become the doctor who no longer looked past the data, the results of the current experiment, to see the person who needed help. Was she any better than Ben?

How does Rachel do it? She asks the real questions, the questions that matter because it's the wellbeing of the patient that's important. There was a time, long ago, when I used to. She hung her head. *When did I give up?*

The walls Sanda had built and reinforced around her heart began to crumble. A lump formed in her throat and tears trickled down her cheeks until she could no longer keep the answer from seeping from her soul. She had always known the answer; she just couldn't, wouldn't, accept it.

She was responsible for the death of her own flesh and blood.

Even back then, she was a Level VI doctor. How did such a thing happen?

It didn't.

Only, it did.

"Sanda? Can you hear me?" Imitar was yelling. "I'm telling you that Rachel is on her way back from Crystal Rim and may need medical support. Are you with me here, Doctor?"

Sanda snapped out of her self-loathing with a shudder. "Yes, of course. I'll be standing by. Fill me in on any further updates."

"Out."

The baby girl. Her baby girl. It happened so many years ago, but the loss remained, like a sharp rock tearing holes in her heart that would never heal. Sanda had been determined to solve the problem, to fix the congenital defect. She had worked steadily, knowing that she would find the solution. But as the days passed and the baby's health continued to fail, her frantic attempts became hopeless. If she could only go back, have another chance. She would have stopped her frenzied search long enough to give her daughter what they both needed the most; her touch. She would have held the infant to her breast, stroked her soft cheek and whispered all the things she should have whispered into that tiny, precious ear.

And then there is Rachel. A grown woman and yet she's

non-judgmental, gives of herself, and is innocent like a child. There is a tenderness about her that seemed to melt the frozen tears of Sanda's heart. Whatever was happening right now on Goliath, didn't matter as much to Sanda anymore. All the research she had worked on before the rejuvenation failures, the countless hours spent hiding behind chemicals and equa tions. It had seemed important. Or had she only told herself that? But there had never been any real healing.

She would go back. Back to Earth and use her gifts to better serve mankind and make a new life for herself. Enough of this world and its lack of sincerity. Goliath needed her more than ever now, but it didn't matter anymore. It was time for her to do what she needed.

Rachel was in trouble and Sanda would be ready, readier than she had ever been in her life.

With shoulders squared, she marched into Medical and ran through the emergency checklist.

* * *

Twenty minutes later, her intercom buzzed. "This is Imitar. Rachel is in the garage, or at least her vehicle is. She's not responding to my calls. I'm sending a transport to bring her to Medical. Status unknown at this time. Please assess and report as soon as possible. Out."

"Wait! Imitar. Can't you bring her in?"

"I'm in charge, and until CPO Schaefer arrives, I have to call the shots. Believe me, I would much rather be there with you. Could you meet Rachel? She may need . . . a friend right now. I wish I could tell you what's going on, but I don't have any details. Sanda, I know you will do what's best. You always do. Thank you."

The stone that had buried itself deep in Sanda's heart so

many years ago, began to push its way to the surface, like a shifting of tectonic plates pushing up a new continent.

* * *

Transport might take too long and Sanda needed to know for herself what was happening. She grabbed her kit and ran for the elevator tube, meeting the hover-gurney in the hallway, the unconscious Rachel curled on her side.

"I'll take her from here. Report back to the commanding officer that I have her."

"We have orders to deliver her to Medical."

"That's where I'm taking her."

Transport shrugged her shoulders, "Will that be all then, Doctor?"

Sanda dismissed Transport with a nod, pulled out her scanner, ran it over Rachel's body and gently inserted a litmus strip under her tongue. There were no contusions, fractures, sprains, no head injury, no detectable wounds of any kind. She inserted the litmus strip into the reader. Rachel's blood chemistries showed an initial high level of stress hormone, now rapidly being broken down by the standard sedative compound found in every first-aid kit.

"My stars, what happened out there? I doubt you self-medicated. Did Ben give you a tranquilizer?"

Hopefully, Rachel would fill her in once she slept off the drug. Until then, Sanda vowed to keep a close watch over her.

CHAPTER 58

Medical
January 11
0900

IT HAD BEEN a week since Rachel had undergone the splicing and ten days since the accident. She moved in bed, trying to redistribute the stiffness to other areas of her body. A dry, nasty taste made her open her eyes in search of a sip of water. As soon as her vision cleared she could tell something was wrong. This was not her room. She was in Medical, as a patient.

It was all starting to come back to her now: meeting Ben on Crystal Rim, the realization that she knew him from back on earth and that she loved him, and then the horrible truth— he was the one who knew the whole story but selfishly kept it to himself. *And now he's dead. I pushed him off that cliff. God forgive me.*

"How are you feeling?" Sanda asked as she stepped beside the bed and touched Rachel's arm. Then Sanda placed her hand on Rachel's brow. "You don't feel hot. That's a good sign."

The palm of Sanda's hand felt comforting but Rachel

frowned. "Why aren't you checking my values from the vitals-bot?" she said between parched lips.

There was no reply from Sanda, just a caring smile. "There is someone here to see you if you're feeling up to having a visitor.

Before Rachel could answer, Imitar breezed into the room with a smile. "How many days are you planning to laze around? About time to get up and get to work, don't you think?"

Something about Imitar always made Rachel feel better. "Hi, Imitar. Thanks for coming. How long have I been here?"

Sanda answered. "Going on three days. You need water." She held the container out to Rachel. "Sorry, it took a few days until I could get free to come visit. I know that you were in good hands with the doc here." He pointed a thumb toward Sanda. "You're sure a lot quieter than the last time I saw you."

"What do you mean?"

"Well, when Zoleta brought you in and the sedative she had given you started to wear off, you started screaming about Ben dying and how it was your fault and—"

"Imitar."

Sanda tried to hush him but he continued, "And then to undergo the splicing again. Craters! You had to be off your orbit. We all tried to stop you, but you were adamant about it being your choice."

"It was my choice. Only mine."

Sanda shook her head, "I was afraid you were going to go through all the pain again just so you could get your memory back, but you told me it had already come back. You remembered your life, family, friends, knowing Ben–everything from before you ended up with us on Goliath." Sanda gave Rachel's hand a quick squeeze. "Even at that, I wasn't so sure you could make an informed decision. And then you said you were doing it because Ben *didn't* ask you to."

"No, he didn't. He never got the chance. I had to do what I could; the splicing was the right thing to do. But I'm still to blame for Ben." Rachel's shoulders sagged. "Will I have to face criminal charges?"

"Hmph. For what? Being vertically challenged?" Zoleta stood in the doorway, leaning against the frame. "Doesn't anyone ever work around here?"

Rachel looked up. "How long have you been standing there? I hear you were responsible for giving me some kind of strong sedative to put me out of my misery when . . ."

"More like *my* misery. Someone had to be responsible. It was the only way to shut you up. You were barking orders: "Bring that vehicle over here! Get a rescue line hooked up! We need to get him out of there. Stat!" Zoleta raised an eyebrow, "But you did move fast and probably saved his life, even though he asked you to let him die."

"You heard that?" Rachel whispered.

"And a bunch of I love you, and I love you, it'll be okay, and hang on. Senseless waste of breath when he didn't have any to spare on meaningless sentiment." She crossed the room and stood next to Imitar until her shoulder touched his.

"You and Ben knew each other back on earth?" Imitar asked.

"Yes, Imitar. We did, and we should have been together, only I wasn't strong enough to make the decision that would have been right for me. I thought I was doing what was best, what I was supposed to do, but it wasn't what I really wanted." She started to pick at her thumbnail, then dropped her hands beside her on the bed. "It was you who sent the vial, wasn't it? Did you read the obituary?"

"I wasn't sure what I was reading at first," he said.

"So, you know I have a son and a daughter somewhere out there?"

"You what?" Sanda and Zoleta said at the same time.

"That's why I need to get stronger. I'm going to find my children."

CHAPTER 59

Goliath
February 10
Two months after the accident

THE NEW RECRUITS arrived the following week, which meant there were only three months left until the space shuttle would be ready for those departing from Goliath. After two days in quarantine, the recruits reported to Command Center where Zoleta briefed them and issued their orders. Imitar said nothing about Zoleta's being fired. She was the most competent to manage operations and second in command as far as anyone else knew. And he'd just as soon leave it at that for as long as he could.

Zoleta had accepted the offer to lead a new world; build the structure, plan the operations, from the ground up on the nearby planet, Delilah, which also circled Gleise 581. She would be instated as CPO and arrange for transport as soon as she was able to put together a start-up team and link communications. Her request to wait until CPO Schaefer was back at the helm on this planet had been granted.

When the recruits had been dismissed, Zoleta turned to

Imitar. "What's got your jet stream caught in a wash? You didn't offer any recommendations or clarification on anything I said. Not that any were needed. You didn't say a word. And, you've been staring at the same code on the halo-screen for ten minutes. Even I could figure it out by now."

Imitar faced her. "I haven't heard if my transfer's been approved or not. I put in for it several months ago."

"Hmph. Then you'll just have to come with me to Delilah and do the initial systems set-up. It'll be a step backward and hard work without any down time for quite a while."

"I don't understand. The CIF is usually prompt— what did you say?"

"I could use a decent programmer, if you're interested."

"Wait . . . you didn't have anything to do with—" He took a hard look at her. "Zo, I'm not so sure."

"I'm asking you. Imitar, will you join me? Please, I need you. You are the best code-buster this side of the galaxy."

"Interesting offer." It would be a tough few years setting up everything on an unexplored planet. A rugged venture to be sure. He could be with Zoleta, but how would she treat him? And what exactly did he want? What could he live with?

"I want you to come with me. To be with me. I've always pretended to know everything. But, Imitar, you're the only person who knows it's just an act. I don't want to be tough anymore. I want to share work, life, love. Even if you won't come with me, and I will understand, will you please forgive me?"

The vulnerability in her tone made him take a deep breath and stare hard at her. "Don't play games with me. Do you really mean what you say?"

"It's exactly what I mean." She crossed the room and touched his face.

Imitar swallowed the knot in his throat, "In that case, I accept—on one condition."

"And it is?"

He stroked his chin and smiled, "I don't want to hear any derogatory remarks about my ability, or lack thereof, to grow a beard, if and when I choose to do so."

"Even if I actually think it's kind of sexy?"

"Wait. What?"

CHAPTER 60

Medical/Intensive Reconstruction
March 30
Three months' post-accident

SANDA BUSIED herself preparing vaccines and writing protocol for the new Research Director and the Life Physician, both of whom would take over her responsibilities. She would leave the formulae and enough vaccine to meet the needs of the workers of Goliath. The rest would be packed up and brought to earth with her. People on other worlds might soon need clean, unmodified genes, or at least drugs that would enable their immune systems to revamp. Scientists back on earth would have the capability to construct more of the vaccine from what was left of Rachel's sample. Maybe Sanda would be able to play a part in saving lives. It was her hope.

The room beeped its alarm; an urgent incoming call on the com above her work table. A wispy, labored voice from the Intensive Reconstruction Unit made her suck in a quick breath. "Room. Increase volume."

"See. Rachel. Must talk. To her." Ben's words faded into a wheeze.

Sanda threw down her instruments, raced down the hall, and into the IRU. Ben's injuries were extensive; she figured it'd still be days before he would be conscious, let alone able to speak.

The soft lighting in the room cast a dim shadow across the emaciated form of CPO Ben Schaefer, lying in the shallow bath of healing solution. Puffy, dark circles underlined his half-mast eyelids. Orange, red, and black bruises ran along the left side of his body, from his shoulder to his groin. Puss oozed from a deep gash near his hip, past his thigh, turning the water murky green. Sanda glanced at the monitors. Yes, he was breathing, but the frail rise and fall of his chest was the only detectable movement. Where did he draw the strength to ask for Rachel?

She leaned over him. "Ben, it's me, Sanda. I'm going to give you another dose of debride-bots, followed by the next phase of reconstruction. Everything looks good." She winced at the discolored water-bath. "At the rate you seem to be healing, I should be able to move you to recovery within the month." Vials of meds were lined out on the hover-tray at the bedside. She picked up the one she needed.

"Rachel . . ."

The mounds of work Sanda still needed to finish before departing Goliath crossed her mind. Rachel would be leaving too. Ben wasn't aware of all the changes that had taken place since his fall, and Sanda was determined to keep it that way until he was out of danger. Instead she said, "Everyone is fine. Rachel is fine. Don't talk. Your job right now is to rest and not worry about anything or anybody."

"Need . . . see . . . her." His lips hardly moved but the monitor emitted a high-pitched beep. His breathing and heart rate had jumped above recovery standards.

"Soon, Ben. You can talk to her soon." She set the purple vial down and picked up the yellow tube. But it wouldn't be today. She waved the sedative under his nose.

* * *

Back at the lab, Sanda continued labeling and storing the vaccine. The harvest from Rachel's second round of splicing, along with the added anti-rejection serum proved to be the right combination. There had been no instances of a rejection or relapse.

Rachel stuck her head in the doorway, "Where did you go? You flew out of here like a bat out of hell."

"I'm at a loss for what that means."

"Oh, sorry, Sanda. It's a cliché. It means you ran out of here really fast. I wonder . . . since no-one says it in this day and age, is it a new phrase and not a cliché anymore? Where did you say you were? Is everything okay?"

"I checked on Ben." Rachel's back went rigid at the mention of his name. "You know you could go see him, sit with him, and talk to him. It might help if he could hear your voice." Sanda stared at her, reading her.

"I know, and I want to. I'm still trying to make sense of everything that has happened now and, in the past, and how I feel about it. I guess I'm afraid that when I see Ben I'll just be confused and make stupid choices. Or worse, not make any. Choose the path of least resistance and let all the decisions be made for me, like I always did before." Rachel's shoulders slumped.

"He asked for you today."

CHAPTER 61

Goliath
Medical/Recovery Room
June 11, T minus 30 hours

RACHEL STOOD BY THE DOOR, trying to decide whether to face
Ben and tell him she was leaving, or let him find out after she
was gone. CPO Schaefer punched in numbers on the holograph floating above his bed in recovery room. "No, that value
is incorrect. The core depth is what needs to be taken into
account. Redo the computations and call me back. CPO Schaefer, out."

She cleared her throat, "Hey there."

The look on his face about killed her. *Keep your feet under
you. Don't fall apart. You're here to tell him what your plans are.
Nothing more.*

"Rache . . ." He closed out the hologram and motioned
toward the hover-stool. "Please."

She sat on the stool, her hands in her lap. "CPO—Ben, I
came to tell you . . . I'm sorry I haven't been in to see you earlier.
There's been so much to do to get ready—"

"Shh. Rachel don't say it. Don't say anything. Let me just

look at you and remember every inch of you. You are so beautiful. I only ever wanted to make you happy. You were the only one who brought out the best in me, brings out the best in me. With you, I feel I could do anything, be anything. Just say the word and I'll do it. I know I was wrong. I should have let you die that day, but I couldn't. I loved you too much. But you didn't let me die either. We . . . we are meant to be together."

Tears threatened to spill down her cheeks as she spoke. "Ben, I have to leave. You have to get this company back on its feet. Maybe . . . someday, but not now. I need to find my own way. I need to find my children, see that they are okay, see that they have a good life. Can you understand that?"

"What about us?" He closed his eyes, opened them again and looked at her. "Do we have a chance?"

Rachel moved close to the bedside and slowly reached for his hand. "When my memories came back, the strongest, most repetitive memory was that I was in love with you, truly and deeply in love with you. And I know it still holds true. All I can say is, I want to be with you, and someday I hope I will be, that we end up growing old together. But for now, I've got to go on this journey alone. To find my children. To find myself."

"It could take years, Rache. I finally have you here, beside me. I can't lose you again. I don't think I can—"

"Years? Years are just a drop in the bucket of time. Living them . . . that's what counts."

"Will I see you again? Will you come back to me?"

"Oh Ben. I have no idea what I'll find out there. But I know I have to try or I'll never be able to live with myself. And then, see, you will have brought me back to life for nothing."

"Never nothing, Rachel. I always wondered if I had met you first, would you have married me."

"Would you have asked me?"

"Yes, and I would have given you the stars. I still will, if you'll let me."

CHAPTER 62

June 11, 2195
Flight Control
T-minus 3.5 hours

THE BODY-SUIT SMELLED LIKE BASIL. Rachel remembered the first time she had ever had bruschetta, her first dinner with Ben, so long ago. She had loved it. She placed a foot into each pant-leg of the suit and wiggled the clingy material up over her hips, ran her arms down into the sleeves, and zipped it closed from her navel to her neck. A row of numbered injectables were lined up on the tray next to her sleep pod. A timer buzzed and she turned toward Sanda, both women raised the vials in a toast and then squeezed the nasal plungers simultaneously.

"You two doing okay?"

It was Imitar over the shuttle com.

"Of course they are. Let them go through the protocol without interruption."

"I was just checking." Imitar replied to Zoleta in the background. The two of them manned the launch from base.

"We're fine, Imitar. Thank you for asking," Sanda replied and smiled at Rachel.

"Receiving a request to deliver undocumented transcript from one Z-Mahn, for Rachel Allison McRae, designated recipient."

"Sure Zoleta. What's the message?"

"Who me? I'm busy with your countdown checks. Imitar read this to Rachel."

He cleared his throat. Rachel pictured him stroking his chin as he tried to decipher cursive writing. "Is it too hard to read?"

"No, I've got this. It's like code once you've got the grip of it. Well, maybe it would be better if I send it to your z-feed."

"Thanks, Imitar. Can I get a hard copy of the letter? I just want to see the words in print and hold it in my hand."

"Sure. Copy coming across. Now."

"And Imitar, I'm really going to miss you. Please send me updates. And I'll miss Zoleta, too."

"Hmph."

The paper was thin and delicate, like the wing of a butterfly. It said:

Rachel of Earth and of Goliath,

What you seek, yours will be. Afraid of the truth hesitation is. Afraid of pain be not, for loss suffer all. Erased compassion time has not, only thickened it as ancient glass melts toward the bottom of the window pane. Precious life is as each person believes it to be. Universal is pain. Ties us together and names us human.

In the palm of the future were you and back to mankind you gave. Yet none of this you chose. No end to time there is, only subsets of centuries, days, hours, and minutes, given are each of us. Increase our lifespan we quest; must we not also strive to increase the value of that life?

Forget us not, Rachel One,

Zuluzimbabanganga

* * *

"Are you okay, Rachel? The timer went off for our next vial."

"Just thinking and wondering if I'll find my children. Or my children's, children's, children. Or my parents. Could they still be alive? And if I do find them, will I matter to any of them? Will I even live long enough to find them?"

"Only you can answer those questions. And they're not easy ones. Right now, it's time to settle in your sleep pod. The next thing you know, we'll be back on Earth. Good luck, Rachel. May your journey be safe and fulfilling."

"Same for you, Sanda. And thank you for everything. See you in fourteen months."

Rachel inhaled the last of her vials and climbed into the sleep-pod. The automatic shield locked into place.

Imitar's voice caught as he said, "T minus three minutes," making Rachel smile as she pictured his boyish face.

As cool air began to fill the capsule, a moment of fear shot through Rachel's mind. Would she, once again be forever un-alive in a frozen state? But then, she thought about the Z-mahn's words, about Ben's love for her and her love for him, and about her quest to find her children. A deep calmness infused her body and soul. "Everything will work out," she whispered as she clutched the silver locket to her breast and closed her eyes.

THANK YOU

To my readers,

Thanks to each and every one of you who read The Time Between Us, my first novel. Hopefully you found the suspense, conflict, and characters I tried to create, entertaining; my purpose for writing.

If you have any comments or questions feel free to drop me a line at jrae57.roberts@gmail.com, or please write a review on Amazon. I would love to hear from you.

Thank you so much,
J. Rae Roberts

ACKNOWLEDGMENTS

So many people played a significant part in bringing this book to life.

I'd like to thank my early readers, Jasmi Vackar, Mark Roberts and Nancy Sayers. If it wasn't for your kudos, I would never have kept going. Thanks for your faith in me.

To my writing group, Writers on the Storm (WOTS): thank you for supporting me in our new writing world, slogging through critiques together and to Susan Rushton who taught us how to edit.

Thanks to fellow authors Robin Rice and June Gillam, who read the entire manuscript, fixed errors and made excellent suggestions.

To fellow author Kristen Billerbeck, along with WOTS member Paddy Lawton: thank you for advising me to start the story closer to the action. Good call.

Chris Phipps, fellow author and WOTS member, I am forever in your debt. Thank you for your help with grammar and punctuation, for great brainstorming sessions, and for providing a place in your home for me to write in peace. Most of all, thank you for the gift of your friendship.

Barbie Valkosky, I couldn't have done it without your

proofing the final draft, asking all the right questions, and finding the errors which slipped past everyone else. Love that lime!

Gia McNutt, artist extraordinaire and friend, I am so grateful for all the hard work you did on the cover. Thank you for the beautiful job and for understanding the story better than I even did. Find Gia at www.giamcnutt.com

To Guy Vackar, Kaeli and Brendan Hogan, Kelden and Emily Roberts, Janet Wheatley, Marianne Quinn, Diane Gilbert, Cynthia Joyce, Tracey Liebig, Jeri Mainer and anyone else who wanted to read the manuscript, or at least said they did, thank you for believing in me.

And finally, to all of my family and friends, I give you my sincere gratitude for your love and support over this long journey.

J. Rae Roberts was the librarian at a K through 8th grade elementary school. Retiring last year eliminated her excuses for finishing this novel.

She graduated from the University of California, Davis with a B.S. in Nutrition Science and worked in research. Continuing her education, she became an RN where she enjoyed working in Family Practice and Sports Medicine.

As a member of Writers on the Storm, Shut Up and Write, and WORMS (book club), J. Roberts continues to enjoy reading, writing, and camaraderie. She is also a member of the Cryonics Institute. Her addictions are: chocolate, Jazzercise, and her grandkids.

Made in the USA
San Bernardino, CA
19 November 2019